Serenity Song

SERENITY SONG

Finn Dervan

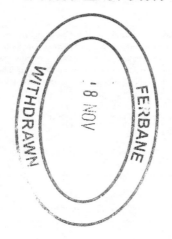

The Book Guild Ltd

First published in Great Britain in 2019 by
The Book Guild Ltd
9 Priory Business Park
Wistow Road, Kibworth
Leicestershire, LE8 0RX
Freephone: 0800 999 2982
www.bookguild.co.uk
Email: info@bookguild.co.uk
Twitter: @bookguild

Typeset in Adobe Garamond Pro

Printed and bound in the UK by TJ International, Padstow, Cornwall

ISBN 978 1912881 338

British Library Cataloguing in Publication Data.
A catalogue record for this book is available from the British Library.

MIX
Paper from
responsible sources
FSC
www.fsc.org   FSC® C013056

For my family and friends on both sides of the Irish Sea

Slàinte mhath.

God Grant me the Serenity to Accept the
Things I Cannot Change,
The Courage to Change the Things I Can,
And the Wisdom to Know the Difference.

Prologue

11th July, 1921
Birr, King's County, Ireland

The curve of orange sun nudged the horizon and inched its way above the pea-green fields that quilted King's County. Silhouetted against it, a young man crouched on a turn of track that emerged from the woods. The flat of his hand lay buried beneath the grass bordering the roadside. With eyes closed and head bowed, he whispered three words to the dark earth that cooled his palm. "For you, Micheál."

———

Ciaran Fahy walked past Craughwells' Bar and turned his push-bike onto Main Street. Looking up the road towards the lonely column on Cumberland Square, he could see that the town of Birr was as still as an oil painting. The only sign of life was a dray-horse pawing the cobbles outside Dooly's Hotel; two men grunting in unison as they hefted barrels of beer from the cart and rolled them into the cellar below. Thin tendrils of smoke curled from chimneys and the peaty aroma of burning turf already permeated the morning air. Ciaran walked halfway up the road and very deliberately turned and leant his bicycle to point the way he had come.

He crossed the cobbles and stepped through the open door of Skelly's General Store. Declan Skelly stood behind the counter poring over the headlines of the *Midland Tribune*, a cup of tea steaming beside him. He looked up and nodded but continued reading as he used a grubby towel to dry a set of tumblers.

Ciaran asked for a lemonade. Declan shuffled to the rear of the shop and returned from the ice-room holding a bottle, dusted with a dandruff of frost. Ciaran thanked the old man, turned his back to the counter and fixed his gaze through the shopfront window onto the red front door across the street.

By now the sun had edged over the roofline opposite and shone directly into the store. The frosted bottleneck began to melt and rivulets of icy water trickled through Ciaran's fingers, collecting and carrying particles of dried mud from his roadside prayer to the bottle's heel where they hung in cloudy pearls before dropping, one by one, to the floorboards.

Ciaran lifted his face upwards, closed his eyes and let the warm light bathe his inner eyelids in kaleidoscopic hues of pink, purple and gold. Taking a long swig, he savoured the tickle of bubbles on his palate and the slow chill that spread down his throat. Opening them again, he saw the sun had caught the bottle in such a way that a pool of flickering light had appeared above the door frame, hovering just below the ceiling.

He smiled, as with the slightest movement, he could send the light sprite dancing back and forth across the length of the shop. Ciaran manoeuvred the bottle so that the bright pin flew outside and across the street where it circled the bronze knocker of the door opposite. Taking another sip of lemonade, he found he couldn't recreate the angle that had given birth to the shimmering pool of sunbeam, and he felt a momentary twinge of irrational loss.

Declan Skelly continued drying glass-ware as he regarded the young man propped against his counter. The flat cap pulled low over brow and the threadbare jacket indicated that the boy he had known since childhood, whom had been hand-picked by the clergy and primed for the priesthood or professional life, had neither taken his vows nor attained the financial success his education should have afforded him. Declan assumed that like so many, he'd been somehow sucked into this wretched conflict. He knew the Fahy family were zealous supporters of an Irish Republic – indeed Declan had been on the wrong end of many a tongue lashing from Ciaran's sisters for continuing to serve soldiers, policemen and their kin – but he'd hoped that Ciaran might have escaped all that when he left to study in Galway years earlier.

As far as the ageing shopkeeper was concerned, this war was like none that he'd read about. He was terrified of what both sides were prepared to do – to each other and to anyone who came between them. The IRA were just as likely to put a bullet in the back of your head as the Black and Tans. The Great War had stirred up unreasonable passions in men and unrealistic notions of freedom: life in Birr had been improving for the working man before all this madness – folk today didn't appreciate how lucky they were. Declan would never forget the raw, gnawing poverty of his youth as droves died in ditches with only nettles in their bellies or fought for air in coffin-ships escaping the Famine: *that* was the time to take up arms and hurl yourself into revolution – and he might have done so too, if only he'd not been so feckin' hungry. Thus he resented that, as peace spread across the rest of Europe, his contrary countrymen had decided to declare war on the British; a war that had ensnared them all in its malicious, vindictive small-mindedness. The papers chronicled an endless litany of assassination, ambush and revenge killings. And always in the background, the insidious drip feed of propaganda that leeched from both sides.

However, Declan hoped that today could be the beginning of the end – the headline on the counter proclaimed as much:

12PM TRUCE ENDS HOSTILITIES BETWEEN CROWN FORCES AND REPUBLICAN REBELS

BRITISH PRIME MINISTER LLOYD GEORGE TO OPEN NEGOTIATIONS WITH SINN FEIN LEADERS

Cautiously, he coughed. "Have ye seen the news? Can it be true? Two years of bloody murder over at last. I'll drink to that, so I will."

Ciaran continued to stare out the window and across the road.

Belatedly the old man realised his mistake – how could he have been so insensitive – was it not Ciaran's younger brother, Micheál, who had been found beaten and broken, like a sack of snapped bones on the Riverstown Road? Declan had heard the poor boy carried on breathing for hours after they found him, but he never spoke another word – he just moaned quietly, his mother clasping his hand until the film of his eyes glassed over, his moans became erratic whistles and then stopped altogether.

"I'm sorry, Ciaran. I forgot myself – I don't mean any offence."

"None taken, Declan. You're right – I'll raise a glass tonight, for sure."

Across the road the door opened and from the shadows within, a uniformed man stepped out. He glanced up and down the street and turned back towards a woman with coal-black hair who had followed him from the house holding the hand of a child. He bent to kiss the girl on the head and whispered something to the woman that made her blush. Gently tracing the curve of her stomach with a finger, he brushed her lips with his and began to walk up Main Street, a battered attaché case arcing alongside him.

Ciaran slammed the bottle on the counter with such force that the lemonade fizzed from the neck, spilling over and blurring the ink of the front page banner. As he strode from the shop without a word, a shocked Declan Skelly haplessly called after him to remind him he wanted paying; but Ciaran couldn't turn back now.

Six strides, right hand in jacket pocket, his heart threatening to burst from his ribcage, he grabbed the shoulder of the policeman with his left, whirled him round and raised the gun to his chest.

A second of utter silence.

"This is for Micheál."

The eyes looking back at him widened in surprise then focused over his shoulder on the woman and child.

Ciaran pulled the trigger twice.

The bullets rent through the rifle-green uniform and the policeman fell, crying words that were forever stolen by the twin cracks of gunfire. The briefcase hit the pavement and burst open sending sheaves of paper twisting through the air like giant confetti. As they settled in the growing puddle of crimson that welled from beneath the stricken man, Ciaran stepped forwards, aimed the gun at the policeman's temple and fired once more.

With the bitter taste of gunpowder catching the back of his throat, his ears ringing and the revolver leaden in his trembling hand, he looked down at the mess of shattered bone and succulent tissue and then at his shoes; black as sin in a pool of sticky red. Ciaran stood statuesque for a heartbeat, transfixed by the spreading tide, so similar in colour to the door behind him.

Screams. A voice yelling his name; the rattling of bicycle chains.

Stabilising a push-bike with each hand, Padraig Nolan hurtled across the cobblestones. "Get on Ciaran! For Christ's sake, get on the feckin' bicycle!"

A frenzied grappling. A metal pedal painfully raking shin. Four unbearably slow thrusts downwards and finally Ciaran generated some momentum.

Gulping air, pumping pedals and gripping handlebars, Ciaran Fahy left Sergeant Joseph Conlon behind him, staring facelessly at the space that would soon be filled by the midday sun and a ceasefire across all Ireland.

However, even as he put distance between himself and his deed, the keening of his first-cousin as she buried her daughter's head in the folds of her skirt only seemed to get louder, and Ciaran realised that fat tears mingled with the stinging sweat that streamed down his face.

Part I

The Courage

We seem to have lost.
We have not lost.
To refuse to fight would have been to lose;
to fight is to win.
We have kept faith with the past, and handed on
a tradition to the future.

Patrick Pearse
Easter, 1916

1

Spring, 2018
York, England

James Lucas knew that he was in trouble.

He'd abandoned Charlie at the opticians as she agonised over a choice of designer frames that looked identical to the untrained eye. His opinion redundant, the shop assistant had assumed the role of professional adviser and he'd made his escape by breezily promising his wife that a cinnamon latte would be waiting for her in their favourite café on the Shambles in half an hour.

That had been over an hour ago.

Once again James had lost all track of time in a bookshop. Sandoval's Rare Books was low-beamed, blissfully quiet and smelt of bound leather, wood polish and aged paper. The copy that he held in his hands he'd come across quite by accident: he'd spotted it as he bent to pick up a coin that winked at him from the grime of the well-trod carpet. Golden lettering on green spine, the book was wedged in the far corner of the very bottom shelf and may have lain undisturbed for decades.

On opening it, a dance of dust particles burst spore-like from the pages. They tumbled and pirouetted, catching flame in a lance of sunlight that pierced the cool umber of the shop. *The Deeds and Exploits of the Irish Republican Army in County Offaly 1918-1923* had been written by someone called Brendan O'Rourke. On the fly-leaf the price had been scribbled in faint pencil and beneath, a short inscription scrawled in ink: *Daithi, Fan Dílis, B.* Tugging his phone from his pocket to translate what he assumed was Irish-Gaelic, James discovered he had three missed calls from Charlie and a tart text message, devastating in its brevity and ripe in its use of invective.

Hurriedly paying up and leaving the penny on the counter for good luck, James stepped into the street and fought his way through the wash of tourists and Saturday shoppers who clogged the narrow arteries of the medieval city.

Charlie was checking her email when she saw James weaving between the banks of parked cars. He wore a sheepish expression and carried a large book under his arm. Automatically Charlie understood the reason for his no-show at the café: her husband was utterly bewitched by the archaic. Their house was at risk of becoming some kind of curiosity shop. Vintage journals lined bookshelves whilst snuffboxes and inkwells crowded the windowsills and mantelpieces. In the garage, a 1966 Morris Minor hunkered needily beneath dust sheets, consuming ever larger chunks of James's teacher salary to remain road-worthy.

Charlie shouldn't complain: she'd known what she was letting herself in for. Almost twenty years earlier, when they'd first met, he was no different. She'd been in the first year of a law degree and James was completing a Masters in Early Modern History. Charlie had stumbled into him – or over him, as it happened – at a house party near the campus. Whilst searching for the bathroom upstairs, she'd tripped over a lanky man slouched against a bookcase, drinking red wine from the bottle and absorbed in a collection of Victorian poetry. He'd helped her to her feet and with

4

wide eyes, animated with flecks of green, had announced, "I think I've discovered a first edition of *Goblin Market and Other Poems* by Christina Rossetti." Blinking and examining his surroundings as though for the first time, he had frowned and asked, "Whose party is this anyway? Do you think I should tell them? This is pretty rare."

Beguiled by his thick black hair and strong jawline, Charlie had joined him at the top of the stairs. They shared wine and James had read to her the poem about the sister seduced by the delicious fruits of the Goblin men. It was strangely erotic and fantastical at the same time – both the poem and it's recitation by this older man. That night they sparred and slurred and flirted and spoke of things that strangers do when they find themselves alone in the shadows with someone they're attracted to. Charlie, nineteen-years-old and already whip-smart and fiercely ambitious, teased James mercilessly over the merits of a post-graduate degree in 17th century witchcraft whilst he in turn gently berated her for embarking on a morally bankrupt path that would see the guilty rich acquitted as they shook hands with their well-paid lawyers.

Almost two decades later, the kernel of truth touched upon in that very first conversation had come to pass: Charlie was partner at a leading law firm in Leeds whilst James toiled away at an academy school in Wetherby, earning a pittance and breeding ulcers.

As James approached the BMW, Charlie's phone began to ring. She connected to Bluetooth, glad that today she'd had her way and they'd driven in her car. James's Morris Minor was draughty, intermittently unreliable and desperately slow. On top of that, her husband harboured an irrational fear of listening to the radio whilst driving, and had installed a cassette machine through which he unapologetically played a finite loop of mix-tapes from his adolescence. Gender and the five years that separated them meant that Charlie didn't necessarily enjoy these nostalgia trips quite as much as she let him believe.

Although James knew that Charlie would never admit to exacting a measure of petty revenge on him for his failure to buy her coffee – he suspected she was doing just that. By the time he reached the car she was deep in conversation with her sister about some works do in a couple of weeks. It became obvious that she had no intention of hanging up any time soon. James opened a bottle of water and started thumbing the book as Charlie reversed from the parking space.

James was a history teacher at a struggling secondary school. He taught everything from the Ides of March to 9/11. However, his sixth form were about to start a module on the Irish struggle for independence, and he'd bought the book in the hope that he might be able to use it in class. A first-hand account of the fight for independence by an IRA Commandant of the South Offaly Brigade was invaluable. The other reason that he hadn't hesitated to slide the book from the shelf was that the period covered by O'Rourke was significant to him; his mother was from County Tipperary, and the branches of her family tree hung heavy with rebel green. But hidden amid the foliage was a forgotten limb – that of her grandfather, Sergeant Joseph Conlon, a policeman in the Royal Irish Constabulary. The story went that he was shot on his way to Mass by a rogue IRA gunman sometime during the 'Tan War' of 1919-21. The juvenile love of a grisly tale had once or twice led James to needle aunts and uncles for details during summer holidays in Cashel, but he'd only ever been met with stony silence or disinterested ignorance. Like bible stories he vaguely remembered from Sunday school, the assassination of his great-grandfather was something he'd been told as a child, accepted uncritically at the time and then almost forgotten. Half-hearted research between assignments at university had left him none the wiser as to the specifics, but it was no coincidence that he was teaching the topic at A-Level a life-time later.

James tapped the Irish phrase written in the flyleaf into his smartphone. The words *Fan Dílis* translated as 'stay loyal' or 'keep the faith'. *Daithi* was the Gaelicised version of the name David. Was the '*B*' beneath the dedication that of Brendan O'Rourke? He hoped so; it gave the work more resonance.

He sipped the water and started to read. It didn't take long for James to discern that O'Rourke's writing was florid and self-reverential – perfect for source analysis in class, but grating after a while. The first couple of chapters described his upbringing in County Offaly, at the time known as King's County – a name that no doubt irked the Irishman. He was one of six children, and the O'Rourke family was steeped in *Fenianism*. The Fenians were die-hard Nationalists who'd stop at nothing to see the British expelled from Ireland. O'Rourke claimed his father and uncles had all been members of the Irish Republican Brotherhood and that he had followed the family tradition by joining the Irish Volunteers.

Hedgerow and rolling fields undulated gently through the passenger window as James read about how O'Rourke and the other rebels of Easter 1916 were forced to surrender at the General Post Office in Dublin. Led at gunpoint from the smoking ruins, the author recalled being jeered at by Dublin women whose husbands and sons were being mown down by German machine gun fire in Flanders. O'Rourke was one of the 1,800 incarcerated without trial in Britain. Sent to Frongoch Prison in North Wales, he recounted a conversation he'd had with Michael Collins, fellow inmate and future leader of military operations in the coming War of Independence. Collins had chuckled at the fact that by throwing hundreds of dedicated revolutionaries into the same prison camp, the British had kindly afforded them the time and the opportunity to plan in earnest for the next stage of the struggle. That next step was to create a 'state of disorder' in Ireland. Armed insurrection in the capital had failed so Collins had looked O'Rourke in the eye and asked, "Brendan, when we get out of here, will you help me unleash merry hell on the Brits? We'll make life so damn hard for them in Ireland that they'll have no choice but to pack their bags and concentrate their cruelty on some other poor bastards less irritating than ourselves."

The car jolted over a pothole and James lost his place. Sipping again from the bottle and flicking back through the pages, something caught his eye. He gasped. Liquid sucked lungward. His trachea spasmed, spouting mineral water back through his mouth and nostrils.

"Gotta go, Bekka. James is choking."

Charlie hung up and swerved the car off the road onto a farm track. The wheels locked and the car skidded to a halt. James, by now rasping and struggling for breath, stared incredulously at the words before him, splattered in spots of saliva and San Pellegrino: *"The Sergeant at that time was an Irishman by birth, but he did more for the British cause in Birr than any from over the sea. A murderer, a torturer and traitor to his motherland, Sergeant Joseph Conlon was a marked man in County Offaly."*

2

May, 1916
Birr, King's County, Ireland

It was St Brendan's Day in Birr and those crammed inside Dooly's Hotel were enveloped in the raucous atmosphere of the evening. Ears assaulted by tin whistles, fiddles and cheers, the stamping of feet and slapping of thighs. The bar besieged; five-men-deep at its thickest as pint jars were passed backwards, hand-to-hand, with the urgency of mariners ladling sea-water from a sinking ship. Blue smoke and even bluer language filled the space between them, and from this melee emerged Constable Joseph Conlon, three tar-black pints of porter locked between fingers and thumbs.

"Tell me Joe, ye'd not have gone soft on those Dublin rebels like Séan here?"

Constable Aidan Lynch, like Joe, was an officer of the RIC. He was in his forties yet had the smooth face of a cherub and the sing-song lilt native to the east coast of Ireland. He was referring to the executions in Kilmainham Gaol of the leaders of the Easter Rebellion. Fifteen of them walked blindfolded to a granite wall and shot without trial by firing squad.

"I was tellin' him that when yer at war, anyone who conspires against ye is a traitor, an' there's only one way to deal with traitors, eh?" He shaped a pistol with his fingers and pulled the trigger against his temple. "Bang!"

Joe regarded Aidan and his friend, Séan Keane, whom he'd known since childhood. Placing the trio of pint glasses on the table, he hitched his trousers at the knee and sat. "It's not so simple as that, Aidan. By doing what the Brits have done, they've made martyrs of them all – and there's naught more reckless than that. For every bullet pumped into Pearse, Connelly and the rest, the Crown will have recruited a hundred more rebels who'll take pot shots from ditches at the likes of you and I. Is that what you want?"

"Of course not, Joe; but I never thought I'd see the day ye'd be siding with a bunch of Sinn Féin Jackeens," Aidan retorted.

"Listen, Aidan: maybe the Shinners had a point, maybe they didn't. But dispatching them the way the government did will cause trouble for us all. This won't go away. I tell you – honestly – I couldn't care less whose arse fills the seat of power in Dublin Castle; English arse or Irish arse, it doesn't matter to me. It will still be fat and round and care little for what happens outside the capital. As long as the men and women of King's County have food on the table, a roof over their head and can sleep in the knowledge they'll not be evicted at dawn, I'm happy with whatever Ireland we live in."

"Well said that man! See he's not so stupid as he looks." Séan tousled Joe's thick head of hair.

Joe acknowledged his friend's backhanded compliment with a wry grin and took a long draught of his pint. "So, yes, Aidan, I'd have gone soft on them – but not for their sakes: for ours. Now, for Christ's sake, the pair of you, let's lay off the politics a while and raise a glass to St Brendan!"

St Brendan the Elder had founded the monastery around which the town of Birr grew in the 6th century. Earlier in the day, the

Catholic and Anglican congregations had filed from their respective churches, both of which shared the saint's name, converging on the ruins of the crumbling monastery in the heart of the town. There, amid the skeleton of sandstone, Father O'Brien and the Anglican rector, the Reverend Joyce, had delivered short homilies on Christian forbearance and commonality. Neighbours and colleagues living cheek by jowl, from the humblest farmhand to landed gentry, smiled thinly at one another across the dogmatic divide. The Anglicans then retired to the high-ceilinged dining rooms of Oxmanton Mall – or in the case of Lady Rosse, Birr Castle itself – whilst the Catholic contingent wound back through the streets to Dooly's. While the Head Constable and Sergeant might sup from bowls of bone-china that night, their Catholic subordinates would have to make do with the longest bar in town. It was here that the great and the not-so-good of Catholic Birr reaffirmed their faith through a communion of whiskey and stout.

Leant in the corner alongside Padraig Nolan, Brendan O'Rourke was scanning the scene that played out before him. He'd read each and every word written about the events in Dublin these last few weeks. He could almost imagine that he'd been part of it, and it shamed him somewhat that he wasn't. What he wouldn't give to be able to say that he'd manned the barricades with Thomas Clarke and Seán MacDiarmada – but had he been, he'd now be suffering the consequences. Instead of standing in Dooly's, surreptitiously pouring home-distilled poitín into his tumbler, he'd be in manacles listing on the Irish Sea on the way to some Godforsaken internment camp on the mainland.

"Padraig, see over there." He nodded across the bar to where Constables Conlon and Lynch sat with Seán Keane. "The enemy within."

"Ah, sure, Brendan, they're not so bad. That Conlon fella did some mighty good work for Pat O'Shea when his mare was rustled by tinkers. I heard he drove all the way out to Roscommon in a motor-car, Pat sittin' beside him all the way, so he was, and knocked some heads in Castlereagh until they gave up the horse."

As Padraig spoke, Brendan observed Father O'Brien, already a little worse for wear, totter towards the policemen and pat their shoulders warmly.

"Hand in glove, Padraig; the church an' police force – as it ever was in this town." He downed the bitter spirit and grimaced. "One day the people here will see Conlon an' the rest of 'em for what they are: King George's patsies, with but one aim; to deny us our freedom. I'm a patient man, Padraig, an' I can wait, because I know that what I believe *will* come to pass. The blood spilt in Dublin won't have been in vain. Mark my words; men like Conlon an' Lynch will be forgotten, because it will be our tales that will be told, not theirs."

On the far side of the room, beyond the band and the space cleared for dancing, Brendan spied Seamus Fahy, a like-minded soul and friend of his father. With him were his daughters, Margaret and Carmel, and somebody whom Brendan had never seen before.

"Jaysus! Would ye look at that, Padraig. If that's not a vision of beauty, I don't know what is!"

Padraig followed his friend's carnivorous gaze. Half a head taller than the Fahy sisters, a woman with porcelain-white skin stood twisting the tips of long black hair between her fingers.

"Sure, on my name-day ye'd think I'm due some luck! Excuse me while I ask the future Mrs Brendan O'Rourke for a dance." He winked and made towards the old Fenian and his family.

Padraig smiled. Like the moonshine he brewed, Brendan O'Rourke was raw spirit; a man distilled into a single notion – that though rough and unpalatable to some – was undeniably intoxicating. He believed in a free Ireland and would fight for it when the chance came. Sure, he could be reckless, but that was why Padraig admired him. Brendan would say and do the things that other men would only contemplate and then regret not doing afterwards. Unlike his father, who was mutable as granite, Brendan had inherited his impulsivity from his gypsy mother – along with her fiery hair, her temper and sharp, bony cheeks. Tamed for a while, her wanderlust hadn't been sated, and before Brendan could crawl, she'd slipped away to re-join the roving caravan, leaving the infant to be raised by his father and grandparents.

Through the twirling couples and swaying drunks, Padraig could see Brendan in conversation with Seamus Fahy. Introductions were made and Brendan took the hand of the mystery woman with a courtly bow. She smiled awkwardly and shook her head. Margaret Fahy thrust her hand towards Brendan, who hesitated for a moment before accepting it. Together they stepped forward and were subsumed into the morass of moving limbs.

———————

Carmel Fahy, with lips screwed into tight red wounds, watched her sister twist arm and arch leg to the beat of the bodhrán, linking hands with Brendan O'Rourke and laughing at each step misplaced.

"Kitty, could ye not see that he liked ye? Why would ye not dance with the man?"

"I'm not one for dancing, Carmel. I don't know how."

"Do ye not find him handsome then?"

"I wouldn't know, cousin. I don't have much to do with men back home in Cashel; other than my brothers, that is." Kitty Sheehan continued coiling locks between delicate fingers.

"Daddy says that ye've been sent to find a husband, so he does."

"That's not true, Carmel!" Kitty replied indignantly. "I'm here to spend time with my cousins and see the world outside Tipperary. Come now; let's you and I dance. Can you teach me?"

But as Carmel explained the difference between reels and jigs, Kitty knew what she said was true. Her father *was* worried that she was on the cusp of taking her vows at the convent. He'd railed that the Sheehans didn't need another feckin' nun among their number – they needed *capital investment*, and that didn't come about through fingering rosary beads and whispering Hail Marys, but from making good marriages. The prospects of that in Cashel were scant and so the Sheehans must look further afield: her aunt had done just that, and now she and Seamus rented land and a farmhouse here in King's County. They could even afford to send their son, Ciaran, to university. So, deep down, she understood that she'd been packed off to this affluent town to catch a man with coin in his pockets.

By now the giddying loops of head to dregs, black beer to froth, had loosened the tongues of the three friends by the bar. Politics behind them, Séan Keane waxed lyrical on unrequited love for a chambermaid at Stoneacre House where he was gamekeeper. Joseph Conlon was listening, but he too had noticed the earlier entrance of the striking stranger who now whirled across the floor with a sister or friend, her head thrown back in glee. He'd been watching from the corner of his eye as she rejected the advances of the red-headed O'Rourke. Conlon had come across the man before: he was a farrier who lived off the Portumna Road on the outskirts of town. Joe didn't care for him much – and it wasn't just his politics. His eyes and actions were quicksilver; his vulpine looks reinforcing a sense of feral cunning. The O'Rourkes were inveterate Fenians but they were probably more renowned for producing blindingly potent moonshine. Head Constable Regan had once told Joe of how, when he'd been sent to wreck the stills and smash the jars of an O'Rourke out-house, he'd tied a thread around a grubby penny and dipped it into one of the pots of noxious spirit. Pulling it out, the penny gleamed as though newly minted that morning.

The breathless reel ended to whoops and whistles, and Joe found himself staring at the ebony-haired woman whose pale cheeks were now coloured by twin bruises of pink. She flapped her hands to her throat, bent to whisper to her friend and wove from the room into the lobby beyond. Conlon saw that a moment later, Brendan O'Rourke drained his glass and stalked after her.

Chivalry emboldened by hops and yeast, Joe sank his pint and followed the farrier into the foyer. It was empty, bar a bored bellboy at the reception desk and a grey-faced nun who stood ramrod straight, perennial disapprobation etched into her features. The hotel doors were wedged open in the vain hope that what little breeze there was might disperse the thick fug of smoke that clung to the ceilings and walls. Joe stepped outside and saw that the woman had walked towards the stone column at the centre of Cumberland Square. The orange glow of cigarette-end illuminated the sharp contours of Brendan O'Rourke as he ambled after her.

Joe kept his distance.

He watched as she turned, startled, and tugged at her shawl to cover the skin that swelled above her bodice. O'Rourke reached for her hand and she recoiled, stepping backwards. Joe couldn't hear the words that passed between them, but it didn't matter. He marched purposefully – and only a little unsteadily – towards them. He grabbed O'Rourke by the shoulder.

"The lady's not interested. I think you've drunk too much of your own poison."

O'Rourke spun; a look of irritation souring to hatred when he saw who it was who'd spoken.

"Who are ye to speak for the lady, or my liver for that matter, *Peeler?*"

Taken aback by the marvellous green of the woman's eyes, Joe ignored the challenge and asked clumsily; "Madam, are you comfortable with this man's overtures? I can leave you to continue your conversation if you'd like."

"No: that is, I should go inside and find my cousins." She turned to leave.

Grabbing her hand, Brendan O'Rourke pulled her back. "Ye can't deny a man a kiss on his name-day."

The policeman stepped between them, uncoupling the clasp. "I wouldn't want to shame you in front of a beautiful woman, nor make you look small before your friend," Conlon nodded toward the hotel entrance where Padraig Nolan was lurking, "but she's made herself clear. I think you should go home."

Brendan lunged at Conlon and gripped his lapels with a wiry strength born of wielding hammer and pumping bellows. "It's yer masters in Dublin Castle who should go home, *slave.*"

Joe could smell the caustic spirit on the man's breath and fully believed Regan's story of the coin de-tarnished. He shoved him with more force than was necessary and O'Rourke staggered backward, tripping and falling against the column's plinth with a crunch.

Clambering up, lip split and twisted in a bloodied leer, Brendan reached to his pocket for the jagged neck of the smashed bottle and considered thrusting it into the throat of this smug policeman. But before he could do anything, he felt the tug of Padraig pulling him back, whispering, "Be patient, Brendan. There's no point pickin' a fight that ye can't yet win. Come on, let's get out of here."

Joseph Conlon watched the pair slope away across the square. He waited until they disappeared into the shadows that converged around Main Street before turning to speak to the woman with hair of jet, but she was already halfway back to the hotel. His heart sank. However, just as she stepped into the halo of light at the entrance, she glanced back over her shoulder. Their eyes met once more and she smiled before being ushered inside by her cousin who cast daggers in his direction.

Joe felt strangely light-headed and saw that his hands were trembling. He found himself snatching shallow breaths, as if the air were too rich all of a sudden. He knew it wasn't the drink or the adrenaline, but something else: a feeling he'd never experienced before. Disorientating, yet not entirely unpleasant. He licked dry lips, rubbed his hands together and smacked his cheeks. Smoothing his uniform, Joe tried to regain some composure before joining Séan and Aidan inside.

3

Spring, 2018
Boroughbridge, North Yorkshire, England

He looked like a fox, the old man on the video. Long-eared and thin-chinned, he clamped tight on a clay pipe with sharp, grey teeth. The caption hovering at the bottom of the black and white film dubbed him *'Red' O'Rourke – Commandant of the 2ⁿᵈ Brigade, South Offaly, 1919-21.* The YouTube clip that James had uncovered had been uploaded from a 1971 RTÉ documentary commemorating fifty years since the signing of the Anglo-Irish Treaty. The pixilated footage showed a crooked man shuffling across a muddy trail in a flat cap, woollen jacket and oversized trousers. He was pointing a roughly-hewn walking stick down the lane to where a dry stone wall curved over a small waterway.

"Two of them, there were, on bicycles. They were returnin' to Kinnity Barracks after deliverin' court summons in Clareen. Me an' the boys were hid just there in a ditch. We only had one pistol an' a shotgun between us. As they passed over that brook, there, I wrapped my face in a scarf an' stood in the road. I shouted at them to stop an' surrender their arms, but the policemen kept comin' at me: Jaysus, we were a shambles that day, so we were! The Peelers didn't stop an' I was knocked into the road, flat on my arse, while one o' the boys took a shot at them with the pistol an' almost killed me, so. I felt the bullet fly past, not an inch from my nose! As they made their escape, I took aim with the shotgun, an' clipped one o' them. He tumbled from his cycle, but climbed straight back on an' the pair o' them pedalled back to Kinnity like the divil himself was behind them. That must have been the spring of 1919 – the very first shot I fired in anger in the Tan War."

Charlie had retreated into the kitchen and James could hear her emptying the dishwasher while speaking on the phone. He assumed she'd called her sister back after his coughing fit in the car. James had his laptop out and O'Rourke's book open. Cursory searches online had thrown up a couple of hits: the YouTube clip he'd just watched, a handful of booksellers with copies of O'Rourke's memoir for sale and a brief article from the *Offaly Independent* about his funeral. The banner-line read, CONTEMPORARY OF TOM BARRY AND DAN BREEN LAID TO REST IN KILCORMAC. James squinted at a grainy photograph taken in 1977, which showed a coffin, draped in the Irish tricolour being carried by a quartet of men in balaclavas. *Provos*, thought James. By 1977 the Troubles in Northern Ireland were at their height and the latest incarnation of the Republican struggle for a united Ireland had evolved in the form of the Provisional IRA – the masked men who darkened the headlines of his childhood with coded warnings, nail bombs and blasted buildings. Although Brendan O'Rourke didn't quite merit his own Wikipedia entry, James realised that in the context of his own family history, this man's story was gold dust. He named the killers of James's great-grandfather as Ciaran Fahy and Padraig Nolan, and described in detail how, as the clock approached midday on the 11th July 1921, they ensured that the man responsible for orchestrating a series of police atrocities in and around Birr paid for his sins. If O'Rourke was to be believed, then Joseph Conlon was a nasty piece of work. Reading the accusations laid against the policeman was an uncomfortable experience, exacerbated by the writer's lurid turn of phrase. No wonder James's enquiries as a boy back in Tipperary had been deflected or ignored – the stigma felt by those who knew, or suspected the truth would be more than enough to temper their tongues.

James felt tainted by association; he was ashamed.

As he scanned the pages, he sensed that familiar spectre of his own private guilt flitting behind the typeface; moving at pace with his focal point, incorporeal, but definitely there.

Always there.

A ghost from the past that stalked him from a distance and now, even years later, could manifest itself when he least expected it, broad-siding him with a numbing sense of culpability. James could fully understand why you wouldn't want to talk of shame that black.

He shook his head and scattered the shadows.

He forced himself to focus on the task in hand; that's what kept him grounded. The work, the job, the opportunity to stop what had happened back then happening to anybody else. He pinched himself hard and counted to five. The dark memories were banished with the sharp sting of pain; all that remained were empty brackets on his skin where his fingernails had dug too deep.

Becalmed for now, he turned back to the text and drowned any residual disquiet in O'Rourke's grandiloquence: The IRA man painted Conlon as the savage ringleader of a murder-squad of Black and Tans. James was well aware of the infamous *'Black and Tans'*: they were mostly ex-servicemen brutalised by the shrapnel and unrelenting horror of the First World War, recruited by the British Government to swell the ranks of the struggling RIC in 1920. The 'Tans' had become the bogey-men of modern Irish history, as hated as Oliver Cromwell. So thoroughly demonised were they that no amount of earnest and even-handed research could ever hope to rehabilitate their cursed name. And that is who Sergeant Joseph Conlon had thrown his lot in with: the baddies, the losers, the ghouls who terrified children. In effect, he'd slid between the cracks of history whilst the gunmen who wore the green of the Republic had documentaries made about them in their dotage and photo-journalists at their funerals.

To the victor go the spoils.

For the first time in his life, James now had the exact date and location of his great-grandfather's murder. He'd been looking in the wrong place all along. He'd uncritically assumed that Conlon – like his great-grandmother, Kitty – must have been a Cashel man from Tipperary, but now James knew that he'd been killed only hours before the truce came into effect in a town called Birr; a place he'd never heard of before today.

He was already hooked.

James let the history wind him in, and in doing so, his nebulous stalker slipped deeper into his subconscious.

After registering his credit card on an Irish ancestry site, it was only a matter of minutes before he had located the scant records pertaining to the murder. Contained on a PDF document, hidden amongst the scores of other men and women who met their maker in the first weeks of July 1921, James found the line that summarised the assassination. The death transcription, as it was called, gave Conlon's rank, home address and a brief comment which simply read: *Waylaid on Main Street, Birr, and killed by gunshot wounds inflicted by members of the IRA. He leaves behind a widow and daughter.*

James frowned. The daughter was James's grandmother, Bridget, but why was there no mention of Pat-Joe, her brother? James typed in criteria for a new search and seconds later saw that Patrick Joseph Conlon hadn't been born until December, 1921 in Cashel, Co. Tipperary. James did the maths and worked out that Kitty must have been four months pregnant with Pat-Joe when her husband had been murdered. Evidently, she'd cut all ties to Birr and returned to her home town to raise her daughter and newborn son.

He took a deep breath: the truth had been hiding in plain sight all these years. It beggared belief that it had taken a chance purchase in a bookshop to reveal any of it. James felt a tinge of resentment that facts so elemental to his family story had become lost – *had been allowed to become lost* – in the space of three generations.

James had never known his grandmother, Bridget Devlin. She had died when his mother, Cate, was barely in her twenties. In the few photographs that existed, she looked thin and nervous; James had always handled her image gingerly – she scared him a little bit – her unsmiling eyes were always fixed on something behind the camera lens and James wondered what it was that made her look so uneasy. By contrast, her husband, Enda Devlin, appraised the photographer with an easy confidence. James's grandfather had outlived his wife by a decade and although James had vague recollections of a thickset man in a knitted cardigan who reeked of pipe-smoke, he too had died before James ever got to know him.

He supposed that's why he was so fond of Pat-Joe Conlon – for it was his great-uncle who'd filled the role vacated by Enda Devlin. Almost a hundred years old, Pat-Joe was seeing out his days in a care home in Clonmel. Although frail, he had his wits about him still and charmed the nurses with stories of an Ireland long forgotten. James remembered how Pat-Joe would sit him on his knee and spin tales of saints and banshees, faeries and kings. Sometimes he'd play the tin whistle and sing melancholy songs about mountains and streams. But never did he speak of his father. On the one occasion James had enquired after the gunned-down policeman, Pat-Joe had looked wounded and replied, "Ah, I wouldn't know about that myself, so I wouldn't. My mammy never talked of it. All ye need to know is that he was a good man caught up in evil times."

That was why James felt so conflicted now: *Was Conlon a good man?*

Unbidden, his guilty past slyly whispered back; Are *you* a good man?

"James, I'm off out. I won't be too late."

James snapped back into reality. "What? Where are you going?"

Charlie stood by the kitchen door with her coat on. "I've told you a thousand times. I promised Bekka that I'd look after the kids for the night. She and Tony haven't had an evening out together since Molly was born. I'm sure they'll be back before ten. If you wait up for me, maybe we could…"

She left the suggestion hanging, but James understood. It had been Charlie who'd chosen not to have children and pursue her career, and James had been more than happy to go along with that; especially in light of what had happened. At the time he didn't think he could handle, or even deserved the responsibility of bringing a child into the world. But now a partner at the firm and fast approaching her late thirties, Charlie had been struck by an unquashable need for progeny, and she'd thrown herself into baby-making with all the vigour and zeal that had served her so well in her professional life. She wasn't to be put off, and at risk of losing her too, James had relented. At first he'd enjoyed the urgent sex at diverse times of night and day, the crumpled sheets and the musky scent of his twenties. But recently it had become too mechanical and desperate, and the crash that Charlie experienced at the end of the month when it had all been in vain again, was wearing on her.

"OK. Send my love to them all. Drive safe!"

He heard the front door close. Technically, he was meant to be avoiding wine to keep his sperm lively, but taking into account the scores of first and second cousins across the water and his Irish family's love of the hard stuff, he reasoned that his genetic makeup demanded alcohol as both aphrodisiac and fertility treatment. Besides, he *really* needed a drink.

He opened a bottle, switched off the laptop and decided to read the book from start to finish. He wanted to inhabit the world that Joseph Conlon had died in, and James knew that the best way to do that was to lose himself in ink and paper.

4

May, 1916
Cashel, Country Tipperary, Ireland

"I wouldn't want to shame you in front of a beautiful woman."
Kitty turned the words over and over in her head. *Beautiful woman*
he'd called her. Stood in the convent yard, dressed all in white,
a starched pinafore brushing her ankles and a scarf covering her
hair, Kitty felt more matronly than alluring. She had returned
home to Cashel and was back with the nuns at the convent school.
There she helped prepare ham and cabbage for the children's lunch
and washed and dried the dishes afterwards. She administered
spoonfuls of foul-tasting tincture to girls with whooping cough
and sometimes even helped with their letters and sums in the
classroom. It was late-morning and Sister Ursula's bible class
had been allowed outside to enjoy ten-minute's worth of spring
air. The pair of them patrolled the courtyard listening for petty
blasphemies and watching for unladylike behaviour.

Kitty was bridling at the fact that apparently another Sheehan
girl married to the Church was preferable to even one of them
courting a policeman. Since the evening when she'd first laid
eyes on Constable Conlon, as she'd discovered he was called,
she couldn't shake the image of him from her head. She bit her
lip to stop the smile that threatened to crack across her face at

the memory of how the tall policeman had swatted away the discourteous red-head with the nonchalance of a prize bull flicking a fly with its tail. God knows why her cousins were so keen on the foxy little fellow. That night she had become lost in her own world as her uncle cracked the whip and the trap conveyed her and her cousins back to the farmhouse on the Riverstown Road. She replayed every word and nuance of expression over and over in her head, and later, alone in the room left empty now Ciaran was away in Galway, she'd poured her thoughts and emotions onto the pages of her diary by the flickering flame of a candle.

The emotions had only seemed to intensify with the passage of time and days later, when Carmel and she had been sent to town to collect provisions from Skelly's, Kitty had snuck away from her cousin, only to be discovered mooning about outside the barracks on John's Mall hoping to catch a glimpse of the policeman. Scolded fiercely by her cousin for harbouring such lunacy, she'd been dragged back home to the farm.

Kitty, who'd never in all her life looked at a man with improper thoughts, found herself prone to flushes and prickly sweats, and impure flights of fancy that both thrilled and shamed her at the same time. She cared not that he was a policeman, and fantasised that like the star-crossed lovers of Verona, their unlikely union could be something purer and stronger than the predictable matches of rural Ireland, bonded as they were by family ties and mutual interest. Something had awoken in her that night that made her feel anxious, elated, giddy and sick at the same time, and she committed all these contrary feelings to the page with a passion that alarmed her.

But five days ago, she had returned from the fields where she and thirteen-year-old Micheál had been foraging for mushrooms. The moment she stepped across the threshold, she could see that something was very wrong. Uncle Seamus was sitting at the rough wooden table slicing potatoes with a razor-sharp blade, his calloused fingers inured to the nicks of the knife. Her diary lay open before him. Hovering at his shoulder, unable to look her in the face, stood Carmel. Seamus never took his eyes from the spud.

"Yer father would fain take poison afore he'd see his daughter court a man of the RIC. These words here, Kitty, they'd break his heart, an' so they're best never read." With that, her uncle sighed, strode slowly to the hearth and placed the bound pages on the smoking turf. "No good could ever come of these wild notions, girl. This can only end badly for everyone. Best forgotten."

The following day, chaperoned by Aunt Mary, Kitty watched from the rattling window as the fields of King's County became the fields of Tipperary and the tiny black tracks of the Great Southern and Western Railway snaked away from her; back towards Birr and the man whom she feared she'd never see again. Late that night as she sobbed silently in the bed she'd known since childhood, she heard the urgent whispers of her father and aunt downstairs, and it was no surprise when the next morning her mother walked her to the convent gates, and she'd donned the white smock and resumed her duties for the Sisters.

Was this what madness was like?

If it was, Joseph Conlon welcomed it with open arms. The last week and a half had been unbearable. He had woken on the morning after St Brendan's Day with the kind of hangover only achieved by drinking your entire bodyweight in stout; a heavy, muddy head that struggled to cast thought at all and a tongue like pumice stone.

The police barracks were just off Cumberland Square and he'd slept that night on a cot alongside the snoring Aidan Lynch. As he made tea and tried to rouse his colleague, he began to piece together shattered recollections of the night before: smoke and music – way too much beer: the bloody leer of the drunkard and the hateful glare of the girl on the steps. But emerging above all this was the pristine image of the pale skinned stranger with eyes of green.

Over the course of the next few days he'd met with resistance, but being a big man who could simulate menace when needed, Constable Conlon had ascertained from the Fenian fraternity that she was Catherine Sheehan from Tipperary, the niece of Seamus Fahy. Moreover, she was unmarried and unbetrothed. However, his clumsy enquiries must have come to the attention of her uncle, because by the end of the week she had been packed off home to Cashel.

Hence the glorious madness that saw him skirting Devil's Bit Mountain on the Cashel Road in a twenty-five horsepower Crossley-Tender. He'd taken the motor-car before the crack of dawn and if questioned by Sergeant Malloy on his return, he had a perfectly feasible tale to hand that involved cock-fighting tinkers who kept crossing county lines to evade justice.

———

Kitty was dabbing a shiny graze on a tiny knee. As the child winced at every touch of the handkerchief, Kitty perceived in the distance a low-pitched thrumming that grew to a growl. One by one the girls closest to the convent gates started squealing with delight.

"Look! It's a real motor car!"

"Miss Catherine there's a policeman come to arrest Sister Ursula!

"He's getting out, so he is!"

Kitty's stomach lurched with a mixture of anticipation and apprehension. "Now be off with you Róisín, it's just a graze. It will be gone by morning. Maud Dolan, NOBODY is going to arrest Sister Ursula. Get away from the gates now, will you!"

Climbing from the long, black motor car was the man who'd not left her thoughts for one moment. Tall and handsome with his cap under his arm, he approached the railings. Kitty supressed a smile as she walked towards him acutely aware of the raptor stare that bore into her from the shadows of the convent door. Sister Ursula was scrutinising her every step, and Kitty knew that a scalding sermon of hellfire and brimstone awaited her later.

Kitty paused, chanced one last timorous look over her shoulder at the old nun and opened the gate.

The policeman examined his polished boots, shuffled uncomfortably, cleared his throat and began: "Miss Sheehan. I…" He coughed again. "Forgive me if this is impertinent and forward, alas, I fear it is both, but I felt impelled to find you. I haven't the words in me to explain why. I just had to. I will understand if you tell me to go, but I knew that if I never saw you again – at least the once – I would drive myself mad with regret. There. I've said it. Forgive me."

A pause.

Kitty breathed deeply and composed herself. She was about to say the bravest thing she had ever said in her life: "There's nothing to forgive, Constable. I'm truly glad that you've found me."

Joe, so solemn and fearful a moment before, broke into a blushing grin. "Do you think that the Sisters would allow me to take you for a spin in my motor-car, unchaperoned?"

"I don't suppose they would, Constable," Joe's face faltered, "but I will come with you anyhow."

Kitty pulled the scarf from her head and unpinned her hair. Tying it to the railings, she slipped through the convent gate without daring to turn. She knew she wasn't going back this time.

———

They drove for what felt like hours. Kitty closed her eyes and let the wind buffet her hair, whipping and tangling it into wild, black knots. She screamed with laughter as they careered over potholes and for a moment she felt weightless. Over the roar of the engine it was impossible to talk without shouting, but it didn't matter; there was no need for conversation. The only thing that mattered was that they were together racing along country lanes, away from the prying eyes of the nuns or her family. Returning towards Cashel, Kitty pointed at the crag that reared up over the town. Joseph slowed and pulled up at the foot of St Patrick's Rock. He walked around her side of the car and helped her out.

"Constable, up here you'll see the best view in all of Ireland. I promise."

Kitty trotted ahead, giddy with excitement and Joe was forced to extend his stride to match her pace. Together the pair began to climb the vertiginous steps that led to the slate grey ruins that watched over the plain of Tipperary. Joe had read about the seat of ancient Irish warrior lords, a fortress sanctuary and the place where St Patrick had baptised King Aengus. Yet he had never climbed this mount, nor wandered through the derelict and roofless cathedral atop it. He felt wonder as he raised his eyes heavenward and followed the curved lines of herring-bone vaulting that arced above them. He felt peace as he watched wispy clouds scud across the skyline framed by empty arches set in stone. And he felt contentment as he looked into those eyes that were the cool-green of pine forests clinging to snow-capped peaks.

Wordlessly they had entwined their hands as they approached the ruin, and just as wordlessly they knew that nothing could now disjoin them.

"I told you that it was the most beautiful view in all of Ireland."

Joe looked past her, through the headstones that cast long blue shadows across the summit of the hill, and beyond to the rolling fields patterned by hedgerow and coppice, bathed in the soft glow of the dying sun.

"They call it the Golden Vale. It's so peaceful. The land of my fore-fathers." Kitty kicked off her shoes and dug her toes into the grass. "All my kin sleep deep in this soil." She caressed the smooth of the marble. "I'd see myself sleep here too, so I would. Maybe beside you, Joseph Conlon?"

"I'd like that, Kitty Sheehan."

Joe very gently tilted her face upwards. He kissed her softly on the lips and the shadow they cast across the graveyard was one.

5

Spring, 2018
Boroughbridge, North Yorkshire, England

"I'm home!"

The house was silent.

Charlie stepped into the living room and saw that James was fast asleep on the sofa, an empty bottle of wine on the coffee table alongside a large glass and the book he'd bought that afternoon. She frowned and took the bottle and glass through to the kitchen. Returning with a cup of tea, she wriggled onto the sofa next to James, but still he didn't wake.

The years hadn't dimmed her love for him. Little flecks of grey were starting to appear on his crown, but his hair was just as thick and he didn't look any different to the man she'd fallen for in her first year of university. She had never resented what others called his lack of ambition. He was a classroom teacher with no interest in climbing the greasy pole. He'd even packed in a cushy job at a private college in Leeds to take up the post at Wetherby after they'd moved in together. That was at the time of his 'wobble'. In the wake of the death of a childhood friend whom she'd never met – Connor, he'd been called – James had accepted a position at a failing Catholic secondary school and thrown himself into teaching with a masochistic fervour. He'd supported her as she took bar exams and worked criminally long hours in the office and he'd never questioned her decision to forge a career before a family. Neither had he openly objected to her need to start one now, albeit she sensed that he wasn't as committed as she to the project – *as the empty bottle of wine indicated.* But they complemented each other well; James was an antidote to the corporate world she inhabited – her very own curiosity, and she needed him more than he'd ever know.

Unlike James, she was no bibliophile, and barely registered the titles on the straining shelves; yet she was intrigued by this battered tome with tawny script on the spine. Besides, any book that made you choke had to pack a punch. Charlie reached across and picked it up. Flicking through the chapters she stopped at a page that seemed interesting. She began to read:

The Catching Flame

The blood of the Dublin martyrs that we had hoped would soak the furrows of our native land, nourish the soil and grow thousands more prepared to die for a Republic, was wasted on those we left behind. From Frongoch prison, we learned that back home there was neither the stomach nor the will to follow our lead. It seems the seeds sown in the cannon fire of Dublin had yet to burgeon in the general populace.

All this changed in 1917: Fighting men like Collins and myself were released from our incarceration and returned to Ireland, reinvigorated, radicalised and determined to succeed. We set about reorganising ourselves and under the leadership of Éamon de Valera, Sinn Féin was reborn. This new Sinn Féin married the threat of violence with the legitimacy and authority of the ballot box, and Irish Volunteers like myself joined the party and agitated in the rural areas for other men to join the movement.

All across Ireland, the native population rented their own fields from men who lived in stately homes on the other side of the Irish Sea. They were sick of the lies that John Redmond and his Irish Parliamentary Party forced down their throats. He talked of the guarantee of Home Rule – a Dublin Parliament that would run Ireland for the Irish. He'd been talking about it for decades but he continued to promise that it was just around the corner. We had seen it delayed, and delayed again. We were not stupid men; we could discern that the Home Rule Bill was a cheque forever post-dated. I was instructed to focus my energies on the rural areas of Offaly, Tipperary and Roscommon where simple farming folk felt the hurt of British rule most. There my words and my passion converted many to the cause.

By October of that year, Sinn Féin membership had swollen to over quarter of a million. Finally the blood let in the streets of Dublin was bearing fruit. Now, reader, you must remember that what was happening in Ireland was only part of a wider picture. 1917 was the year of revolution: in Russia the Tsar had abdicated and the Bolsheviks led by Lenin and Trotsky had seized power in Petrograd. For the first time in history, the common man was taking power from the wealthy. The dream of a workers' republic that had led James Connelly to bear arms on the bank of the Liffey was now reality.

When I look back, all these years later, I believe that a candle was lit in 1916. That flicker showed us the way, but it was only in 1918 that the flame caught and the fire began to burn uncontrollably across this land.

Always a good Catholic, I knew well the story of Saul and his Damascene conversion. For me, the conscription crisis was such an example of divine intervention. For it wasn't solely our tireless work that led so many into the light, but the sheer arrogance of the English themselves: They saw fit to force young Irishmen, who had no quarrel with the Germans, to don the uniform of the British Army and die ignoble deaths in rain-soaked holes in Flanders for a master who had oppressed them these four hundred years past. I must admit that when I heard the news, I laughed the heartiest laugh I had for months and raised a toast to Lloyd George! As Yeats, with words more eloquent than those of an honest soldier, wrote, "It seems to me a strangely wanton thing that England, for the sake of fifty thousand Irish soldiers, is prepared to hollow another trench between the countries and fill it with blood."

Belatedly across Ireland those intellectual 'nationalists', whom to my mind were no better than those we sought to expel, joined with us. Even that old fraud of an Irish politician, that stooge of the status quo, John Dillon, walked out of the vipers' nest in Westminster and returned to Dublin to work alongside Sinn Féin. The unions, the priests and the bishops united, and came to see the truth: *that unless we rid ourselves of these parasites, we would never be a nation.*

And so in every hamlet, market town and city, thousands attended rallies, took the anti-conscription pledge and brought the machinery of British government to a standstill in a General Strike. And what did the fools do? They arrested scores of Sinn Féin representatives including De Valera himself, and held them on trumped up charges of treason.

The outrage was deafening. The men were released, the Bill was dropped, but the damage inflicted on the British was irrevocable.

In the November 1918 elections, Sinn Féin won seventy–three seats from just over a hundred. The people had spoken.

The Republic had awoken.

As Charlie read the last lines, she looked up to see James smiling at her through heavy lids, massaging his neck.

"What do you think?"

"He's a bit preachy, isn't he?"

"Just a little." He rubbed her thigh. "He was one of the men who murdered my great-grandfather."

"How can you bear to read it?"

James considered for a moment. "I wanted to understand the rationale for killing Conlon just minutes before the truce. They must have wanted him dead pretty badly and I needed to know what he'd done; and O'Rourke explains it all. It's a grimly fascinating read. I mean this guy makes Conlon out to be a monster – in fact his description of him makes Himmler look compassionate. It's so over the top; and that made me think, how much can I trust O'Rourke's account? So I did some digging."

James reached for his laptop and turned to a page in the book that he'd bookmarked with a Post-it Note. Charlie smiled at his enthusiasm. It reminded her of the night on the stairs with the first edition of the Christina Rossetti anthology.

"Look, O'Rourke writes here that he was arrested in Dublin along with all the others during the Easter Rising of 1916. He goes on to describe his year in Frongoch prison in Wales and how he pow-wowed with the big-fella, Michael Collins. But since the centenary of the Rising all the records of those incarcerated have been released online and he is not there. I've checked and re-checked. There was no Brendan O'Rourke ever arrested in Dublin, or sent to an internment camp in Britain."

"OK, so what does that mean?"

"Well it means that he's prepared to lie about a big chunk of his life, confident that he could get away with it. And he almost has – at the time he wrote this book most of the men involved in the Tan War were either dead or senile, and before the declassification of official government records or the internet, who could challenge his version of events? So if he's lying about that, he could be lying about lots of other things. Maybe Sergeant Joseph Conlon wasn't a monster after all. *The winners weave their own narratives* – look at the Normans with the Bayeux Tapestry."

Charlie yawned. "You've lost me."

James warmed to the analogy. "Basically, I think that if I tug at the frayed edges of this man's fabrication – then I might uncover what lies beneath."

"That would be a wall, James."

"OK, that doesn't quite work – I mean the truth, Charlie."

"Do you mean *your* truth, James?"

James shrugged. "Well, it can't hurt to do a little research can it? Next week is Phoebe's birthday and while we are down in London I could nip in to the National Archives and really get stuck in. I could quiz Mum too, and see if she knows any more than she's told me."

"Whatever rocks your boat." Charlie pulled her bra-strap down over her shoulder and fluttered her eyelashes coquettishly. "Husband, can we go to bed now, or has that *entire* bottle of wine made you as muddled as your metaphors?"

James smiled. "If you grab this bull by the horns, he'll take you to heaven and back."

Charlie cackled as she took his hand and led him upstairs.

6

May, 1918
Galway City, Ireland

Two young men in grey caps, hands buried deep in their pockets strode at speed up Quay Street, the briny tang of salt, seaweed and oyster shells sweeping up the bay through the Spanish Arch. They were talking excitedly as they crossed the rushing River Corrib ducking past hawkers, tinkers and gypsies who thrust brightly coloured scarves, matches and posies of heather before them. Galway city, with its pastel-coloured facades and cacophony of street calls and fiddles, was a world away from the sedate avenues of Birr; and as Ciaran and fellow student, Dermot Rooney, emerged from Quay Street onto Cross Street, Ciaran had to grab hold of his friend to stop him being crushed by a huge, lumbering horse-drawn tram that trundled before them.

As they approached Eyre Square, the crowds thickened and Dermot had to raise his voice to be heard above the hub-bub around them. "We'll never hear a thing back here, Ciaran. We'll have to make our way through the crush. Sure, I can't even see the podium. Come on, follow me!" With that, he dove into the throng and started weaving, apologising and squeezing his way forward.

When they could make no more headway, halted by an impassable wall of tightly-packed shoulders, Ciaran made for a lamp post. Half perching on Dermot's shoulder, arm wrapped around the iron column, he pulled himself up and surveyed the multitude. He had never seen so many souls in one place at the same time. It was hard to believe that there were this many people in all Ireland, let alone that they could crush into one square in the centre of Galway. Ciaran observed that the crowd was almost entirely made up of men: bowlers, flat caps and even boaters undulated gently before him as far as the eye could see. Interspersed amongst them a handful of larger, more colourful hats, garlanded with native foliage were worn by women clutching bouquets tied with ribbons of green, white and orange. Above the shifting swathes, like main masts with sails unfurled, huge banners affirmed anti-conscription slogans; each one held aloft by men who wore the dark-green armbands of Sinn Féin. Ciaran, unlike his father and sisters, was no radical. He believed in the rule of law, and until this crisis over conscription he'd held firm in the belief that Britain would honour the Home Rule Act, passed in 1914 but postponed for the duration of the conflict with Germany. No more men need die in Ireland to obtain what had already been decided constitutionally. His moderate views had caused untold strife at home and it was a relief to be away in Galway, a day's journey from the opprobrium of his father and sharp tongues of his sisters; both of whom now wore the uniform of *Cumann na mBan*, the women's wing of the Irish Volunteers.

The atmosphere was charged: all around him eyes shone brightly while throats were hoarse with the strain of chanting slogans or shouting to be heard over the roar of the crowd. Ciaran couldn't help but notice the armoured cars of the RIC who were setting up a perimeter around the demonstrators. More ominously, as he raised his line of sight, he spotted the tell-tale glints of sun catching glass on the rooftops of the grand shops that lined Eyre Square. He prayed that they were field-glasses and not sniper sights.

The clamour quelled and a suited gentleman with a neatly trimmed white beard stepped out onto the wooden dias before them all. He held no notes in his hand and stood patiently until even the hushing had subsided.

John Dillon, until recently a Member of Parliament in Westminster, began in a measured tone that was clearly audible to the thousands listening. "Irishmen and Irishwomen, I say with all my soul that it is good to stand in front of you today. It is heartening to see such a multitude united in one aim. We have assembled, all of us, to take the Anti-Conscription Pledge. This pledge is our mantra and we must stand by it; for these words are binding. The Pledge runs thus: *Denying the right of the British government to enforce compulsory service in this country, we pledge ourselves solemnly to one another to resist conscription by the most effective means at our disposal.*"

The crowd erupted in thunderous cheers and applause.

"It was but a few short months ago that those who seek to deny us our place in the world rubbed their hands in glee to see how this land was divided. Fragmented politics had weakened us all; and brother had turned on brother, sister on sister. But no more! I am glad to say that on this issue, I and the Irish Parliamentary Party stand hand in hand with Sinn Féin!" Cries of support were shouted amid much whistling. "We stand hand in hand with the ancient Roman Catholic Church! We stand alongside the men of the Unions!" Banners trembled and baritone mutterings of support rumbled amongst the dockers and factory workers. "United we stand and together we condemn this conscription bill! We will not allow one drop of Irish blood to be spilled in consequence of this blundering act of tyranny!"

From all around Ciaran's vantage point screams of, "We take the pledge!" "We'll not go to die in foreign fields!" rang out. Balled fists were pumped. Strangers embraced. On the far side of the square, Ciaran saw a detachment of RIC attempt to drag a man from amongst the multitude. He resisted. Others stepped in to pull him back from the policemen's grip. A wave of uniforms charged at the crowd, truncheons raised and began to cudgel men and boys. A woman stepped between them and was knocked to the ground and dragged, kicking and screaming, towards the armoured cars. Ciaran watched as a surge of angry muscle made for the policemen, who backed off, wisely releasing those whom they'd pulled from the melee. A wall of Irish defiance formed before them and Ciaran heard himself chanting with everyone else; "We'll not go! We'll not go!" He was laughing wildly now, tingling with transformative ardour. His heart was pounding and pumped an altered, renewed, even redder blood. He could feel it flooding the labyrinthine network of his mind, washing away reservation and trepidation; allowing him for the first time to perceive truths for so long hidden. His father was right: he'd always said that parties like Dillon's IPP were part of the problem – by accepting office in the House of Commons, Irish Nationalism was forever diluted and compromised. Sinn Féin refused to take up their seats in Westminster, and if men like John Dillon had decided to throw their lot in with them, then Ciaran believed that it was time for him to join the movement too.

When all the speeches had ended, flushed and exhilarated, Ciaran and Dermot were sucked up by the current and moved as one with the hordes. From Eyre Square to the suburbs, a rush of humanity poured through the thoroughfares of Galway; and though the streams split and followed different courses through the city streets, like the gushing tributaries of the River Corrib, they were truly flowing in the same direction.

7

May, 1918
Birr, King's County, Ireland

Kitty screamed in agony.

She thought that she may pass out the pain was so intense.

Bloodied rags lay sodden on the blankets at the foot of the bed. Kitty gripped Biddy Fitzpatrick so tightly that she feared she'd snap the brittle bones of the midwife's hand. Peering up at her, framed by the V of her pale-white thighs, Biddy's daughter, a pock-faced girl with fingers too fat for her choice of profession, probed inside Kitty and shot a concerned look towards her mother.

"Mam, there's too much blood, so there is, an' I can't see the child."

"Don't fret, Claire. This one's strong. She has the grip of a wrestler, so she does. The child will come in its own time. Have ye not seen the size of her man? Kitty here is going to be the mother of a giant, so."

Kitty grimaced and moaned as another wave of contractions shuddered through her frame. Biddy stroked her soaking hair. "Hush now, girl. Breathe in, and breathe out. Think of something that fills ye with joy, the happiest thoughts ye can, an' then push with all yer might when I tell ye."

So Kitty thought of her wedding day – a year ago this month, celebrated at St Brendan's on the banks of the Camcor River. She remembered Father O'Brien shaking the hand of her husband – so splendid in his uniform – and their first kiss as man and wife. She fought the darts of pain shooting from her core and focused instead on the moment they passed between the ranks of RIC who formed a guard of honour. And how a great gust of wind had shaken the bows of an apple blossom, sending hundreds of pink-white petals fluttering down over them. A bittersweet moment; God had seen to grant them confetti although there was no one there to throw it. Only Sister Ursula had travelled from Cashel that day, carrying with her a letter that Kitty's mother had smuggled from the house in the folds of her skirt. As for the Fahys of Birr, they could barely look Kitty in the eye when they passed her on the street – that is apart from Ciaran. On the rare occasions he returned to his home town, he would always see fit to contact his cousin by letter, and they would meet at Dooly's, where he would treat her to Darjeeling and finely cut cucumber sandwiches. She would listen as he told her about life in Galway and the smell of the sea, and how on a clear day, if you looked really hard, you could make out the tips of New York skyscrapers peaking over the rim of the Atlantic Ocean. She didn't believe him of course, but she craved the chance to stand tip-toed on the rocks of the West Coast and see for herself.

The memory was doubly joyous because later on, after Head Constable Regan had toasted the couple in his spacious drawing room on Oxmanton Mall, he had taken Joseph to one side and talked of promotion. Her husband's exam results had been amongst the highest in the land, and with the imminent departure of Sergeant Malloy, the vacant position was his; if he wanted it. Molloy had confided in Regan that he was too long in the tooth to face the animosity towards the RIC that was hardening across the county. The day he'd witnessed a constable knocked unconscious from a tree, pelted with rocks by men and women whom he'd considered peaceable folk because the lad had been sent to pull down an Irish tricolour, was the same day that he'd handed in his notice. For Kitty and Joseph that meant that they wouldn't have to live in the crowded police barracks on John's Mall but in the private accommodation that came with the promotion. If they were lucky enough to be blessed with children, their sons and daughters wouldn't grow up 'barrack-rats', but be brought up in the fine looking house on Main Street with the red front door and bronze knocker.

A violent contraction saw the corners of the room flicker and fall into shade as Kitty faltered between states of consciousness.

"Now, girl! For the love of God, push!"

Kitty balled her fists and screamed.

Downstairs, Sergeant Joseph Conlon paced the kitchen. He was lighting another cigarette before he'd stubbed the last. He examined his pocket watch and calculated that nothing other than tobacco smoke had passed his lips in six hours. He wasn't hungry and it didn't matter how many jugs of water he consumed, his mouth was desert-dry – so he'd given up even trying. From time to time, Claire Fitzpatrick had stomped down the stairs with a handful of bloody rags to collect more hot water, and each time she'd said, "Nothing yet, Sergeant. Have patience."

But the last scream had shaken him. It sounded as if Kitty was dying upstairs. Joe couldn't help himself. He bounded three-stairs-to-a-stride up to the bedroom door, and turning the handle, he heard the reedy wails of a newborn.

Composing himself, his hand froze and he knocked gently on the door. Biddy Fitzpatrick called out, "Sergeant, you're very welcome in here now, so you are. Come inside and meet your daughter, Bridget Conlon."

8

Spring, 2018
Richmond-upon-Thames, London, England

Cate Lucas paled. "What are you saying?" The champagne flute frozen an inch from her lips. "Are you telling me that my own mother watched as her father was shot dead right before her very eyes?"

"Yes, Mum." James fidgeted with a napkin.

Cate Lucas stared blankly for a moment at her son and tipped the remaining champagne down in one. "Waiter! Another bottle please. Thank you."

A silent claxon blared, painfully audible to all at the table bar Cate herself. Worried looks passed between the rest of the family as the waiter returned and popped the cork. Cate allowed her glass to be refilled and took a large sip. "She never breathed a word. Not once in her entire life. It explains so much: her coldness, her distance, her…" Cate grasped at the ether with her fingers for a phrase, "her inability to *connect*. That's why I left Ireland so young – to get away from the *insularity*. Sometimes when she and I were alone in a room, I'd close my eyes and it was easy to imagine that there was nobody there but me. She barely breathed. She occupied another space. If it wasn't for the cigarette smoke that clung to her, you wouldn't know she was in the house at all."

Cate Lucas was still in her fifties if you believed her Facebook profile, and on looks alone she could almost get away with the lie. She wore skinny jeans and Chanel No. 5; her pearl-white bob complementing the string of plump orbs around her throat. She'd fled the Devlin home in Cashel when she was seventeen to train in London as a nurse. It was there in the mid-60s she'd met a junior doctor with prospects and through acts and acrobatics that the priests back home would condemn as mortal sins (but had nevertheless served their purpose), she accepted the proposal of the ambitious, young registrar. At a time when the words, *'No Blacks, No Dogs, No Irish'* were pasted inside the front windows of rental properties across the capital, she'd clipped her consonants, rounded her vowels and buried her Tipperary past in a shallow grave along with her catechisms and her communion dress. In time, Catherine Devlin became Cate Lucas, wife of spinal surgeon, Frank Lucas and mother to James and Phoebe; and her hometown of Cashel became a mere holiday destination, exotic in its unfamiliarity.

Now, half a century later, sitting in a French restaurant on the banks of the Thames, sipping Bollinger and picking at salade niçoise, Cate could feel the lightly shovelled soil tremble, as what lay beneath stirred.

"How do you know this, James?"

James cast a glance towards Charlie, who had advised against bringing any of this up during Phoebe's birthday meal, but she refused to meet his gaze, pretending instead to examine the tasting menu.

James considered how much to tell his mother about what he had discovered in the last week. Since reading the book from cover to cover he had subscribed to a number of archive databases, and during free periods at school had been downloading articles and documents that tallied with the events that O'Rourke described. On the front page of *The Irish Independent* under the banner, *SERIES OF GHASTLY CRIMES,* halfway down one of the crowded columns was the headline, *SERGEANT SHOT OUTSIDE HIS HOME*. It read:

> *On Monday morning, Sergeant Joseph Conlon of the RIC was shot dead outside his house on Main Street, Birr, King's County. He was only yards from his front door when he was accosted by an unknown assailant who fired three revolver shots into his chest. The act was witnessed by his wife and child. Two suspects were seen making their escape by bicycle in the direction of Bridge Street.*

You could be forgiven for missing it amid the maelstrom of minute, black typeface crushed onto the page. It was clear that in the final days before the truce, an orgy of violence erupted across Ireland. In just one column a relentless litany of deadpan banners declared, *FOUR UNARMED SOLDIERS KIDNAPPED ON STREETS OF CORK, MAJOR O'CONNOR MURDERED, UNARMED PRIVATE SLAIN, GIRL OF 15 MURDERED, COLD BLOODED SKIBBEREEN CRIME, FARMER DRAGGED OUT AND SHOT, REVENGE KILLING IN QUEEN'S COUNTY, FAMILY BURNED TO DEATH*. Amongst so many who grew cold on mortuary slabs that week, it was no wonder that the death of Joseph Conlon had been reduced to four sentences, buried beneath an avalanche of tragedy. This contrasted markedly with the reporting two years earlier of the first blood spilled in the war: two RIC constables had been ambushed at Soloheadbeg in Co. Tipperary in early 1919 escorting a cache of gelignite to a quarry, and pages and pages were devoted to their assassination. One of the men responsible, Dan Breen, had a £1000 bounty placed on his head and a nationwide manhunt was put in place. The thousands of wanted-posters pinned inside pubs and outside RIC barracks described Breen as, '*about 12 stone, clean shaven; sulky bulldog appearance; looks rather like a blacksmith coming from work*'. But such was the vicious end-game of this conflict that in the space of less than thirty months, killing a policeman in front of his family earned barely an inch of ink.

Frank Lucas watched from the corner of his eye as his wife swilled back another two fingers of Champagne. "Yes, James. Why now? Where's all this suddenly come from?"

James was already regretting bringing this up tonight. It had been a bad call. "It's a long story, but I'll cut it short; I found this book written by an old IRA man back in the '50s and it tells the story of the Anglo-Irish War in County Offaly. The writer claims that Mum's grandfather, Sergeant Joseph Conlon, was a marked man in the town of Birr. His crimes were so bad that the IRA were determined to execute him before the truce came into effect on the 11th July, 1921. That's why with only hours to go before an armistice, two assassins were posted outside his house and when he came out, they shot him dead. The newspapers report that his wife and daughter witnessed it all."

"But, what crimes are you talking about, James? Nobody has ever spoken to me about any *crimes* of my grandfather." Cate's voice had developed an edge that was familiar to the Lucas family and only manifested itself after alcohol and before some kind of scene. Her glass empty again, Cate reached towards the ice bucket.

"Some water, Mum?" Phoebe thrust a water jug in her direction and shot James a glance that spoke volumes.

"No thank you, Phoebe, it's your birthday and I'd like some more bubbles please."

James waited while her glass was refilled, and tried back pedalling. "What was she like? Your grandma, Kitty Conlon? You've never really spoken of her. Have you any photographs?"

Mollified for a moment, Cate considered the questions. "I am not sure that I do." She frowned. "Maybe in the loft: I'll get your father to look. Your Uncle Noel will have some back at the shop in Cashel. I never knew her. Like my mother, she passed too soon. Pat-Joe said she'd died of a broken heart, and my mother never spoke of the past, but there was one photograph I remember she kept in a tin frame on the dresser in her bedroom. We weren't allowed in there, but I used to sneak in when she was serving customers downstairs to try on high heels and scents. It was a very formal portrait taken after my mother's christening. My grandmother, Kitty, was a rare beauty; she had long, black hair and delicate features. I can see some of her in you, Phoebe."

James's sister smiled and twisted her hair.

"Although she wasn't gurning like everybody seems to nowadays, you could see in her eyes that she was so happy and proud – of the child in her arms and her husband, the policeman."

"Could you describe him for me, Mum?" James asked.

"He was tall; big chested too. He wore a dark uniform, a peaked cap and I remember, he wore a silver pocket-watch chain that looped into his breast pocket. One large hand rested on my grandmother's shoulder, almost protectively I always thought. It pained me that my mother never opened up about her parents, and Pat-Joe was no better. But I can understand, given the times: ignorant old biddies about town used to hiss at the Conlons whenever they passed them in the street. That happened for years. There were those in Cashel that wouldn't let Pat-Joe cross their threshold, even for a wake. For some, those old hatreds were impossible to shake, I suppose."

Cate stared into the middle distance for a moment.

The hovering waiter took his opportunity to dive in and replenish glasses and collect plates. "But, James, you still haven't explained what crimes you think my grandfather responsible of. I was told he was a fine man; a devout Catholic, murdered for no more reason than the uniform he wore. The man on my mother's dresser didn't look like a criminal."

James hesitated.

49

"*I want to know*, James." Cate's demand was delivered with enough volume to quell the conversations of other diners around their table.

"OK. Now, Mum, remember, these are just the allegations of one man; a man whom I know can be liberal with the truth, so take all this with a pinch of salt." James took a deep breath. "They say that Sergeant Joseph Conlon ran a 'Murder Squad' in Birr. He led and took part in reprisal raids where rebels were much more likely to end up six feet under than behind bars. In the week before he died an IRA safe-house was razed to the ground and an entire family perished in the flames. Oh, and there was a priest inside at the time too."

"NO!"

This time, across the restaurant, couples stopped. Clauses and cutlery arrested mid-sentence, mid-air.

"I don't believe it. That can't be true. He went to Mass every Sunday of his life!"

"Mum, calm down." Phoebe rubbed her mother's shoulder. "James doesn't believe it either. In fact he's going to go to the National Archives tomorrow to see what he can find. He's confident that the original documentation might show an entirely different side to the story." Phoebe smiled at James through gritted teeth. "*Although he did say he wouldn't talk about it tonight before he had checked first.*"

"Phoebe's right, Mum. I shouldn't have said anything until I knew a little bit more. I might even nip over to Ireland in the school holidays and see what I can dig up in Birr."

Cate's eyes darkened and she suddenly looked very serious. "I don't want you to, James. Let it go. You and Phoebe have no idea. I've got cousins who served time in Long Kesh during the Troubles. Don't be meddling with those people. Outside of your books and libraries, James, there's a real world where killers walk free – released after the Good Friday Agreement – but killers none the less. I've seen it from both sides of the mirror."

"What do you mean, Mum?" Phoebe asked.

Cate's voice began to tremble. "My brother, Mikey, here in London, beaten half to death after the IRA bombs in Birmingham because he drank Guinness and spoke with a Tipperary brogue. Your own father dragged from a spit and sawdust saloon in Cashel when his English accent riled some locals the year you were born." She turned to her son and spoke very slowly. "There are long shadows out there, James, darkening green fields and one-horse towns, and if you wade in there asking questions about a dead RIC man, they won't care whether you have Irish blood running through your veins, they'll listen to your accent and spill it anyway."

She grasped at her glass too quickly and knocked it over, spilling half a flute's worth of Champagne over her blouse. Charlie jumped up and handed her mother-in-law a napkin. "Come on, Cate, let's nip to the loo and clean you up." As she walked away she turned to James and swished her index finger back and forth across her throat. *Kill the conversation.*

Frank, Phoebe and James were left at the table. Nobody spoke for a second.

"She's right you know, son. There is a darkness in that family, like she said: secrets and silence. I have felt it – sitting in that parlour at the back of Noel's shop – I say the wrong thing and you can almost hear the tumbleweed. He and Caitriona would look at each other and Cate would have to rescue me, like Charlie's just done for you." Frank pulled at a hardened glob of candlewax and rubbed it between his fingers. "Sometimes it's best to leave the shadows alone – you shine a torch into them and you don't know what you might see. From all the years married to your mother and visiting her brothers in Tipperary, I have learned that those shadows are there for a reason: to hide the ghosts. So leave it now. When she comes back let's talk about something jolly shall we? It's not the time for you to be dredging up the dead." Frank stood up.

"Now, I think I'll nip to the loo too while your mother's cleaning up."

When he was out of earshot, Phoebe regarded James and asked, "This mission you're on hasn't got anything to do with what happened to Connor has it? You've got the same look in your eye as you did back then. That suicide-bomber stare. It scares me, James."

"What? No; of course not. Why would it?" James picked up the menu. "I take it we are having dessert?"

Phoebe nodded.

"Sorry, Sis. I won't say anything else. Promise."

Phoebe smiled thinly at her brother, and only half-jokingly said, "So, James, are you available same time next year to ruin my birthday party again, or should I look to hire a professional party-pooper next time?"

9

February, 1919
The O'Donagh Farm, Galross, King's County, Ireland

Some called Tommy O'Donagh a half-wit; a beautiful half-wit. But to his younger sister Bronagh, he was neither beautiful nor stupid. She saw in him an animal cunning – he always got what he wanted and their parents doted on him – that wasn't stupid! He was given more milk, more cheese, and when they slaughtered their livestock, the choicest cuts of flesh, whilst Bronagh fished for gristle in her thin broth. Mammy and Daddy said that was because farming was all he would ever be good for and he needed the strength to help his father on the land. What he lacked in wit, they said, he made up for in strength and brawn. As for being beautiful, well he was her brother, and the Casey girls who peered over the hedgerow at harvest time calling Tommy's name as he swung the scythe, his sun-bronzed torso glistening with sweat, didn't have to smell the reek of him afterwards.

She was meant to be feeding the chickens and collecting the eggs, but as her mother wouldn't be able to see her from the kitchen window, she had followed the men to the barn. Whilst they entered, closing the great barn door behind them, Bronagh had snuck around the building and, with the sun on her back, was peering inside through a crack that ran between two long slats. She could see her father, Eamonn, standing alongside her brother. Next to him was baby-faced Micheál Fahy who looked years younger than Tommy even though they had both just turned sixteen. Even with his back to her she couldn't help but recognise the carrot-coloured hair of Brendan O'Rourke, who often visited her father late at night and held court in their kitchen, drinking home-distilled poitín and talking politics. To his right stood Padraig Nolan who was often with O'Rourke and two other men whom she didn't recognise. When they began speaking she found that she could hear every word they said.

"Brendan, I have some cots up in the haymow, ye'll be able to sleep five or six comfortably. An' it's warm, so it is – there'll be hay enough to cover ye if the wind gets up."

"Many thanks Eamonn." He nodded towards Tommy. "Can yer lad be trusted?"

"He's a fine boy – he'll not say a word to anyone and he's good at followin' orders, aren't ye son?"

Tommy nodded and took a step towards his father.

Brendan considered for a moment and then continued, "Where can we hide the guns an' ammo?"

"See there in the corner stall. I have dug down beneath it an' under the hay is a trap door. There's a fine amount of space under there. Enough for ye to hide an arsenal, so there is."

"Yer a good man Eamonn O'Donagh – a patriot." Brendan looked around at the men before him, thin slits of orange slicing the dusty gloom, striping their faces like tigers. "We knew this was comin'. Padraig over there told me to bide my time – he was right. I did, an' it hurt me sore to sit on my hands. But it has begun. Dan Breen an' the Tipperary boys have started a war an' now we must fight. But what do we need to fight a war, boys?"

"We'll need guns," proffered Micheál in the deepest voice he could muster.

"Aye. Weapons an' bullets. An' we've no more than one shotgun an' Paedar's service revolver with four rounds in it." He nodded towards the older of the two men that Bronagh didn't recognise. His face looked young enough, but his short hair was salt-white. There was a low murmur of agreement amongst the men.

"Now we must do here what our boys did in Tipperary. They ambushed the Peelers, stole their gelignite an' they took the rifles from their cold, dead fingers. In a day's work they've secured guns, bombs an' bullets; an' without them, we don't stand a chance. If we're to be soldiers of the Irish Republican Army then we'll need what the Crown Forces have. We'll strike the RIC barracks across the county. We'll start with the culchie stations – sure, some of them are only manned with two Peelers. We'll take what they've got an' we'll wage war on these bastards with their own bullets."

"Will we have to take lives, Brendan?" Eamonn asked, his hand on Tommy's shoulder. "It's a mortal sin, so."

"Eamonn, we'll do what we have to do to get the British out of this county an' out of this country. We need to make men think twice about workin' for the British." Bronagh could hear that he was warming to his role as leader – she knew from the nights she listened at the top of the stairs that Brendan liked the sound of his own voice. "They must be told that they're traitors. They must be made to understand the consequences that come with war. If they won't hand over their weapons, they must be made to. We are not murderers, Eamonn – I've no wish to take a man's life unnecessarily – but see where words have got us?"

"So how will we do it Brendan? There's almost twenty thousand RIC and how many of us? We could all be dead before we ever get our hands on a single British bullet." The other man she didn't recognise spoke with a reedy whine. "We can't take on the Empire with a half-empty pistol and some ol' farmer's shotgun. It's plain madness!" He looked around the circle of men imploringly.

"Liam, I need to know that ye are with me. It is fear and apathy that has allowed the British to throttle the life out of this land. D'ye not suppose that thousands of men and women, just like ourselves, believe what we believe, want what we want? But they're just like ye: too damn scared to do anything about it. They need to be woken, and when they are, it will be the British who'll fear that every footfall on the street behind them could be the last sound they ever hear. From this moment on we are brothers. Look on each other now, and be prepared to die for that man."

Bronagh watched as the group regarded each other. There was a flurry of brusque shoulder slapping. Micheál Fahy looked so out of place she thought – a boy amongst men; trying desperately to be something he was not. And as for her brother, she couldn't imagine that he understood a word of what was going on.

O'Rourke continued, relishing the spotlight. "Conlon an' the RIC know full well the Fenians in this county – so we *will* be targeted. Expect that. Be prepared. We need to protect our loved ones, so don't keep anything that could get ye arrested at your homes. We have this barn for starters, so we have, but we'll build a network of safe-houses here an' across the river in Tipperary and up the road in Galway. But remember, for every good soul who'll give us bed an' shelter there'll be another who'll spill their guts an' see us hanged." Brendan stopped and looked each man in the eye. "If anyone here betrays us, I will kill them. This is no game now – we are soldiers and this is a war."

Liam Kavanagh swallowed; his mouth was dry and little beads of perspiration ran down the side of his face. Ex-Private Peadar Moran's expression was impassive as he spat a mouthful of chewing tobacco onto the dried mud and cow-muck at his feet. Eamonn O'Donagh nodded grimly, his hand still resting defensively on Tommy's shoulder. Padraig Nolan stared straight ahead; Bronagh caught her breath for a second, suddenly terrified he might have spotted her. Micheál stood beside her brother appropriating what he considered to be the manliest expression possible but actually made him look like he was straining to pass wind.

Grinning, his big, blank eyes squinting against the sunbeams that slashed his face, Tommy asked, "If we are to be soldiers, will I get to wear a uniform with brass buttons and a tin helmet?"

Bronagh realised that her brother might well be a beautiful half-wit after all.

10

27th August, 1919
Birr Castle, King's County, Ireland

Sergeant Joseph Conlon was uncomfortable. This was despite the fact that his backside had never been more comfortable. The upholstered armchair, striped like a boating blazer, was perfectly sprung with generous armrests and its high back allowed him to tilt his head and examine in detail the gilt fluting of the ceiling and the giant chandelier that hung above him. He had never seen so many thousands of pieces of cut glass. It was as though an exploding star had frozen in space and time. Each hurtling shard, sharp and mercurial, had been tamed and chained, trapped forever in looping necklaces of glittering ice, whilst larger rocks dove dramatically downwards, their terminal velocity arrested by the silver links that suspended them above Joseph's head.

The wallpaper was textured with bronzed ferns and game birds on a bed of olive green. Around him, ten generations of the Parsons family, all haughtily sporting dusted wigs, observed him nonchalantly from behind oval mounts housed in heavy gilden frames.

Before him, three arched windows, stretching from floor to ceiling, looked out onto the sculpted demesne that sloped gracefully down to the Camcor River. The largest of the three opened out onto a sun-kissed terrace and a late summer breeze blew gently through the room caressing the crystals above him that tinkled like faerie laughter.

He knew why he was here: his presence had been requested by Colonel-Commandant Edward Sutherland, the Commanding Officer of the Leinster Region. Joseph had been told by Head Constable Regan that the Englishman wanted to *'assess his suitability in the role as Sergeant in light of the deteriorating situation in and around King's County'*. It had been implied that Sutherland wasn't convinced that Conlon was up to the job. Certainly Joseph was one of the youngest appointed to the role in the history of the RIC, and this was further complicated by the fact that, contrary to the usual protocol, he was serving in a district where he had grown up. There was also no denying that since February the role of Sergeant had become significantly more trying. Across the county sporadic attacks had been made on policemen; solitary shots taken from behind boulders on craggy passes or aimed at police barracks in the dead of night. Death threats were being posted to magistrates and landlords; farms had been raided and firearms stolen. Shopkeepers and bartenders were being pressurised not to serve officers of the Crown and – not just here in Birr but all across Ireland – men of the RIC were retiring in droves, or even worse, aiding the enemy. In Dublin, the seventy-three Sinn Féin deputies elected in 1918 had refused to take up their seats in Westminster and instead set up an alternative government known as *Dáil Éireann* – the Assembly of Ireland. By April, Éamon de Valera had become President of this fledgling legislature and only a few weeks ago, Joseph had learned that the Irish Volunteers had formally assumed the nomenclature of the *Irish Republican Army* and had duly sworn allegiance to both the Dáil and the notional Republic of Ireland. Of course, none of this was to the liking of Joseph's English superiors and he appreciated that they might well have reservations about a local man who broke bread every Sunday with many individuals whom would see this notion a reality.

Through the drawing room door he could hear the abrupt and clear-cut intonation of the Colonel. Joseph imagined that he was conversing with the newly-widowed Countess Frances Parsons. Last year, her twelve-year-old son, Laurence, had inherited the Earldom of Rosse after his father had strayed into the sights of a German sniper. Joseph wasn't old enough to remember a time when Birr had been named Parsonstown, but it was common knowledge that since the 1600s the fortunes of the town had been inextricably entwined with those of the Parsons family.

The Georgian townhouses on the broad curves of John's Mall, Rosse Row and William Street told the story of a town considered to be *the* bastion of forward-thinking Britishness in a backward, Gaelic hinterland. Only two or three miles from where Joseph was sitting were Crinkill Barracks where the Prince of Wales's Leinster Regiment had been based for as long as anyone could remember. From this depot, thousands of young men from every corner of Great Britain had been trained and sent to Faizabad, Salonika, Egypt and Palestine during the Great War. It had been those with Scottish blood who had seen to it that in 1915 the hated statue of the Butcher of Culloden that tilted so menacingly atop the column on Cumberland Square had been pulled down. Now the Doric pillar stood strangely bereft of adornment in the centre of the Square – as though a sculpture had been lifted from a plinth in an art gallery and never replaced.

On the other side of the door the conversation came to an end. Joseph heard a throat being cleared and he jumped to attention as Colonel Sutherland stepped inside the room, closing the door behind him.

"At ease, Sergeant."

"Sir."

The colonel had sandy hair, so solidly lacquered it might well be shrapnel-proof. A severe side-parting traversed the left side of his skull and handle-bar sideburns, peppered with russet, framed his face. Beneath a long, aquiline nose was a finely trimmed moustache. Joseph reckoned him to be in his late forties.

"Conlon isn't it?"

"Sir."

"I used to know the Countess before she married. She comes from good stock – the Lister-Kayes – you know them?" Joseph shook his head. Sutherland ignored him. "I know her father well – damned good chap, great spin bowler too. Anyway, terrible business with her husband. Terrible."

Joe didn't feel he could say anything.

"Well, I suppose you are wondering why I summoned you here, Conlon? It's no secret that this country is going to the dogs and you are the man-on-the ground, so to speak, who has to arrest that decline in this part of King's County. Now I have read your file and it does throw up some concerns."

Joseph waited.

"You're a local man. A left-footer, no less."

Joseph's brow furrowed.

"A left-footer, man – beholden to the Roman Church. You are a Catholic, aren't you?"

"Yes, sir."

Sutherland could barely conceal his distaste. "I have to admit that I'm surprised you haven't been posted further afield. We don't usually allow our men to serve where they have connections. Compromises them, see. They can be got to."

"Yes, sir. My posting here was a charitable act amid wretched circumstances. I was already serving the Crown in County Clare, but Head Constable Regan saw fit to arrange a transfer so I could return home to nurse my mother after my father, a serving constable here in Birr died suddenly – a brain haemorrhage it was.

She was unable to cope with the loss, and as she had no family to speak of either here or back in Limerick, the transfer was agreed on compassionate grounds. Rather than a hindrance, I believe that my familiarity with the people of the town has enabled me to serve the Crown more effectively. Sir."

"Very good, Conlon, but as I say, it is that very familiarity that I am worried about. Now that Shinners are taking pot-shots at police, how do I know that you won't turn a blind eye?"

Joe provided exactly the kind of response that he hoped the Englishman needed to hear. "Sir, granted, I am Irish, and a Catholic too. But I am a policeman as my father was before me. I pledge myself to keeping the peace and ensuring the safety of every man, woman and child of this town. Anybody who threatens that peace, or desires to spill blood in the name of greed or politics will be arrested and feel the full force of the law upon them. I will not shy away from my duty as a policeman. That I can assure you."

Sutherland reflected for a moment, his mandible moving from side to side making his moustache arc like the eyebrows of one mildly amused. Then he nodded almost imperceptibly to himself and looked Joseph in the eyes.

"Conlon, come with me. I would like to take a walk." Sutherland gestured towards the French door in the central window.

The two men stepped outside the drawing room onto a paved terrace that overlooked the gardens. A set of stone steps led down to the lawn below. Conlon followed Sutherland down the steps and, half a pace behind him, crossed the croquet green where brightly coloured balls, hoops and mallets had been discarded by the children.

Abruptly, Sutherland stopped and turned. In a school-masterly tone, he began an oration that he had devised this morning and would take no little pleasure in delivering: "Do you appreciate history, Conlon? I know your lot like a story. Well here is a story for you. Almost a thousand years ago, while your Irish ancestors were beating each other to death with wooden clubs over horses, women or sheep, the Anglo-Normans came to this sodden isle with chainmail, trebuchets and battle-steeds and built this castle. Now, they made the mistake of breeding with the natives and unsurprisingly they too fell into fighting each other, and over the years this grand old building slumped into rack and ruin. It was King James I who gave this land to a God-fearing, loyal, English, Protestant family – the Parsons. And look what they have done to it." He indicated towards the huge gateway, flanked on either side by rounded grey towers carved with ominous looking embrasures. Like a mountain range, the multi-layered roofline soared above them; jagged peaks of crenellations and chimney pots vying with each other to avoid being caught in shade.

Sutherland turned and continued to walk through the gardens towards the Camcor River. Conlon duly followed. As they rounded a set of rhododendron bushes, sun-blushed in bottle green and hot pink, the 'Leviathon' loomed into their line of sight. From a distance this giant telescope looked like a medieval siege engine. Ladders and suspension wires criss-crossed the stone structure, a gargantuan gear locked into a massive rack of iron teeth. Huge supporting walls reared up forty feet high and between them the hulking telescope balanced at an angle secured with chain and counterweight.

Sutherland continued. "William Parsons, the third Earl, built this. It took him three years, but when he was finished, Conlon, this was the largest telescope in the world. For seventy years scientists and scholars came from the four corners of the globe to study here and unlock the secrets of our galaxy. And it is not just here in King's County that science and industry have thrived. The Titanic, forged and welded by Irish boiler-makers in the same Belfast shipyards that have supplied the Empire with battleships and cruise liners for the last half-century. Surely, Conlon, you can see that *England is good for Ireland*. Without us, no doubt you'd still be dancing around naked, sacrificing each other to trees and speaking that gibberish you call a language."

Again, Joseph didn't know what response was appropriate – certainly not the honest one that welled up inside him like hot, black mud from the bowels of the earth. Was the Colonel goading him? Was he testing his allegiance to the Crown?

The momentary silence irked the Colonel. "Well, man, do you agree?"

Conlon chose his words carefully: "Sir, it is hard to deny the material benefits and progress enjoyed by some in the larger cities, especially in the North. Equally, here in King's County there are very many people indebted to the generosity of the Parsons family."

"Good man. Now, England doesn't want to lose Ireland, and, by God, you can't afford to lose us; so together we have to deal with these *rebels* for everybody's sake. Now, I hear that the police force in Birr is somewhat depleted. How many men have you managed to lose this year, Sergeant?"

"Five since the spring, sir. Two of them felt that they were physically unable to continue to serve. They were approaching retirement age and I believe that they resented the fact that their Sergeant was so much younger than them. However, there have been three more since then."

"Could you enlighten me on why that might be, Sergeant?"

"There has obviously been a campaign of intimidation. In March, I think it was, a general warning note was pinned to the station door in the dead of night addressed to 'The Traitors of the RIC' and signed on behalf of the 'Offaly Brigade of the IRA'."

Sutherland snorted with derision at the use of the Gaelic name for the county.

"The men reported that shopkeepers were refusing to serve them and that they were denied drinks in some public houses. Although I have visited the shops and bars in question and warned those concerned about their behaviour – it has got to the men, sir, and I can't arrest half the town for being reluctant to serve the police a pint of Guinness. Morale has been flagging in the force. Of the two most recent to leave, I believe that the last was approached by masked men holding shotguns who told him that he could choose the uniform and at the same time choose a casket, or he could go home to his family and lead a full life. They were only boys, sir. They were scared and they chose to resign."

"Surely you know who these Shinners are? Why haven't they been arrested, or even better, shot? That's why you were promoted, man! The whole point of making you Sergeant was because we needed somebody with his ear to the ground."

"Sir, we are aware of those with Fenian sympathies, but we have no proof that they've been involved in any wrong doing; and so far nobody is willing to come forward and name names. For the authority of the police to hold firm, I have to tread a fine line. If I was to arrest and charge people with no evidence then all respect for me and my men would be eroded. We can't keep control if we lose the support of the people."

"Damn it, man. Do you think the Indians want us there either? We don't need the bloody consent of the people to rule them! As far as I'm concerned, General Dyer did a first class job at Amritsar to show those wogs who was boss – it's a damn shame they're calling it a massacre. We need some of that same medicine here, Sergeant, and you'll be pleased to hear that we're going to give you the tools you'll need to administer it – a timely fillip, so to speak."

Joseph suspected that what he was about to hear would bring him no pleasure at all; he hoped this wasn't written all over his face.

Sutherland's jaw tightened sinuously at the apparent lack of enthusiasm emanating from the Irishman. "The enemy have got their hands on a significant amount of weaponry, and as it has become impossible to defend the rural RIC outposts, GHQ in Dublin has decided to centralise operations in the county towns. I have received orders to bolster our presence in Birr. For the time being, Conlon, you will remain in charge of the day to day running of the force under the supervision of Head Constable Regan, but I will be closely monitoring your actions. You'll be getting seventeen more men from all across the country. You will use the RIC Station on John's Mall as operational HQ but we will fortify the workhouse and transform it into a secondary barracks. I will expect regular patrols and liaison with your counterparts across the borders in Tipperary and Galway. I want the Shinners hunted down, the weapons returned and the rebel threat eradicated in King's County. Can I rely on you, Sergeant?"

"Yes, sir."

Sutherland handed Sergeant Conlon a list of constables who would be drafted to Birr. "They will be with you Monday week. Sandbags, beds, barbed wire, weapons and ammunition will be with you in due course. I have been told that an armoured vehicle is on its way from Dublin. I am still waiting for the General to sign off on a couple of items, but you should be fully operational within a fortnight. Have you any questions, Sergeant?"

Conlon shook his head, slightly queasy at the gravity of the situation. "No, sir."

"Good. Now, do your duty, Sergeant: for your country and mine. As you said yourself, do it for the good of this town. You have a wife and a child, I hear? Well, do it for them as well. We can't have a bunch of mad men running around with guns and explosives thinking they're above the law, can we?"

Joe regarded his superior. *No, that role's already been taken*, he thought.

11

Spring, 2018
The National Archives, Kew, London, England

As the glass door sealed behind him with a faint hiss, James could feel the change of atmosphere – both physically and metaphorically. The air was drier and slightly cooler and those who sat in front of stacks of ancient-looking box files packed with time-bleached paper exuded an air of professional purpose. He was in the inner sanctum of the National Archives in Kew holding nothing but a transparent plastic bag filled with the few essential items allowed through the full length body-scan. All he could hear was the occasional cough, the sound of pencil lead on paper and whisper of pages being turned.

At the help desk he presented his reader's card to a young woman with duskily-kohled eyes wearing a silken hijab of brilliant azure. She swiped the card, peered at the screen, typed a couple of keystrokes, hummed very quietly, typed some more and clicked a mouse. Walking to the printer, in one graceful movement she plucked a pen from her top pocket, picked up the printout and circled three lines of text. James could see from her expression that there was some sort of complication.

"Hi, Mr Lucas. OK; it seems that not all the records that you want to view are currently available. I have just checked the system and it seems as though some of them are 'pending digitisation'. It looks as though you are researching post-1916 Ireland, and obviously since the centenary of the Easter Rising, there has been a huge upsurge in interest. Hence, for the foreseeable future, the archives team downstairs are scanning and uploading a range of documents – some of which, I see here, are the ones that you have requested to access."

Confusion and mild consternation must have clouded James's expression. "Basically, they are going through the box files in a broadly chronological order and scanning into PDF format those documents that are most likely to be used by researchers, but don't worry, Mr Lucas; half the records you want to view are ready for you now and the ones you won't be able to see today will be online within the next twenty-eight days. In fact, as they become available, you will receive an automated email that will contain a link to access them – so you can view them at home."

James nodded, visibly crestfallen.

She tried to rally him; "To be fair, you'll have enough to be getting on with today; there are three box files waiting for you in locker 21b. As each one contains about two hundred separate documents, you'll have to use the last digits of your reference codes to find the exact ones that you are looking for." She underlined the relevant numbers on the printout and turned the page towards him. "I would like to say that they are in numerical sequence, but some readers do see fit to place them back in the boxes in, let's say, *a less than logical order* – so patience and resilience are your watchwords for the day." She flashed him a professional smile. "Oh, and your locker number matches your workspace, so you will be sat at table 21b. Again, sorry for the inconvenience."

James thanked her and went in search of his locker. As he strained to gain purchase on the weighty boxes crammed within it, he appreciated that trying to work his way through six of them would have been impossible today anyway. He carried them to his workspace and plonked them a touch too heavily on the table, silently apologising to those who looked up with surprise and no little irritation. Swiftly taking his seat and ducking behind them, he cross-referenced the catalogue codes on boxes with his search requests. His heart sank as he realised that the document he craved to examine the most, the Court of Inquests' findings on Conlon's assassination, was amongst those being digitised in the bowels of the basement.

That was a massive blow.

He had wanted to return to Phoebe's flat with some real answers.

Today.

After last night's spoiled birthday meal, he felt he owed his family a little bit more than supposition and gut instinct.

He sighed and looked about him at the researchers buried deep in reams of brittle, bone-dry paper, all of them scanning every word methodically, turning pages with licked fingers, standing to angle phones to capture the best shot of text; sitting, thinking, scribbling, and turning back to the source material. James reluctantly accepted that if answers were as easy to find as he imagined, then there would be no secrets left. The woman at the counter was right, he needed *patience and resilience*, and to that end, he decided to start at the beginning and work his way through the paperwork chronologically.

The earliest document of any worth was dated the 25th August, 1919, and was a single sheet of carbonless copy paper. Two circular stamps of dark pink could be made out above the typed title, '*RIC Reinforcements: Birr Barracks*'; below, a list of seventeen names in alphabetical order. It was signed by the Commanding Officer of Troops in the Leinster Region, a Colonel-Commandant Edward Sutherland. Beside each surname was service number, town/county of origin and religious affiliation. Of the seventeen, eleven of them were Catholic and the remaining six were Protestant. A Daly, a Donovan, a Fallon, a McGee, a Ryan, a Shaunessy and eleven others had been sent from the four provinces, from afar afield as Donegal, Wicklow, Kerry and Antrim. James opened his note pad, scribbled down the date of the document, a brief description of the contents and, for good measure, he took a photograph with his phone.

The next record that he looked for amongst the hundreds of sheets of fragile paper, punctured and bound with treasury tags, was referenced WO/35/132A/7 and had been listed on the catalogue search as *"Account by Sergeant Joseph Conlon, RIC of IRA Raid on Birr Barracks, September 17th, 1919."* James ascertained that this box file was one of those that had been repacked by some rushed researcher in a particularly haphazard way. Document /7 wasn't anywhere near document /6, nor was it to be found in the first thirty that he came across. Gingerly flipping each unique account of ambush, assassination or accident, he became lost in unrelenting tragedy. So much death: Catholic, Protestant, civilian or soldier; each and every one of them sent to their graves early, leaving grieving wives, mothers and sons. Quarter of an hour later, he found it: WO/35/132A/7 – words written in black ink by the hand of his great-grandfather a century before. Not too dissimilar from his own, it was easy to decipher Conlon's script, especially as the policeman had capitalised key names and places for clarification.

Account by Sergeant Joseph Conlon RIC concerning IRA Raid on John's Mall Barracks, Birr, King's County Wednesday, September 17th, 1919

Following interviews with Constables DALY and FALLON and with diverse residents of John's Mall, I vouch that the following statement is an accurate account of the events of the 17th September, 1919.

In light of numerous written threats to MAJOR TERENCE DAVENPORT, once of the Prince of Wales's Leinster Regiment, residing at STONEACRE HOUSE, SHARAVOGUE, coupled with what I considered at the time to be credible intelligence from a trusted informant, I came to strongly believe that an IRA attack was planned on said residence on the night of the 17th September. Both within the house and in the gamekeeper's lodge, it was common knowledge that a number of firearms were kept by the Major, including shotguns, hunting rifles and revolvers. Major Terence also owned a collection of antique pistols and retained a significant cache of ammunition under lock and key. Hence I led a force of eighteen RIC to ambush the expected IRA operation, thwart the robbery, apprehend the perpetrators and recover stolen weaponry from them.

Under cover of darkness, I split our forces into three units: Unit 1, led by Acting-Sergeant RYAN was positioned on the Birr-Sharavogue Road and Unit 2, under Acting-Sergeant SHAUNESSY on the Sharavogue-Roscrea Road. In this way all routes of ingress and egress to the property were monitored. Four RIC constables along with myself were positioned in the grounds of Stoneacre House.

A skeleton crew were to remain on guard at the newly established WORKHOUSE BARRACKS on Townsend Street and at JOHN'S MALL BARRACKS.

At approximately 10.30pm, Constables Daly and Fallon who had been tasked with manning the barracks on John's Mall heard uproar on the street outside, and from the station window identified a known drunkard by the name of GERARD O'HANLON. He was observed throwing stones at the houses opposite and heard singing rebel songs loudly. Three windows were smashed at Nos 7, 9 and 11.

Residents from the adjoining houses had exited their homes to see what the commotion was and MRS DOTTIE FOLEY approached the barracks to seek assistance. Both Daly and Fallon then left the station to apprehend the drunkard, despite being given strict orders that one of them should remain inside the station at all times. They became embroiled in a struggle with Mr O'Hanlon and it was during the course of this struggle that four masked men carrying shotguns and what have been identified as RIC Carbines approached and accosted them.

Both officers were dragged from Mr O'Hanlon and one member of the group, assumed to be the leader, told the small crowd of onlookers to return to their houses and pull their curtains if they, *"ever wanted to see another sunrise."* Constables Daly and Fallon were walked back into the barracks at gunpoint where they were told, *"The guns, the ammunition, all of it – give them to us gentlemen, or we will blow your brains out and we will take them anyway."*

A consignment of arms and ammunition had been delivered to the station only three days earlier and were being kept under lock and key. Constables Daly and Fallon were ordered to open the cell where they were being stored and to carry the three chests, containing 12 Lee Enfield Carbines along with 350 rounds of ammunition, outside and to load them onto a horse and trap.

Both Constables were then led back inside the station and beaten almost unconscious with their own batons by two of the masked men. They were told to strip to their underwear and were locked in the cells. The masked men took the keys with them and the same man who spoke before said, "*Tell Conlon that no member of the RIC is safe here anymore. We are the South Offaly Brigade of the Irish Republican Army and if any of ye's want to live, ye'll hang up yer uniforms of yer own volition!*" He then proceeded to hang their uniforms on the hat stand by the door as he left.

Neither police officer could tell in which direction the assailants made their escape and residents of John's Mall refused to comment when asked for fear of retribution.

Both policemen suffered bruising, mild concussion and a few cracked ribs and Dr Burke was called to tend to their injuries in the early hours when both men were discovered.

There was no attempt made by the IRA to attack Stoneacre House, and it became apparent that the supposed raid was a decoy to draw the main bulk of the force from the town.

The informant, whom I can vouch for personally, has been brought in for questioning this morning (18th September, 1919) but strenuously denies that he/she has falsified information. It is my opinion that he/she was misled purposefully. There is also the very real possibility that the rebels have an informant inside the RIC as they knew exactly where to look for the weaponry.

Head Constable Regan and I are committed to following up leads and interviewing suspects. We will double our patrols and fortify our positions both at the Barracks on John's Mall and on Townsend Street. We are confident that the criminals will be found and the arms recovered.

I hereby certify that to my knowledge this is an accurate account of the events of Wednesday 17th September, 1919,

Signed

Sergeant Joseph Conlon, RIC

18th September, 1919

Interesting, thought James; his great-grandfather had been well and truly duped. The underlining of the word <u>strongly</u> and Conlon's defence of the informant implied some sort of personal relationship. Who was it? More pertinently, who was the leak in the RIC? Could this person have helped the assassins plan the policeman's murder? Would the documents stacked before him reveal those answers?

Greedily he slipped the elasticated band from the next box file and dived in.

———

Like the first, this wodge of documents wasn't organised in any discernible order. James knew that somewhere amongst the faded leaves of paper was hidden the Inquest Inquiry into the death of Micheál Fahy – the crime that set in motion the series of events that would see his great-grandfather riddled with bullets on his doorstep.

What struck him as he turned page after page was how the legal process failed to deliver any sort of closure: whether it was soldier or civilian, nine out of every ten Inquest Inquiries recorded a verdict of death by gunshot wound, or blunt force trauma at the hands of '*person or persons unknown*'. In one such case, it beggared belief that despite seven sworn testimonies, each identical in their description of a gang of Black and Tans '*setting upon*' a boy with rifle butts on a busy Cork thoroughfare an hour before the unfortunate lad was found slumped on a street corner with severe swelling of the brain, his death was deemed by the coroner to have been caused by '*a pre-existing medical condition*'. By the same token, it was equally unlikely that in rural County Clare, a pub-full of witnesses were unable to identify or give anything other than wildly conflicting descriptions of the unmasked man who calmly finished his pint before marching over and pumping lead into a local magistrate taking supper at a coaching inn. Unwilling witnesses and bureaucratic whitewashes thwarting justice at every turn – no wonder both sides lashed out at each other with increasing fury.

When he finally found it, James experienced a nervous excitement underscored by a queasy sense of foreboding. James noted that the assault on Micheál Fahy occurred less than a week after the IRA raid on the barracks. *Was it a reprisal killing carried out by an embarrassed and angry Sergeant, determined to wreak revenge on the one he suspected had bested him?* James sharpened his pencil and turned to a fresh page in his pad and started to read.

Court of Inquest into the Death of Micheál Fahy, aged 16, of the Riverstown Road, Birr Pronounced dead on Monday 22nd September, 1919.

1st Witness: Daniel O'Flaherty, farmer of the Riverstown Road, being duly sworn states:

Myself and my son, Patrick O'Flaherty, were together carrying a cartload of cut peat from the scrubland. It must have been six or seven of the clock on the Sunday evening as the sun was setting over Loch Derg. As we rounded the corner on the road that leads up the Fahy farm, we saw a trap that was tipped forwards and a dead horse still bridled to it. As we came closer, we saw there was a man laid out on the track covered in blood. Patrick jumped off the cart and ran to the body and we could see that it was young Micheál Fahy. He was in a bad way. We could not wake him. We emptied the cart of turf and laid him on it. I took him up to the Fahy farm and sent Patrick to run for the priest and the doctor. We saw nobody else.

2nd Witness: Dr F.G. Burke, of Oxmantown Mall, Birr, being duly sworn states:

Patrick O'Flaherty knocked on my front door at 8pm on Sunday, 21st of September, 1919. He told me that Micheál Fahy had taken a 'terrible beating' on the Riverstown Road. I made my way to the Fahy farm to find Micheál unconscious and laid out on a bed. He was breathing normally. His mother, Mary Fahy, had cleaned his face of blood, but it was clear that he had suffered severe lacerations to the face, extensive bruising and fractures to the cheekbones, eye sockets and skull and a number of his teeth were missing. There was also significant trauma to the torso. I administered a tincture of laudanum to arrest the pain and advised that he be propped on a pillow for the duration of the night. His mother sat with him. When I returned the following morning his breathing had become more erratic. As far as I am aware, he never regained consciousness and I proclaimed him dead at 12.02pm on the 22nd September, 1919.

3rd Witness: Fr O'Brien of St Brendan's RC Church, Birr, being duly sworn states:

I was called to the Fahy farm by Patrick O'Flaherty. I did not arrive there until almost 9pm. I saw Dr Burke leaving and went to sit with Mrs Fahy at her son's bedside. Micheál was in a very sorry way and we prayed for his soul together. I asked Mrs Fahy whether she would like me to perform the last rites. She told me to wait a little while yet. She said there was still life in him. I spent the night on an arm chair in the corner of the room. In the dead of the night I was awoken by a moaning. Mrs Fahy held her son's hand and I heard him say, "Please, please, please." He never said another word and in the morning I performed the last rites. I was there when Dr Burke pronounced him dead at lunchtime.

4th Witness: Sergeant Joseph Conlon, RIC, of Main Street, Birr, being duly sworn states:

On the afternoon of the 22nd September, in my capacity as Sergeant of the RIC in Birr, I was required to attend the home of the Fahy family of Riverstown Road to initiate preliminary investigations into the death of their son, Micheál Fahy. On my way to the farm, I examined the scene of the attack and ascertained that the Fahy's horse had been shot behind the left ear with what looked like a rifle or revolver bullet – but certainly not with shotgun shot. The track was dry so there were no discernible foot prints.

When I arrived at the house, Mary Fahy and her husband, Seamus, along with their two daughters, Carmel and Margaret, were present at the scene. Micheál was lying beneath a sheet. When I lifted it, I could see that he had been badly beaten. Seamus Fahy told me not to touch him and acted in a threatening and aggressive manner.

When interviewed, it became apparent that they had not witnessed the attack but they believed that the assault was the work of the RIC or the soldiers at the barracks at Crinkill. I was told that I was not welcome in their house and Carmel Fahy spat at me. I assured the family that I would find out who did this to their son and the criminals would be brought to justice. Mary Fahy laughed and said, "*What, ye'll reach through the looking glass and arrest yer very self?*"

In the following 48 hours I spoke with the O'Flahertys, Dr Burke and Fr O'Brien and every one of my constables. I was unable to shed any more light on the incident. Investigations are ongoing.

Opinion

The Court, having carefully considered the evidence, are of the opinion that Micheál Fahy, aged 16 years, of Riverstown Road, Birr, died at said location at 12.02pm on the 22nd September, 1919 from shock and haemorrhage caused by a vicious physical attack by person or persons unknown.

Signed at Birr on this 26th day of September 1919.

James could make out an array of signatures that all seemed to have military prefixes. It was stamped and countersigned on the 14th October by Colonel-Commandant Edward Sutherland.

So what did that tell him?

Well, it told him that nobody was charged, and that the killer or killers walked free.

It told him that Sergeant Conlon was either covering up his own actions or those of his men, or that he genuinely didn't have anything to do with it.

It told him that the family thought that Conlon was responsible, and that might have been enough to seal his death warrant twenty-two months later when Ciaran Fahy emptied three bullets into him.

But in the final analysis, it didn't really tell James very much at all. He was no closer to confirming or debunking O'Rourke's claim that his great-grandfather was a murderer.

James was exhausted. He could read no more today.

He captured images of all relevant documents with his phone and spent some time noting down his thoughts – questions he would like answered and possible directions of enquiry. He stretched and felt his back click. He packed up the records, slipped the elasticated bands around the box files, and with all three folders wedged between his forearms and chin, walked back to locker 21b, unsure what he would be able to tell his mother when he went to see her the following day.

12

27th September, 1919
Birr, King's County, Ireland

The sick, grey light leeched in between rough wooden slats that had been hastily nailed to the inside of the workhouse window frames after the attack on the police station ten days earlier. Designed to protect the barracks from firebombs sent hurtling through the glass, the horizontal slats threw the room into semi-darkness and had merely reinforced the sense of surreal dislocation that seeped into every waking moment of the RIC constables. Young men, a day or two at most from the towns of their birth and their mothers' cooking; yet here they were, secluded in the shadows, hiding behind sandbags and barbed wire while outside a picturesque and vibrant Irish market town got on with the business of living.

Lying rigid on his cot, Constable Daniel Fallon awoke with a start, sweat slick on his back and chest, the grubby sheets clinging to him. Peeling them off like dead white skin from a blister, he gasped for air, sat up and shook his head in an attempt to rid himself of the images that haunted him. The sounds and colours were so real, the nightmare so vivid; but why shouldn't it be, because it wasn't really a nightmare, merely a memory replayed in excruciating detail every night since Daly and himself had chanced upon the boy and horse on the Riverstown Road.

He could see it still, every second etched violently into his consciousness.

The pair of them on patrol.

Both still bruised and sore, on bicycles, carbines hanging from their shoulders.

No conversation.

The straight road through the woods; twisted branches and foliage knotted above them obscuring any sunlight.

The trap ahead, a boy sat holding the reins and the piebald horse trotting towards the turn in the road and the open slopes beyond.

"That's the one!" Daly spat, his Belfast diction hammered and hardened on the Shankill Road. "That's the feckin' horse and trap from the station! That's one o' the wee bastards who stripped us. Cunt!"

Without warning, Daly stopped: his bicycle clattered to the rocky track. With military fluidity, the rifle slung over shoulder swung round in a lethal trajectory.

The bark of the bullet; amplified by its singularity and the silence of the woods.

And then the shrill, otherworldly whinnying – a sound as alien as a dragon speared; tumbling earthward – and then the dull thud of lifeless flesh on sun-baked mud.

Danny could still see the smile of satisfaction curl on Jonathon Daly's lips, his face in profile, locked to the stock of the rifle, a little wisp of gunpowder smoke caressing his cheekbone.

The stupid boy didn't even run. He jumped off the trap to the stricken beast and buried his face in her neck. He didn't move as they approached him. He still didn't move as they cocked their carbines and stood over him. He just kept running his hand through the horse's mane and whispering into her ear.

"Hands up ye Fenian fecker!"

Nothing.

Daly: irritated now. "I said, get up, boy, and put yer hands above yer head unless ye want to join the little horsey here."

At that the boy whirled to his feet, wild-eyed, his hair matted in sticky clumps, half his face dripping with the warm crimson of the mare. For a moment Danny thought he would hurl himself at the pair of them and tear at their faces with bare hands. But he didn't – staring down the barrels of the two rifles trained on his nose, something gave; he looked scared. He looked caught. He looked about twelve.

He didn't speak as he was turned and cuffed and Danny wished with all his heart that the recurring dream could have stopped right there; at that precise moment. Had it, an entire alternative history would have been forged: *They take him back to the station. Sergeant Conlon praises their police work and restraint. The boy is questioned. He gives up valuable information. The Shinners are rounded up, the guns recovered and Danny Fallon and Jonathon Daly are heroes.*

But no: a handful of incendiary words, negligently strewn onto the dying embers of an inflammatory situation – and what had been contained was unleashed. A life was lost and history followed its callous course: *There are no 'what-ifs', there is only ever what is.*

"Yer goin' to pay for what ye did to us last week ye little gobshite. By the time I've finished with ye, ye'll be wishing my bullet had hit ye and not your nag."

Suddenly defiant, his youthful bravado rekindled. "Oh, 'tis ye two, so. I didn't recognise the pair of ye with yer trousers on."

And then it all happened so quickly.

A wet thud as the butt of Daly's rifle connected with the side of the boy's skull. He dropped heavily, handcuffed and unable to deflect the deluge of kicks and blows that rained hard upon him. He barely made a sound, just the grunts of the broken as Jonathon Daly stamped on him again and again.

Frozen by the turn of events and the horror unravelling before him, Danny Fallon did nothing, and when he unlocked the blood-spattered cuffs from the shattered wrists of the boy, Danny Fallon said nothing either.

And that was the most disturbing part of his dream.

The silence.

The silence that followed him back to the barracks as they left the bleeding boy lying next to his dead horse.

The silence they shared as they stood outside Head Constable Regan's office the day after the boy was pronounced dead.

The silence as the Sergeant informed him that the deceased was his own wife's first cousin and looked long and hard into Danny's eyes to catch tell-tale flickers of truth lurking behind his blank stare.

The silence he felt envelop him now as he lay one cot away from a killer; cold sweat crystallising into fine salt on his chest, on this, the day of the boy's funeral.

13

Spring, 2018
Kilburn, London

The bus from Phoebe's to his parents' flat passed through Kilburn, where James had grown up. When his mother had first arrived in London, 'County Kilburn' as it was known, was home from home for the displaced of the four provinces, and widely accepted as Ireland's thirty-third county. It had been here, at St Mary's Roman Catholic Infant School that he'd met Connor McCleary, the boy who was to become his best friend and whose death he was responsible for.

It had been the very first day of the autumn term and Miss Clarke was asking the class what they had done over the summer. The new boy, Connor, boasted of riding a pony bareback in Connemara. One of the girls excitedly described eating ice cream and building sandcastles in Worthing. Another bested her by sharing a story of a plane trip to Tenerife and a camel ride. James had told of climbing St Patrick's Rock in Cashel with his mother and cousins in the rain. When all the children had finished their tales, Connor had approached James and asked; "If ye've been to Ireland, an' yer mammy's Irish, why d'ye sound like the Prime Minister?" The Prime Minister at the time was Margaret Thatcher, so this was no compliment.

"My mum says that only navvies speak Irish in London."

Connor frowned. "What's a navvy?"

James shrugged.

"Well I'll be one of them I suppose. I'm Connor. Me an' my mammy have just moved from Liverpool; maybe that's why we speak Irish, like?"

The seven-year-old James smiled. "Maybe." He proffered his hand. "I can be your friend if you want."

Connor had grinned. "Alright, Maggie. We'll be tick as tieves, so." He spat in his palm, took James's hand and shook it vigorously.

And they were as thick as thieves: despite Cate's alarm that her son was mixing with the wrong sort, they were inseparable throughout infant, and into junior school. Connor was easily the most articulate boy that James had ever met, though he struggled with reading and writing. He was prone to bouts of melancholy, and would lash out if the other kids teased him about having no father. But he was the most loyal friend that James could ever want. By the time that they finished junior school, Cate and Frank Lucas had become so concerned about the bond that had developed between the pair that they enrolled James in Gray's College for Boys whilst Connor moved on to Aylestone Community School. If anything, this only served to strengthen their friendship.

Looking out the bus window now, Kilburn had changed a great deal since the 1980s: there were still a couple of the old Irish pubs on the High Road and a handful of shops with Gaelic script. But chain stores and charity shops were the order of the day. You were much more likely to find food from the Middle East or West Africa than you were boiled ham and cabbage. The Irish diaspora had evaporated; just another minority amongst all the other minorities who together made up the majority of modern day London. Amongst the 'evaporated' were his parents, who had moved out of Kilburn after he left school. Frank and Cate now lived in a town house in Hampstead that James had once calculated was worth forty years of his teacher's salary; and that was if he didn't pay any tax or national insurance and lived off air for four decades. The girl from Cashel had done well for herself; certainly better than Mrs McCleary, whom James suspected still lived in the same flat in the grotty high rise off Belsize Road.

As the bus idled in traffic, James could make out the small park where he and Connor had shared their first cigarettes and swigged neat vodka decanted into tonic water bottles from his dad's drinks cabinet. Despite their separation during the school day, nothing could stop them meeting up in the late afternoons, where they slouched on park benches, passed roll-ups back and forth and leant in on one another to share James's Walkman headphones and listen to the latest mix-tape of hits recorded from the radio. Cate's assumption that the fatherless boy from Liverpool was a bad influence on her son couldn't have been further from the truth. It had been James who had introduced Connor to almost every vice that teenagers indulged in; strong cider, joints, bottles of strangely flavoured 20/20, and later, little wraps of speed that James had procured from a sixth former at Gray's College. The problem was that Connor just had a greater appetite for it all, and once he had a taste for something there was no-one at home capable of reining him in. With his mother working most nights, Connor enjoyed a freedom that James just didn't have; a freedom that James had envied at the time, but in retrospect could see had been his friend's undoing.

As the memories flooded back, James reproached himself; he'd been coping so much better recently. He hadn't thought about Connor for months. Somehow the Joseph Conlon investigation had become tangled up with his guilty secret. He realised that it had been a mistake to come this way – he should have got the Tube – or not come to London at all *because London was dangerous.* Up in Yorkshire, he was insulated, surrounded by books, antiques and countryside; a world away from the streets that made him sick with shame.

From his jeans pocket, James's phone began to vibrate and the muffled first bars of a Smiths song fractured the stuffy silence of the bus journey. Self-consciously, James grappled with his trousers and pulled it out to see that it was his mother. With RP clarity that carried the length of the deck, despite the fact that the phone was pressed to his face with the in-call volume right down, Cate announced to his fellow passengers that she'd appreciate it if he could pick up some avocados on his way, and a pink grapefruit – if they had one – for the gin.

Sticky with embarrassment, James mumbled in the affirmative, hung up and didn't dare look up until the bus reached Hampstead Heath.

14

27th September, 1919
Birr, King's County, Ireland

The bells of St Brendan's knelled as the congregation filed out of the church and into the cemetery. Purple storm clouds tinged with livid orange clotted the solid sky; it hadn't yet rained and every lungful of air dripped with humidity. The eerie light and soot-black mourning clothes made those who stood around the open grave appear pallid and waxy; cholera victims patiently waiting their turn to faint and pitch forwards into the earth's maw where they'd join the dead amongst knotty roots, rocks and worms.

Ciaran Fahy held his mother. Sisters, Carmel and Maggie, sobbed behind black lace while his father, Seamus, stood apart, his prominent chin jutting defiantly as he clenched his teeth; individual tears traversing the lines of his face and falling onto his shirt. Cousins, aunts, uncles and a huddle of men with dark green ribbons tied around their arms stood on the other side of the grave. Ciaran looked around the churchyard to see if they were being watched by the army or the RIC, but could see no one – at least Kitty's husband had the sense to let them mourn in peace. Ciaran genuinely didn't know what would have happened if anyone in uniform was seen near the church, for nobody in Birr was in any doubt as to who was responsible for his brother's murder – his mother said that he had only spoken one word after the attack, which he repeated three times: "Police, police, police." With these, his final words, Micheál had made it impossible for Ciaran to stand back while men braver than he took up arms.

It was almost a year since the Sinn Féin election victory of 1918 and nine months since Dáil Éireann had established itself as the legitimate government in Ireland. Ciaran hadn't told his mother, but he had given up his law degree the day the election results came in. What use was English law in a country that Ciaran now believed was destined to throw off the shackles of colonialism? Since then he had been part of a Republican cell producing propaganda and news sheets from a printing press in Galway. He'd clung to the vain hope that pressure from the USA would force the British government to concede more liberty to Ireland in this post-war world, but the Amritsar Massacre in India had demonstrated that Britain was in no mood to loosen its stranglehold on Empire anytime soon. Ciaran had started to question whether it could ever be possible to attain liberty without first showing the courage to take up arms. As he held his mother's shaking shoulders and looked at the wooden casket that contained the bruised and broken remains of his little brother – the question was answered.

He regarded the grim-faced boys and men on the other side of the grave and, catching the gaze of Brendan O'Rourke, he nodded. He was in.

The gravediggers lowered the coffin. Ashes were scattered over the lid and before the first spadeful of soil was tossed, Seamus Fahy pulled a tricolour from his jacket and let it flutter into the abyss.

———

From behind an ancient yew tree, forty yards from the funeral party, Kitty Conlon watched numbly. She cried silent tears, terrified that anyone would hear her sobs. As her cousins passed within touching distance of her hiding place, walking slowly towards the church gates, she saw that Ciaran's beautiful grey eyes had hardened to flint. Kitty shifted her weight, snapping a twig and for a horrible moment thought she saw Aunt Mary stare directly at her through the daggers of dark green leaves. Heart in mouth, she held her breath and pinned herself behind the tree trunk, never knowing that only a year before, Aunt Mary had slunk behind the very same boughs and watched as Kitty and Joseph had passed the yew, bursting with joy, holding a baby wrapped in the silk of a christening gown.

15

Summer, 2018
Boroughbridge, North Yorkshire, England

James knew that he'd really fucked up this time.

As he sat in their kitchen, nursing a third large scotch since he arrived home from school, James explored the myriad ways in which he could explain to Charlie what had transpired.

He supposed that the only saving grace was that unwittingly she had played a part in it herself – in fact the whiskey whispered seductively to him that her culpability outweighed even his, as it had been her works do that had placed him in the position he now found himself – *and* he hadn't even wanted to go. But that wouldn't cut it, and he knew it. He was going to have to come clean, take it on the chin and tell his wife the truth. Because of his naivety – or drunken stupidity – depending on how you looked at it (and Charlie would definitely look at it through the prism of the latter), he was currently suspended from school pending an investigation and could well find himself virtually unemployable within the education sector all together. He'd been in a state of agitated panic all day – without the work, what could he do to smother the memories or alleviate the guilt? What else was he good for?

He had arrived at St Wilfred's Academy that Monday morning feeling absolutely wretched. Bilious waves of nausea washed over him as he unpacked his briefcase and feebly arranged the day's resources across his desk. The art-display at the back of the classroom swelled and rolled disconcertingly; the kids' colours too garish and bright – their depictions of medieval battles too graphic and gory for his spirit-poisoned stomach lining. James had virtually no recollection of Saturday night, nor much of Sunday, for that matter – he had stayed in bed most of the day desperately trying to rehydrate his prune-like brain and stop his skull caving in on it. The night before he had been lured by the promise of free drinks to Charlie's big works do in Leeds. Charlie wasn't drinking – determined as she was to conjure the coloured line on the pregnancy test – so James reasoned that he could do the drinking for the pair of them. A boozy meal had been followed by a trail of bars on Park Row before they had ended up in some monstrous space where tonic water glowed and conversations were devoured whole by ravenous beats and deafening basslines. The details were a blank. Sunday had been a write-off, and he was starting to think that he should have pulled a sickie today.

James was just preparing a form-time activity when Yvonne, the Headteacher's PA, poked her head around his classroom door.

"Mr Lucas? Jane needs to see you in her office immediately. Don't worry about your lessons this morning – everything is in hand. If you would follow me?"

Bewildered, James had followed the click-clack of sturdy heels on gum-smeared linoleum. A handful of students who had arrived on one of the early buses loitered outside their form-rooms surreptitiously fingering phones, and James could have sworn they were smiling at him slyly as he passed them by.

Gamely trying to tame dishevelled hair with sweaty palms, James asked, "What's this all about, Yvonne?"

"I have no idea, Mr Lucas. I know that she's got your union rep in with her and some school governors. You'll find out soon enough."

Not much of a comfort. James wracked his brains to work out what the hell was happening. Could it have something to do with his lessons on Catholic collusion with Fascism in Franco's Spain and Nazi Germany? St Wilfred's was nominally a Roman Catholic academy but he doubted that the governors were unleashing the Spanish Inquisition on him over some lessons that were an integral part of the new GCSE. Was it to do with his outburst during the school briefing when the humanities staff had been told that they were losing teaching time again and he'd demanded to know exactly how much more maths could feasibly be squeezed into a single day? (The answer: a lot more.) But again, dragging him before the Head first thing on a Monday morning over something so trivial would be excessive – even by Jane's standards.

No, it had to be something more serious than that.

Stepping past Yvonne into Jane Wainwright's office, James saw the image projected on the wall behind her, and realised that it was.

———————

It all came back to him.

It was well after midnight on Saturday night and James was returning from the bar with his umpteenth gin and tonic. It was criminally expensive but the tab was being picked up by Charlie's Managing Partner, Tim Barton. James had decided that his wife looked too glum sipping at Perrier water all night so he had bought her the most elaborate mocktail that her law firm's money could buy. Decorated with fruit and umbrellas, it looked like a small beach resort. He was on his way back when he bumped into Zara Thomas; only three weeks ago a stressed out A-Level student at

St Wilfred's, but tonight, celebrating her final exam by trying to break the world record for displaying the greatest percentage of bare flesh while technically fully clothed.

"Come in, James. Take a seat."

James looked around the room, trying to avoid the image that dominated the far wall. He recognised a couple of parent governors who couldn't meet his eye. There was somebody official-looking who wore a red lanyard along with an expression of particular distaste. His local NUT representative, Barbara Something-Or-Other, who only popped in to school once a year to ensure that she was re-elected, sat nibbling a Hobnob next to the empty chair that he assumed was for him.

Projected onto the wall was an Instagram image of a ruddy cheeked James, bloodshot and blurred, gurning into the camera lens that had been expertly angled by Zara Thomas to capture a portrait of wanton insobriety. James was holding a ludicrous cocktail in one hand and a G&T in the other, while Zara hung from his shoulder, puckered lips grazing his right cheek and pale breasts fighting to be free from the plunge-neck top she wore. Damningly, underneath the image, she had posted the caption:

Look who I pulled 2nite! #sexonabeachwithMrLucas

Below that, James could see that the image had been liked over six hundred times since Saturday night.

Bugger, he thought.

His belongings had been collected for him and were waiting at reception. Jane didn't want him being spotted by any of the six hundred students who had gleefully watched the image go viral across North Yorkshire. Despite the fact that by Sunday afternoon when Zara had woken to discover what mischief she'd caused, and had hurriedly posted, '**Just Jesting. Soz!**' and '**OMG! It woz only a selfie #MrLisinnocent**', the damage had been done. Outraged parents had seen all they wanted to see and bombarded the school voicemail with demands for a lynching, or a permanent dismissal at the very least. A local journalist had somehow even heard about it and had contacted Jane Wainwright at home on Sunday evening for comment. He had been told in no uncertain terms that if they so much as printed a single word they would be sued into insolvency by the academy's lawyers.

The upshot was that James was sitting in his kitchen, now starting his fourth generous scotch, which he justified by the fact that he didn't have school to go to in the morning, waiting for Charlie to return home.

There would be an argument, and she would win.

The next few weeks would be hell.

And it wouldn't get any better.

So that was why he had booked a ferry crossing to Ireland.

Somewhere deep inside of him he suspected his psyche needed some sort of crusade; something to occupy his mind and keep that demon guilt shackled. If he couldn't fight the good fight at St Wilfred's in a daily attempt to save cohorts of modern-day Connors, then he needed to save something else: he could try to save Sergeant Joseph Conlon.

Since he had returned from London he hadn't made any headway in the search for clarity over the policeman's murder. He had reread O'Rourke's account of the raid on the John's Mall Barracks and it had tallied with Conlon's testimony, although of course O'Rourke had made much greater mileage out of the fact that he had hoodwinked the police with his misdirection at Stoneacre House. O'Rourke was also adamant that Conlon himself had taken part in the murder of Micheál Fahy, although it was never quite clear how he was so sure. However, what had been revealed by the re-read was the identity of the informant that Joseph Conlon had trusted so implicitly. O'Rourke named him as one Séan Keane, a local gamekeeper whom James discovered met a particularly nasty end in a later chapter.

James understood that if he was to disentangle fact from hearsay and rumour, he couldn't rely solely on a sixty-year-old book and what he could access with the click of a mouse. He was going to have to go to Cashel and speak with his family. He was going to have to go to Birr and walk the streets his great-grandfather had trod. Maybe 'Mocktailgate' had happened for a reason; it might be the push that he needed to uncover the truth about Conlon. *And James, of all people, knew how toxic burying the truth could be.*

At that moment Charlie's car swung into the driveway. *Dutch courage*, he thought, draining the dregs of his whiskey.

Part II

The Wisdom

If suffering brings wisdom,
I would wish to be less wise.

William Butler Yeats

16

Summer, 2018
Cashel, County Tipperary, Eire

It was almost midday when James pulled up outside Pat-Joe's empty cottage a couple of miles south of Cashel. It was a typical Irish crofter's home; squat whitewashed walls three-foot-thick, topped with a grey slate roof. James had a set of keys, as did most of the immediate family. Pat-Joe had lived here all his life and had owned the cottage along with the barn, paddock and three surrounding fields. However, almost ten years ago the land and outbuildings had been sold to a distant cousin who grazed his livestock in the thick grass and stored his farm machinery in the barn. The money raised from the sale helped contribute to the costs of keeping Pat-Joe in the nursing home in Clonmel.

A couple of years shy of a century, nobody expected the last Conlon in the family to be around for very much longer, even though the ravages of time had been kind to his body and mind. He was still able to shuffle up and down the corridors of the Golden Glade care home without the need for anything more than the gnarled walking stick that tapped a sedate pace in the infinitely patient rhythm of the ancient. Indeed, James couldn't recall ever seeing his great-uncle without this trusted cane and suspected that over the years it might have somehow fused into the gossamer-soft skin of his palm, and was now as much a part of the old man as his dry wit and even drier breath.

The upkeep of the house was shared between Noel and Mikey Devlin, James's uncles, both of whom lived in Cashel. It had been Noel who had inherited the family business from his father, Enda Devlin, and still lived above the jewellery shop on Friar Street. Mikey had returned to Cashel after an attempt to make a life for himself in London had ended prematurely after the beating at the hands of National Front thugs in the wake of the IRA bombing campaign of 1974. The last child born to Bridget and Enda Devlin was John, who had emigrated to Boston in the '80s and only returned home to Cashel sporadically. The Devlin siblings had argued long and hard about whether to sell the cottage along with the land, but as the eldest, and backed somewhat by her husband's money, James's mother, Cate, had persuaded her brothers to keep it on as a base for when she or John came to visit. Hence it was Noel or Mikey's responsibility to pop in before any family arrived, open the windows and fire the oil-stove to dry the damp from the walls.

James, despite having called in advance, opened the door to be hit with a musty funk that made him recoil. Holding his nose and gagging, he ran around the house opening all the windows. Once he had dispersed the worst of it, he knelt on the cold slate floor and fiddled with the oil faucet that fed the stove from a tank out the back. At least there was now electricity and running water. James could remember the days when buckets carried from a pump in the field were lined up along the kitchen wall filled with water for cooking and washing. He would never forget the numb fear he experienced an hour or two into a Lucas family visit, when, with Pat-Joe in full flow and gallons of tea sloshing around insides his guts, it became impossible to cross his legs any longer and the trip to the outhouse on the far side of the yard became inevitable. Invariably it was raining, and as the wearing of shorts was apparently compulsory for boys under ten back then, his pale legs were soaked as he scampered across the slippery yard and into the dark, wind-swept toilet, with wailing, rusty hinges and gaps in the door slats large enough to accommodate small birds.

There were always spiders.

Everywhere.

Above you, motionless in the centre of their webs; below you, scuttling across the floor; and beside you, hiding behind what passed for toilet tissue but was in fact more akin to grease-proof paper.

By the time James was twelve he had chosen to sneak behind the outhouse and relieve himself against the aging brickwork rather than face the legion of fanged arachnids that lay in wait for him inside. He knew that as a toddler, Phoebe had unrepentantly wet herself on more than one occasion as she sat grinning on a wooden stool in the kitchen, and to be fair, he didn't blame her – there was no way he would ever have let his bare buttocks come into contact with the rickety wooden seat, warped and stained with urine, mould and years of being exposed to the elements.

As James gingerly began to sweep up the desiccated flies and cockroaches that had flocked in their hundreds to this empty house and now crusted the window sills in an apparent last minute bid to escape it again, he switched on the radio. A reedy organ played mournfully as the death notices were read out. After less than a minute of listening to which corpse would repose at which chapel and where you could send your floral tributes, James switched it off. It reminded him why he never listened to the radio in the car. If, God forbid, he were ever to find himself strung upside-down by his seatbelt, choking on petrol fumes and exsanguinating slowly, he didn't want the last thing he ever heard to be the weather, the latest boy band or the death notices – he wanted to meet his maker serenaded by a song worthy of that moment, and there wasn't a track on any of his tape cassettes that didn't fit the bill. Charlie seemed to like them too. On the rare occasions that she relented and let him drive her someplace in the Morris Minor there was nothing she liked more than a bit of Morrissey or My Bloody Valentine.

Driving the mile and a half from Pat-Joe's into town could take an age if you were unlucky enough to get caught behind one of the many huge tour coaches that squeezed their way around the byways of the Irish countryside like greasy clots through cholesterol clogged arteries.

Cashel was barely recognisable to the place that James remembered as a child – of course people had always travelled to visit St Patrick's Rock and the ruins atop it – but not in the vast numbers they did now. Each one of these coaches would disgorge a shuffle of orthopaedic-shoed tourists in sun-visors who would be greeted with fiddle music played through tinny speakers and stalls selling shamrock fridge magnets, Guinness badges and 'Cashel Rocks!' T-shirts.

Directly in front of him, as James edged in first gear towards the junction causing the hold up, was a green minibus, tight-packed with young travellers. Cans of Heineken were held aloft and swayed in time to the familiar bassline of a U2 anthem that throbbed insistently from within the rocking vehicle. Suddenly, with a slickness worthy of one of the boy bands that James so disdained, they all turned and simultaneously started to wave at him. Some of those on the back row pulled faces and gave the thumbs up and behind them, James thought he saw a flash of pink bra and lily-white belly. Taken aback, James blushed and smiled lopsidedly before waving back. As the bus peeled off towards St Patrick's Rock, he saw emblazoned on the side panelling an image of a dancing leprechaun alongside gaudy yellow text that read,

'*The Little Green Party Bus – Ye want Great Craic? – We've Got It!*'
Visualising this drunken posse staggering around the wonders of
Ireland, a guide book in one hand and a can of lager in the other,
James smiled sadly, and sympathised with the poor bugger who
had to drive them around.

A minute later and James was pulling up on Friar Street.
He gazed up at the shop front of *Devlin's Fine Jewellery* and was
pleased to see that Noel had splashed the cash since he had last
been home and treated the building to a lick of paint. However,
stepping inside the shop to the dull tinkle of a pewter bell, James
saw that no such radical change had occurred inside. Indeed, if
Enda Devlin were to be dragged from his grave, he'd notice not a
jot of difference from the shop he opened in 1943. The sun never
seemed to shine through the windows and the polished floorboards
and mahogany cabinets lining the walls made the space more
museum than retail experience. Glass display cases housed an array
of delicate trinkets, each with tiny handwritten price labels tied
to them with thread. Earrings, necklaces and wedding rings lay
on a wash of cream silk, now furred with a fine coating of dust,
along with an array of Catholic paraphernalia designed to reduce
time spent in purgatory. The hard edges of the room amplified
the customers' whispers, creating an uncomfortable hush that can't
have been helped by the fact that Noel, in his charcoal-grey three
piece suit, looked more like a funeral director than someone from
whom you'd wish to purchase a declaration of undying love.

Rather atypically, James thought, there were actual customers
in the shop today; two couples in fact – olive skinned, dark
haired and all sporting incongruously bright clothing for the
dismal surroundings they found themselves in. Whilst one couple
were speaking to Noel in faltering English, the second seemed
transfixed by the variety of rosary beads and crucifixes displayed
in the show-case by the window. Without stopping his sales pitch,
Noel, with only the expressive use of his bushy eyebrows, ushered

James around the counter and through the door into the parlour at the back of the shop.

Aunt Caitriona was drinking tea and peering over her reading glasses at a small television set that shared the crowded sideboard with toaster, kettle, microwave and mini-fridge. The room was warm, as always; an electric two-bar heater squatting on the floor and glowering angrily. A chaos of leads snaked across and over each other, converging on a lone adaptor pierced from all sides by a range of finger-smudged plugs. A heavy odour of old upholstery, burnt toast and dogfood hung in the air. Colm, their giant Irish wolfhound, lay at Caitriona's feet, his outstretched paws almost touching both walls. With the same enthusiasm to see James as Noel had displayed moments earlier, Colm opened one disinterested eye, ascertained that neither food nor danger was forthcoming and then lazily let it slide shut again.

Caitriona struggled to extricate herself from the threadbare armchair, fumbled with the remote control to mute the last black and white television in Europe and stood to greet her nephew. Taking both of James's hands between hers she stretched to plant a wet kiss on his proffered cheek.

"Ah – you're very welcome, James. Glad to see you home. Was the journey long? I'll bet it was. I'm after making some tea for myself. You will have some tea now, will you? I'll make a fresh pot. Sit down now, lovey, and I'll put the kettle on. And a biscuit? You'll have a biscuit? Jaysus, you look too thin. I've got some grand biscuits from Supervalu – coconut, chocolate *and* cherry, would you believe it? Ah, they're awful clever with biscuits now, so they are."

As Caitriona busied herself with boiling water and positioning biscuits in a round on a chipped china plate, she continued with a breathless stream of questions, statements and indeed answers too, in her melodious Tipperary brogue.

"And how's your dear mother? We've not seen her home for a while now. I heard she's stiffness in her back. I am a martyr to that myself. It's all those years bending over cabinets that did for me. The doctor says it's chronic. And your father, Frank? Is he well? And your beautiful sister – has she a man? Tell me now, are you not after getting your wife pregnant yet?"

James felt like a tennis player facing a malfunctioning ball machine that was launching unreturnable aces five to the second. Snatching at one wildly, he blurted, "They're all good, Caitriona. All well – they send their love."

"It's a terrible business in England at the moment, isn't it? All these Islamics blowing themselves up for God-knows-what, and running round with knives and the like. I've seen it on the television. You'd imagine that Mohammad Ali, or whatever they call the fella they worship, wouldn't be bothered with all that business, so you'd think. I doubt you'll see any of that nonsense over here in Ireland; the priests wouldn't allow it. I pray every day for your poor mother and father, so I do. They've not been caught up in any of that, have they?"

"No, Catriona. The *Islamists* seem to have ignored the garden centres and car boot sales of the suburbs, so Mum and Dad are doing just fine."

"Well God be praised for that at least." She placed the tray on the table. "And yourself? How are you? I heard that… Well, Aoife told me that… something to do with some pictures?"

For maybe the first time James could remember, Caitriona seemed genuinely lost for words. Her eyes were hooded and she couldn't meet his gaze. Her daughter, Aoife, was close to Charlie and James was a little annoyed the story had arrived in Tipperary before him. *Thanks for that one, honey*, he thought.

"Oh, it's nothing, Catriona." He picked up a biscuit and brushed a dog hair from it. "A genuine misunderstanding. Charlie has looked into it and legally, I am utterly in the clear. The school just has to be seen to be taking safeguarding seriously. It will all be ironed out, and in the meantime I get to visit you lot." He smiled and hoped that his nonchalant explanation hid the real fear he felt scald his innards. He topped it off with a bare-faced lie: "Besides, teaching has lost its lustre for me anyway. I could do with some time to re-evaluate my career. Teaching's not the same business as when I started."

"Everything changes, James. Look out the window. Cashel's full of folk from all over – and not just the tourists. We have Polish shops and Spanish waiters. We've got Latvian taxi drivers for the love of God and *Sheedy's Hardware* is run by a couple from Romania. A lovely couple, so – good Catholics too – but I feel I'm after waking up in a foreign country every time I go out to buy bread. I don't even understand the till girls at the supermarket. God knows what language they're speaking at me! When I was a girl nobody in their right mind would dream of moving to Tipperary to better their lot. It is us who all wanted to get out – so we did!"

His ageing aunt stared wistfully at the wall. "Your mother, your Uncle Johnny, and even Mikey for a time, two of my brothers, Pat and Tony, and now my own little Liam on the other side of the world with grandchildren I never see."

James knew that both Noel and Caitriona had never left Ireland and never would. Indeed, they had only strayed outside Tipperary by accident. Even their youngest, Liam, a software developer from San Francisco, had been forced to bring his American fiancée back to Cashel to marry or he wouldn't have had his parents in any of the wedding photos.

Just then the door swung open and Noel strode in.

"Feckin' Claddagh rings! I sell nothing but feckin' Claddagh rings nowadays. I never even saw one of them till a couple of years ago, so I didn't. Anyhow – how are ye, James? You have tea? Good. So how long ye home for?"

"I am well, Noel. I don't know how long I'll be about. A week or so, maybe? I am staying out at Pat-Joe's."

The two men shook hands.

"Ah – sorry about that, James. Caitriona told me ye were coming. It's been awful busy like. We've not had the chance to get out there and give the house a good airing."

"Don't worry. It's liveable and I haven't got Charlie with me – so that makes it easier."

Noel nodded, remembering the arsenal of industrial cleaning products that the pair had brought with them last time they stayed, then glanced across at his wife. "Caitriona, would ye go out there and mind the shop while I talk with my nephew?"

As the door closed, Noel turned towards James with an even more sombre expression than normal on his long, solemn face. "So yer mother tells me that ye are set on digging up the past, so I hear?"

So it wasn't just Charlie who was blabbing about him. James couldn't help but feel a little intimidated at the tone. "Yes, well I am trying to find out a little bit more about Mum's... and your granddad – Sergeant Conlon. I did some digging and I discovered that..."

"I don't want to know what ye discovered, James. I know enough about it already. My grandmammy came home to Cashel after the Tan War to be with her kin – Volunteers in the 3rd Tipperary Brigade some of them were: Fenians through an' through. Walk to the Folk Museum on Chapel Street an' ye'll see their faces lookin' back at ye from photographs, so. Ye'll see their belts and their bullets, their rusting revolvers. Ye will also see their obituaries." He prodded the table with a fat, white forefinger; "This one, killed by the RIC in 1920 aged 23. That one, shot by the Black and Tans in '21 leaving behind a widow and three children. The other, executed by the Free State Army in '22 for resisting the Treaty." Noel picked up his wife's cup of lukewarm tea. "Once she was home, Kitty Conlon wouldn't insult their memory by talking of her dead policeman husband, and my mammy knew better than to ask her about it. Now I can't speak for yer own mother, but I grew up with uncles around me who knew of Conlon's deeds across the way in Offaly and they told me I wouldn't want to know the half of it. So I am telling ye now: I know all I need to know, so I do – an' yer books and documents won't change the past nor change my mind. The only thing they'll do is stir up trouble. For ye. For us. For everyone."

He slurped from the cup and licked his lips. "Here in Tipperary, James, the Devlins, the Sheehans, the lot of them; they were all Republicans through an' through. Cut them and they'd bleed green, so they would. An' not just the men in the photographs either. What d'ye think happened to all the gunrunners an' kneecappers after the Good Friday Agreement? They didn't just disappear into thin air, so. They're still about. Maybe a bit greyer. Maybe a bit fatter. Maybe even a bit slower on the trigger, but they're still twisted with feckin' hatred, James. *And* they've sons an' grandsons they've poisoned with the same shite. These are bad men who put too much store on the words and actions of others long dead – they're like yerself in that way. I have cousins who I know would take exception to an Englishman prancin' around the twenty-six counties asking questions about an RIC marked man. Ye've got to be awful careful. In small-town Ireland, yesterday is today and tomorrow will still be yesterday; you can't change it, James, because nobody wants it changed."

Reaching down to stroke Colm, he finished portentously; "If ye want my advice, over here there's no better motto to live by than '*Let sleeping dogs lie.*' If livin' is yer aim, of course."

A dry chuckle followed by a long silence.

A shiver ran the length of James's spine despite the warmth of the parlour.

At that very moment the door burst open and a leprechaun sprang into the room gripping an oversized, polystyrene pipe and proceeded to perform a little jig in front of James.

"Begora! It's grand to see ye, cousin James! You're very welcome home to auld Oirland, so ye are!"

Beaming from beneath an emerald-green top hat and hidden behind a synthetic ginger beard was Noel's youngest daughter, Aoife. Dropping her cod-Irish accent, she asked, "Did you not see me on the bus? Sure, I got all the punters to wave at you. I'd recognise you and your old banger anywhere!"

Like an advert break in a horror movie, Aoife's arrival banished the disquiet of Noel's warning with such immediacy that James found it hard to believe that only a couple of seconds ago he had been experiencing a genuine sense of creeping dread.

He couldn't help but laugh. "Why on earth are you dressed like a leprechaun, Aoife?"

"Hey, you've got to give the punters what they want. We promise good craic and a taste of 'Auld Ireland' on the Little Green Bus, and that's what they get – along with a cool-box of beer and an awful lot of toilet stops. We keep this outfit for selfies. I thought it may tickle you."

She gave James a warm hug. "Anyway, I've only got two hours before I'm back on the feckin' thing and down to Cork for a night at the races, so you better not disappoint! Tell me all the gossip from across the water. How are my gals? How's Charlie? How's Phoebe?" She paused, her eyes twinkling mischieviously; "And, please explain to me, James, how the feck did you end up crashing Instagram with a picture of some school girl's tits?"

17

Almost imperceptibly, blue and gold morphed into green and gold. The county hurling colours that hung flaccidly from flagpoles outside identikit houses, told James that he had left Tipperary and he was now in Offaly. It seemed strange to him that in all his visits to Ireland, he'd never ventured northwards to the region known as King's County during the days his great-grandfather policed the streets of Birr. He assumed that Pat-Joe at the very least must be aware that Joseph Conlon was buried in the churchyard of St Brendan's, but James doubted that anybody else had even visited the grave – certainly his mother was surprised when he told her that he had located her grandfather's headstone. *To be so utterly forgotten in the space of two generations* – it was heart-breaking.

James circled the column on Emmet Square and couldn't help but think that, bereft of the statue that once adorned it, it resembled a solitary, granite candlestick abandoned at a crossroads by an ancient giant. He pulled into one of the parking spaces outside Dooly's Hotel and ejected the tape cassette, cutting off the Cocteau

Twins mid verse. It was an impressive building. Dove-grey and punctuated with white window frames, it ran the entire length of one side of the square. Celtic script above the entrance told him that the hotel had been established in 1747. James wondered whether Joseph or Kitty had ever enjoyed a drink inside, and imagined that they probably had.

He checked in, and as his room was ready, James dumped his suitcase and laptop upstairs. Armed with a battered satchel and a virgin guidebook, he stepped out into the Georgian town. The first thing that struck James was how much Birr reminded him of the twee market towns of North Yorkshire where you could enjoy high tea before nipping into a Barbour shop to buy a wax jacket or a pair of posh wellies. Birr boasted two squares from which a confusion of thoroughfares radiated. The larger of the two, once named Cumberland Square, had been rechristened Emmet Square in honour of the Irish Nationalist, Robert Emmet, whom like so many others had swung on the hangman's noose, before being cut down and beheaded for treason. The less grand Market Square was situated on the banks of the Camcor and was dominated by a monument commemorating the similarly dispatched Manchester Martyrs. Palatial houses lined the leafy avenue of Oxmantown Mall which sloped gently up to Birr Castle and James was surprised to discover that the Assembly Hall that now housed the Civic Arts Centre had originally been built as an *Orange Lodge*. That, in itself, indicated that the Birr of Joseph Conlon had been controlled by those who would die before seeing the union of Britain and Ireland rent asunder. Quite frankly, Birr was the most thoroughly *British* town James had ever come across this side of the Irish Sea.

Despite the sun, the shoppers and the traffic, Noel's warning gnawed at the periphery of his consciousness. Against his better judgement, James found himself stopping from time to time to check that his movements weren't being watched by greying ex-soldiers of the Provisional IRA. Ridiculously, this mild paranoia grew as he approached St Brendan's churchyard, the final resting place of Sergeant Joseph Conlon.

As he opened the gate and passed a giant yew that must have been ancient a hundred years ago, the church loomed before him. St Brendan's was a sombre looking edifice, built in the gothic-revival style with dark turrets and sharp steeples that wouldn't look out of place in a Bavarian forest. Head stones, some ravaged by wind and rain, others the same polished granite that adorned kitchen work surfaces the world over, ran parallel to an ivied wall separating the graveyard from the convent next door. James had absolutely no idea where his great-grandfather was buried. Looking at the number of headstones stretching all the way down to the far wall and around the back of the church towards the river, he resigned himself to spending more time here than he had at first calculated. Having decided to start near the banks of the Camcor where the tilting tombstones appeared more ancient and then work his way back towards the road, he spied an old woman in a thick winter coat emerge from the shadows of the church porch. James called out, but she didn't hear him. He called again and trotted up behind her, catching her as she reached the gate.

"I'm sorry. Excuse me?"

She turned and smiled a toothless grin.

"I was wondering whether you could help? Do you know this church well? You see, I am looking for a specific headstone and I have no idea where to start."

The woman rummaged in her pocket and pulled out a set of dentures. She manoeuvred them onto her gums and peered through thick lenses at James.

"Do I know this church well ye ask? I was christened here, took my first communion, married, christened seven of my own an' will be buried here, so I will. I have arranged the flowers for Father John, an' before him for Father Thomas for forty years an' more; so I'd say that I know this church as well as anybody alive."

112

"Brilliant! I've bumped into the right person then. I am James, James Lucas, and I am researching a little bit of family history."

"Ah! Another of Erin's lost children. Welcome home. This whirl-wise-web or such like, that everyone's clicking an' a' proddin' on their telephones has every Tom, Dick an' Harry looking for dead ancestors – like treasure-hunters, so. Hundred's o' them. Mostly Americans; big, loud voices, an' very well fed. A lot of them Mulroneys, I seem to remember. We've had folk from Australia – a strange lot they are – and others from England. By the sounds o' it, I'd imagine that's where ye'll be from." She shuffled forward, stood on her tiptoes and scrutinised his features. Her breath smelt fetid; James tried not to gag. "Ye look like ye have some Mulroney in ye, so ye do."

Stepping back, sucking air from the side of his mouth, James replied, "Yes, I am from England. Yorkshire, actually; although I don't think there's any Mulroney in me."

She seemed disappointed with that. "'Tis a pity; they're a fine Offaly family, the Mulroneys. Blood relatives of mine, so they are. But yer kin are from Birr, ye say?"

"Yes; my great-grandfather is buried here somewhere. A policeman by the name of Sergeant Joseph Conlon."

She shook her head and tutted. "Another one after lookin' for the auld Peeler?" As if a cloud had passed over the face of the sun, the old woman's expression darkened and she bit her lip before continuing.

"I'll not speak ill of the dead – especially of a Catholic who is buried in consecrated ground with his poor mother beside him. What I will say is that yer man was after puttin' a good few of the young fellas buried here into the cold earth himself, so he was. If I were ye, James Lucas from England, I would pay yer respects quickly an' get yerself back home to yer loved ones, an' leave this place be." She leant forward again and whispered, "An' I wouldn't go round tellin' anyone ye are kin to Sergeant Joe either. Ye never know who might be listenin'."

Noel's warning gnawed all the harder and James felt a flutter of anxiety deep within him: the dead wings of ghostly moths disturbed in the dark.

"The Conlon plot is over there, behind that mausoleum." She pointed towards the gravestones clustered in the shade of the convent wall. Peering through thick lenses, her tongue snaked across her upper lip. "Ye seem a nice young fella, James from Yorkshire. I can see the Irish in ye – ye have the good looks of a son of Erin, so. In a bookish sort of way, mind. It would be a sore pity if anything were to befall ye because of *him*." She spat the last word like you would a mouthful of rancid fish.

"When ye've made yer peace, go home, an' may God go with ye. Then forget this place, an' forget the dead Peeler, who caused nothin' but pain in this town."

And with that she opened her mouth in a silent scream, drew back her lips and thrust her thumb into her palate. With a slippery click, she pulled the top row of teeth from her mouth, trailing creamy tendrils of saliva as she did so. Wiping the spittle from the yellowing dentures, she wrapped them in a handkerchief and deposited them in her pocket. She gave James a last gummy grin – or grimace – he couldn't tell; turned and walked towards the church gate.

James was stunned.

He took three deep breaths and began to walk towards the convent wall. *His poor mother beside him.* So, it wasn't just Joseph buried behind the mausoleum.

It was a family plot the size of a double bed, edged in white marble and scattered with gravel. There were no flowers or sentimental trinkets strewn beneath the headstone. The epitaphs simply read:

Here lie the remains of
CONSTABLE THOMAS CONLON, RIC, BIRR
OF KILFINNY, LIMERICK
1857-1909

His wife,
SARAH CONLON (Nee DONELLY)
OF KILFINNY, LIMERICK
1862-1915

And their son,
SERGEANT JOSEPH CONLON, RIC
OF BIRR
1885-1921

For maybe five or six minutes James stood as still as the stone before him.

He didn't know how to feel.

He didn't know how he *should* feel.

If anything, he felt numb. Before this moment he hadn't even considered the existence of Joseph's parents. It hadn't been important to him – they weren't assassinated on the final day of the Anglo-Irish War and had never been written about in books by IRA gunmen. But because of the actions of their son, they too had been forgotten; abandoned beneath ivy, unmourned and unnoticed for more than a century.

Rather clumsily, James stepped over the edging, crunching gravel underfoot as he leant forward and placed his left hand on the headstone. He closed his eyes and whispered to whoever was listening, "I'll find the truth. I promise."

The truth.

The last time he'd stood by a gravestone, he hadn't told the truth.

Mrs McCleary, a locum priest and a handful of antipodeans in tie-dye had stood at Connor's headstone in Paddington Old Cemetery; everyone damp in the thin drizzle. Brenda McCleary had clasped James's hand and thrust a worn strip of photo-booth snaps into his palm. "He always talked of ye, James. He loved ye like a brother. He had these on him when they found him. I know ye did everything ye could for Connor. Thank ye."

She was led away by the priest.

James nodded grimly at the inappropriately dressed mourners as they filed past him. Strangers, all. When he was sure that he was alone, he unclenched his fist and examined the photographs: A trio of passport sized images stacked one atop the other: Connor and he in their teens, probably high, certainly tipsy; both sporting sunglasses and grinning manically. James was wearing bright yellow Walkman headphones and Connor his favourite baseball cap. In the last image, Connor had James locked in a neck-hold and he was kissing his head. They looked so happy.

Why hadn't he told Mrs McCleary that he'd killed her son?

James clamped his eyes tight; so tight his jaw ached and his nostrils flared. He breathed in deeply. And again. The panic began to subside. He was an old hand at caging the beast now. Focus on something else; kid yourself you're saving others: A-Level results as panaceas, antiques and bookshops as therapy, alcohol as anaesthetic.

He stepped back; re-focused. He shot a self-conscious glance around thechurchyard and took a couple of photographs of the tombstone before nodding at his ancestors and winding his way back through the graveyard. And then he was stopped in his tracks by a name familiar to him.

Micheál Fahy
1903-1919
Stolen from his loving parents,
Seamus and Mary, too soon

Only metres apart in death.

Jesus, what am I doing to myself, he thought. Another young man, dead before life had really begun.

He couldn't let Sergeant Joseph Conlon be guilty of all this – James somehow had to prove him innocent – for his own sake as much as Conlon's.

As he passed the giant yew that had been collecting shadows beneath its boughs for centuries he asked himself, what did the old woman mean by the words, *another one after lookin' for the auld Peeler?* Who else had been to visit the Conlon grave?

Standing at an upstairs window in the converted convent chapel, now the Birr Civic Library, someone had been watching James's every move and had in turn been capturing images of the family reunion with his smartphone. As the churchyard gate swung shut behind James, the stranger made a call.

18

27th September, 1919
St John's Convent of Mercy, Birr, King's County, Ireland

Sergeant Joseph Conlon was squinting through field glasses at the funeral party in St Brendan's churchyard. He was perched on a pew in the gallery above the chapel of the Sisters of Mercy Convent. He could see the Fahy family clustered together with heads bowed, clutching one another with pale white hands, the exception being the pugnacious Seamus, who stood apart and seemed to be fighting a dark rage, his left fist clenched blue. Micheál's elder brother, Ciaran, was staring blankly across at aunts, uncles, cousins and kin who surrounded the dark shadow that divided them.

Joe had a notebook and pen and was recording everybody present at the funeral. Out of respect for his wife's family he had ordered for there to be no RIC presence at St Brendan's. Better to observe, identify, record and follow up leads discreetly afterwards. That way he wouldn't lose the last vestiges of support that the police force retained after the death of Micheál Fahy, and he would avoid the possibility of a shoot-out on consecrated ground, a sin that would surely damn him to hell for all eternity. But he also had an ulterior motive for giving the order that there would be no police presence at the funeral, a reason that he had only shared with Head Constable Regan: Joe now strongly suspected that one of his men was passing information to the South Offaly Brigade of the IRA. How else would they have known exactly where to look for the chests of weaponry and ammunition when they raided the barracks last month? If the message got back to them that there was to be no official surveillance, then it was likely that the more prominent members of the Fenian community would crawl out of the woodwork.

Joe could recognise the fiery red hair of O'Rourke, with his perennial side-kick, Padraig Nolan, alongside him. He had expected the pair of them to be in attendance – both had been prominent Irish Volunteers and Joe was certain that they were now rebels.

Wasn't that the miller's son, Liam Kavanagh? He scribbled his name down and annotated a faint question mark next to it.

He knew well the military bearing of Peadar Moran – a tough bastard who had been dishonourably discharged from the Leinster Regiment for slicing off another man's ear lobe in a drunken brawl – Joe had accommodated Moran in the cells on John's Mall on numerous occasions after the whiskey had turned him mean and a publican had sent for the Peelers. Joe had listened with disgusted fascination as Moran had shaken the iron bars, bloodied knuckles like limpet shells locked in lines, cursing into the early hours a litany of obscenities that were impressive even for a squaddie.

Beside him, an ageing, white-whiskered man in crumpled clothing stood protectively alongside a good looking boy. His eyes never stopped surveying the perimeter of the churchyard. He reminded Joe of a hoary rabbit, ears bolt upright, watching and listening for any movement in the sky or rustle in the gorse; hind feet ready to thump out warning at the slightest indication of danger. Joe knew that he had seen the old man at market with some half-starved bullocks and thought he came from the hills on the road to Athlone, but he couldn't place his name.

Beneath dark caps were some other young lads whom Joe couldn't identify at all. Each of them had a green ribbon tied above their elbows. Joe knew that membership of Sinn Féin was now an arrestable offence in some parts of the island, but he didn't believe that imprisoning the majority of the Irish population whom had returned seventy-three Sinn Féin deputies in free elections was in the interests of democracy. Nor would it help in the policing of the land.

As he observed the funeral party, he found himself panning the field glasses across the churchyard towards the mausoleum in the corner and the white headstone that marked where his mother and father were buried. To lose them both before he gave them grandchildren still stung. For them never to have seen the beauty of Kitty nor heard the sweet laughter of Bridget reinforced his belief in the terrible symmetry of existence. He reasoned that man could only experience so much happiness at any given moment, and that on God's cruel balance sheet withdrawals had to be made before any significant wealth of joy was allowed to be deposited. This grim logic was the only way he could rationalise their loss and it made him appreciate more the bliss he felt in the arms of his wife.

If he was honest with himself, there had been precious few embraces in the previous weeks and none since the death of Micheál Fahy. Kitty looked at him like a stranger and didn't need to speak to communicate to him that he should sleep in the barracks for the time being. She claimed to have heard from one of the few women who would still talk to her that the last words her younger cousin had spoken, damned the police thrice. Joe had cried, he had knelt at Kitty's feet, he had rent his hair like a wild man, he had lost his temper and cursed and sworn on everything holy that he had nothing at all to do with the death of her cousin.

But he knew that she didn't believe him.

And in a way, she was right not to, because he *was* complicit in Micheál's murder. Nobody had been charged. He had wanted to beat the truth out of each and every one of his constables, and drag the battered perpetrators before Kitty so that they could spit out admissions through smashed teeth and so prove his innocence. But what Sergeant in their right mind would do that? Besides, Head Constable Regan had taken him to one side and let him know that the orders had come through from Dublin that investigations into the homicide of suspected rebel operatives, especially when the police themselves were suspects should, of course be investigated, *'but maybe not with the rigour of a normal investigation.'* The last thing that the RIC needed in this time of turmoil was its own officers on trial for murder. Conlon had tried to argue that being seen to serve justice could only strengthen their standing within the community, but Regan had regarded Conlon wearily and replied, "Joseph, do you really think for one moment that locking up our boys would stop the killings or the ambushes or the raids on barracks? If it would, I would do it. But you know it won't. It will deplete our numbers, make us impotent and serve as definitive evidence that we can't beat these bastards through policing alone. Back in Westminster they have their heads in the sand. They don't want to be engaged in a war, and they don't want to consider rebels as combatants. They most certainly do not want British newspapers reporting on the murder trials of policemen with penny dreadful headlines. All that can do is swell the support of those against us. Think of it this way, Joseph, perhaps one of the Fenians themselves was responsible – maybe Micheál, with his first cousin married to a policeman was a liability? They're using our guns and our bullets. Who is to say who pulled the trigger on the horse or beat the boy?"

Joe didn't know.

He might never know; and that made a mockery of him being a policeman. What he did know was that the bruising around the boy's wrists suggested that he had been cuffed before he died and he could only think of one organisation that used handcuffs – and it wasn't the so called Irish Republican Army.

As Father O'Brien closed his missal and the mourners turned to follow the priest from the graveside, Joe saw Seamus Fahy pull a tricolour from his jacket, and drop it into the blackness that embraced his son.

A tough man like Joe shouldn't cry, but when he saw Kitty cautiously emerge from the shadows of the yew, and slip through the church gate after the funeral party, the tears came heavily. Saltwater pooled in the field-glass lens blurring the scene before him into an impressionist nightmare of dead greys, greens and sickly orange.

19

Summer, 2018
Birr Civic Library, Co. Offaly, Eire

Why was it always the men who strode straight past her and into the early readers' section as if they knew the library intimately? How long would it take for this one to realise that there was nought downstairs but Peppa Pig, David Walliams and out-dated children's encyclopaedias, comically redundant in their ignorance of DNA, nanotechnology or the end of the Cold War? Dervla liked to play a game with herself each time this happened. The man with the battered satchel didn't look like he was from around here – he resembled a university professor or something – would that give him an edge? Dervla wagered that he might break the sixty second barrier; she started counting under her breath.

She had only reached fourteen when the man with the scruffy hair gave up scanning shelf labels and walked over to the help desk. A winner!

"Hi, I was wondering whether you could help me?"

Dervla glanced at the oft-ignored signage that clearly stated what kind of desk she manned, "I should be able to, so."

The dark-haired stranger smiled. "Of course – sorry. I am looking for anything you might have on local history. Especially anything relating to the War of Independence."

"We have a cabinet upstairs full of local history — there are some rare first editions so we keep the cabinet locked." Dervla opened a drawer and rooted around. "Ah, there's someone with the key up there at the moment. It should already be open. If I could get ye to just sign in here with your name and address and then it is up to the top of the stairs, make a right and then down to the end."

He bent and scribbled his name and address on the ledger. *She was right.* Dervla knew he wasn't Irish. *James Lucas from Yorkshire.* Dervla considered the boast — the small claim to fame that she enjoyed revealing to those who asked after books on this period. Flushing somewhat, pink cheeks and freckles under a tangle of copper, she smiled self-consciously, revealing twin tracks of orthodontic braces. "There's a book up there written by a relative of mine; if ye are interested?"

"Oh?"

"My great granddaddy was one of the heroes of 1916 and leader of an IRA unit here in Birr, so he was. He wrote a book called…"

The Englishman cut her off. "*The Deeds and Exploits of The Irish Republican Army in County Offaly?*" He stared at her strangely, as though he'd seen a ghost. "Your great-grandfather was Brendan O'Rourke?"

Dervla beamed, her cheeks now throbbing crimson. "That's mad, so it is! How did ye know?" She felt a swell of pride that somebody from so far afield had heard of her ancestor.

"Just a hunch."

"Wait till I tell my mammy — she won't believe it." Regaining her composure, she added professionally, "Of course, if ye need any help in locating anything else, please just ask."

As the man all the way from Yorkshire stalked up the stairs swinging a brown satchel, Dervla started tapping away on her iPhone. *Surely this story was too good to keep to herself?*

To all intents and purposes, James *had* seen a ghost. Noel's words haunted him as he passed banks of computer screens peopled by Leaving Cert students. How could he have been so naïve? In smoke-box Irish towns, the past and present would forever collide in endless Brownian motion, and he'd stepped right into the middle of it. From the top of the stairs James had turned to catch the flame-haired librarian working her phone furiously, a wide grin across her face – and that worried him. Did he really need the current crop of O'Rourkes to know that there was an Englishman sniffing around in Birr? Especially as the toothless woman from the churchyard knew exactly whose history he was digging up?

More than ever, James was starting to understand the wisdom of his elders. He would try to keep a low profile from now on.

The cabinet was unlocked as promised. James could see that there were a wealth of tomes on the Earls of Rosse and the Parsons family. Manuscripts mapping the evolution of Birr from Parsonstown lay alongside ecclesiastical histories of St Brendan the Elder. Reference books tabulating population and demographics were stacked beside works on Georgian architecture. But then his eyes alighted on what he was looking for: propped against a copy of O'Rourke's memoirs was a darkly bound book entitled 'Policing in West Offaly – 1814-1922' by Thomas Mannion. The book was dedicated to, 'All the men who served in the Royal Irish Constabulary and their families. Policemen erased from this nation's history.' James hoped it might challenge the Republican account of Joseph Conlon's death. Sitting at a table near the window, he pulled pad and pen from his satchel and began to take notes.

An hour later James had discovered that by 1920 all of rural barracks in King's County had been abandoned and the number of policemen posted to Birr had peaked at twenty-four in January, 1921. But at the same time as this centralisation, the overall picture for the Crown Forces was grim: over 2,750 men resigned or were dismissed for harbouring nationalist sympathies. James wondered what had stopped his great-grandfather from resigning. Was he just another British stooge or was there a nobler reason for his continued employment in an organisation that was becoming marginalised within Ireland? James sighed, this book was no more than a collection of statistics and anecdotes about barrack life. The chapter on the weeks running up to the truce merely regurgitated lists of men shot and newspaper headlines. There was nothing new here.

Spotting an empty workstation, James took the opportunity to check his email, something that he hadn't had a chance to do since leaving Boroughbridge. Logging on, he saw that two days ago he had received an automated message from the National Archives with a link to one of the newly digitised documents he had requested. *Finally!* It was the big one; the Court of Inquest findings into the assassination of Joseph Conlon. There was no point downloading the PDF file to a public PC, so James decided to print it off. A laminated sign on the desk told him that it was 20c per page, and print-outs could be collected at the help desk downstairs. James pressed print, and began to pack up his stuff – he needed a breath of fresh air and a bite to eat. He'd read the document in situ, on Main Street.

He was in the process of logging off when he felt a tap on his shoulder and heard a soft spoken voice enquire, "Would I be wrong in supposing that you are looking into the death of Sergeant Joseph Conlon?"

So much for keeping a low profile.

———————

For a second James felt like a child caught in the act of pilfering penny-chews from a sweetshop. He froze. A thin reflection hovered behind his shoulder in the PC monitor, the face obscured by shadow. With a disproportionate sense of foreboding, James swivelled on the desk-chair to find himself before a well-dressed man with feminine lips, pale skin and eyes of glacier-blue. His hair was long and dark and poured behind his ears and over his collar like Guinness.

"Oisín Ó Súilleabháin is my name," the young man continued, "and I couldn't help but notice from the window that you were taking photographs of the Conlon grave and browsing through Mannion's work on the RIC. I put two and two together. Forgive me if I have come to five."

James was too taken aback to reply anything other than, "No, not at all, you're right. I am. But, why are you watching me?"

"Don't fear. I am sorry if I have unnerved you; let me explain myself. I am a PhD student from University College, Dublin. Over the last few months, I have been back and forth to Birr to access the Rosse Papers and this library's cache of original documents, and you are the very first person I have come across who seems to be thumbing the same books as I. My thesis focuses on reprisal killings in the last weeks of the Tan War, so Sergeant Joseph Conlon has always been very much in my cross-hairs, so to speak. He was the most senior policeman to be executed on the last day of the conflict, but I think you already know that, don't you?" A hint of a smile. "There I was, dreamily staring through the window trying to reword a clumsy paragraph, when I saw you talking to Maebh Kinahan, and then her directing you to Sergeant Conlon's grave. I probably had the very same conversation with her the first time I came to Birr."

Oisín's delicate lilt, melodious and soft, his elven features and his otherworldly eyes reminded James of Pat-Joe's tales of the *Sidhe*, ancient Irish faery folk, both beautiful and treacherous. James understood that he was talking to '*the other one*' of the old woman's mutterings.

"Dervla downstairs was telling me that you are interested in the Tan War. Are you a fellow historian like myself, or are you perhaps related to the unfortunate policeman? Your surname, Lucas, doesn't sound very Irish."

James began to feel a prickle of discomfort and not a little indignation. "I am sorry, but I am finding this all a tad uncomfortable, Oisín. I don't like the thought of being watched from a window while I pay respects at a grave, nor do I take kindly to being observed whilst I browse books in a library. But sneaking downstairs to snoop at the library register to garner my name and address is a step too far."

Oisín smiled disarmingly, the light dancing in his eyes, "Oh don't mind me, James – can I call you James? Please forgive me. Months of following dead men's trails have murdered my manners. I believe that I may be losing my humanity amongst all the bloodshed."

A flash of brilliant, white teeth. "Of course, I should have approached you directly and introduced myself from the outset. No harm done, I hope? So, are you an historian, or relative? 'Paying respects' leads me to suspect that you are the latter."

"Well, you're right again," James bristled, "Sergeant Joseph Conlon was my great-grandfather."

"Come now, James. Please, let there be no coldness between us. Meeting the descendant of the last man killed in the war of Independence is an honour. And, if I may say so, an opportunity too. We are obviously both men who chase the past and we know the value of evidence. Dry documents that grow old in archives may form the skeleton of our theses, but it is the real men and women who lurk behind the text that we must tease out to give flesh to our theories. Chancing upon you could be the making of my doctorate. You may be in possession of an oral history to the assassination I am unaware of. Maybe letters, diary entries, family photographs? I would be grateful for anything you could share with me about the death of your Sergeant Conlon. Oh, and of course, I will share with you all that I have learned. We could pool our knowledge to each other's mutual benefit."

James considered Oisín with a steady gaze. He discerned the barely-concealed affront that the young academic had at another historian stumbling onto his patch. Yet he recognised the greedy look in the man's eyes at the thought that his own quest could be furthered. And James reasoned that he would learn a lot more from Oisín than the student would from he: James decided to ignore the territorial pissings for now. "I haven't any unique insights – Sergeant Conlon seems to have been whitewashed from my family history. In actual fact, I only learned of the details of his death a couple of weeks ago. Since then I have begun to build up a picture of the man, but you may be disappointed in what I have to share. Obviously you know what O'Rourke accuses him of – I have managed to get my hands on a handful of documents from The National Archives that pose some interesting questions."

Oisín's eyes lit up. "Student finances being what they are, I haven't as yet had the chance to travel to London, so you would be saving me time and money if I could examine those files. I have spent five or six full days here in Birr annotating and making copies of documents about the RIC, the Black and Tans and the Auxiliaries in County Offaly – I am willing to give you access to all that I have found that may be pertinent to you."

A trade of information would save him valuable time and reveal to him aspects of the story that he didn't know even existed. What were the Rosse Papers? What original documents did the library here in Birr hold? James felt like an amateur trespassing in the realm of professional academia.

"OK. I haven't got my laptop with me – it's up in my hotel room, but I could pop back across town and grab it."

"Don't worry yourself now, James. I have to go over to the castle in the next half hour or so. The Rosse papers are part of an archive that they keep there and you can only examine them by appointment – by the end of the afternoon I imagine that I will have gleaned all that I need to know for this part of my thesis and then I'm done with Birr. I believe that it is always best to do business with a pint in one's hand, and as this is my last night, might I suggest that we meet later on tonight?"

After the day he was having, James knew he'd end up drinking tonight anyway. Better to drink on the job with a lead than alone with the demons. Even though he didn't trust this suave post-grad student, James agreed.

"Grand, so! I am staying in a room above Craughwell's on Castle Street – it has good food, great music and beer so fine that Yeats himself would struggle to find words to do it justice. If you bring a USB stick with your data from the National Archives, then we can copy things back and forth and both go to bed happy men. Shall we say 7.30?"

James considered telling him that he had just printed off Conlon's Inquest report, but decided that he wanted to analyse it himself before he shared it with a stranger.

"Yes, that seems like a good idea. See you at 7.30 then."

"*Slán leat, Seamus.*" Oisín smiled and winked as he headed off towards the stairs.

'*Goodbye James*' in Gaelic – that was about as far as his knowledge of the language of his forebears went; that and '*sláinte*' of course. Hopefully he would get to practice the pronunciation of the latter a fair few times later that evening.

James packed the last of his belongings into his satchel and made for the stairway. All morning he had avoided the place that Sergeant Conlon had been murdered. He'd traversed the town by twists and turns, glimpsing through parked cars and shifting faces the spot it occurred, but never set foot on Main Street.

He couldn't put it off any longer: It was finally time to follow in the very last footsteps of his great-grandfather. Ignoring the fact that the red-head at the help desk held the printed pages as though they were infectious, and pointedly didn't smile as she accepted his money, James stepped outside into the afternoon.

20

1ˢᵗ October, 1919
Mill Island, Birr, King's County, Ireland

As Séan Keane opened his eyes, or more accurately, opened his left eye, as his right was swollen shut and caked with dried blood, it didn't seem to get any brighter.

Slowly growing accustomed to the gloom, he could make out that he was propped against some jute sacks on rough floorboards. Thin streams of weak sunlight filtered through cracks in the wood-frame revealing a lazy mist of minute white particles suspended in the air.

Séan's hands and feet were bound, his fingers cold and numb. His head throbbed with an intensity that threatened to send him crashing back under and he thought he might vomit.

He could smell dust and damp and algae and something else that reminded him of childhood, an incongruously reassuring smell that evaded his grasp like elvers slipping through wet fingers.

His jaw ached and his mouth was stuffed with dry rags. A tight gag tore painfully at the corners of his lips. He tried to generate some saliva to swallow, but couldn't. He began to panic, choking on the stale cloth that scratched his palate. Summoning some composure from within, Séan inhaled slowly through his nostrils, thankful that they weren't clogged with blood.

In and out.

In and out.

And he listened.

First to his thudding heart which, sensing it might be cheated of years of steady pulsing, seemed set on drumming out a lifetime of beats in the remaining minutes he had left. And then to the deep, monotonous tremor that rumbled from the bowels of the building setting the floating white particles a-quivering. Behind that he could hear the rhythmic creaking of ancient timber, the rush of water and the voices of men hissing words at each other close by.

As the layers of sound made themselves known to him, Séan cleared his head and tried to work out what had happened. The last thing he remembered was leaving Treacy's Tavern in Portumna and heading down the track that led from the town around the lake to the small farmstead where he had been living – if you could call it living – for the past fortnight. He had been sleeping on a makeshift cot in the byre of his brother's rented farm and working the land for board and lodging.

For the first week after the raid on the barracks that had forced him to flee Birr, Séan had dined nightly with Vincent and his family and never once set foot outside his brother's land. But five nights ago he had slipped for the first time from the byre after the Keanes had gone to sleep to the tavern on the lake road. All he had wanted was a couple of jars, some fiddle-music and some time away from Vincent who couldn't help but look at him with a sorrowful gaze reflecting disappointment, confliction and fear all at the same time.

And he had enjoyed himself. The convivial atmosphere – and more pertinently the beer – had helped him forget his own fears, and when he spoke to the farmers and fishermen who frequented the spit and sawdust pub, he told them he was a travelling salesman out of Cork City just passing through.

So Séan had returned.

Twice more since then; and that was why he was where he was now, gagged and bound and waiting for a bullet to the back of his head.

Somebody must have recognised him, or guessed, because the face that shifted in and out of focus as he was dragged from the track and thrown into the trap before losing consciousness, was that of Brendan O'Rourke.

Stroking Séan's hair almost maternally he had whispered, "Ah… Séan. We've found ye at last. I'd have thought ye'd have gone farther. We're goin' home to Birr, Séan, an' ye'll be pleased to know that now ye can be buried next to yer father."

What could he have done?

What options did he really have?

When O'Rourke and Nolan had sidled up to him in O'Hegarty's in Sharanvogue a month past and bought him pint after pint and smilingly talked of hunting and fishing and hurling and his days as one of the most promising corner-backs in King's County, he'd been flattered. The conversation flowed as quickly as the Guinness: his work as gamekeeper at Stoneacre House, Sir Terence Davenport, childhood sweethearts and old friendships. Séan, like the rats he caught on the estate, had been lured into a trap. As he accepted his eighth pint, his tongue now thoroughly loosened, he heard the cage door snap shut behind him.

"We like ye, Séan. Yer one of us, so you are, an' we'd never want to see ye hurt. But ye have to know, ye work for a parasite. A man who has grown fat on the toil an' misery of fellow Irishmen, like yerself, like me, like Padraig over here. Ye know who we are, ye know what we stand for, and ye know what we're willin' to do to achieve that end. We're givin' ye fair warnin' that Stonacre House will be burned to the ground. Orders have come through and will be carried out. All the weapons that Davenport possesses will be seized an' that corrupt landlord an' his family, a brood of bastards that have looked down on the likes of us for centuries, will go to the flames too. Now, me an' Padraig here are tellin' ye this because we don't want the blood of a good Irish patriot like yerself on our hands. This work is grim enough as it is, so help me God. So, we'd like ye to be away on the night of the 17th September. I'm sure ye can come up with somethin'. An' we'd like ye to leave the gates unchained, the doors unlocked, the gun cabinets open an' the cartridges out in a place where we will be able to find them. Ye'll do that for yer country, won't ye, Séan?"

What could he do?

Let Sir Terence, his wife, their widowed daughter and grandchildren be murdered in their beds? And, Nora, the chambermaid – he'd not see a hair on her head touched.

Three generations of Keanes had been the estate's gamekeepers and when Sir Terrence had bought the place he had kept the family on. Séan was even fond of the retired major. Yes, he could be blunt – and he didn't hide the fact that he considered Séan a subordinate – but there was a degree of soldierly affection between the pair born of spending innumerable hours tramping the fields and forests around the estate discussing fences, fishing and pest control. Séan knew that he couldn't let the old bluffer and his family die at the hands of the wild eyed extremist leering next to him.

So he did the only thing he could do. He downed his pint, wiped his lips with the sleeve of his jacket, grinned and said, "The 17th you say? I can make myself scarce that night, sure. I could be here all night if I only had the money to spare."

He shook the hands of Brendan and Padraig, accepted the bribe and the following day, while picking up supplies in Birr, he had slipped a note through the red door on Main Street that belonged to Joseph Conlon.

Of course, now he knew that he had been used. The attack on Stoneacre House had merely been a diversion so that the IRA could raid the barracks on John's Mall and seize the cache of weaponry. The morning after, Joe had called Séan in and interviewed him formally. Although Joe committed to keeping his identity hidden in the official documentation, he acknowledged that Séan was in very real danger if he stayed in Birr. The two old friends had embraced, and Joe had sworn that when this ragged band of Fenians were safely behind bars then he would send for him.

Shifting uncomfortably and trying to relieve the pressure on his aching arms, Séan rued that O'Rourke had used their childhood friendship to get at the Sergeant. Joe and Séan had known each other for more than twenty years. Back before all this hatred started, when the priest and the local policeman were respected as the moral authority of the town, Joe's father, Constable Thomas Conlon, had come to know Séan's father well. There wasn't much crime in Birr back then, but what little there was was focused on poaching, cattle rustling and property theft, so naturally the gamekeeper and policeman came into contact regularly. Over the years they became friends, and by the time that Séan was five, Constable Conlon was bringing his own son, Joseph, around to Stoneacre House to learn the craft of the countryside from Séan's father. Over the long hot summers, the two boys became inseparable. They swam, they fished, they played war games in the woods, and it was during one of those summers that Joe Conlon saved Séan's life.

They had been out firing catapults at rabbits when they had decided to construct the greatest treehouse ever built. It would be the tallest, largest, most secret treehouse in all of King's County and it would command views over every field, boreen, stream, cottage and hill. Séan had provided nails, rope, a large bucket, slats of wood and various other pieces of equipment liberated from his father's shed. Joe had supplied boiled sweets and bottles of lemonade. Séan, a couple of years younger than Joe, ascended the tree with the agility of a squirrel, the rope looped over his shoulders. Higher and higher he climbed until Joe was just a speck below him looking up through the foliage.

"Séan, don't climb too high! We won't have enough rope! Loop it around a branch and throw it back down."

And so it began: Joe tying slats of wood to one end of the rope and hoisting them up with the other. Séan collecting each one and stacking them, one atop the other, wedged between two branches. Then bucketful by bucketful, twine, jam-jars of nails, hammer and saw, lemonade and confectionery were sent swinging upwards through the leaves until sixty feet up, the boys had all they needed teetering precariously on the swaying branches that shifted in the summer breeze.

Using the rope, Joe laboriously pulled himself up towards Séan who smiled at the look of trepidation on the elder boy's face as he checked each foothold and handhold before releasing his full weight. Séan had never seen his friend look scared before and it made him feel proud that for the first time it was he, and not Joe, who seemed to be captain.

When Joe reached him, he looked physically ill and hugged the trunk with the desperation of a shipwrecked sailor clinging to a broken mast. "Maybe this wasn't such a good idea after all, Séan."

"Ah – don't worry. It's a grand idea, and once we have a floor put down it will be as solid as a cobbled street, so it will."

Half an hour later a platform, about six foot by six, was nailed into the upper branches and Séan remembered dancing a jig to reassure Joe of the solidity of the structure. Joe had smiled at that and said, "It's not too shabby after all."

The boys had then reclined against the tree-trunk, bathed in verdant dappling, sipping lemonade and sucking strawberry lozenges. They listened as the breeze rustled the leaves which shivered and whispered like distant waves caressing pebbled shores.

"I think I can hear the sea, Joe."

"You eejit. Birr must be the farthest point from the sea in all of Ireland."

Séan clambered up onto the next branch and then the one above. "I can too! It's on the other side of that hill, so it is. Ye wouldn't be able to see it from all the way down there, mind!"

He sat two branches up, swinging his legs and enjoying the way the power dynamic had shifted ever so slightly back in his favour.

Then the branch snapped.

Séan could still recall with absolute clarity that split second of weightlessness as he hung suspended in the treeline before the laws of gravity followed their awful logic and his stomach lurched up his throat as the rest of his body began to accelerate towards the forest floor sixty feet below.

Séan would never forget that one second; the second between the starting-pistol report of the branch snapping, the downward momentum and the rough jerk at his collar as the strong right hand of Joseph Conlon arrested his fall. Grunting with effort, his friend held him by the scruff of his shirt and with buttons popping and legs kicking helplessly at the nothingness of the void, Joe dragged him back over the edge of the lookout.

"Feck Séan, what's the rush to get down all of a sudden? Sure, I'm only starting to enjoy it up here now." Joe gave a lopsided grin and then looked earnestly at Séan. "Seriously, don't go scaring me like that again."

Séan remembered that he had started laughing and crying at the same time. Gasps of air, sobs, snot, tears and manic laughter; a symphony of shock. Joe had ruffled his hair and told him not to worry: he'd always be there to catch him when he fell.

The dynamic was irrevocably restored.

Well, this time, thought Séan, even the strong hands of Sergeant Conlon couldn't save him. He was a dead man for sure – death was never cheated, only ever delayed.

These bittersweet memories faded as he heard the angry whispers next door getting louder as the conversation became more heated. Séan shuffled painfully across the floorboards and pressed his ear to the wall. He could make out three or four voices, but there were two that were dominant. One of those was the familiar voice of Brendan O'Rourke, rural and unpolished yet confident and clear. His sentences were punctuated with pauses and dramatic intonation, like a priest or politician. The second voice, he couldn't quite pin down, but there was finesse to the elocution that suggested that the owner had trod more streets than just those of Birr.

"I want no part in this, Brendan. Murdering a man in cold blood is not what I signed up for."

"Ciaran, did ye really think that the bastards who run our country would just roll over an' let us have our land back after shootin' a handful of policemen and burnin' some culchie barracks? Hell, Lloyd George won't even admit that the British are fightin' a war. To him we're just criminals, we're outlaws runnin' around murderin' and burnin' an' we just need to be policed properly. This *is* a feckin' war, Ciaran, an' that man is a feckin' spy. In wars spies are shot."

"But he did exactly what you wanted him to. He was just a pawn! You got the guns, you got the ammo. You made the Peelers look like fools. You won. Why kill him now?"

"Ciaran, if we don't kill him we are tellin' everyone that it's fine to go chirpin' to the RIC about legitimate Republican activity. Feck, this town is the most establishment town in all of Ireland, so it is. There's Irishmen an' women here who'd rather this land was run from London, than run by ourselves, for ourselves. D'ye think there's one of the fine folk of Oxmanton Mall or William Street who wouldn't go straight to Conlon if they knew who we were or what we planned? If we can't win their loyalty by the nobility of our cause, at least we can guarantee their co-operation through the barrels of our guns. So yer man next door: he's a *message*. A very necessary message."

"Brendan, look me in the eyes and tell me that you are not going to murder that man because he is a friend of Sergeant Conlon's. Tell me you are not doing this out of spite for a man you hate because Kitty chose him over you."

There was a dark silence and Séan heard the unmistakable sound of a revolver hammer being cocked.

"As yer ranking officer, soldier, I am askin' ye to mind yer words. I sup with yer father and am steppin' out with yer sister. We're practically family. I haven't forgot who was responsible for Micheál's death, although it seems to me that ye have. Yer own mother heard his last words: *Police*. Now who's the police in this town? If Conlon didn't beat the life out of yer kid brother, then he certainly ordered it. If anyone should be committed to the cause, it should be ye. Here, take this gun an' go do it yerself – if yer man enough."

Séan heard a pause and a shuffling of feet on floorboards.

"No? I didn't think so. Let me tell ye somethin', Ciaran, we know we can't win this war on the open battlefield, although the Brits would love to see us try. No: we have one chance to win this war an' success rests on the unholy trinity of guerrilla warfare. D'ye know what that unholy trinity is, Ciaran?"

"I am sure that you are about to tell me, Brendan."

"Feck off, Ciaran, with yer sarcasm. Will ye listen for once? God the Father is *Fury*. He is Old Testament physical force. We fight our enemy only when an' where we can win. We ambush, we assassinate, we raid an' we burn. An' then we just melt away into the hills an' hamlets of this beautiful isle.

"God the Son is *Fear*. He's more subtle than his old man, but just as deadly. We intimidate our enemy. We scare him, we put him on edge. We keep him there. We let all those who would challenge us, both soldier and civilian, know that no-one they love is safe anymore.

"And God the Holy Ghost is *Hopelessness*. We ostracise the Peelers. We make it so they don't feel part of God's earth anymore. We won't pour them drinks, nor serve them in shops. We will see them locked behind the grim bars of their barracks, with all the freedom of prisoners. We make it so that they come to see that winnin' this war is in fact to lose. If they prevail they will forever cower behind barbed wire an' walk alone in a land that used to be theirs.

"Ye want to beat the greatest Empire this world has ever seen? Then ye crush it's morale – *intimidate, ostracise, attack*! Now this single bullet that I will use on Séan Keane will do more damage to the RIC an' those in Birr who don't share our convictions than a thousand rounds fired in anger."

Séan heard one pair of palms slow clapping; "So ends the sermon of St Brendan. But all your fine words won't change the fact that what you're about to do is no better than what they did to Micheál. We're meant to be *better* than them, Brendan! Pontificate all you want: I'll have no part in this murder."

A door slammed, followed by five heartbeats of silence. For a moment Séan had a glimmer of hope.

"If I didn't think that his sister would never let me taste what she keeps inside her drawers again, I swear I'd have that little gobshite shot for insubordination!"

Some nervous bar-room laughter.

"Come now. Let's get this thing done."

Séan began to pray.

21

Summer, 2018
Main Street, Birr, Co. Offaly, Eire

The rain pounded the pavement with such ferocity that it looked as though the torrent was erupting skyward from the drains beneath the street. Bare-legged women tottered past the window in high heels, diaphanous knee-socks of watercolour-grey streaming down their calves, small leather jackets held over heads and pummelled from above in a relentless tribal drumbeat. Faceless suits sprinted along shopfronts, hurdling puddles, hidden under umbrellas while teens in T-shirts and sodden trainers squelched unhurried towards a destination that as yet remained unknown to even themselves.

James was sitting in a café, printed pages spilling across the table before him. He had dived inside as the strip of blue above the street darkened to purple and the first heavy drops of rain began to fall. The inquest report had made things very real, and his appetite had withered. An untouched panini sat on a greasy napkin beside a cold mug of coffee. The first witness was a shopkeeper named Declan Skelly who had watched the assassination unfold from the very same spot that James was now sitting. Number 42, Main Street was the address given, and unless the council had seen fit to change the street numbers in the last century, Saoirse's Sandwich Stop occupied the building which had once been Skelly's General

Store. The shopkeeper reported seeing an unmasked man whom he did not recognise approach Sergeant Conlon and shoot him three times. An accomplice, whom he was also unable to identify, appeared with two bicycles and both assailants made off in the direction of Bridge Street. According to Skelly, after the shooting, he ran out to check on the prone policeman, but there was nothing he could do. He claimed to have sent a boy from three doors down to fetch a priest and a doctor whilst he consoled Mrs Catherine Conlon and their daughter, Bridget.

James looked out across the street, through the driving rain and blurred limbs at what must have been Sergeant Conlon's house but was now a Thai Nail Bar. From the report, it was clear that Sergeant Joseph Conlon had been walking up Main Street towards what was then Cumberland Square and was ten or fifteen yards from his front door when he was attacked, so he must have died somewhere between the Paddy Power betting shop and Supermac's Burgers. Fixing his gaze to where a group of youths huddled in the portico of the fast food joint, chain-smoking and ramming fries down their throats, James conceded that it wasn't the most august location to meet your maker.

The second witness to give evidence at the inquest was Head Constable Regan who identified the body shown to the court as that of Station Sergeant Joseph Conlon of Birr. He went on to explain that investigations carried out immediately after the assassination showed that two roadblocks had been constructed on Oxmantown Bridge and on Bridge Street and that the assassins had proceeded towards the obstruction on Bridge Street, abandoned their cycles and then made their escape by motor car across the border into Tipperary.

Smart, thought James – *it was well thought out.*

The final witness was Dr Burke who, in a couple of clinically sterile stanzas, related how he was woken and called to the scene, but due to massive blood loss and a fatal shot to the temple,

143

Sergeant Joseph Conlon was dead when he arrived and formally pronounced so immediately afterwards.

James wondered why there was no testimony from Kitty Conlon – was she too distraught to appear in court or was she unwilling to implicate her first cousin, Ciaran Fahy? Like so many verdicts that James had read over the last four weeks, the court concluded that Sergeant Joseph Conlon had died, *'from shock and haemorrhage caused by gunshot wounds to the chest and temple. Death was instantaneous. This court being in a verdict of wilful murder by members of the IRA whose identities are unknown at present.'* Beneath their concluding remarks he could make out a number of regimental ranks amongst the signatories and again the stamp of Colonel Commandant Edward Sutherland who signed off the report on the 26th July, 1921.

Draining the dregs of his coffee, James felt a wave of exhaustion roll over him. He looked across the street to where the teenagers were now flicking dying fag-butts at each other, kicking puddles and screaming obscenities, and he felt the sting of saltwater.

This little fragment of history that had robbed Kitty of a husband and Bridget and Pat-Joe of a father, and had been hidden from his family for a century, had now become a little piece of his present, and his future. It was something James couldn't *unforget*: yet another piece of unwanted emotional baggage to go with the rest. *But this time he could change the script.* He still had the power to make this story end well, unlike those last twelve hours of Connor McCleary's short life.

Dabbing his lashes with the oily serviette, he recalled a phrase from the Faulkner novel: *'The past is never dead. It's not even past'*.

It felt like that today.

22

Summer, 2018
Birr, Co. Offaly, Eire

"Sir? Excuse me but are you Mr Lucas?"

James removed his soaking jacket, folded it over his arm and brushed the sodden strands of hair that hung over his brow back behind his ears. Cold trickles of rainwater snuck beneath his shirt collar and raced down his spine.

"Yes, Room 21, I think."

The receptionist, sporting a trendy quiff, hipster beard and wearing a name-badge that dubbed him Ronan, sorted through a pile of Post-it Notes and, finding the relevant one, squinted at his own hand-writing. "Your wife, Charlotte Lucas, has called three times today already. She wants to know why your phone is switched off and asks whether you could call her at work."

"Bugger!" James fumbled in his pockets and realised that he had turned the phone off when he'd entered the library and had forgotten to switch it back on again. "Thank you. What time was her last call?"

"About forty minutes ago, sir. I told her that I would get the message to you the moment you walked in." He paused, looked James up and down and continued, "She gave me a remarkably good description of you actually – you are the only man I have seen today with a grey wool jacket and a battered brown satchel, and you do kinda look like a teacher too."

James smiled wryly at his sartorial predictability and lifting his phone above his head and waving it slowly from side to side explained, "Still searching for a signal. It's an old phone. This could take some time."

"Oh, you can call her from reception if you want. Just press 9 and then add your international code." Ronan placed the telephone on the desk and turned to deal with somebody on the other side of the kiosk.

The phone rang four times before Charlie picked up. "Barton-Fawcett, Charlotte Lucas speaking."

"Hi Charlie, it's me. Sorry, my phone was switched off all morning. I got your messages. Thanks for reminding me that I need a fashion makeover by the way. The hip young dude on reception took great pleasure in identifying that I dress like a teacher."

Charlie chuckled huskily, "Darling, you've always looked like a teacher – even before you were a teacher. Maybe that's why I fell for you – I always had a thing for older men."

"So were you calling just to tease me or did you just need to hear my dulcet tones to get you through the day?"

"Well it *is* nice to hear your voice, James – you haven't been exactly bombarding me with calls since you left. Besides, your mother called. She said that she hasn't been able to reach you either. She said that she'd finally persuaded Frank to root around in the loft to look for pictures of the Conlons and he has found some. They are a bit faded, but she got him to scan them and email them to you – she sent them about an hour ago. I told her I would catch you at the hotel and pass on the message."

"Cheers, honey; it's been strange following my great-grandfather's trail all these weeks without the vaguest idea of what he looks like."

James paused and lowered his voice. "I was at his grave this morning. His father was a policeman as well – Constable Thomas Conlon – his parents are buried here in Birr too. In fact, I have just got back from the spot where he was shot. I got quite emotional, Charlie. He died somewhere between a bookies and a bin rammed with paper cups and milkshake straws. It was quite sad really. I don't know what I was expecting; I knew there wasn't going to be a plaque or anything but I just thought that…" James tailed off unable to articulate what he thought and saw that Ronan had finished dealing with the guest and had returned to his seat where he stared into his computer screen, his head cocked slightly to the left.

"Hey, James, I am proud of you – you're over there and you're doing something that nobody else has taken the time to do. And remember – don't think in terms of innocence or guilt – think in terms of 'mitigating circumstances'. What wouldn't we do to protect our own in a time of conflict? You just find out what you can and frame your findings in the context of the time."

"Thank you, Charlie. What would we do without lawyers to paint in shades of grey? I miss you. Look, I am soaked and I am feeling washed out and I have to meet somebody at a bar on Castle Street later. I'm going to lie down for a bit and I'll check out the photos of Sergeant Conlon. Sorry my phone was switched off. Love you."

"I love you too. Stay safe. Bye!"

Charlie hung up and James passed the phone back to Ronan, who in turn handed him his room key. As James waited by the elevator, Ronan pulled his own mobile from his pocket and started tapping out a text.

If Oisín was trying to play mind games with James, he couldn't have chosen a better place to play them than in Craughwell's Bar. James stepped over the threshold into what could only be described as a shrine to Republicanism. All that was missing were votive candles and collection boxes. Crowding the walls were black and white photographs of the Easter Rising, a framed copy of the Declaration on Independence and charcoal portraits of Wolfe Tone, Parnell, DeValera and Collins. Green, white and orange tricolours hung from the bar and bunting the blue and gold of County Offaly looped between the light fittings on the rough stone wall. More recent photos of hurling teams grinned back manfully alongside faded images of white whiskered men playing fiddles, smoking pipes or gripping on black pints with wind-chapped hands. Polaroids of younger men in polo shirts holding bottles of Becks aloft were starting to peel at the edges over a bronze fireplace in which a small peat fire smouldered. A middle-aged crooner with slate-grey goatie and matching pony tail perched on a stool in the far-corner strumming an acoustic guitar and singing a plaintive ballad in Gaelic.

James could see Oisín tucked into a booth, the digital glow of a laptop illuminating his face an avatar-blue, reinforcing his otherworldly looks. An empty glass and a ketchup smeared plate on which three fat chips lay abandoned had been pushed to the side as the student tapped the keyboard.

"James, glad you came. Sorry, I had a fierce hunger an hour ago and I couldn't hold it off a moment longer, so I have eaten – I hope you don't mind."

"Not at all. Whilst I am standing, can I get you a drink?"

"Ahh, you're a true gentleman, James. Another pint of the black stuff would be grand. If you're hungry, I'd order at the bar now – they are not the hastiest of cooks here, but what they do is worth the wait. Maybe if you have the USB stick, I could transfer things back and forth whilst you grab the drinks?"

James dug around in the satchel for the memory stick and handed it over explaining which folder held the relevant documents and approached the bar.

He ordered some food and whilst the beer settled he requested a double Bushmills. He downed the whiskey in one and ordered another. This second shot disappeared just as quickly. James turned and leant back against the bar and listened to the strange rhythm and undulations of the Gaelic language in the melancholy song that had hushed the tavern. The whiskey warmed him, and he could feel the day's tension slipping away. The balladeer sung in a doleful tenor and James wondered what the words meant. Returning to the table with the pints of Guinness, he asked Oisín, "Do you speak fluent Gaelic?"

"That I do, James. I'm a Connemara boy from one of the last communities in Ireland that still speak it as a matter of course. You should try it. *Is fearr Gaeilge briste, ná Béarla clíste.*"

James stared blankly at the Irishman.

"That means, 'Broken Irish is better than clever English' – the very words Obama spoke in when he came to Ireland in 2011. You have to fight to keep the last flickers of a dying culture alive, whatever the cost. A hundred and fifty years ago the English had all but snuffed out our traditional sports and spoken word, but look around you now. Hurling flags outside every house and Gaelic compulsory in schools again." He patted his hand against a reproduced image of Irish Volunteers emerging from fog in greatcoats and peaked caps. "The men in this photograph would be mighty proud to see the Ireland that they died for in the Tan War."

"So what's this song about?"

"Ah, 'tis a sad one, so. It is a song about two brothers during the Hunger. They both loved the same girl but she chose to be with the elder of the two. The younger brother cursed his sibling and set sail to America where he made his fortune whilst the elder opted to remain in the old country to raise a family. When the younger returned many years later, all that was left of this family was a line of gravestones next to the crumbling wall of an abandoned church. Shamed, the young American joins the IRB and vows to take back his homeland from the British. The song is about guilt and loss and revenge." He supped the beer. "Do you know much about the famine years, James?"

"Not much, but more than most, I suspect: *'The Almighty, indeed, sent the potato blight, but the English created the famine'* – however, as historians, we both know, Oisín, that that wasn't strictly true."

Oisín smiled, impressed.

James clarified. "I am a history teacher back in England. We study the Famine, the Land Wars and the struggle for independence, but I am no expert. In a classroom full of teenagers, you can only scratch the surface and cross your fingers that they retain some of what you've taught them."

"Don't put yourself down, James. Where would we be without our teachers? So you'll understand how tragedy and glory forever go hand in hand with one another in Ireland. Our tragedies celebrated and our successes brushed beneath the carpet. Is it not strange how Wolfe Tone's failed rebellion of 1798 and the military disaster of 1916 are glorified in our national consciousness whereas a successful guerrilla campaign that formed the bedrock of our Republic is condemned today by many as our darkest hour – a time when we forgot ourselves and turned to terrorism? The famous faces you may recognise on these walls arguably did less to bring about what we have now than the photographs here of anonymous old men in caps, drinking porter and telling tales; all of them thoroughly ignored by history textbooks. They were the boys of 1921 who brought Britain to her knees and forced the truce of July…"

James interjected, "And put three bullets into my great-grandfather…"

"Yes, that they did, but would you begrudge Ireland her freedom for the sake of five hundred policemen? *One and a half million* Irish starved in the space of four years during the famine. Even as historians we can never comprehend what that must have been like."

Oisín drew deep on his pint and licked the head from his top lip with a thin pink tongue. "I am here in Birr because it is an anomaly in Irish history as far as I can see. Generally, it was where Republican support was strong that the most vicious reprisals occurred. The Sinn Féin counties of Cork, Tipperary, Clare and Galway – it got very nasty there indeed. The Black and Tans, the Auxiliaries, the RIC and the IRA all locked at each other's throats like pitbulls, giving no quarter and drowning in a sea of blood. But here in Birr, the majority of the population were staunch supporters of the status quo. Yet, incongruously there was a disproportionate amount of violence here – and I think that is down to one 'bad apple', as they say. Unfortunately, James, I think that the 'bad apple' was your great-grandfather, Sergeant Joseph Conlon."

James countered. "But history is always written by the winners, Oisín. As far as I can see we only have the spurious claims of Brendan O'Rourke to substantiate the accusations levelled against Conlon. There is nothing in the National Archives to corroborate a word that he writes. He lied about being in Dublin in '16 and he certainly wasn't sent to Frongoch with Collins. The man's a fantasist. At Micheál Fahy's inquest, where Conlon is called as witness, it's clear that the family had no proof the RIC had anything to do with his death. They merely *believed* it was the police, and, as you will appreciate, suspicion isn't fact."

"Ah Jaysus, James! Don't tell me you are after rehabilitating the name of your long dead ancestor! I know it's a cliché, but there is no smoke without fire. It was his wife's first-cousin who pulled the trigger for Christ's sake! Do you really think Ciaran Fahy is going to execute his own kin because of a vague suspicion of guilt? Besides, I have had access to documents that you haven't seen yet. Look here."

Oisín moved the cursor across the screen and clicked on a photograph of what looked like a series of diary entries from July 1921. He turned the laptop round so that James could see more clearly.

"OK, I told you that I have been looking at the Rosse Papers and some of the original documents at the library. Well one of the sets of records donated to the Civic Hall are the diaries of some of the parish priests at St Brendan's. For the period that covers the Tan War, the priest here was one Father Patrick O'Brien; the very same priest found shot and burned up in a farmhouse near Galross. Father O'Brien writes here that; and I'll quote directly:

"5th of July 1921 – Fitful sleep again last night. Tossed and turned and had to kneel at the foot of my bed for hours asking for guidance. What was told me in the confessional disturbs me greatly. If it is true, then there is corruption in the Crown Forces that needs extirpating. Should I speak with the bishop and seek his blessing? For surely, revealing the secrets of the confessional is a mortal sin? I am torn.

"9th of July 1921 – With the Truce now common knowledge, it is possible that the policeman whom I know has committed the most unspeakable acts might escape his rightful justice. Tomorrow at Mass I will impress upon the individual concerned the importance of revealing the secret that fills them with shame and unmask this monster for what he is.

"The following day, James, was Sunday the 10th of July. The very same day that Father O'Brien and the O'Donagh family were executed at the farmhouse in Galross and the building razed to the ground. There is no coincidence that within 12 hours the man responsible, *'the policeman who has committed unspeakable acts'*, was shot on his doorstep on Main Street. O'Rourke clearly states that the Galross Massacre was carried out by Conlon and it was that which sealed his fate as the clock ticked down to the truce. You can't deny that the priest's diary supports that interpretation of events."

James was about to argue that the priest's words could have been about anyone and were at best only circumstantial evidence, but Oisín raised his hand and continued. "Look, this might sting a little, James, but I think you need to hear something. I'll only be a minute."

Oisín walked to the corner of the room. He bent and whispered something into the ear of the singer who was plucking at strings, expertly translating ancient harp to acoustic guitar. He nodded and Oisín returned, scrolled down a list of Word documents, clicked on one and spun the laptop back to face James.

The first powerful chords of the next song saw a number of heads snap up across the bar. Two old-timers collaborating on a table barely large enough to hold their collection of pints slapped their thighs in time to the jaunty beat and even the barman began to tap the till with pudgy fingers.

"Ye'll all know this one, so ye will. A wee bit of local history about a terribly bad fella. It's called, *Ol' Wild Eyed Joe o' the RIC*. Feel free to join me in the chorus."

Even though around him he could hear whoops and claps and, in the periphery of his vision, some agitated swaying, James couldn't drag his eyes from the lyrics that snaked down the page:

Ol' Wild Eyed Joe o' the RIC

There was a man
With eyes of brown
Who wore the uniform
Of the Crown
And in Birr, it is said
He filled good Fenians with plenty dread.

He knew their names
He knew their mothers
He knew their sisters
And knew their brothers
Ye'd fain cross this man of law
For fear of terror brought to yer door

Chorus
Ol' Sergeant Joe o' the RIC
The scourge of County Offaly.
He liked his fists
And he liked his fire,
An' he left that farm
A burnin' pyre

He shot a priest
He killed a child
Those eyes of his
So mad, so wild

But come July '21
This traitor faced the Irish gun
He never heard the noontime bell
Three bullets sent him back to Hell

Chorus x 2

The song finished to a round of applause and someone yelled, "Another! Play that one about Cromwell – Ned o' the Hill!" and the pony-tailed singer realised that his crowd tonight were in the mood for rebel songs – a happy audience meant more beer at the bar when his set was over.

James was just stunned.

Stunned at the cruel simplicity of the lyrics.

Stunned at the pure joy that the song had given everybody sitting around him, especially as Sergeant Joe was sent 'back to Hell' in the final verse.

But more deeply unnerved by the fact that this song had undoubtedly been played in bars and taverns and folk clubs across Ireland for at least half a century, if not longer. A nightly incantation on the evil of the man who gave his grandmother, and through her, his mother, himself and his sister the gift of life – and nobody in his immediate family had ever known a thing about it.

James realised that from this moment on he might find himself lying awake next to Charlie, knowing that somewhere across the water a dentist, a teaching assistant, a plumber or a journalist might be sat in a folk-club tapping their feet, smiling and clapping to the chorus. And after the song was finished, intrigued by the back story, they might find themselves Googling the title of the song and being led to one of the many sites – each of which cited O'Rourke's work – that confidently named Sergeant Joseph Conlon as the head of a murder squad in Birr most notable for the Galross Massacre.

And so suspicion *does* become 'fact'.

"A bitter pill to swallow I imagine, James. I didn't want to shock you, just to illustrate that we all choose our versions of the past. All the statistics in the world on British agrarian policy won't shake a Republican's belief that the Famine was Ireland's Holocaust and the British were the 19th century Nazis who caused it. The people of Birr have *chosen* to paint your great-grandfather as the incarnation of evil. That's what they know, and that's all they *want* to know, and you snooping around the town with some misplaced sense of loyalty to a man who caused such pain here can only put you at risk. I will speak candidly to you, James. Do you have family here in Ireland?"

James nodded.

"Well, I am surprised that they haven't tried to dissuade you from sticking your nose into a hornet's nest. You and I can sit and have an academic debate about interpretations of the past and the likelihood of one version of events over another, but there are men, and for that matter, women in this town, *in this very bar*, who would take much more than an academic interest in your quest to rehabilitate the name of Sergeant Joseph Conlon."

Oisín drained his pint. "You'll have another?"

James felt sucker-punched. "No thank you. I don't think I will. I might just head back to the hotel and check out some of the stuff on this memory stick. I may not prove Conlon's innocence but at least I can use it in my A-Level classes – you can never have too much material in teaching, so thanks again."

"No; thank *you*, James." Oisín scrolled down through the transferred National Archives documents, photographs of obscure inquests and screen-saved newspaper headlines. His eyes gleamed. "Have you an email address that I could contact you on? I might send you a copy of my thesis when it's done."

As James scribbled it down on a page in his pad and ripped it off, Oisín asked, "And did you not order food just now?"

"I've lost my appetite to be honest. Feel free to have it when it comes – if you're still hungry, that is."

"I'm always hungry, so I am. Well so long, James, and heed my advice: a man's chosen history is like a suit of armour – it defines and defends him, but viewing the world through a visor distorts his perception, and to prise it off the man, you'll have to kill him first."

He winked and smiled with sharp, white teeth.

Outside Craughwell's it had finally stopped raining although the gutters and drains continued to drip in metronomic rhythm. It was quiet and unusually dark for the time of year, the streetlights projecting a sickly orange shimmer onto the surface of the puddles. The whiskey and beer, drunk quickly on an empty stomach had made James feel a little lightheaded and the shock of the song had intensified his senses. His mother would have told him he was 'overwrought' again. Turning onto Main Street, James looked up the road towards Emmet Square and couldn't see a soul. On his way to meet Oisín it had still been raining and he had passed down the other side of the street huddled under his brolly without really taking much notice of the stretch of pavement between the Nail Bar and Supermac's. Now he found himself walking towards the spot, his heart audibly pounding. Counting out fifteen steps from the door that Joseph Conlon pulled shut a century earlier, James inspected the patch of pavement that straddled Paddy Power and the fast food restaurant. A crumpled burger wrapper, a hunk of uneaten meat still glazed with unnaturally yellow cheese and a sole gherkin lay washed up in a hollow next to the curb.

It had been here.

Again an inexplicable urge to genuflect and connect with something solid overpowered him, and James watched himself in the sheen of a parked car as he crouched and splayed the fingers of his hand across the wet concrete in the same way a sprinter waiting for a starting pistol might. The words of the song didn't in any way reflect the image of the man he had examined only hours before. His mother's photographs had shown a kind-faced giant of a man, dressed in uniform with huge hands resting gently on the shoulders of a beautiful woman who held a child in a cotton-cream christening gown. Although neither was smiling, they betrayed a warmth and love that was almost palpable. James was convinced that something had become lost in translation along the way – the eyes gazing serenely from the family photograph just weren't the 'wild eyes' of a stone cold killer.

Rising from a kneeling position, James glimpsed in the side mirror a flash of colour and the unmistakable lava-glow of a cigarette. Wheeling around, he caught a heel of trainer disappearing down an alley about twenty metres behind him and heard rapid splashing, then silence.

James stepped into the electric light that poured from Supermac's. A handful of tables were filled with kids chewing and talking simultaneously, whilst behind the counter, acne-pocked youths stared dead-eyed into the night. Checking that there was nobody behind him, James walked briskly up the street towards the hotel.

Once in his room, he double locked the door and peered out the window onto Emmet Square. A couple meandered hand in hand past the column, they stopped and kissed. A white van turned from the junction on Main Street and crawled in the direction of John's Mall, but other than that, nothing.

He was imagining things.

James switched on his laptop. Whilst copying Oisín's files and organising them into folders, he heard the familiar ping that told him he had a message. Again the automated email from the National Archives informed him that another of his requested documents had been uploaded. He opened the file to see that it was an incident report into the events of the 2nd October 1919 – a day that started with the discovery of the body of Séan Keane and ended with two constables and four suspected members of the IRA taking turns on Dr Burke's mortuary slab.

Oisín was right: the spectre of death hung unnaturally close to Sergeant Joseph Conlon.

23

2nd October, 1919
Birr, King's County, Ireland

The first that anybody knew that something was wrong was the ungodly screeching that pierced the fog that had rolled in from the Camcor River, enveloping Cumberland Square. So thick was this fog that even from Dooly's Hotel the giant pedestal was no more than a blurred shadow in the heart of an evil, dank mist.

John Butler owned the bakery on Cumberland Street and prided himself on being the first awake in the town. He had begun to prepare the dough and light the fires in the early morning gloom, but after fifteen minutes could abide the relentless cawing no more. It sounded like some poor soul being delivered a death blow again and again and again – but never dying; just doomed to grunt the same guttural croak as the blade ripped skin for eternity.

He had to do something about it, and as any right-minded man would, he decided to send his wife across the road to see what was making the God-awful racket. A minute later, her own blood-curdling scream joined the chorus of cawing and John raced to the bakery door and peered into the murk. Her screams only served to agitate the frequency and volume of the hellish croaking and like main-sail torn from its riggings in a storm-force gale, a violent flapping erupted as a murder of crows burst free from the fog and flew over his head.

Sergeant Conlon approached Cumberland Square by foot. He was still sleeping in the barracks on John's Mall and had heard the woman's screams long before a runner had pounded on the station doors yelling that there was a body tied to the monument. Aware that such a large open space was the perfect spot for a sniper to take a shot at the inevitable policeman at the scene, he exercised some caution, but reasoned that you would have to be more than just the best marksman in the world to hit anybody in this pea-souper, but guided by the hand of God, so he took his chances.

Through the fog he could make out the shape of a man slouched at the foot of the pillar. If there hadn't been a crow sat on his shoulder pecking his ear and thick rope looped around his neck, he could have been just another drunk passed out in the town square. As he got closer, the Sergeant could see a placard cut from card and pinned to his chest. He knew what it would say before he read the words, capitalised and daubed in black ink: EXECUTED BY THE IRA – SPIES AND TRAITORS BEWARE!

Stepping forward he shooed the bird, who turned and glared at him malevolently before cawing and disappearing into the mist. He slowly reached forward to tilt the drooping head of the corpse. The neck cracked as rigour mortis resisted his action and Conlon was forced to snap it up like a stiff gear stick catching in the Crossley-Tender. The dead white face and pallid skin now waxy and cold to the touch was the canvas for an obscenity of red, blue and black. The carrion had entirely plucked out the left eyeball leaving a gaping cavity tinged in fresh red tissue, blue-grey tendrils of his optic nerve dangling horrifically and hanging down his cheek. Where his other eye should have been there was just a swollen knot of livid bruising from which protruded a fan of eyelashes glued together in dark, congealed blood. On the right side of his temple just above his ear, where the crow had been feasting moments earlier, shattered white bone and slick indigo brain matter indicated the spot where the bullet had entered the body.

Joseph fell to his knees and howled.

He held Séan's face in both hands and pressed his forehead to that of his oldest friend and heard his men running up behind him concern in their voices, "Sergeant? Sir? Are you alright?"

"No, I am not." Focussing on the white smudges on his friend's lapels and the fine white powder in his hairline, he stood and turned to his Acting Sergeants, "But I will be soon. Ryan – wake everybody in the station and arm the men now. Have them ready in ten minutes at the top of Main Street. Shaunessy, run down to the workhouse barracks and bring the Crossley to the top of the street with the rest of the boys. We are going to get the men who did this before they wake. I think I have an idea where they are."

"Sir?"

"Yes, Ryan?"

"Shouldn't we wait till the fog lifts? At least give the boys some breakfast before we go to fight?"

"Ten minutes, I said! GO!"

————

The Crossley-Tender with Conlon, Ryan and Shaunessy up front and eight armed constables in the back crossed the Camcor at Bridge Street and followed the river downstream along Moorpath Road to the outskirts of town where Conlon ordered the driver to kill the engine.

About a third of a mile away, where the current was much stronger, the river was split by a sliver of land that ran for about four hundred metres in its dead centre. The old mill crouched on the near-side bank and could only be accessed from the mainland by a rickety wooden bridge. Conlon ordered complete silence as his men jumped from the back of the Tender and started to follow the river towards the mill.

The fog hung thick and gave them good cover, muting the sounds of their approach. Conlon anticipated that, dependent on where the rebels had stationed their lookout and how effectively his men could silence him, they could be inside the mill before anybody had even woken. The Sergeant was cool with rage, calm even. The fine layer of white dusting that powdered the corpse of Séan Keane had vindicated his decision to observe the funeral alone and his haste in arriving here had stopped the RIC mole, if indeed there was one, from having time to warn the rebels whom he was sure were hiding out in the Teddy Kavanagh's mill.

His men struggled to stay upright as roots and branches waylaid their way and decomposing autumnal leaves and sodden ground made the approach treacherous. Conlon could taste the mud of the river and the rot of the foliage in the back of his mouth, and something else...

It was tobacco smoke.

He signalled for his men to stop and surveyed the area on both sides of the bridge with field glasses. They didn't really help – he could now perceive the wispy tendrils of fog in sharper focus.

But then on their side of the river, about sixty yards away, he spotted the tell-tale flash of a match being lit and then the pulsating glow as the smoker puffed furiously to get the cigarette to catch in the moist air.

"Shaunessy. Use your bayonet. Quiet now. Don't let off a shot."

His Acting Sergeant stalked off silently into the undergrowth. Conlon turned to his men. "Alright, listen up. Once we're across the bridge, Acting Sergeant Ryan will take O'Farrell and Pierce to the rear of the mill, the rest of us will fan out from left to right and approach the mill from the front. The aim is to take them all alive – but as it is themselves who are so desperate for a war, if they resist, we will give it to them. Remember lads, they have our guns and ammunition – some high quality weaponry, so be careful. If we do this right we could finish this here."

Conlon poked his head above a tree stump to see that Shaunessy was only a matter of metres from the pin prick of scarlet. Then, without warning, Ryan lost his footing and started to slip down the bank. Totally off balance, his arms flailed and with a loud yelp he went crashing into the vegetation.

It was enough to warn the sentry who dropped the cigarette and made for the bridge screaming "Wake up! Peelers! Peelers!"

As his footsteps clattered over the wooden boards a single shot rang out and the man crumpled. Startled birds exploded from bushes shrieking in alarm and Shaunessy exclaimed, "Sir, I've got him come on!"

Conlon cast a look of disgust at Ryan who was being pulled up the bank by Fallon. "Fool! That's going to make things a lot feckin' harder for us now. Come on, we've got to get across. Run!"

The unit charged through the ferns and across the bridge, vaulting over the body that was still twitching. Conlon stopped and knelt beside the fallen man, rolling him over to check for a pulse. A mere child's face looked back at him. The boy was choking on a reservoir of rich, ruby-red blood that welled from his lungs and spilled over his lips. Before Joe had even managed to find the carotid artery, his fingers slick with the boy's blood, the terrified eyes that stared heavenwards dulled, and Joe realised that there was no point.

"Ryan, take your men and try to get round the back – go! Shaunessy, Murphy, Daly, McGee go left and give them cover. Mooney, Dwyer and Fallon, to the right with me."

The pincer movement he was trying to effect was halted abruptly when a volley of shots rang out from the mill and his constables dived frantically for cover and started to return fire.

Conlon prayed the fog would give them a cloak of invisibility which might just save all their lives – but he doubted it: good men were going to die today.

With the covering fire given by Shaunessy and his unit, Conlon could see that Ryan, Pierce and O'Farrell seemed to be making headway skirting around to the left of the mill and were now disappearing into the mist. He saw Shaunessy take a shot and then scramble forwards, ducking behind a small conifer.

From the mill another volley of gunfire rang out and Conlon heard a grunt and Shaunessy shout, "I'm hit! I'm hit."

Constable McGee broke cover and ran to where his Acting Sergeant was propped against the fir tree, black blood oozing from his midriff. McGee pulled a handkerchief from his pocket and said, "Hold this to the wound, sir. Hold it tight. I'm going to get you out of here."

"Give him some cover!" Conlon shouted as McGee began to drag the prone figure of Shaunessy towards a rocky outcrop that would grant them reprieve from the pot-shots coming from the mill. Then another shot rang out and the side of Constable McGee's head imploded in a mist of crimson and he slumped atop his Acting Sergeant. Four or five more bullets were then pumped into the two bodies and there was a moment of utter silence.

And that was when all hell broke loose.

"Fenian feckers!" Daly screamed. From all sides Conlon's men let lose a barrage of bullets that peppered the mill, splitting the wood-slatted wall in a shower of splinters.

In the midst of this maelstrom Conlon heard a quiet splash and looked to his right to see that the copper-haired Brendan O'Rourke had jumped from a mill window and was now wading shoulder deep across the river holding a Lee Enfield rifle above his head. Realising that the current was too fast in the centre of the Camcor, O'Rourke opted to round the millwheel and follow the near-bank to the relative safety of the woods behind the mill.

Conlon shouted to Dwyer to cover him and sprinted across the ten metres of open ground to the bank, bullets whizzing past him. Hearing them thud into the other side of the oak tree that he had managed to pin himself behind, he pulled out his Webley revolver and aimed it between O'Rourke's shoulder blades.

"Stop or I'll shoot. You're surrounded!"

O'Rourke ignored him and carried on wading into the mist. Conlon fired and heard his bullet splash into the river. He squinted through the churning fog and saw the smudged upturned triangle of the rebel disappear from his line of sight around the static millwheel.

Conlon had no choice. He scrambled down the bank and tried to edge into the water but slipped and tumbled into the freezing cold Camcor smashing the back of his head on a rock.

For a handful of heartbeats he was utterly submerged and the gunfire, the screams, the fog, the blood and the war were all gone. It was dark and quiet and, as wraith-like curls of algae floated before him weightlessly, Joe had the urge to inhale and leave them all behind. But primal instinct kicked in and he hauled himself up, trying to gain purchase on the slimy riverbed pebbles. Joe too began to wade along the bank and around the mill holding his Webley clear of the choppy water.

In the distance he could see that O'Rourke was a good way ahead of him and had managed to clamber up into the undergrowth. So Joe made a split decision. He strode out towards the middle of the river where the current was fierce and released himself to the torrent. He allowed it to carry him about forty yards downstream of the spot where he had seen O'Rourke emerge, and then with every ounce of his strength he fought the course of the Camcor and splashed his way to shore.

Grabbing hold of an ancient tree root, he dragged himself up the bank, holstered his dripping revolver and charged into the vegetation in pursuit of O'Rourke.

Ferns, brambles and low lying branches whipped his face as he thundered through the foliage. He could hear shots and screams far behind him, but they were dulled in the mist and seemed a world away now. He had but one thing on his mind: to get his hands on Brendan O'Rourke.

Stumbling out of the treeline he emerged onto a stretch of silty sand at the far end of the island. A fallen tree bisected the muddy beach and acted as a makeshift jetty for a little rowing boat that was tied to it. O'Rourke had lain his rifle on the tree whilst he struggled to untie the knot, so Conlon took his chance and threw himself headlong at the rebel.

The pair of them bounced off the tree and began to struggle on the ground. Joe tried to use his superior weight to pin O'Rourke down but the farrier writhed like an eel and managed to wriggle out of Joe's grasp and reach for his rifle.

Conlon stretched out an arm and, digging his fingers deep into the soaking material of the smaller man's jacket, dragged him away from the weapon.

Rolling him over, Conlon straddled him, pinning the rebel's arms beneath his thighs so that he could unclip his handcuffs.

"Ahh, so ye've got me, so you have. I wonder how ye managed that. How did ye know where we were? I thought last night we rid ourselves of the little birdy who's been tweeting to the Peelers."

A cold hatred coursed through Conlon's veins and he stopped trying to unclip the cuffs and instead dragged the wiry man to his feet and held him tight by the collar with his big left hand. He stared straight into the rebel's eyes; his own clouded with poison and swung a right fist into O'Rourke's cheekbone hearing a satisfying crack.

O'Rourke went down heavily and landed face first in the foamy scum of the river and didn't move. For a moment Joe thought that he had killed him outright with one blow. Then he heard a spluttering and without turning the IRA man said,

"There's a real rage in ye, Sergeant Joseph Conlon. Did ye look Micheál Fahy in the eyes like that before ye beat him to death? How could ye kill Kitty's first-cousin?"

Conlon didn't even dignify the slur with a denial – he just growled threateningly, enunciating each word with unhidden menace. "Don't you ever mention my wife's name, O'Rourke. This has nothing to do with her. This is between me and you. Between the law and the outlaw. And it ends here."

A little chuckle bubbled from O'Rourke. "From what I hear, she's no wife to ye anymore, Joe. She has eyes of Fenian green and she's seen through your lies – an' that's why ye are sleepin' in a barracks with a bunch o' boys while she lies alone in her big bed on Main Street. Maybe I'll see fit to join her in it someday…"

O'Rourke lunged for the rifle and almost had it at the tips of his fingers before Conlon kicked it into the shallows and crushed his knee into the small of his back. The anger that he had struggled to control since finding the body of his friend tied to Cumberland Monument erupted into a vindictive, mindless rage. He leant forward and pressed O'Rourke's head deep into the muddy silt, "I'll kill you. I'll feckin' kill you… I swear I will…"

Joe would never discover whether he would have followed through on his threat because the hard nose of a rifle jabbed the back of his neck and he heard the recognisable Kerry lilt of Acting Sergeant Ryan.

"No ye won't, sir. Stand up and put your hands on yer head. Gently does it now."

"Ryan, what are you doing?"

"What every decent Irishman should be doing: resisting the Crown."

And suddenly it became clear: it had been Ryan all along. The tip off to the IRA about the cache of arms delivered to the barracks. The confidence the rebels had that the RIC had fallen for the bait at Stoneacre House. Ryan's reticence this morning and his theatrical fall into the bushes that alerted the sentry.

"Come on now, sir. Stand up."

Joe released the pressure on the back of O'Rourke's skull and stood with his hands raised above his head. Whilst O'Rourke gasped for air and spat out grit and sand, Ryan relieved his Sergeant of the Webly.

"Well, it seems like the tables have turned, does it not?" O'Rourke retrieved the rifle from the shallows and placed it in the rowing boat. "Give me that gun, Ryan, and get in the feckin' boat."

O'Rourke cocked the revolver and trained it on Conlon's heart as he loosened the moorings and stepped into the rocking rowing boat that immediately began to pull away from the bank.

"There's nobody more receptive to a bit of lovin' than a grievin' widow, Sergeant. Think on that before you die."

He pulled the trigger.

The hammer fell with a dull metallic click – but nothing happened.

O'Rourke pulled the trigger again.

Seizing his chance, Conlon dived behind the fallen tree as the rowing boat was dragged by the current into the mist. Behind him, he could hear police whistles being blown. A second later, two bullets came screaming over his head, one of which splintered the top corner of the boat's transom.

"Feckin' row, Ryan, row!"

By the time that Pierce and O'Farrell reached him, Conlon could barely see the rowing boat but knew that the powerful current of the Camcor would carry O'Rourke and Ryan through the mist all the way to the safety of Tipperary.

24

Summer, 2018
Dooly's Hotel, Birr, Co. Offaly, Eire

James always found taking breakfast in a hotel to be a grim experience. More often than not he was nursing a hangover and sheepishly examining every arch of eyebrow or twist of lip to augur from Charlie's body language whether he had said or done anything the night before that merited the contagious awkwardness between them that also seemed to be afflicting everybody else in the room. This morning was no different: a subdued and oppressive atmosphere hung leaden in the gloom. Grey drizzle drummed the skylight and the dull clink of cutlery on tableware tinkled out asymmetric percussion to the hushed conversations whispered across tables.

Some of the older couples chewed in stony silence or flicked through guide books whilst everybody else stared fixedly into phones, scrolling, tapping and smiling thinly from time to time. Waitresses with Eastern European accents hovered in corners keenly watching for a last piece of toast to be reached for or a teapot to be tipped to the critical angle that demanded fresh hot water.

James was feeling emotionally fragile. The hateful song he'd heard in Craughwell's and Oisín's conviction that Conlon was guilty as charged had shaken his resolve. He was starting to question what he was realistically hoping to achieve over here. The incident report of the shoot-out at the mill had only reaffirmed the suspicion that the deeper he dug, the more evidence he would find incriminating Sergeant Conlon. The dispassionate report had stated how Liam Kavanagh, his father, Teddy, and two teenage brothers, Donal and Finbar Gallagher had, '*whilst in opposition to the Crown Forces, died of gunshot wounds inflicted by members of the Royal Irish Constabulary in the execution of their duty.*' The document had finished with the unsurprising ruling that, '*This Court being in the unanimous verdict of justifiable homicide.*' James remembered having seen the same judgement again and again as he sat all those weeks ago in the National Archives and it beggared belief to imagine that every RIC kill was in self-defence and not one teenage boy of the IRA had raised his hands in surrender as their front door was kicked in.

On top of this, before he'd turned in, he'd peered once more through a slit in the curtains and, behind the monument, he could make out the tip of a baseball cap poking from beneath a hood, shrouding a face in shadow; a single, glowing eye of burning tobacco staring directly at his hotel. For a horrible moment, he imagined it was Connor the night before he died, watching him now from beyond the grave. Unnerved, James pulled the curtains tightly shut and checked the bedroom door once more before he climbed into bed.

But he hadn't slept well: he'd endured a surreal nightmare that had left him exhausted and was unpleasantly vivid even now. He had dreamed he was in a court room, standing in the dock. The bench and the witness stands were the dark mahogany of Devlin's Fine Jewellery and it was Noel who sat in the judge's seat, wielding a heavy gavel. It crashed down on the woodwork sending sharp splinters shooting out across the court, one of which lodged with excruciating reality in James's eye. A cavalcade of witnesses were called to give testimony, amongst them the red-head from the library, her orthodontic brace a tangle of barbed wire, and a parade of old men with hard eyes and flat caps who flickered through his dream tinged in sepia.

Oisín Ó Súilleabháin and Zara Thomas appeared hand in hand, terrifyingly beautiful as Oberon and Titania; his ex-student revealing ample cleavage that sparkled with glitter. The pair of them kissed and laughed faery laughter, revealing sharp incisors and, as James tried to speak, he found that he could only bray ignorantly, a matted ass's head where once his face had been.

Suddenly he was a child in Pat-Joe's outhouse scratching furiously at a fetid, purple wound on his arm and there was blood on his fingernails, but he kept on scratching. He scratched harder and deeper. But the itch wouldn't go away.

Then he was back in the court room again and the toothless woman from the churchyard was pointing at him with a preternaturally long finger, rasping, "Traitor! Spy! Traitor! Spy!" and above her Noel glowered as he donned the black cap for sentencing. James felt something sticky on his chest and when he looked down he could see a growing rose of crimson swell from beneath a crumpled note pinned to his heart which read, 'Executed by the IRA'. The last thing he could remember seeing in the court room was Connor's mother, dressed in black lace, smiling ferociously at the verdict, mouthing the words 'murderer' over and over.

And then he was back in the outhouse with the spiders and the itch and he was picking and ripping at stitching and pulling the flesh apart to get at what lay beneath. And that was when the gaping wound disgorged a relentless vomit of maggots that poured fat and white and hungry all over the screaming boy in the toilet.

So he had woken, shivering and fearful in a strange bed and texted Charlie to tell her that he might try to catch an earlier ferry home later that week.

It was over.

He had failed.

He couldn't change a thing.

He still had to visit Pat-Joe in Clonmel and he should do the rounds of all the cousins before he left, but the defiant certainty that Conlon was innocent was gone. In the cold light of day he had come to the conclusion that he was clutching at straws and he should follow the advice that everyone had given him, and just go home and forget about it.

He could box it up and bury it deep along with everything else.

He was good at that.

25

3ʳᵈ October, 1919
Birr, King's County, Ireland

Kitty's eyes opened to the darkness that enveloped the bedroom with a sudden gasp, a sense of misgiving gnawing away on the periphery of her consciousness. Half asleep, she instinctively reached out and found only hard, cold flatness where the warm bulk of her husband should have been. Rousing herself, she stretched for the oil lamp that cast a dim amber glow on the space between her bedside table and the cot in which Bridget slept. Slipping from beneath the warmth of her bedcovers, Kitty felt the chill of the early morning on the soles of her feet as she padded across the wooden floorboards and looked down on her child. Her daughter was sleeping soundly and breathing with a steady rhythm – *all was well*. Tiptoeing to the curtains, Kitty peered through the opaque mist that had penetrated every crack and cranny of Main Street, obscuring the fuzzy glow of the street lights to such an extent that it was quite impossible to even make out the words 'Skelly's General Store' that she knew should be quite visible above the shop front opposite. Main Street was empty and quiet and Kitty could make out no menacing shadows lurking shark-like beneath the fog outside her window.

Yet, something wasn't right in the house. Kitty stood perfectly still listening to the sounds of the building.

There was somebody downstairs.

Despite the damp draught that seeped in from underneath the window pane, she could feel warmer air on her feet, wafting into the room from beneath the door frame, carrying with it the fecund smell of wet animal.

Kitty checked again on her daughter, and leaving the door ajar, crept downstairs, the oil lamp casting a quivering arc of ochre on the walls and bannisters as she descended. At the foot of the stairs she could perceive a slit of light coming from the other side of the kitchen door and a stronger smell of warm damp and wood smoke.

She pulled it open to find the room ashade. A fire crackled in the hearth sending shadows dancing across the walls. Joe was crouching on a stool in front of the flames in his undergarments. His head was in his hands and his elbows on his knees. His police uniform was draped over the back of a chair, caked in mud and slime. Copper drops the size of penny coins collected on the flagstones beneath. The tin bath was half full of lukewarm water and a large pot hanging from the chimney crane above the flames simmered. On the table a bottle of Tullamore Dew stood next to a full tumbler of whiskey and a single sheet of paper sparsely populated with black ink.

Kitty approached her husband and held the lamp above his head, his hair matted in clumps of sludge.

"Joe? What's happened?"

Joe looked up at her. His face was mud-smeared, cut, bruised and swollen. Clean streaks of pale skin tracked through the grime where giant tears had fled his haunted eyes.

"Joe, whatever have you done?"

He flinched at the question and blinked.

"I almost killed a man in cold blood yesterday, Kitty. I wanted to. I really did. And I would have killed him too if I hadn't been stopped by the muzzle of a gun at the back of my neck." He regarded the dancing tongues of flame. "A minute later and I would have been shot dead with my own revolver had it not been wet through with river water."

Shaking his head dreamily. "Such fine margins, Kitty, between his life and mine. To kill or be killed – that's what it all boils down to now – and I have had enough."

"What do you mean, Joe?"

Conlon stared deep into the burning logs and rubbed the rough stubble on his jaw. "And my men; I realise now that they're no better nor worse than me. They're scared and angry and seek revenge on those who make them feel that way. Whilst I was selfishly filling the dirty mouth of Brendan O'Rourke with sand and river water so that I never need hear him utter your name again, my boys were taking no prisoners back at the mill. I left them to do the Devil's work and wasn't there to stop them, Kitty. A father and a son, and two brothers only eighteen and nineteen years of age, for Christ's sake."

Joe reached for the tumbler and drained the contents in one. He poured another. "Jesus, I saw Patrick Shaunessy and Gregory McGee shot in front of me and feckin' birds pecking at the brains of my best friend, Séan Keane."

Kitty gasped and stroked his hair.

"And don't forget your own cousin, Micheál: probably killed by one of mine and I unable to do anything about it, about any of it, Kitty."

He choked an anguished sob and sniffed, another fat tear rolled down his cheek. He gazed imploringly up at his wife. "I've never killed a man, Kitty, you must believe me, but that hasn't stopped me becoming a killer. Their blood is on my hands. We've all become animals and I want no more part of it."

He nodded towards the letter pinned beneath the whiskey bottle. Slowly he stood, unhooked the bubbling pot and poured the boiling water into the tin bath. With his back to his wife as she read his resignation letter he wearily pulled his vest over his head, stepped out of his underpants and into the bath.

"I do this for us, Kitty. For you and for Bridget and, God-willing, for the large and happy family we will build together. The work I do now is no longer policing – I never wanted to be a soldier fighting a war – just a man keeping the peace. It's over for me."

He closed his eyes and sunk as deep into the bath as his large frame could, enjoying the warmth of the water on his cold skin.

Kitty placed the letter back on the table and knelt down beside the bath. "I believe you, Joseph."

"What do you believe?"

"I believe that you are a good man and I should never have doubted you for a second. You couldn't have harmed Micheál. I'm ashamed that I ever allowed myself to think such things. Can you forgive me?"

"Hush now." Joe gently touched her lips with his forefinger. "Kitty, you have nothing to be sorry for. It is I who should be seeking your forgiveness. Was it not me who chased you to Tipperary and stole you from your family, my work that has turned your kin against you, and my inability to find your cousin's killers that has seen us take to separate beds?"

Joe reached for the flannel folded over the lip of the bath.

"Here, let me." Kitty prised it from his hands and soaked it in water before softly dabbing at the muddy cuts and bruises on his face. With an almost imperceptible sigh, she wet the sponge again before washing his neck and strong shoulders, watching the bathwater trickle in glistening streams over his biceps, golden in the candlelight. Lathering the flannel with soap, she ran it through his chest hair and around his nipples and asked, "And what will become of us, Joe? Where will we live? What will you do?"

"We could go anywhere, Kitty, do anything. We could move to Cashel to be with your family. I could start again, set up a shop or start a business. I have savings and you know that I will work hard…"

And until her dying day, Kitty would always remember what she said next. Even at the time it seemed as though she was watching herself speaking the words that sealed her husband's fate and although she didn't know where the sudden conviction came from, she believed every single word that passed her lips at the time.

"Joe, you're dreaming. Do you really think you'd last a day in Tipperary? It's wilder than here. My Republican cousins back in Cashel won't care whether you wear a uniform still: the fact you once wore one will be enough to widow me. I know that you didn't hurt Micheál – but they don't, and do you really think that they will believe me when I tell them all you've told me tonight?"

"Kitty, but we could go anywhere. Dublin, Belfast, Liverpool – London even?"

"Look at me, Joseph Conlon. I fell in love with you and I married you because you made me feel safe, and you still do. You're the biggest, bravest man I've ever known. We have a house, and a child and some standing in this community. Why should we throw that all away to live on the run? We can't spend the rest of our lives wondering whether every man who approaches you on the street with his hands in his pocket means to use them to shoot you or shake your hand.

"Joe, the only way to guarantee our safety is to finish this. You must win this war and make these streets safe, whatever it takes. I never thought I would hear myself say these words but, Joe, you can't resign. You must stay a policeman – I can see of no other way for you to keep your wife and daughter safe."

By now Kitty's hand had slipped under the waterline and was gently massaging his taut belly with the soapy flannel. As she leaned in over the bath her nightgown opened at the neck revealing to Joe a glimpse of the smooth white contours of her breasts and the warm, dark shadow between. Kitty followed his gaze and let go of the flannel, tracing her fingertips down through the soft hair below his belly button and touching upon the growing affirmation of his love for her.

"Now, dry yourself off quickly, Joseph Conlon, and come to bed. You have a daughter sound asleep who misses her father and an aching wife who wants her husband back."

Kitty pulled her hand from the water, picked up the oil lamp and walked towards the door.

"And make sure you burn that letter before you come to bed."

Joe was going to do anything she told him.

26

Summer, 2018
The Golden Glade Retirement Home,
Clonmel, Eire

"Let me tell you a story, Seamus."

For, even now, Pat-Joe refused to call him James, blaming the last three hundred years of misfortune on the vainglorious king who lost the Battle of the Boyne and then fled Ireland hidden under a woman's shawl.

"A long, long time ago, when giants still roamed this land, there was a great warrior called Oisín. One day whilst he was hunting he spied the most beautiful woman he had ever seen riding a white horse through the forest. She wore a long dress of palest blue. It glittered with a thousand stars and her hair tumbled over her shoulders like sunbeams. A golden glow followed her through the gloom of the wood and Oisín was transfixed.

"He spurred on his mare to meet her and as he approached her, she gazed into his eyes and spoke. 'My name is Niamh and my father rules the kingdom of Tír Na nÓg, a magical land where there is neither pain nor sorrow nor death and where nobody ever ages. Even there we hear the fantastical tales of bravery told about you, Oisín, and I have come to rescue you from this world of suffering and take you back with me to the Land of Eternal Youth.'"

Pat-Joe hacked and with trembling fingers, held a handkerchief to his lips and spat out some phlegm. Sipping from a plastic beaker, he licked his cracked lips and continued.

"Now Oisín didn't want to leave his father, Finn MacCool, nor his family, but he had fallen in love with Niamh and agreed to go with her, knowing that one day he would return. So off they set across the silver seas that separated this world from the next. They lived together in ageless bliss for three summers and three winters. Now, although Oisín missed the green fields and plentiful streams of Ireland, it was his father and family whom he ached to see the most, so he begged Niamh to let him return to visit them. Reluctantly she agreed, telling him to ride her white horse across the sea, but she warned him that if even one of his feet were to touch the ground in Ireland, he would never be able to return to Tír Na nÓg.

"So Oisín rode the silver waves once more to this world and the place of his birth to find that there were no longer any giants in Ireland, his father's castle was now just a crumbling ruin and nobody remembered the stories of Finn MacCool or Oisín. Indeed, Seamus, *three centuries* had passed since he had first crossed over to Tír Na nÓg."

Pat-Joe stared through James as if in a dream, and for a moment James wondered whether that was the end of the story. But his great-uncle wasn't finished.

"As he trotted back towards the shores and his faery queen, he came upon some old men trying to lift a heavy stone and in trying to help them, he fell from his horse and immediately aged three hundred years. Lying on the turf, bearded, wrinkled and ancient, with his dying breath he managed to share the stories that had become lost. St Patrick himself recorded them and now that they are written down, they will never be forgotten again."

He paused and looked at James, "Do you know why I have told you this story?"

James suspected it was because only a few minutes before he had been telling Pat-Joe about his encounter with Oisín Ó Súilleabháin in Birr, but shook his head anyway.

"It is because the last duty that Oisín performed before he passed over was to tell forgotten tales. I know that my time is fast approaching, Seamus, and fear, shame and the wrath of your grandmother have prevented me from sharing what I know of the past; a story that will be forever lost if I don't tell it to someone with an inclination to listen."

James felt his stomach lurch in anticipation.

"You've come here today and told me about documents in London and songs in bars and priests' diaries and my daddy's grave, and you've made me realise that I have spent my entire life telling every story from the past but my own. I think that of all my kin, you're the only one who will listen, who might understand. So this story is the story of our family, a story told to me by my mother, Kitty Conlon, and a story that I feel I must share with you."

James saw that his great-uncle's eyes had regained the lustre that he remembered from days sat on his knee next to the fire in the cottage – the lustre of a weaver of tales who knows that his audience hangs upon his every word.

"Now your Granny Bridget, my sister, took our father's death very hard, so she did. I can only imagine what it must have been like to watch your own daddy shot before your very eyes. But I never knew him – I didn't wake in the night screaming like Bridget. I never associated his memory with a moment of bloody murder. So my mammy would tell me things that she never shared with my sister, and before she died, she entrusted to me items that Bridget would have nothing to do with.

"Seamus, would you go over to the wardrobe in the corner, and on the top shelf above the coat rail you'll find a briefcase – would you bring it to me, please?"

James did as he was told and returned to the chair by the bed with a battered, black attaché case. He laid it on top of the sheets and Pat-Joe asked him to open it.

Within the case were a number of faded photographs – a few in frames, but most of them tied loosely with frayed pieces of grey string. Names and dates were written on their reverse in faint pencil. There was a birth certificate, a copy of *Irish Fairy Tales for Children,* a brass whistle and one single sheet of cream paper, ancient and brittle and stained around the edges with what looked like spilled black ink.

James examined the photographs: there was the one that he had seen before that showed the infant Bridget in her christening gown, her father standing proudly behind his wife, but there were many more that James supposed hadn't been seen by anybody for half a century. Some showed Joseph Conlon as a young man – one was from his RIC training in Dublin at Phoenix Park, another showed him standing outside his barracks in County Clare before he had been transferred to Birr. The framed photograph was an image of Kitty and Joseph on their wedding day – it was a little blurred but it couldn't hide the beauty of James's great grandmother. There were even Victorian hard-backed cards that carried the misty image of Joseph's parents, Thomas and Mary Conlon, dated from the 1890s.

James found himself holding his breath as he picked up the book of fairy stories and turned to the flyleaves at the front. There in a bold script, he could make out the words,

December 1920,
To my Darling Wife, Kitty,
I pray that you will read these tales to our daughter, Bridget,
on those long evenings when I am waylaid at the barracks.
I love you with all my heart,
Your own Joseph

James examined the whistle, turning it over in his fingers and tracing the words, 'The Metropolitan Patent – Royal Irish Constabulary' followed presumably by the name of the manufacturer, 'J Hudson' and an address in Birmingham.

Pat-Joe sipped again at the plastic beaker. "My father was wearing that whistle on the day he was shot."

Finally James picked up the fragile slip of paper with the edges of his fingertips. It was typewritten and many of the words were obscured by the dried black substance that framed the entire left-hand side of the sheet. An oval-shaped stain nosed its way from the top right hand corner, but the words beneath this bruising were still legible.

"Mammy told me that when he was murdered, he was holding this very briefcase. She said that when it hit the cobbles it burst open and sent a shower of papers flying up in the air – like New York ticker-tape from the newsreels at the cinema, she said. And while she is screaming and my father is lying dead on the pavement, his blood spilled in the gutter, and the old shopkeeper from across the road is yelling at a boy to fetch a priest and doctor, two policemen appear from nowhere, as if they had been there all along. She told me that despite the fact she was screaming her cousin's name and pointing towards the river, they seemed more intent on containing the scene. She remembers one of them telling her and Bridget to step away from the evidence whilst the other picked up each sheet of paper, his fingers dripping with my father's blood. Within minutes a Crossley-Tender had hurtled past them in the direction of Bridge Street and, heralded by the shrills of police whistles, Dr Burke and Head Constable Regan arrived outside her house with three or four more constables. She thinks she must have fallen into some sort of swoon because the next thing she can remember was being picked up from the pavement, her dress soaked red and a single sheet of bloodstained paper stuck beneath the sole of her shoe. In all the confusion the policeman who had been collecting the papers had slipped away and she didn't know what to do with it, so she peeled it off her foot and carried inside where Dr Burke sedated her. After the funeral she placed it inside the attaché case that had been left open and empty beside her husband's corpse along with all the other keepsakes that she had of him. She took it back to Cashel with her a few weeks later when she left Birr for good.

"Now, Bridget couldn't bear to lay eyes on the thing, and I'm told that she would start screaming if ever she saw her mother looking through it, so my mammy put it away and forgot about it. When she closed those hasps, she locked inside all the pain and guilt and she never spoke a word of it to me until Bridget moved out to marry Enda Devlin and it was only the two of us in the house. When she died, it passed to me, but Bridget told me plain that if ever I brought that briefcase to her home or spoke of its contents to her children, she would disown me – and I believed her. Your grandmother could be cold, Seamus. So I told tales of the Fianna, I sang songs inspired by famine and read poems about the Sidhe, but I never spoke of this strange black briefcase and the bloodstained letter within until now…"

A single tear ran down the old man's face. "So now, like Oisín, I have shared my stories with you before I breathe my last. Maybe you will make some sense of this twisted history if you have the wisdom to understand it."

He gently took the letter from James's fingers, placed it in the case and clicked the hasps closed and pushed it along the bed towards his great-nephew.

Pat-Joe gazed with rheumy eyes at the pulleys and rigging that hung from the wall bracket at the head of his bed and then at the wheelchair that was folded under the windowsill and smiled a wry smile that transformed into a throaty chuckle.

"Poor fecker: thrown from a flighty white mare. He never had a chance. I imagine half of the folk in here won't touch the ground again until they're put in it. Who'd have thought it? If Oisín had only wheeled himself across the silver seas in that nasty contraption, he could have made it back again to Niamh and eternal youth."

His chuckling turned to coughing, which in turn became wheezy gasps for air. James jumped up not knowing whether to call for assistance or to start slapping his great-uncle's back, but Pat-Joe waved him back to his seat. Slowly the old man regained control of his ragged breathing, reached for his beaker of water and took a greedy gulp.

"Ah, but can you imagine never growing old until that one moment when all your yesterdays come rushing to catch you up in a heartbeat? Surely that's the way to go."

James flinched at the memory of Connor's gaunt face the day before he died.

"Are you talking about Oisín or Joseph Conlon, Pat-Joe?"

His great-uncle blinked and stared at the wall.

Part III

The Difference

'The dark shadow we seem to see in the distance is not really a mountain ahead, but the shadow of the mountain behind – a shadow from the past thrown forward into our future. It is a dark sludge of historical sectarianism.'

David Trimble,
First Minister of Northern Ireland,
December 1998

27

12*th* *June, 1920*
Birr, King's County, Ireland

He could still remember the first time he had stuck a blade into a man; the penetration, the delicious thrust and slide to the hilt – the intimacy of it all.

Looking back, almost a decade later, it was no wonder he considered the act akin to copulation. The way he saw it, stabbing and fucking were essentially the same thing: an unbidden plunge into another's being, a release of pent up frustration. Victory and contentment; irresistible urges sated – for a time, at least.

He smiled as he pictured the look of surprise on the big man's face – a tough bastard he was too – but he had underestimated the resolve of twelve-year-old Billy Jardine.

It had been January, 1913 and the Catholics on Abercromby Street in the East End of Glasgow were flying flags and playing fiddles in celebration of the passage through Commons of the Third Home Rule Bill. Their music and laughter carried on the icy wind that blew off the Clyde, through the blackened tenements of London Road and down the alleys lurking off Dalmarnock, amplifying street by street their unbridled joy. Every cheer that whipped across the city and seeped in through cracked glass and warped window frames of Unionist households was a defiant battle cry that filled the Protestants of the East End with fear and hatred.

His Da, a boiler-maker at the shipyards, had hacked up a ball of grey phlegm, sooty and poisoned from a lifetime spent smoking and breathing asbestos, and spat it through the open window. He followed it up with a mouthful of bilious curses, hurled just as hatefully as the glob of mucus. His cat-calls were joined by dozens of others from above, from below and across them in the seething slum blocks of Bridgeton Cross:

"To Hell with Dan!"

"Fuck Dan!"

"Mick Bastards!"

Billy was old enough to understand that 'Dan' was Daniel O'Connell, a dead Irishman who had managed to obtain for the Catholics of Ireland the vote. In this corner of Glasgow, you were either a 'Billy' or a 'Dan' – a Protestant or a Catholic – and the Jardines were sash wearing, flute playing, banner waving, die-hard, Unionist Billies.

And today it looked as if their world was crumbling around them. His Da had explained that even though the right-minded House of Lords would block this bill – it would eventually become law, and the Irish would be granted Home Rule. For families like the Jardines, this meant *Rome Rule*: their God-fearing Protestant brothers and sisters in Londonderry and Belfast would soon be ruled by a Catholic clique from Dublin, who in turn would take orders from the Anti-Christ in Rome himself. What was worse, of course, was that the Dans of Glasgow would finally have one over them for the first time since 1690 when good King Billy had crushed the Catholic hordes at the Battle of the Boyne, and cemented a Protestant ascendancy in Ireland.

Two hundred and twenty-three years of bragging rights, a quarter of a millennia of Orange Order parades and tradition now teetered on the precipice. Everything Billy had ever known or understood was about to be trampled on and spoiled. And all this serenaded by a wretched underclass, drunkenly and spitefully pouring rebel songs into the chill of the night, infecting the very air his family breathed.

He had to do something.

Leaving his Da staring at the unchanging words on the newspaper, a toxic brew of whiskey and loathing churning behind disbelieving eyes, Billy Jardine knew what he would do: he was going out to kill a Dan.

Billy ran with the Derry Boys: the juniors who one day would step up to become fully fledged members of the Brigton Billy Boys. He was one of the youngest in the gang, but his size and maturity belied his age, and most considered him to be five or six years older. At twelve, he already boasted broad shoulders, wispy hairs on his chest and he shaved with his Da's razor every other day.

On the corner where London Road meets Dalmarnock, Billy spied the boys. Sour-faced, they regarded the icy pavement glumly, smoking roll-ups and stamping their feet to keep warm. The fiddle music wafting from the Catholic enclave of the Calton was even louder here and people passed him with pained expressions etched onto their faces.

"Lads, I cannae take it no longer. Let's gan an' sen' a message to the Dans – let's wipe the wee smiles aff their Mick faces."

They had followed the Clyde towards Salt Market, sticking to alleyways and avoiding the residential streets where they knew the Calton Entry Boys would be on the lookout for strangers. If they were spotted deep in the Irish quarter, where the San Toy and Kent Star held sway, then they would face a kicking, but Billy was counting on the fact that tonight the enemy would have their guard down, stupefied by whiskey and what they thought was victory, and would be unwilling to act on the sighting of four wee bairns slipping through their territory.

Crouching behind steel kegs welded together by frost in the shadows behind O'Hare's Tavern, the boys watched as a rectangle of light folded open across the frozen alleyway. A big man, green handkerchief in top pocket, lurched outside whistling a Gaelic tune. He stumbled, stopped, righted himself, and started to fumble with his trousers. They heard a low moan and a tinkling trickle turn to spluttering gush. Billy nodded and the group fanned out, casting four small shadows onto the steaming wall. Without interrupting his stream, the man rotated and observed the boys with unhidden scorn.

"Wha' yea fuckin' lookin' at? Fuck aff ya wee cunts," he slurred, and sprayed an arc of amber on their shins and shoes.

"We've come tae tell ye that there'll be nae surrender from the Brigton Billy Boys."

The Catholic snorted. With that, Billy Jardine stepped through the stream of piss and calmly stabbed the man in the guts. He collapsed to his knees, holding his cock and wearing that look of shock that Billy still smiled at now. As blood and urine pumped from him in erratic spurts, Billy turned and said, "Come on lads, let's leave the big man tae finish his pish and get oot o' this shithole."

Billy never found out what had happened to him. He knew his letters and he'd scoured the papers in vain looking for gory tales of murder in the Catholic quarter. He had hoped to read of baffled policemen coming to dead ends in their enquiries and the incident being chalked up as just another unsolved gangland act of violence. But there was nothing – not in the papers nor even the word on the street – so he reluctantly supposed that the wound hadn't been fatal, or even that deep. The drunken Mick must have survived the night and maybe woke up with a banging hangover and no recollection how he had pissed himself and gashed his stomach.

Billy couldn't deny he was disappointed.

However, the other lads who'd watched him do it testified to the act with an air of reverence. In the billiard rooms and on the street corners of Bridgeton, Billy's reputation was made amongst those of the East End who believed such a deed was understandable, if not even commendable on such a grim day as that.

Today, sat in the back of a Crossley-Tender on his way to Birr, wearing the mismatched uniform of army khaki and RIC green – which had led some Limerick wit to dub them the 'Black and Tans' – Billy Jardine grinned, knowing he was being paid to do what he had risked arrest for back in Glasgow. He had signed up to serve in Ireland so he could strangle the life out of this Fenian rebellion, and in doing so, ensure that the Dans back home never got to see an independent Ireland.

He was going to put as many of them in the ground as he could, and all with the consent of the British government.

Life didn't get any better than this.

28

12th June, 1920
Galway, Ireland

A clean shaven and blue-eyed gentleman wearing a bowler hat and three piece suit idled beneath the station clock pulling restlessly on another cigarette. At his feet, a large suitcase and six butts, crushed and twisted into black and white question marks. Despite his position directly underneath the grand timepiece, he repeatedly dug a watch from his pocket to scrutinise the second hand as it raced with alarming speed ever clockwise. His eyes darted from figure to figure, scanning faces and gaits as they emerged from the ticket office and made their way down the platform to the waiting locomotive. He flipped his watch once more and felt a flutter of panic realising there were only two minutes before the train left. Beneath the bowler an uncomfortable prickle of perspiration irritated his scalp.

Calm down.

Don't make yourself conspicuous.

Take a deep breath.

Slowly, he began to breathe more regularly.

An explosion of white steam hissed from the engine, startling him. It billowed, cloud-like, along the platform, obscuring porters and passengers who trotted alongside claret carriages in a

12th June, 1920

cacophony of clicking heels and rolling wheels. From this drifting bank of steam emerged a figure robed in black habit and white wimple; waddling penguin-like and lopsided, unbalanced by a huge suitcase.

The young man snapped his pocket-watch shut, ground his cigarette and, picking up his own suitcase, strode towards the struggling nun.

"Sister, may I be of some assistance?"

"God bless you, my son. Although my will is strong, I fear my flesh is weak. Thank you."

The suited gentleman strained as he took the weight of both suitcases and half-tottered along the platform.

"Mine is the next carriage, my son."

He hefted the cases into the vestibule, stuck his head out the door and peered one last time at the faces of those running for the train and those who milled around the platform. Satisfied, he shunted the cases down the corridor towards the compartment door outside which the young nun was waiting.

"If you would be so kind? This is me in here."

"Strange; I believe that I am in this compartment too – what a coincidence, Sister."

Forced into using a weightlifting technique which at one point posed the very real danger of splitting his suit trousers, he managed to raise the nun's suitcase high enough to slip it onto the overhead luggage rack.

"Sister," he gasped, "what have you got in there? Lead?"

"Something like that," she chuckled. "My, you are a strong, young man."

He smiled, lifting his own marginally lighter case up onto the opposite rack, and heard the soft click of the compartment door closing behind him and the rusty squeak of roller blinds as the nun shut out the world outside.

"For your troubles my son, would a kiss suffice?"

Padraig Nolan turned and gently tucked a stray lock of hair underneath Margaret Fahy's wimple and cupped her breast through the coarse fabric of the habit.

"I think a kiss would do very nicely indeed."

The tips of their tongues touched before slipping inside the other's wet mouth. Greedily they devoured each other, caught up in the danger of what they were doing and the delicious sacrilege of the moment.

They were still kissing as the whistle blew. A sudden lurch sent them tumbling in fits of giggles onto the carriage seat and the train pulled out of Galway Central station on its way to Banagher, where an IRA car would pick them up and transport the pair to Birr.

The unsuspecting observer, however, would never have guessed that in the suitcase perched above the suited businessman were twenty-four grenades, six Webley revolvers and twenty nine copies of the *Western Gazette*, whilst hidden beneath a second habit and selection of austere undergarments, the nun's suitcase was leaden with 600 rounds of .303 cartridges for Lee Enfield rifles and 80 rounds of .455 Webley revolver ammunition.

Padraig had removed his bowler as the locomotive had pulled from the station and run his hands through his thick sandy locks. Now he slept, his head resting against the window pane, brow creased in small folds and skin taut over cheekbones. Margaret, flushed with guilty arousal, watched the fields and rivers race away through and behind his pale reflection, and swore to herself that she would never let him go.

She had hardly seen anything of him since both he and Brendan O'Rourke had fled Birr after the shoot-out at the mill. To think she'd held a torch for Brendan at one point. She should be grateful her sister had outmanoeuvred her on that score. When Carmel wanted something, there was no point fighting her. In that respect, Carmel and Brendan were well-suited – they shared an intensity that she and Padraig lacked. Padraig was altogether a different type of man to Brendan: he made her laugh, and Maggie couldn't imagine that Brendan O'Rourke could induce a smile in anyone anymore. Thank the Lord that her Padraig hadn't been at the mill that morning – from what she'd heard, Brendan was lucky to have made it out alive. Almost murdered at the hands of that bastard, Conlon. Meanwhile Ciaran, who'd clashed with Brendan over the spy, had returned to Galway where he assuaged his conscience by inciting violence rather than being honest about it and picking up the gun he encouraged others to use.

The shoot-out had been a setback, for sure, and Republican activity in Birr had been restricted to low level agitation ever since. Shallow graves had been sunk into the manicured lawns of the establishment, a handful of hussies seen stepping out with Peelers had been dragged from beds and tarred and feathered, but no blood had been spilt in months. Nor any successful operations against the enemy, and it pained Maggie to see that life in Birr had reverted to how it had been before Dan Breen fired the first shot in January, 1919. It seemed that Micheál's death had been in vain and those responsible were going to get away scot-free.

Although Ciaran was too yellow to fight alongside men like Padraig and Brendan, Maggie had to grudgingly admit that he was highly regarded amongst the clandestine circle of IRA big-wigs and Sinn Féin TDs in Galway. Ciaran not only wrote and edited the *Western Gazette*, a weekly news-sheet chronicling British atrocities and communicating directives from Dublin, but also sat as judge in one of the Dáil Courts set up to administer fair and distinctly *Irish* justice to the Irish people. The one case she'd watched saw an IRA battalion commander charged with damage to property, assault and abusive language towards women. She had never heard the like, and naturally assumed the fighting man would scoff at the spectacled waifs who dared judge him, refusing to recognise the authority of the court. But no, the battle-scarred commander, with bowed head, admitted his part in the bar-room brawl and accepted the guilty verdict. Apologising to the publican and his daughter, he promised to reimburse them for damage done. The women in the courtroom burst into spontaneous applause as the commander vowed never again to use such crude language towards a sister in the struggle against the common oppressor. This was a new type of justice; one unthinkable under British law and Ciaran was at the vanguard of the movement. So in his own way, she supposed, her brother was doing his bit for the revolution.

Brendan and Padraig, on the other hand, had spent the intervening months temporarily seconded to the North Tipperary Brigade, which was larger, better organised and more rigorously regimented than the South Offaly Brigade. Since November Padraig had slipped across the border to visit her as much as he could and he had recounted with pride how they drilled and trained and studied strategy. He talked of life on the run, as one of a flying-column, days and nights spent shivering in dug-outs before an ambush. He boasted of successful raids on RIC barracks in Thurles and Templemore, and the last time she had seen him, holed up in the O'Donagh barn in Galross, she had noticed a change. The adolescent she once knew was now a man – and this man was a soldier. A real soldier of the Irish Republican Army, and she loved him.

Maggie and Carmel had stayed at the Fahy farm. Both members of Cumann na mBan, they had worn their uniforms openly to begin with, campaigning for Sinn Féin in the council elections. Carmel had once been dragged, kicking and cursing, from a soapbox by a couple of Peelers at the foot of the memorial to the Manchester Martyrs on Market Square. But that wasn't safe anymore: they were more useful to the cause in the shadows.

They dressed as civilians, transporting arms, ammunition, rations and intelligence between regional HQs and local militias. The reasoning was that they were less likely than their menfolk to be stopped and searched – but even that old courtesy was becoming redundant in the wake of the wave of new recruits to the RIC; *the Black and Tans*. Since late spring these Great War veterans had been filtering into police barracks across Ireland, and they didn't adhere to the niceties of gallantry when it came to women – the exact opposite, in fact. The horrific tales told of these fiends only made her more determined to resist the invader. Surreptitiously holding the *Western Gazette* within the pages of the thoroughly respectable *Irish Times,* Maggie acknowledged that with each well-pitched phrase, her brother wounded the British incrementally and just as effectively as the brave boys who slept in barns and cellars and could look a man in the eye before pulling the trigger.

His latest article was no exception:

BLACK AND TANS RESPONSIBLE
FOR CONNEMARA ATROCITY

On the night of the 29th May, a detachment of Black and Tans entered the premises of O'Briain's Bar in Spiddal, Connemara. That particular evening an Irish literature festival was being held and notable writers and poets of the Gaelic language were reciting their works in our native tongue. Shots were fired and significant damage caused to glass and tableware. Brothers, Ruaidhrí and Máirtín Ní Mháille were arrested and ostensibly taken into custody at Barna Barracks.

Despite entreaties from their family, the local RIC refused to allow Máire Ní Mháille, their mother, any access to, nor, indeed, any contact with her sons.

On the 4th June, two corpses were discovered partially buried in the Moycullen Bog. The bodies were identified as those of the two unfortunate brothers. Both cadavers displayed evidence of torture and almost every bone in their bodies had been broken. Flesh hung loose from their skeletons and the preponderance of grit and small stones embedded in their tissue, along with stretch marks and bruising to the neck, suggest that the pair were tied to the back of a motor vehicle and 'run'. This is a practice used by the Black and Tans to elicit fear and encourage confessions from those they suspect are members of the Irish Republican Army, *and in direct contravention of the Geneva code*. Although the RIC attest that both men were suspected gunmen whom escaped from custody in Barna on the night of the 2nd June, witnesses claim to have seen headlights and heard, *'inhuman wailing'* and *'screams like banshees'* on the Barna-Moycullen road at approximately 11pm on the night of the 30th May: **THREE DAYS BEFORE THEIR SUPPOSED ESCAPE!**

Máire Ní Mháille contests the RIC version of events and claims her sons were arrested in O'Briain's purely because they refused to respond to questioning in English. Numerous witnesses, including eminent and respected writers and poets attending the literature festival, concur with Mrs Ní Mháille's account of events.

As yet, no-one has been charged with the double homicide, and this journalist suspects that nobody will be charged.

Are we to suppose that speaking our native tongue now warrants a death sentence? How long are we prepared to accept this tyranny?

Maggie closed the paper and wiped a tear from her cheek. *What kind of monsters had been unleashed on them by the British? Who could do such things to a fellow man?* The uninvited image of a crow pecking the empty socket of an executed gamekeeper clouded her conviction for a moment, so she turned back to the *Western Gazette* to steel herself with more hatred.

29

12ᵗʰ June, 1920
Birr, King's County, Ireland

"Ten shillings a day, full board and lodging, no poison gas, nor mortars to contend with. Just a bunch of Paddies sharing a revolver! It will be like shooting tin ducks at a summer fair."

Underneath the tarpaulin in the back of the Crossley-Tender, spirits were high amongst the men wearing the mismatched uniforms of the Black and Tans.

Eddie Miller, a ruddy-faced boy from the Fens still couldn't believe his good fortune. Ten whole shillings a day! He would go home rich when this was over. He was the only one of the eight men in the truck who hadn't fought in the Great War. Turning eighteen as the conflict ground itself to an exhausted end, he'd never left the training barracks in Cambridgeshire. Post-war cuts had seen him demobbed and, along with the thousands of other men looking for work, he'd struggled to find it. He had lived with his parents for a while longer and helped with the harvests the previous year, but nothing that earned him enough money to set up home on his own. And then he had seen the adverts: They seemed too good to be true. In bold letters they asked,

'DO YOU WANT A JOB?'

Well, yes, thought Eddie.

'JOIN THE RIC, THE FINEST CONSTABULARY IN THE WORLD.'

The poster pinned outside the town hall had promised ample pay, free uniform, generous leave, opportunity for promotion, compensation for injury and the guarantee that if the job wasn't for you, then with one month's notice, you could just leave. What wasn't to like? So he had signed up immediately. He'd been shipped over to Dublin just over three months ago where he'd enjoyed the basic training and the camaraderie and now, finally, he was off into the field to fight for real.

Eddie didn't know nor understand too much about the Irish, or what their grievance was, but he did know that whilst British blood had irrigated the battlefields of the Somme, these treacherous Micks had staged a rebellion in Dublin, and now that the war against the Kaiser was over, they had started another one by shooting at the army and police over here. The papers back home had told him as much.

He kept quiet when the older men talked about religion for fear of being revealed as ignorant. Of course, he'd gone to church with his parents each Sunday, but had spent every turgid second insensibly bored, day-dreaming of petticoats and footballs and cavalry charges. He had no real idea what a *Roman Catholic* was – he doubted he'd ever met one – and wouldn't even know if he had. But some of the men here were experts on the subject; and most of them seemed to really hate these Catholics. The moustached Scot with the vicious scar running from lip to ear-lobe, whom Eddie thought was called Billy McDeen or something like that – the man was barely comprehensible – seemed to have an especially strong aversion to them. He was quite unnerving really: the way he stroked his bayonet, which he had named *Ripper*, boasting that it was '*belly-slicingly sharp.*' The man had spent most of the journey wearing a strange expression, his eyes animated with black flame as though reliving some secret and sordid memory. To be honest, all the men who'd served in France or Turkey had a darkness lurking just below the surface; Eddie couldn't help but notice the sourness in their eyes, when he, the uninitiated – the *virgin* as they called him at training camp in Phoenix Park – talked of mortars or poison gas.

He felt stupid now and shut up.

———————

Billy Jardine jumped from the Crossley-Tender, stretched his back and listened to it pop. He released his genitals from the sweaty knot they had formed in the humidity of the truck and pulled his underpants from the crack of his arse.

He already had the measure of the men he was with: some good soldiers and some cannon fodder. Taggart and Ross were Scots like himself and both Presbyterians. He could work with them. There was a Taffy that went by the name of Evans – a Methodist, and the four English lads, West, Pallister, Miller and Simons. Jardine assumed that they weren't Catholic – he'd not seen any rosary beads or crucifixes – but you could never tell: Anglicans south of the Tweed were so wishy-washy about their religion they might as well be left-footers. The fact that they had signed up to fight the Fenians implied they were all Unionists at least – and that was good enough for the time being.

One by one the new recruits fell out of the truck, weighed down by rucksacks, rifles and mess equipment. They organised themselves into a dishevelled line. Before them stood four officers wearing the dark-green of the RIC and equally sombre expressions. Billy cast his eyes around the barracks. An armoured car was parked at the foot of a foreboding portico that led into what he assumed was an old workhouse. The building was large and grey and even less inviting than the four Irishmen who stood to greet them. Iron bars and wooden shutters locked in window-panes on the lower floors, whilst upstairs he spied uneven slats of timber nailed inside the window-frames. A makeshift sentry post had been constructed to the left of the entrance gate and barbed wire looped through spears of Victorian fencing fronting the road. Sandbags were piled inside the perimeter fence and a heavy chain and padlock hung from the gate. The middle window of the second floor had been completely removed and the muzzle of a Lewis machine gun poked aggressively from behind another bank of sandbags. Billy was both impressed and surprised at the levels of defensive fortification and, for the first time, began to appreciate that this might be more than just a rag-tag insurrection of local-yokels with a grievance against their landlords. These Shinners were obviously serious and it looked like they had the RIC on the back foot.

Well, not for long, if he had anything to do about it. He was determined to bring the war to them.

The eldest of the four coughed conspicuously and the new recruits stopped murmuring between themselves. He had thin white hair, lamb-chop sideburns and a bulbous nose that told Billy that the man liked a drink. *What Mick didn't?*

"I am Head Constable Regan. The RIC is renowned as the best police force in the world because we follow orders to the letter and we exercise our duty with tact and fairness – but we do not shirk from our responsibilities to maintain law and order. You will not run amok here in King's County. You will uphold the proud tradition that this force has spent decades earning. More often than not, I will be in Tullamore, co-ordinating operations with the District Commissioner – but when I am in Birr, you will find me in the barracks on John's Mall where the married officers are billeted. As single men, you will be based here under the direct supervision of Sergeant Conlon – who is *de facto* operational commander of the Birr District police force. He is ably assisted by Acting Sergeants Daly and Flynn. If you have any problems or questions, they will be your 'go-to' men.

"You are here to help keep the peace, and contrary to what you may have heard across the water, the rule of law still applies here. And by God, you will keep to it. Do I make myself clear?"

Nobody said anything.

"Do I make myself clear?" Regan bellowed.

"Yes, sir!"

"Daly, Flynn! Show the men to the dormitories."

As the eight recruits trooped into the barracks, Jardine remembered the words his training officer had shared with him before he left Dublin, and they jarred with those of old 'whisker-face' here. *'If the natives approach you with their hands in their pockets – shoot them. If they don't put their hands up when you ask them – shoot them. You might make mistakes from time to time, but you're not here to make friends. You are here to make life hell for those whose trade is agitation and whose method is murder. The more you shoot – the more I will like you – and don't worry, no policeman will get into trouble for shooting anyone.'*

Jardine wondered how it was going to play out here.

Regan turned to Conlon. "So, what do you think, Joseph?"

"I don't like the look of them, sir."

"Joseph – I am not asking you to like them: I am asking you to *use* them. Let them be your Rottweilers. If we are to bloody our hands – *if we have to* – let them do it, because when this war is won we can send them home to their Manchester slums and London ghettos and we can get back to policing the good people of Ireland. We've lost too many men in the last year – and not to

IRA bullets, but to the realisation that this is a dirty war. We *need* these men to do what our own consciences won't allow us to do."

Regan stared through the wrought-iron and barbed wire. "Does that make us as bad as them, or the IRA? Possibly. But at least we are doing it for the right reason: to save this country from its wildest notions. Now I have given these boys the official spiel – *you* have to ensure that the rebels quake with fear at the sound of their bark and the sight of their champing teeth. You can give your dogs some slack, and at times you'll need to, but God help us if you let them off the leash completely. Are you still up for the job, Joe? Have you got what it takes?"

Joe thought of his wife, his daughter, of poor Séan Keane and then of Brendan O'Rourke, and he looked the Head Constable square in the eyes and replied, "Yes, I have. I can use these men."

30

Summer, 2018
Derry City Walls, Northern Ireland

"You'd think the council would wash that shite off the roof – but why would they? They're just ex-Provos in suits anyhow."

Sticking the vape back between her lips, the young mother balletically extended her right arm and angled it over the city walls. Shaping her fingers into the outline of a gun, she squinted through bracelets and pulled the trigger. She blew a lungful of cherry-flavoured vapour over the tips of her fingers and winked at James with the parting words, "Fuck 'em all." She turned and continued pushing the baby-buggy along the city walls towards Loyalist West Londonderry.

James followed the trajectory of her imaginary bullet into the Catholic Bogside and saw, daubed eight feet high in white paint on roof slates, the letters 'IRA'.

Visiting Pat-Joe and examining Conlon's letter had given James cause for hope, and set him on a quest that had led him north of the border. Admittedly chunks of text were obscured beneath inky staining, and it was obviously only one page from a much longer document, but what was legible implied that Conlon suspected his men of corruption and maybe even murder. He wrote at one point, *'God knows I have blood on my hands and that*

I haven't always acted with the dignity that this uniform demands, but...' and the next few lines were hidden beneath crusty black blood. James had considered taking the document to a lab to see if there was some kind of spectograph that could reveal the words beneath – but realised he didn't have the vaguest idea where to start. Besides, further down the page were more tangible clues that he could pursue. *'I suspect that Acting Sergeant Daly and Constable Fallon know a great deal more about the incident than they have admitted...'* then again some missing words, before, *'let slip about shooting a horse...'* Towards the bottom of the page the tone darkened: *'sectarian split developing,'* and then the words, *'chief amongst the agitators is Constable William Jardine who has been accused of heinous crimes by one of the most respected members of the community. I intend to follow this up...'* The last section on the page read, *'...this is proved to be correct then a court martial and summary dismissal, followed by a criminal investigation can be the only course of acti(on)...'*

Whilst in Cashel, James had spent hours in an internet café constructing the family trees of the Birr RIC using Oisín's service records and an Irish ancestry website. Constable Daniel Fallon had survived the conflict, returned to Donegal and married. He still had descendants living in the region now. James had struggled to discover any more on Acting Sergeant Daly other than that he had been a Belfast man from the Shankill Road and had died in 1922 leaving no dependants. With his service number, however, James knew he'd be able to delve a little deeper if he paid a visit to the Public Records Office of Northern Ireland in Belfast. As for Jardine, he was Scottish, born in Glasgow in 1900, and as most of the Black and Tan records had been destroyed by fire in Dublin Castle, there was no record of court martial or criminal investigation. James acknowledged that he had hit a dead end there. None-the-less, *the game was afoot* and he was itching to hit the phones to see if he could make contact with any of Fallon's descendants in Donegal.

James reasoned that if one of Fallon's grandchildren was willing to speak to him, he could drive northwards to Donegal, flip back into Belfast and then, if he had found out what he needed, it was only a short drive down the coast to Dublin and the ferry home. He may not even need to chase up the Jardine lead if Conlon was right in his belief that *Daly and Fallon know a great deal more about the incident than they have admitted* – James might well have uncovered the *'heinous crime'* levelled against the Scotsman without having to make the journey to Glasgow at all.

That evening, across the road in O'Malley's with a pint and a copy of the Irish phonebook to hand, he had almost drained his battery and his will to live calling each and every offshoot of the Fallon family in County Donegal. From the ancestry website, James knew that Constable Daniel Fallon had sired three sons and two daughters, and although he had their initials, he discovered that not only was the surname, Fallon, particularly popular up there, but his daughters had married a Murphy and a Kelly respectively, and that had made the task nigh on impossible. Just before he was going to give up for the day and retire to Pat-Joe's, he had struck lucky when he got through to a very talkative octogenarian called Margaret Fallon. It transpired that she was the widow of a Thomas Fallon, and her Tommy was indeed the son of the man he was enquiring after. Constable Daniel Fallon had done well for himself after leaving the RIC; she boasted that he'd set up his own electrical business in the 1930s. *Fallon's Electricals* had become a well-known brand in the northern counties by the '60s, and by the time she was courting Tommy, they had stores all across Ulster. Of course the Troubles had seen the business suffer, but there was still one remaining store in the Waterside in Londonderry Town, as she called it, run by Kenneth Fallon, Daniel's grandson – himself now in his late sixties she'd wager. The old man had moved in with Kenneth and his wife, Alison, as he succumbed to dementia – mad as a brush he was towards the end – but the two of them were close. The entire business had been left to him and if anybody knew anything at all about Constable Fallon's past, it would be his grandson, Kenneth. The chatty pensioner didn't have a number for her nephew-in-law but told James that he could look the shop up on his computer and it should be there. James thanked her profusely and said his goodbyes. He tried to hang up but was forced to listen to a story involving a flat tyre and a rainy border crossing in 1978. By the time he put the phone down, his ears were hot and his pint warm. However, he felt he was on the verge of something.

So now he stood on Derry City walls watching Protestant mums shoot imaginary bullets into Catholic houses in the Bogside, on his way to meet a man who may hold the key to his great-grandfather's murder.

31

Summer, 2018
Fallon's Electricals, The Waterside, Derry City, Northern Ireland

When the call had come, Kenneth Fallon had been showing a couple of old sceptics the basic functions of a microwave oven. The decrepit pair eyed it warily, and asked about radiation – they didn't want cancer, they told him more than once. He had tried to explain to Mark, one of his (frankly useless) employees, that he was *with customers,* but the shaven-headed youth persisted, saying it was an Englishman on the phone asking for him by name. And it sounded important too – he was some sort of historian writing a book on Protestant heroes of some war – Mark hadn't quite caught which one – but the Englishman wanted to know about Kenneth's granddaddy, Daniel Fallon.

Kenneth had taken the call; he was nothing if not dutiful. He had never shirked a responsibility towards his family, his religion or his community. As top officer in the Drumahoe Orange Lodge, he impressed upon all the young men and women of the Order the need to respect God, Christian values and their elders.

Kenneth had loved his grandfather, and owed this business to him too – hence he had willingly taken him in when it became clear that he couldn't cope on his own anymore. But Kenneth believed that he had let his grandfather down, and failed his wife at the same time. It had been the job – it had taken up every last second God had granted him – and to his abiding shame, he had left his wife, Alison, to nurse his dying grandfather whilst he manned the tills and checked stock. By then the kids were at school – so it was she who spent the week days spooning food into his mouth, washing soiled sheets and dealing with his increasingly aggressive behaviour.

Daniel Fallon had degenerative dementia and barely recognised his grandson, but he was responsive to Alison, and Kenneth couldn't help but feel a little jealous. So it seemed natural that when the household awoke to screams that sounded as though somebody was being flayed alive, it was Alison who got up to calm Daniel and whisper in his ear that everything would be fine.

Before they had married, Alison had been a psychiatric nurse at the Waterside Hospital. She had dutifully relinquished this job without too much fuss after Kenneth explained she was to be wife, mother and homemaker; and that that was more than enough to be getting on with. So she had started playing amateur psychiatrist with Daniel in the still of the night while the rest of the family fell back to sleep after another of his night terrors. She had bought a drawing pad, charcoals and chalks, coloured pencils, crayons and felt tips, and when he woke, screaming and unable to articulate what had terrified him so, she had passed him the art materials and whispered, "Draw it, Grandad. Your dreams are like poison – you'll be able to sleep peacefully when the nightmares are sucked from you onto the page."

And Daniel had drawn and shaded and emblazoned in primary colours graphic horrorscapes that reminded Alison of the most unsettling trench art of WWI – bodies, barbed wire, dead horses and fire.

In the morning, after Kenneth had gone to work and the kids sent off to school, she would sit with Daniel and show him the images he'd drawn the night before. Playing professional psychiatrist, she'd recorded their conversations on tape cassette and tallied each tape with its corresponding sketch.

For the last six months of the old man's life, she had followed this process religiously – and to her credit, it seemed to have worked. By the end, Daniel was less agitated. It was as though he'd managed to get something off his chest. In fact Alison had spotted that the very last image he'd drawn was markedly different from all that came before. In each and every one, a tormented figure with lips sewn together watched impotently as scenes of depravity played out before him – but in the final sketch, this recognisable figure – whom she knew represented Fallon himself – looked as though he was speaking. The rough twine that had ripped through his lips, knotting them tight together, was gone, and the expression on the figure's face looked very much like that of Daniel in these, his final days – as though, both then and now, he had found some sort of redemption.

So that was why Kenneth felt guilty: in the last half year before Daniel died, he had barely seen his grandfather, and when he did, the old man didn't recognise him. More than that – and to his eternal shame – God had seen fit to take this saint-like woman from him only eight months later.

Leukaemia.

Kenneth had been destroyed, and secretly harboured suicidal thoughts. But his religious conviction, his children and the support of the Orange Order had pulled him through and – much like Daniel must have done – he bottled up his emotions and trudged on through life stoically and unhappily. He had never opened the plastic storage box filled with mad art and tape cassettes and he had never once been tempted to listen to the last recordings of the two souls whom he'd loved most in the world. But neither had he the strength to throw away the box; and so for the last thirty years it had sat upstairs in an attic. Today he was going to give it to this English historian, James Lucas, with his very best wishes. Maybe it was time his grandfather's story was heard after all.

32

Summer, 2018
The Waterside, Derry City, Northern Ireland

The anonymous text had come through a couple of days ago. He didn't need to know who it was from: he just needed to follow the instructions.

A name: James Lucas. His vehicle details: make, model and license plate. The words, 'Dooly's Hotel, Birr' and the letters OO/SHU. Thirty seconds after the first, a second arrived: an image of a man waiting by a lift, oblivious to the fact that someone was sneaking a photograph of him. It was a bit blurred, but it would do. OO meant 'Observation Op', and depending on who you spoke to, SHU stood for *Shut him up* or *Shit him up*. No point splitting hairs; they both meant the same thing. This Lucas must have ruffled feathers somewhere higher up the food chain and somebody wanted to find out what he was up to and, if necessary, persuade him to back off and stay quiet.

So he'd got a squad together – a couple of lads; a bit raw and green, but keen nonetheless – and he'd gone through the usual protocol to rent the van. They'd made it to Birr the same evening. They'd watched Lucas leave the hotel just before 7.30 and he'd left the lads in the back of the Ford Transit and followed by foot. He'd watched from the corner of the bar as the mark swapped data with some strange looking fella who looked like he loved himself too much, and then he'd followed him back up Main Street. He'd got sloppy and was almost spotted when Lucas had stopped to tie his shoelace; but in this business, that wasn't necessarily a bad thing – it was good to let them get a little paranoid. Put them on edge.

Since then they'd driven down to Tipperary, idled in a carpark of a Clonmel care-home and watched as Lucas pottered around Cashel having coffee with friends or family. Now they were parked up behind an electrical store in West Derry. This was not a part of town he wanted to be in – Unionist bullshit was painted all over the walls; bollocks slogans and murals goaded him from every corner. The last time he'd been here, half a decade ago, he'd been planting a pipe-bomb underneath a PSNI officer's car – unfortunately it didn't detonate properly and the policeman got away with cuts, bruises and minor burns. A shame, but best laid plans and all that. It's a pity he didn't have orders to use one of them now to blow up one of the many Orange Halls he'd passed as he'd trailed Lucas's conveniently conspicuous vintage car.

He missed the good old days.

His phone buzzed; a message from the same anonymous sender. He read the text. This Lucas was indeed a lucky boy: it seemed that his mother was kin to some old timers back in Cashel who'd served time for the cause and were still well respected in the movement – although Lucas probably wasn't aware of this – and they wanted kid-gloves used on him.

For the time being at least.

33

28th October, 1920
St Cillian's Priory, King's County, Ireland

"My baby," Mary Fahy cooed, straightening the ivy wreath that sat atop her daughter's restless brown locks, "I'd never have dreamed ye'd look so beautiful as ye do today. A princess, so."

Carmel Fahy, wearing her best dress beneath a thick green shawl into which her sister had knotted white and orange ribbons, felt more like Marian from the English textbooks they'd been forced to read at school. This was her own outlaw wedding, the woods around the ruined priory her Sherwood forest, and Brendan O'Rourke her rebel groom.

As a man on the run, theirs could never be a traditional wedding so Father Francis, a priest sympathetic to the movement – their own Friar Tuck no less – had agreed to marry them in secret. Her mother had fretted that this unconventional union would be a mortal sin, but the young priest had assured her that on the consecrated ground of the monastery and celebrated by an ordained priest, in the eyes of the Lord, the marriage would be absolutely binding. Carmel's brother, Ciaran, and other members of the Sinn Féin judiciary from Galway were here to recognise the legality of the ceremony on behalf of the government in Dublin. So Carmel was covered by both church and state, *and thank the blessed Virgin for that*; for although her father and mother didn't know it, she was eight weeks pregnant with Brendan's child. Even in these heady, revolutionary days where women could carry guns and sit as judges in Dáil courts, bearing a child out of wedlock was still a step too far.

Carmel was glad she was wearing the woollen shawl: not only did it disguise the barely noticeable bulge pressing tightly against her dress, but it repelled the autumnal chill borne on a breeze that descended from the Slieve Bloom mountains, dislodging the last russet leaves from the trees around them.

Milling about St Cillian's Cross and the mossy stone sarcophagus that was to act as their altar, the men smoked and smirked – a few of the more senior amongst them wearing tattered Volunteer uniforms from 1916. She noticed a shade of vulnerability in Brendan as he pulled too deeply on his cigarette and laughed too loudly at what Padraig whispered in his ear. Carmel couldn't help but swell with pride that this hardened soldier had been softened by the prospect of wedding his sweetheart.

She recognised most of the men around Brendan: Padraig of course, the O'Donaghs, Peadar Moran, the ex-Peeler, Ryan and the culchie boys from Killeen. There was a sizeable representation from the Tipperary Brigade and even some of the young lads from town, only recruited in the last couple of months, yet had seen fit to show solidarity with their brigade chief. The mood was upbeat in the Republican camp. Since the arrival of the Tans in June, the rebels had consolidated their hold on the countryside surrounding the town of Birr. In the rare sorties that the police had made to burn crofts, beat up farm boys and seize weapons, a hail of bullets fired from invisible snipers in the hills had sent them scurrying back to the bolt hole of their barracks, where they cowed behind barbed wire and sandbags in the old workhouse.

More than that, the aggression and lack of understanding towards the community shown by the Black and Tans, along with the horror stories heard or read in the secretly distributed newssheets from Galway had transformed previously supine Irish citizens into fervent republicans. For the first time ever, politically conservative Birr was starting to perceive the Crown Forces for what they were – not agents of peace, but instruments of repression.

The sun was setting; the crumbling stone and climbing ivy bathed a wan golden. Brendan, hair aflame in the dying rays, stood before the priest. Seamus Fahy took his daughter's arm and asked, "Are ye ready to marry yer soldier?"

"Yes, Daddy, I am."

A fiddler drew horsehair across string, conversation ceased and cigarettes were stubbed as father and daughter made their way through the parting crowd of Fenians. Looking at the smiling men and women who stepped back and allowed the pair to pass, Carmel felt an irrepressible wave of optimism for the future. By the time her baby was born, Ireland could be free and the outlaws of today would be the leaders of tomorrow. *Her child would be no British subject*, she thought as she took her place next to Brendan under the Celtic cross that glowed with the last shafts of autumn sunlight.

34

28th October, 1920
Birr, King's County, Ireland

"If ye willnae tell me wha' I wannae ken, I swear I will beat ye so bad yer own mammy willnea recognise ye, ye bog-trottin' bastard."

Vinny McMahon was terrified that he was to be hospitalised – or very much worse – purely because he didn't understand a word the Scotsman was saying to him. Christ, if he knew what he wanted, he would tell him and feck the consequences.

Constable Daniel Fallon, in his slightly more decipherable Donegal dialect translated: "Vinny, my colleague here is asking ye to tell him where yer wee pal Tommy O'Donagh can be found. We know the boy's a Shinner an' Constable Jardine would like to speak with him."

Billy Jardine had spent the last month greasing greedy Irish palms with silver, threatening, intimidating, picking on and probing the young men of Birr; looking for weakness, avarice or gullibility. He had a good mind now as to who was ripe for turning, who had Sinn Féin connections and who would die afore they said a word to the Peelers. Vincent McMahon was as soft as porridge and would spill his guts at the sight of a raised fist let alone the ink-black eye of a revolver – and the IRA knew that too. That's why the lad was useless for any detailed intelligence on them, but he did know those who would know more.

Tommy O'Donagh was a name that had come up regularly in Billy's street-corner interrogations. By all accounts he was a half-wit, but his pals said that he boasted that he was a real soldier of the IRA. To Billy's mind someone that stupid was worth much more alive to him than dead – and Billy was determined to gather as much information on the enemy as he could. Conlon was sitting on his hands – he was clearly conflicted – and Billy thought he knew why: the man was a dirty Catholic! How could they put a left-footer in charge of the barracks? How did they expect you to win a war against terrorists when your own Sergeant was rubbing shoulders with them on the pews at Mass every fucking Sunday?

So Billy and Daly and a handful of other men – obviously all of whom were of the reformed church – had taken it upon themselves to do what they felt Conlon wasn't; and establish a network of informers. He had heard that Conlon had lost a close friend, shot as a spy by the IRA – boo-hoo – but still no excuse for not pressing the locals. If the Fenians wanted to knock off a few of their own for talking to the police, so be it. A couple less potato-eaters to deal with and the townsfolk got to see these 'Republican heroes' in their true colours – cowardly murderers. Surely *win-win*?

Billy knew from his days running with the Derry Boys back in the East End of Glasgow that it was virtually impossible to best your enemy on their own turf. You were asking for a beating if you ventured into San Toy territory without knowing what you would find. Here in Ireland *everywhere* outside the town walls was enemy territory: every farmstead, hamlet, village or valley was a potential ambush waiting to happen. So Billy reasoned that not only did the IRA need to be provoked into a major operation, but that the police needed to know in advance exactly what their plans were.

This Tommy O'Donagh could be the key and Vinny *was* going to tell him where to find the boy.

"Let me introduce ye to a pal o' mine. Meet '*Ripper*'. Now, if ye willnae spill your guts, then Ripper will do it for ye."

Vinny regarded the eight inch bayonet blade and didn't need any translation from Fallon to know what was at stake here.

"He lives up at Galross, on a farm on the Athlone Road, so he does. Him, his mammy, daddy and sister. But you won't find him there so you won't," Vinny stammered. "A wedding, he said. A Fenian wedding he's after goin' to. Up in the hills somewhere."

"Where?"

"I don't know where, I swear! Towards the hills – that's all I know." Tears were streaming down Vinny's cheeks. "He said all the fightin' men would be there – even some in uniforms he said, and... and..."

"Who was tae be hitched?"

An uncomprehending glance towards Fallon.

"Who was getting married, Vincent?"

"I don't know – I heard no names! I don't know. I can't think..."

Billy lifted the boy's shirt and almost tenderly traced a line across his heaving, white belly with his finger. "Just here. Ye'll live long enough tae see yer guts at yer feet afore ye die. So think!"

"Red!" shrieked the terrified child. "Yes, Red!" A glimmer of triumph and relief flashed across his face. "'*Red's wedding*' is what he said. Captain Red O'Rourke! I remember now. He was to marry some Cumann na mBan woman – from near Riverstown or somewhere – but I swear I never heard her name. Not once. I swear it."

"Red O'Rourke eh?" Jardine looked at Fallon.

"That would be Brendan O'Rourke, Billy. He's a known Fenian – he's been on the run since last winter. He's the very man who killed the Sergeant's friend. Conlon would fain see him dead, so he would."

Billy smiled, beginning to formulate a plan that might provoke O'Rourke into acting rashly. He gently pulled the trembling boy's shirt back over his stomach and patted his belly. Sniffing the air, he lowered his gaze to the child's crotch where a well of damp was growing from his undergarments.

"For fuck's sake, laddie, ye've gone an' pished yersel'. Run away wee man! Ye stink."

Vinny understood every word of this last sentence and obliged. Shame, hot and wet, ran down his cheeks and his trouser legs.

35

Summer, 2018
Belfast, Northern Ireland

Grubby white light flickered apologetically, barely penetrating the gloomy corners of the cavernous multi-storey carpark on Waring Street. James was sitting in the front seat of the Morris Minor with a plastic container full of drawings and tape cassettes. He was wearing a head torch, and in a move that he knew would have impressed his wife's Yorkshire sensibilities, he had even prepared a flask of coffee in his hotel room before walking around the corner to the fourth floor of this concrete tower block. It was late and other than the humming of the strip lights that dripped murky pools of grey luminescence over bonnets and boots, the place was eerily silent and deserted.

He lifted the lid and delved into the box. Kenneth had promised that his late wife, Alison, had been methodical in her cross-referencing of images to interviews, and James found this to be the case. Bless you, Alison Fallon, he thought as he examined a child-like image of two men, some trees, a blood-smeared face of a boy and what looked like a dead cow, or maybe a horse? He slipped the cassette into the tape deck and listened as the faint hiss of thirty-odd years was arrested by a crystal clear voice...

James hadn't arrived in Belfast until late the night before. The traffic had been a nightmare in Derry – roadworks had closed a section of the orbital ring sending thousands of cars nose to tail through the same stretch of the medieval town as James was parked. In fact, on his way out of Fallon's Electricals he had almost been knocked over as he attempted to dart between cars with the large storage box full of Daniel Fallon's art and interviews rattling in his arms. A white rental van had flown from a side street behind the shop as he stepped off the pavement and had to swerve to avoid him. A woman walking on the other side of the road had waved her walking stick yelling, "Southern yahoos" after the van as, with squeal of wheel and whiff of scorched rubber, it darted down another side street ahead. Rush hour made everybody aggressive, James had thought, and clearly that became magnified if you bore Republic of Ireland plates in the staunchly Loyalist enclave of West Londonderry.

By the time he was out of Derry and on the A6 towards Belfast the sky had darkened. Thick, black clouds herded together and unleashed a violent downpour on the stream of traffic trying to make up for lost time. The inevitable accident closed a lane on the M22 and resulted in James belatedly arriving in Belfast hours later than he had hoped, stiff, tired and hungry. To top it all, he discovered that the phrase *parking available* on the hotel website actually translated as *park three streets away in a public carpark, lug your baggage to the hotel in the driving rain and pay £15 a day for the privilege*. Thus he decided to leave Kenneth Fallon's box unexamined in the boot of the car until the following day. Chewing chicken skewers in the overloud hotel bar half an hour later and exacerbating his headache with every sip of tannic wine, he wondered what he hoped to achieve here in Belfast. Then, irritable with himself for letting an arduous journey undermine his own resolve, he'd taken himself to bed.

However, this morning, waking to clear blue skies over the River Lagan, the sun glinting off mirrored prows in the Titanic

Quarter, James regarded a city that encapsulated the eddy of the Irish saga in much the same way that Berlin had come to epitomise the Cold War. With sunbeams flooding through the window and room service already ordered, James reasoned that sitting in a Morris Minor in a multi-storey carpark, listening to the demented ramblings of a dead man came a distant second to spending the day visiting parts of a city that he felt he knew through teaching but had never set foot in: it was going to be like meeting a pen pal in the flesh for the very first time.

Well versed in the art of research since his visit to London, James had already registered online for a visitor's pass to PRONI, the Public Records Office of Northern Ireland. Arriving by foot, his ragged satchel holding pencils and paper, he was issued with a reading card and climbed the stairs to see what, if anything, he could find out about Acting Sergeant Jonathon Daly.

It didn't take long.

Daly, it transpired, had left the RIC in 1921 and joined the Ulster Special Constabulary in Belfast. The USC were overwhelmingly Protestant and Unionist and came to be seen in nationalist circles as the *'dregs of the Orange Lodges, armed to the teeth and unafraid to unleash their ire on innocent Catholic men, women and children alike.'* From the few documents that mentioned him by name, it became apparent that Daly was a committed Orangeman himself and had been involved in a number of incidents in West Belfast resulting in either, *'the wilful murder of six civilians'* or *'the justifiable homicide of six IRA suspects'*, dependent on who was writing the report. He hadn't even lasted a year – he'd been stabbed to death in the toilets of a Shankill bar in late 1922 by *'person or persons unknown'*. The inquest stated that the lavatories could be accessed directly from a rear courtyard and that witnesses had seen two men running up Northumberland Street in the direction of the Falls Road. The assumption was that he had been assassinated by members of the

IRA. He left no family or dependants and he was only twenty-four when he died.

James felt no sympathy.

So it was another dead end; but it did support Conlon's assertion that the Birr RIC had become split down sectarian lines by July 1921. Surely it couldn't be a coincidence that the final letter that the Catholic Conlon composed the night before his murder revealed grave misgivings over the Donegal Protestant, Fallon, the Belfast Orangeman, Daly, and the Glaswegian Black and Tan, Jardine? And hadn't his grandmother seen two policemen appear on the scene as if by magic stooping to scoop up the scattered sheaves with bloodied hands? If it was them on Main Street that morning, what was it they were trying to hide, and could the remaining pages still exist? James reasoned that it was unlikely – surely they would have destroyed anything that incriminated them? What was clear was that there was nothing more to find out about Daly inside this building and, as James had a taxi tour of the Belfast murals booked for the afternoon, he needed to grab some lunch and get back to the hotel in time to meet his driver.

The driver who pulled up outside the Marriot an hour later was called Doug and he had thick, heavily inked forearms and a couple of ounces of gold on each finger. He must have been in his late fifties or early sixties, James thought, and although he had no hair on his smooth, bald pate, he sported a bushy, silver moustache, brittle as a pan scourer. Doug had started the taxi tour with the usual patter outlining the history of the city, regurgitating the well-worn, company-line account of the causes of the Troubles that stuck doggedly to documented facts and betrayed no emotion. However, the accidental use of personal pronouns was enough for James to infer that Doug had been brought up as part of the

Protestant community. Slipping into conversation that he was a history teacher from Yorkshire whose own great-grandfather had been assassinated by the IRA had the desired effect: Doug began to drop the rehearsed, non-partisan stage setting at each stop, and by the time they reached the Falls Road, the pair were conversing candidly about the history and legacy of sectarian violence in Belfast.

"To my mind, sectarianism became divorced from religious conviction a long, long time ago, son. Do I go to church? No, I don't. But would I consider myself a Protestant? Yes, certainly. Would I treat a fella differently the first time I met him if I knew he was a Catholic from around here?" He worked the gum in his mouth ruminatively. "Yes and no: No, because I don't care two hoots whether ye worship with priest or pastor. Buddhists, Muslims, Christians; aye, even those Hare Krishnas – it's all the same to me what ye believe in – see? So a Catholic's no different. Each to their own, I say. But, yes, because..." he shuffled awkwardly and articulated each word with considerable care, "... because I know that here in Belfast – if they were of a similar age to myself – they can't help but have watched what's played out in this province from the other side of the looking-glass, so to speak."

James nodded, encouraging him to carry on.

"I grew up in Fermanagh, right on the border with the Republic. Men were dragged from their beds prayin' and cursin' and shot by the Provos for no more than doin' business with squaddies. My own uncle was found in a field in '72, a bullet buried in his brain because he was a UDR man – a volunteer, like. He kept the peace and looked out for his own durin' the Troubles. He was off duty, tendin' cows in a field – he was just a farmer, but the Catholics wanted our land, ye see."

Doug's voice dropped a notch: "I tell ye, some would call it *ethnic cleansing*. They targeted the sons. They ensured that Protestant families had no-one to leave their land to, and in time they were displaced and the Catholics bought up their farms. Fuckin' brutal it was. That's why me mammy and daddy moved to Shankill when I was a kid – livin' on the border got too dangerous and they thought Shankill could give 'em some security. And if ye minded yer own business and kept to yerself, like, it probably was safer than the bandit-country I was brought up in."

He wound down the window and spat the gum onto the road. "It really was the Wild West back then, and what I saw growin' up in Fermanagh made me hate the IRA." He paused, "And Catholics too, I suppose. So naturally I'm more wary of 'em – more cautious, like – until I get to know 'em. And I know lots of 'em now, and I'd even count some of 'em as friends – of a sort. But's that's how it is here, sonny – certainly for folk of my age at least. Don't be fooled by this shiny new Belfast full of micro-breweries and tasting menus; peel away the fresh paint and plaster and you'll find a pox of bullet holes and a rawness that never goes away."

Doug had explained all of this as the pair pulled up beside the 200 foot tall Divis Tower – the top two floors of which had been converted into a British Army observation post in the 1970s giving their surveillance teams, and their snipers, a panoramic view of the sprawl of buildings that fractured off the Republican Falls Road and Loyalist Shankill.

"A wee lad was gunned to death in this very building in '69. Patrick Rooney – only nine years of age. Taken out with a volley of machine gun fire from an RUC armoured truck parked right over there." He nodded across the road. "The police said they were bein' fired at by an IRA sniper – they probably were – but turnin' a machine gun on a block of flats is cracked by anyone's standards; but back then, it was just another day."

They continued down the Falls Road. Spray painted murals flashed past them in colourful explosions of shamrock green, white and orange. Celtic knots bordered heroic scenes of Easter 1916. James recognised Collins and de Valera standing amongst the ruins of the General Post Office. Starving crofters stared listlessly from rural hovels, Gaelic script condemning the British of genocide. Long haired men in donkey jackets marched beneath Civil Rights banners, the faces of hunger strikers hovering benevolently above them. James saw a group of Far-Eastern tourists clustered below the image of Bobby Sands. They wore white grins as one of them balanced a selfie-stick. They cheered as the photo was taken, before a girl in pigtails broke rank and exchanged the camera at the end with her own. The grins were switched back on and the process repeated. James wondered whether any of them knew that the saintly-looking man floating above them took sixty-six days to wither away and die in the Maze prison. He kind of hoped they didn't.

"Clever lad that Bobby Sands," said Doug. "I remember the time well. It got awful bad in the '80s, for sure. A lot of drivers who do this tour are Catholics from around here, an' some of 'em knew the boy well. They tell me he was an artist; he used his body as a canvas. They say that he was one of the first to realise that Provo gunmen wearing balaclavas, shootin' soldiers and blowin' up pubs had turned them into hate figures, even within their own communities. And Sands wasn't wrong: everyone hated the Provisional IRA then."

He slowed the cab, so that James could make out the details of the mural.

"Now this Bobby Sands has a think and decides to become a martyr to the cause. There's naught a Catholic loves more than a martyr – there's barely one of their saints doesn't meet a grisly end at the hands of a lion or a Roman Emperor or some other heathen. What Sands wants to do by starvin' himself to death is to *take the gun out of equation*, see? Nobody gets hurt but him and his sacrifice makes more waves than some poor squaddie being shot up at an army checkpoint. And all he has to do for the IRA to claim the moral high ground is not eat – sounds easy right? Well, maybe not – but fair play to him: he stuck it out to the end and got what he wanted."

Doug barely took a breath. "Suddenly Provo murderers are saints, the British government are cold-hearted bastards and Maggie Thatcher's a war criminal. Then the Yanks pile in and condemn British policy, and obviously the Catholic Church makes out like Sands is fucking Jesus." His look hardened, and James saw a shadow of something unpleasant. "But we shed no tears back in Shankill. We raised a glass, cheered and wished him a speedy trip to hell. See, Sands *chose* to take his life which was a choice he never gave his victims. Got to hand it to him though – a clever ol' bastard. Anyway, let's drive ye somewhere that will look a little more like home."

But as the cab flitted past the red, white and blue kerb stones of Shankill and the Unionist murals of King Billy at the Boyne; the red hand of Ulster waving at him from every wall, James didn't feel any more at home than he would in Communist China, and he wondered why.

"Ye'll be glad to see some friendly faces, eh?" Doug nodded towards a twenty foot high depiction of the royal family. "Ye'll have lots of them in Yorkshire, I'll bet? What else? Let me guess – Trafalgar? The Falklands? Surely Waterloo?"

James didn't want to shatter Doug's illusion that mainland Britain and Northern Ireland were two peas in a pod, so he stammered, "We don't do the mural thing quite as much – but we, er…" Wracking his brains to think of some examples of nationalistic fervour, all that came to mind were EDL marches or visions of tipsy middle-Englanders waving flags at the Royal Albert Hall. "We're big on Remembrance Day," James came up with. "Poppies, bugles and TV schedules jam-packed with World War One documentaries come November."

"Oh, aye. We do the same – ye'll want to see this then…" Doug pulled up at the end of a terrace overlooking a large open space on which a half constructed tower of pallets was growing by the second as scruffy boys dragged anything even vaguely flammable towards the giant pyre.

"This is our Remembrance Day – if ye will. They're gettin' ready for the Eleventh. At midnight on Friday, we'll light the fires to welcome the Twelfth and then Belfast will see all the marchin' bands and Orange Lodges out and about celebratin' King Billy's victory in 1690."

James spied the green, white and orange of Eire's flag pinned to the sixty-foot construction and thought about mentioning the fact that the Queen didn't ceremonially burn a German flag as she laid a wreath at the cenotaph, but thought better of it. "Doesn't it stir up unneeded animosity with everybody over there?" James nodded back towards the Falls Road.

"Ach! It's just tradition, son! It's like Independence Day in the States – hell, we don't stop 'em going wild on Paddy's Day and drinkin' green Guinness or wearin' Easter lilies to remember the Sinn Féin Rebellion. Christ, we spent thirty years blowin' each other up, son, so a couple of wee fires and some flute music isn't goin' to start WWIII."

Completely covering the façade of the end terrace, James couldn't help but notice the huge mural depicting what looked like Ulster's answer to Eminem. Cool eyes appraised him from beneath a baseball cap worn back to front. A fat gold chain hung around a thick neck. Doug followed his gaze and his smile soured.

"Now that's what I was talkin' about before. Sectarianism divorced from any sense of tradition or religion. That's Stevie '*Top Gun*' McKeag: a bad man. He called himself an Ulster Freedom Fighter, but most of us older ones recognised him for what he was: a gangster and murderer, plain and simple. The wee lads you see about you watch too many Hollywood movies and listen to all this rap music and they think he was a hard man – a Loyalist hero. They idolise him. There's nothin' hard or heroic about shootin' women and shopkeepers and sellin' smack to your own community. *A bad man*: I raised a glass the night he died as well – in the quiet of my own home, obviously."

Doug shook his head and pulled out of the cul-de-sac and, as the image of Stevie McKeag shrank behind him, James wondered how far history had moulded the man he'd become or how much the man had chosen to pin a convenient history to his murderous nature.

"I am showing Daniel, *Image One.* Daniel, can you tell me what is happening here? Who is this person?"

The tape hissed.

"Daniel, this will help you. If you tell me about it, you will stop having nightmares. You'll sleep again. Is this a cow? Who is the man with the gun, Daniel?"

Again a sibilant pause.

And then, for the first time, James heard the voice of a man who had lived with, and worked for his great-grandfather a century earlier. He was surprised by the timbre of the old man's voice: he had been expecting to hear the frail and confused whispers of a geriatric teetering between this life and the next, but instead, Fallon spoke with a gruff Londonderry growl, paradoxically aggressive and defensive at the same time – like a bully whose voice had broken but still slept with the lights on for fear of wetting the bed.

"No one."

"Come on. These pictures you drew mean something. What do they mean, Daniel?"

"Nothing."

"Why is there blood on the boy's face? *Why* is he bleeding?"

"It's not his blood, ye stupid girl. It's the horse's. Idiot child shouldn't have talked back."

"Who hurt the horse Daniel? Was it you who…?"

233

"No." His voice sounded smug and superior. "Shootin' a horse isn't a crime in a time of war, is it?"

"Of course not. You were a soldier. You were fighting rebels. I understand. You must have fought alongside lots of other soldiers. Who is this soldier?"

Without hesitation this time. "Daly."

James realised that Alison was asking the same questions in different ways in order to trick the ravaged synapses into giving up their secrets.

"So Daly shot the horse as the rebel escaped – that's fine. What else could he do to stop him? It was war. What happened next, Daniel?"

James held his breath as the tape reels turned.

The bully broke and the bed-wetter croaked. "I watched. I just watched."

James heard sobbing now.

"Watched what, Daniel?"

From the speakers a sudden smashing. Thumps and grunts and stamping of feet collided together on tape.

"For the record," Alison half-shouted over the commotion, "Daniel has become very agitated and he is kicking and stamping and, I can only best describe it as rowing, like he is in a canoe – or punting."

An ear piercing howl cut her off and Daniel screamed. "Just watched. Always watching. So many."

"Daniel, calm down, calm down. Hush now. Well done. Come here, Daniel. OK, I will stop it here."

A dull click brought the interview to an end and James breathed deeply.

He realised that he had just heard a first-hand account of the murder of Michael Fahy. It *had* to be. It all tallied with the inquest report that he had read in Kew. The Riverstown Road as it emerged from the woods, the dead horse, the beaten boy.

Shit, this *was* huge. James was sitting with a box full of atrocities and a witness to them all. He realised that the shattered recollections of a dementia sufferer pieced together by an amateur psychologist wouldn't stand up in a court of law, but they didn't need to. They cast an entirely different perspective on the dry and brittle documents that had lain in dusty boxes on both sides of the Irish Sea since 1921. They were his means to reinterpret the past and maybe rehabilitate Sergeant Joseph Conlon. In the absence of any contrary evidence, James might be closer to the truth than anybody else in the last century.

This is for Pat-Joe, he thought as he slipped in the next tape and shuffled through the drawings to find the image that tallied.

"OK. It is the 4th April, 1986, and I am showing Daniel *image thirteen.*"

James examined the surreal scene before him. Dead centre, a giant face dominated the drawing. A man with dark hair and parting stared back at him, a scar stretched from his left ear towards his chin. He held an index finger to his mouth, bisecting a neatly coiffed moustache. In the background the sealed lips of the man representing Fallon held a gun towards a woman, whilst on the other side of the image another (or was it the same?) woman lay on the ground. Wire-like strands of hair snaked from her scalp and her white legs were splayed open, a puddle of blood between them.

"Daniel, what is happening here? Who is this man? Is this what I think it is? Daniel?"

Once more the tape hissed before the old man started to speak.

"Shhh!" he whispered into the microphone. "Billy told me, 'Shhh! Or else'."

Alison's voice again: "For the tape, Daniel is drawing a finger across his throat."

36

26th November, 1920
Slattery's Bar, Birr, King's County, Ireland

It was ten days since they'd been stopped on the road.

Ten days since Maggie Fahy had watched as her sister was dragged by her hair into the bushes by the side of the track.

Ten days since she had stared into the obsidian blackness of the barrel of the gun, trying to block out the grunts and slaps she heard coming from the agitated undergrowth.

And only six days since Carmel had stopped bleeding.

And when she looked at her younger sister, Maggie could see that the child wasn't the only thing that had died in Carmel that day.

In Dublin, less than a week before, a detachment of Black and Tans had opened fire on spectators at a Gaelic football match. Twelve died and scores more were injured in the stampede that followed. So Maggie was acutely aware that her sister's personal tragedy at the hands of the Tan had been cruelly reflected and amplified by what the national press were already calling 'Bloody Sunday'. Maggie dreaded to think what thoughts smouldered behind her sister's lightless eyes.

Carmel watched the group of Englishmen in the corner of the bar unblinkingly. She exhaled; cigarette smoke curled from her nostrils, snaking across her line of sight, as solid as silk and white as snow. And still Carmel didn't blink.

The iron tang of blood clung to her still: she could taste it when she swallowed and smell it on her skin and in her hair, and no amount of scrubbing could shake off its insidious stench. She could even *see* it, flushing the cheeks of the drunken Tans, pulsing through the swollen veins in their throats.

Waiting to be spilt.

It was nice to get away from the claustrophobic atmosphere of the barracks, and if he was honest, Eddie Miller thought to himself, it was nice to get away from some of the men with whom he shared a uniform. That Billy Jardine unnerved him and the complicated religious divisions that simmered beneath the surface made Eddie terrified to say anything for fear of offending someone over something he just didn't understand. At least Pallister, West and Simons didn't seem to be too religious. Like him they were all Englishmen, and the way Eddie saw it, all the more civilised for that. They liked beer, football and playing cards. Simple things that Eddie could understand.

So they had come to Slattery's tonight. Unlike most of the pubs around here, they seemed very welcome. Ted Slattery had shaken their hands as they came in and sat them at a table in the corner. Frothing pints and a rough loaf had arrived almost as soon as they'd sat down and the stoat-faced publican told them they could settle the tab at the end of the night and winked. It was West who'd brought them here: he had gleaned that Slattery's offered a very different type of evening to what they had experienced heretofore in Birr. He said that it was a '*Parisian establishment*', and those who'd served in France nodded, smiling slyly at one another. Eddie understood what had made them leer as soon as he walked in.

There were women here.

Eddie had never been to a public house frequented by women before. Back home, although daughters or wives sometimes slipped through saloon doors and timidly approached the bar to buy take-out pots for husbands or fathers, they'd never dare sit unchaperoned to have a drink themselves. But here couples skulked in shadowy booths, women sat at bar stools sipping half pints, and single girls stood at the bar smiling at the men as they ordered drinks.

In fact, on the far side of the room, Eddie had noticed one girl who couldn't take her eyes off him. She was smoking a cigarette and sitting with a friend who seemed nervous. Eddie had never been good with words, but she was looking at him almost *hungrily*. He felt his cheeks redden and his mouth dry. Eddie smiled back, and almost choked on his beer. He had heard Jardine damn the local womenfolk as 'dirty Fenian sluts' – but from where he was sitting, surely this was a good thing. If these were Catholic girls, then Eddie wished there were a few more of them back home in the Fens.

———

In the end it had almost been too easy. Christ, men were stupid – or they didn't think with anything other than what they kept in their trousers. But wasn't that why she had chosen him in the first place? Easy prey; naïve, unsuspecting and so very keen.

A conversation at the bar as he bought some cigarettes, a round of drinks and an accepted request to walk her home: that's all it took.

She had watched as he turned and grinned at the other Tans and thrown a handful of coins across the table. She shivered with revulsion as he slipped his arm into hers. As the door closed behind them and Carmel felt the cold breath of the November night on her bare chest, he asked whether she was worried about being seen with him as he wouldn't want her to get into trouble with the Shinners. She laughed a little too sharply and told him there was no chance of that, and he looked puzzled for a moment.

They walked arm in arm along Compton Road and Carmel almost lost her nerve, but she forced herself to relive each stabbing thrust, to feel the stubble rake her neck, the muscular fingers smothering her and the rancid whisper spat into her ear as the Scotsman finished: *"Sergeant Conlon sends his regards to yer husband, Mrs O'Rourke. I'm jus' the delivery boy."*

And she could taste the blood in the back of her throat again and the ache in her womb; so she led the Englishman onwards toward the river.

When they reached the Oxmantown Bridge, Carmel checked to see that there was nobody watching them, other than her sister of course, who'd followed discreetly and kept to the shadows.

"Under here. It's dry and nobody will hear us," she said, leading the policeman under the arches. She turned her back to him and asked, "Could ye unhook me, there's a clasp at the top?"

Feeling his sweaty fingers fumble with the hook, she took the Webley revolver from her clutch bag and turned back to face him.

"I know yer not the one, but ye'll have to do, so you will. I am sorry, soldier."

The blood drained from the ruddy cheeks of Eddie Miller as he faced death in exactly the same way as he'd stumbled through most of his life: thoroughly baffled by this strange turn of events.

37

Summer, 2018
Belfast, Northern Ireland

James had listened, taken notes and was beginning to understand the cyclical nature of action and reaction – of atrocity and reprisal – that had stained the streets and charred the buildings of Birr between 1919-21. He had heard Daniel Fallon, both in bursts of cathartic clarity and in drawn out minutes of confused and defensive obfuscation, recount a catalogue of crimes that included rape, torture, reprisal and murder. James had pored over disturbing images of drowned men, smoking crofts and bullet pocked townhouses and using O'Rourke's book, he'd been able to match a number of Fallon's wild nightmares to events mentioned by the IRA man.

The body floating in the water, referred to on tape as '*wee Eddie from England*' must have been Constable Edward Miller. O'Rourke claimed he had been executed by an unnamed IRA operative in November 1920, his body dumped in the Camcor River. According to the book, this in turn led to a reprisal raid by the Black and Tans on a bar called Slattery's. Fallon's drawing of a building belching smoke from a shattered doorframe above which an illegible sign swung, tallied with O'Rourke's typically lurid description of a drunken posse of Black and Tans razing the bar to the ground later that same month.

It was disheartening all this death and hatred. The number of tapes he must still listen to was daunting, and a cursory glance through the remaining sketches gave James a very good idea what was coming. His stomach twisted with anxiety as he held an image of a dead policeman lying in a pool of blood beneath a bright red door. A woman and a girl stood over his body. Equally distressing was an image that he was sure represented the Galross Massacre: bodies outside a burning farmhouse, one of whom wore a cross around his neck whilst blood trickled from a hole in his forehead. Upstairs in a window, a blond-haired girl screamed. And in all of these crude images there was pretty much one constant: the zip-lipped figure of Fallon and the moustached character whose eyes seemed to become more demonic in each depiction – the man that James assumed must be the Glaswegian, William Jardine. The one who would slit Fallon's throat if he talked about what he'd seen.

James sighed and picked up the next cassette. He was leafing through the drawings, searching for the corresponding image when he heard the shrill rubber yelp of tyres turning sharply. A powerful engine whined, accelerating towards him at speed. Bright beams of light flashed across concrete before focusing their blinding glare directly into his rear view mirror. James squinted and covered his eyes. A bank of white flooded his peripheral vision as a van screeched to a halt a mere half metre from his right ear.

Irritated that in an empty carpark some idiots had pulled up so close that he couldn't open his door, James glared up at the face in the passenger seat window and was unsurprised to see a feral youth eye him coldly.

All at once he heard the slamming of doors, the squeak of trainers; a splash of colour flitted across his rear window before simultaneously both far side doors opened and two men bundled in. The man in the front swept the tapes and sketches into the foot well and lunged at him whilst the blur in the backseat dove behind the driver's seat and James felt ice-cold steel nuzzle his neck.

It had all happened so quickly that the simple exclamation, "Wha…" remained unfinished – James just swallowed and looked at the man who leant across and grinned at him with stained teeth.

"James Lucas. How are ye? We've been watchin' ye – for a good while now, so we have – and we thought it time we had a little chat wit' ye."

And suddenly all the horrors on the pages and on the net, on the tapes and in the archives and in his head – always once-removed from reality – manifested themselves into this man of flesh and bone, who leered at him from the passenger seat.

38

Summer, 2018
Belfast, Northern Ireland

"It seems to me that ye've been keepin' some very poor company, Jimmy. It's not so nice for me to see an Englishman trottin' about our island, sobbin' at the graves of traitors, rubbin' shoulders with Orangemen in West Derry an' crusin' round the Shankill Road takin' pictures of pyres with tricolours pinned to the top o' them. Especially considerin' that it was yer traitor great-grandaddy that murdered plenty of patriots, made their wives widows and left their kids fatherless."

The man was thin and sinewy – his complexion grey and unhealthy. White stubble grew over his narrow chin and gaunt cheekbones and his closely cropped hair was peppered with nicotine-coloured strands of fading ginger. He smelt of stale sweat; his sour breath reeked of cigarettes, cheap whiskey and fried chicken.

"Aye, we've been followin' ye, wonderin' what yer game is. See we don't want you comin' over here, twistin' truths an' stickin' yer nose into things that are none o' yer business, Englishman. Yer Sergeant Conlon was a murderin' traitor, an' yer ol' man in the home knows it well, so he does. And if he thinks any different, at least he's been wise enough to keep his mouth shut about his daddy all these years. But ye're a different kettle o' fish entirely. Ye are open about it, like. Challengin' us on our own feckin' history. An' that's gonna piss us off, so it is.

"Ye can tell by the gun at yer neck that we are deadly serious. An' let me tell ye – I *have* killed men in the name of the Republic, so don't think I'll sweat over one more."

He paused to let that sink in.

"I hear ye've some good family back in Tipperary – so my colleagues down there tell me anyhow – an' that's the only reason I am givin' ye a warnin' first. Feck off back to England, Jimmy, an' never set foot in County Offaly again, or, so-help-me-God, I will do to ye what Ciaran Fahy did to your great-granddaddy."

James heard a metallic click below his left ear. The muzzle of the gun kissed him coldly.

"Consider yerself a marked man, Jimmy boy."

And with that he was gone.

Only the foulness of his words hung in the air.

As the white van with southern plates reversed and, with shriek of wheels, lurched forwards and around the ramp, James finally breathed out.

His car doors were still open and a gust of wind caught Fallon's drawings, whirled them round the foot well and dropped them, lifeless again.

James shivered.

He had naïvely likened the poisonous legacy of the Irish struggle to a decomposing corpse weighed to the bottom of a bog: conveniently invisible but still capable of fomenting rancid bubbles that surfaced in the backroom bars of the Bogside and the Orange Lodges of Fermanagh. Sat here in the pallid light of a Belfast carpark, having come face to face with some splinter group of the Real IRA, James realised that this corpse had dislodged itself from its ghastly moorings and was surging, bloated and gaseous, upwards into his present.

And, more than that, he acknowledged that Noel, Oisín, his mother and even the old woman in the graveyard had all been right – had he cared to listen: if you go prodding stagnant waters, there's a very real chance the dead will reach out to drag you down with them.

Part IV

The Things I Cannot Change

Hello, Hello
We are the Billy Boys
Hello, Hello
You'll know us by our noise
We're up to our knees in Fenian blood
Surrender or you'll die
For we are the Brigton Billy Boys

39

Summer, 2018
The Belfast-Cairnryan Ferry

"And you didn't call the police?! You're not bloody Robert Langdon from the Da Vinci Code, James. You are a secondary school teacher from Wetherby, and this is real life!"

James winced, creating a little space between his right ear and the mobile phone.

"Charlie, I couldn't. They obviously know who I am, and who my family are. They were stalking me – they almost ran me over in Derry, and they must have even followed me to Clonmel. What can the police do anyway? It was a rented white van, probably hired under a false name – and even if they got lucky and caught the guy who warned me off, do you think he hasn't got friends who might finish what he started?"

"And how exactly do they know who you are?"

"I've told you: I don't know. It could have been anyone." James realised that this was an understatement. "I had to leave my name and address at the library – with a descendant of O'Rourke as it happens. Oisín knew what I was researching and where I was staying. Dooley's had my details too and I'm sure that lad on reception was listening as I told you about the spot where Conlon was shot. Christ, even the scary lady I met in a graveyard knew who I was and what I was doing in Birr. It's a small place, Charlie, and I wasn't very subtle in my investigations. I'm sorry."

"Well if you are so sorry, why are you on your way to Glasgow and not just coming home?"

A good question. He couldn't tell her the truth: that his guilt over Connor's death had somehow transposed itself onto his need to see Conlon vindicated. For his own sake, he *had* to prove that Joseph Conlon was innocent; he had no choice. However, James recognised that another factor was also at play: once the shock of the encounter in the carpark had dissipated, James had experienced what could only be described as an irrational frisson of excitement. He might not be on the verge of debunking two thousand years of Christian dogma like the fictional Robert Langdon, but he *had* genuinely uncovered a secret; one that had lain hidden for over four generations. He was within touching distance of finishing something that had started a century ago.

And Billy Jardine was the key to it all.

There were still Jardines in Glasgow: William Jardine had married in 1939 and had a son and daughter. His daughter had never married and died in the early '90s but his son, Alec, was still alive and, according to the family tree that James had built using Jardine's service number and date of birth, he had fathered two sons, another William and a Robert.

"I am going to Glasgow because I am *so* close, honey. I really think my great-grandfather was innocent. I believe it was this Jardine. I just don't quite understand how Sergeant Conlon came to be blamed for it whilst the real criminals escaped justice. Even if I can't clear his name, I need to know how it happened."

Charlie was silent on the other end of the phone. He could picture her lips, pursed in disapproval.

"Look, I might not find anything, in which case I'll be home in a couple of days and I swear that I will forget all about it. But, Charlie, I have spent the last twenty years of my life studying history, reading other people's books and recycling other people's arguments; but by doing this, for the very first time, I could change the past. *I would be rewriting history*, Charlie."

"Listen to yourself, James. I'm worried about you. I think that being suspended from work has unhinged you or something. It's dangerous!"

"I admit I was naïve in Birr. I didn't listen to advice and I put myself in a vulnerable position, but I am going to be much more discreet in Glasgow. I have booked a B&B on the outskirts of town that only takes cash. I have given a false name. I picked up a pay-as-you-go mobile this morning and I am going to make sure that I leave no clues about who I am if I end up treading on anybody's toes. Trust me, Charlie, it will be OK. I promise."

"It's not OK, James. You're playing detective, and maybe putting your life at risk, and to what end? What's the ultimate goal here? Are you going to the press with this? Are you planning to write a book? Make a bloody documentary? And if you do, won't the IRA come and find you? Can't you see this is crazy?"

It didn't matter, as long as he found out the truth.

He'd told himself that if he did go public, he would ensure that there was no paper trail. He could publish in some obscure historical periodical. He wouldn't use his own name, of course – and even if the IRA did chance upon the article, the fact that Jardine was a Black and Tan would surely give them an even more credible focus for their hatred anyway. James had toyed with a title: *The Breaking and the Making of a Villain: Reinterpreting the Galross Massacre, by Sarah Dexter.* He had decided to swap gender to muddy the waters even further. But first he had to track down the surviving Jardines and quiz them on their progenitor.

"Charlie, you're breaking up," James fibbed. "My signal is cutting in and out. Look, I'll call you tomorrow when I am in Glasgow, OK? I love you."

"James? James?"

251

He hung up.

He looked out the window at the rolling blackness of the Irish Sea: a solitary pin-prick of light winked on the horizon. The bar was closing for the night and a lonely-looking man in tracksuit and trainers wobbled across the deck gripping two plastic glasses half full with amber liquid and ice. James watched as he sat and downed the first, then savoured the second. From a holdall on the floor, the man rummaged around and dug out a cap. He put it on, pulling the peak low over his eyes and wriggled back into the chair, propping his feet on the seat opposite. It was a New York Yankees cap – almost exactly the same as Connor had been wearing the night before he died. James didn't know if it was a sudden swell in the sea, or something else, but his stomach turned and he suddenly felt very sick.

That final evening together had been awkward to begin with despite the familiar sounds and smells of their favourite pub off Kilburn High Road. The friends hadn't seen each other for a while and James was acutely aware that Connor had just done a stretch at Wormwood Scrubs for handling stolen goods. James, by comparison, was in his second year of teaching at King Henry's Grammar School and had recently bought a flat with Charlie. He'd done a lot of growing up in the time they'd been together and that night he'd been anxious that Connor was high, but his friend swore blind that he was clean; nothing harder than the odd line from time to time – and the weed of course.

QPR were on the big screen and the green glare from the pitch made Connor look even more pallid than he was. He was on the Jamesons as he said his digestive system couldn't cope with pints anymore. James was worried about him; but as the evening wore on, the two friends had relaxed and fell back into the comfortable banter that had characterised their adolescence. By the time James stood to order a fifth round, it felt like old times again.

Connor suggested they nip outside for a quick spliff. James declined, almost bashfully, explaining that since he'd started teaching he'd given it all up. It felt a bit hypocritical; besides there was nothing worse than experiencing the Tuesday Blues in front of a class of precocious teenagers.

Inevitably the conversation turned to Connor's moment of mad self-sacrifice when he'd allowed the trajectory of James's life to continue without deviation whilst ensuring his own was sent into tail-spin. It had been the summer of '93. Connor had long before dropped out of school with a handful of qualifications, whereas James was virtually guaranteed a place at Newcastle University as long as he didn't crash and burn in his A-Levels. They'd spent the afternoon cruising bars in Kilburn; Connor still using fake ID as he wasn't quite eighteen. Earlier, James had hooked up with a friend of a friend to procure a festival-pack of goodies; a freezer-bag filled with enough chemical stimulants to see him and four fellow school-leavers through their post exam blowout at Glastonbury. Unwisely, the pair had decided to sample the wares in a pub around the corner from Connor's flat. They were none too subtle either. About twenty minutes later, a uniform strolled in and the barman nodded towards their booth.

James had his back to the door, but Connor had clocked the tip-off. He hissed, "Quick! Pass me the baggie! Now! Pass it under the table. There's a copper comin'."

James protested weakly.

"For fuck's sake, James, gimme it! What have I gotta lose compared to ye? You can owe me one. Right?"

James had slipped the bag under the table shamefully.

Neither of them could have predicted the consequences: the magistrate came down on Connor like a tonne of bricks. He was sentenced with possession with intent to supply and served six weeks in a Young Offenders Institute. He was never the same again; when he came out, it was obvious that he'd graduated to harder drugs. James went to university and Connor went back to the building sites and their lives diverged for the first time since they were seven years old. They saw each other less frequently, and that wasn't just because of the distance between London and the North East. Despite the eternal gratitude that James would feel towards Connor, he couldn't handle the burden of responsibility that he felt had been thrust upon him by Connor's act of selflessness.

So that is why he didn't hesitate when Connor asked him, that last night of his life, if there was any chance that James could sub him some rent money – just fifty quid until the foreman paid him at the end of the week. James didn't have the cash on him, but they finished their drinks and walked up to an ATM by the Tube station. Connor seemed twitchy as James entered his PIN number; he was dragging deeply on a cigarette and bouncing on the balls of his feet. When James handed over the notes, they had embraced and he'd wondered at how skinny his friend was and questioned what use he'd be on a building site.

Naïve fool.

He should have known that Connor was still using. It was obvious.

Strangely, it had been James's mother who'd called him in Leeds a few days later to break the news. She'd kept in touch with Brenda McCleary – not socially of course – but through Christmas cards and letters, some containing small cheques. James was touched that Cate, on some level at least, still had an affinity for those who'd come to London like her from the boreens of Ireland, yet not experienced the same good fortune.

She told him that Connor had been found on Sunday morning behind a curtain in a squat he co-habited with dead-beats and travellers from Australia and New-Zealand. He was stone cold, eyes wide open; a needle hanging limply from his arm.

James was beyond consolable.

At the time Charlie had been bewildered by his mad grief, but had stood by him as he ditched his job at King Henry's and scoured the TES for teaching positions in the toughest schools in the region. Was it self-flagellation? James didn't know; but it had helped numb the guilt; and now he might not even have the job to go back to.

All the more reason to make this count.

He *was* going to follow this through to the end; whatever it took.

The man in the baseball cap started to snore. James flipped open his laptop and connected to the on-board WiFi. He typed the name 'Billy Jardine' into the search engine and started to scroll through the thousands of hits; looking for anything that could help him. Hidden amongst the myriad of Facebook and Linkedin profiles, James came across something that chilled and thrilled him in equal measure.

Charlie was right.

This *was* crazy.

40

THE GLASGOW TRIBUNE

Monday 2nd December 2007

The Enduring Legacy of
Sectarian Violence On The Streets
of Glasgow

*Part One of a Two Part Exposé on Three Generations of the
Most Dangerous Family in Scotland*
By Moira Dunn

They sat, drinking pints and cheering on their team in the Highlander's Arms in the Calton. It was the 26th May, 2007 and for Celtic supporters not lucky enough to get tickets for the game at Hampden Park, this pub was where they would watch their team attempt to win the Scottish Cup for a record 34th time.

Hopes were high.

A month earlier Celtic had secured their second consecutive title, beating Rangers with four matches to spare; and their opponents in the Cup Final were lowly Dunfermline Athletic who had finished at the foot of the table and were duly relegated.

However, the game wasn't as one-sided as they had hoped. The deadlock was only broken in the 84th minute courtesy of a Jean-Joël Perrier-Doumbé strike. As the ball hit the back of the net, the pub exploded with joy.

Little did anyone know, that had Robert 'Rabb' Jardine had his way, there would have been a very different kind of explosion in the Highlander's Arms that afternoon and that very few Celtic supporters would have been alive in the 84th minute to celebrate the winning goal.

Unbeknownst to the general public, Strathclyde Police had raided a flat in the Bridgeton area of East Glasgow three days earlier after an anonymous tip off. There they had arrested Rabb Jardine on charges of terrorism, attempted murder and membership of a proscribed organisation. The organisation in question has been named as the Red Hand Defenders (RHD), an Ulster Loyalist paramilitary group responsible for a number of killings since the Good Friday Agreement of 1998. Within the Bridgeton flat, police discovered bomb-making equipment, plans of the Highlander's Arms, a Celtic shirt and sports bag which contained an explosive device primed with a timer that could be set for any time up to an hour.

Last Thursday, the jury at the High Court trial, held in Edinburgh due to the sensitivity of the case in the Strathclyde area, unanimously returned a verdict of guilty on all charges. The following day, Judge Lord Cameron sentenced Mr Jardine to 27 years imprisonment.

However, Rabb Jardine is not the first member of his family to face charges originating from religious hatred. He is just the latest in a long line of Jardines who have targeted Catholics and Irish Republicans both in Scotland and Ulster over the last 80 years.

'BILLY' JARDINE AND THE RISE OF THE RAZOR GANGS

At the end of WWI, William Robert Jardine was demobbed and returned home to Glasgow. He had signed up in 1916 after lying about his age on his enlistment form. When he was deployed in August 1917 at the Third Battle of Ypres, more commonly known as Passchendaele, he had just turned seventeen. We will never know whether the horrors he witnessed in the mud of Flanders brutalised him or the tough tenements of the East End of Glasgow; but brutalised he was. From the moment of his return to Scotland in November 1918, his long and colourful life was to be characterised by violence; violence of a distinctly *sectarian* nature.

'Billy' Jardine struggled to find work in the slump that followed the armistice of 1918 and public records show that he was arrested and charged with affray in 1919. He was one of many involved in a fracas at Tollbooth Cross, in the course of which he sustained a serious facial injury. However, the case collapsed due to the inconsistency of witness statements.

Aged only nineteen and already a veteran of the Great War, Jardine enlisted to join the Royal Irish Constabulary (RIC) in 1920 where he served for the duration of the Irish War of Independence. Jardine was one of many 'Black and Tans' who were sent to crush the burgeoning Irish Republican Army that was being directed from Dublin by Michael Collins. The 'Tans' carved out a fearsome reputation for themselves and Jardine would have been able to act upon his extreme prejudice against the Roman Catholic majority of the island. As most official documents relating to Black and Tan atrocities were destroyed in the storming of the Four Courts in 1922, many of the tales told are apocryphal and this chapter of Billy Jardine's life is shrouded in mystery.

We do know that when Billy Jardine returned to Bridgeton in 1922, the sectarian violence endemic across Ireland was very much alive and kicking on the streets of Glasgow. The overcrowding and poverty the city was experiencing in those years was blamed in some quarters on the influx of Irish immigrants seeking employment in the shipyards of the Clyde.

The *Glasgow Herald* wrote in 1922 that, *"Ireland has been responsible for more of our social trouble in Glasgow than the war and Bolshevist propaganda combined."*

It seems clear that Jardine concurred with this opinion as court records show that he was first sent to the 'Big House' – that is Barlinnie prison on the Eastern outskirts of the city – for six months' hard labour after being found guilty of slashing the face of one John Shannon on the 17th March, 1923. Shannon had been a member of the Catholic gang, the Calton Kent Star, and had been celebrating St. Patrick's Day. Witnesses claim to have heard Jardine scream, "This will wipe the smile aff yer Fenian face, ye Mick bastard!"

The next time that Jardine came to the attentions of the police was in 1925 and the circumstances were also deeply mired in sectarian hatred. It was Saturday, 11th July and almost 50,000 had gathered on Cathedral Street for the annual Orange Walk from the Grand Lodge Headquarters to Springboig and back. As the procession of marching bands moved through the Calton, a small number of Orangemen broke off the main phalanx and made their way to Abercromby Street. Considered a hotbed of Republicanism after the alleged Sinn Féin killers of Detective Inspector Robert Johnstone were discovered there in 1921, these Orangemen intended to vent their hatred on the Catholic residents of this *'Shinner Street'*.

That day Sinn Féin flags hung proudly from the tenement windows of Abercromby Street and the sound of Irish fiddles drowned out the brass of the marching bands. Bottles and stones were hurled at these flags by the rogue Orangemen and a street fight began in which fifty were arrested. One of those was Billy Jardine who was using his own flute to beat a sixteen-year-old boy, Séan Creasey, about the head. He was found guilty of affray and sentenced to thirty days back in the 'Big House'.

Evidently, in the latter years of the 1920s, Billy Jardine was rising through the ranks of the Brigton Billy Boys: the largest and most organised of the 'razor gangs' of Glasgow. Led by the charismatic Billy Fullerton, the gang numbered between 500 and 800 at its peak. The organisation included committees, secretaries and treasurers along with a strict code of discipline. Membership cards pledged to 'uphold King and Country' and 'to defend other Protestants', and if these basic tenets were breached then court-martials could be held and a range of punishments meted out on the transgressor. Each gang member paid a weekly subscription, which not only covered fines accrued by the 'foot soldiers' for street violence but also ensured that they could count on the representation of the city's best lawyers when their more prominent members were sent to court.

Evidence that Billy Jardine was amongst the elite of the organisation is demonstrated by his miraculous acquittal in 1929: After being arrested for the attempted murder of a San Toy gangster, Kieran Doughty, who had been stabbed three times with a bayonet, Jardine was brought before the court. Doughty survived the attack, naming Billy Jardine as his attacker. The case collapsed after Jardine's lawyer belatedly produced seven witnesses who testified that Jardine spent the entire evening in *The Duke*, a popular public house near Bridgeton Cross. These witnesses notwithstanding, Jardine's lawyer somehow managed to persuade Kieran Doughty to retract his statement. Doughty claimed that in retrospect he realised that Jardine had been wrongfully arrested by the 'busies' in a case of mistaken identity. Despite the judge having reservations about the veracity of these new depositions, without a single witness willing to testify against him, the case was thrown out of court and Billy Jardine walked free.

It seemed as if Billy Jardine had got away with an awful lot, thought James.

He skimmed through the rest of the article. According to Moira Dunn, Jardine had assumed an *'air of respectability'* in the 1930s. He opened a laundry business on London Road in 1931 and formally joined the Orange Order becoming a *Brother* at the Hall on Worcester Street in the East End of the city. The journalist implied that despite widespread acknowledgement that Jardine was heavily financed by the criminal underworld, his public association with respectable Presbyterian ministers and other establishment Unionists, including Glasgow's Tory MPs, kept him at arm's length from Chief Constable Percy Sillitoe – the fabled 'gang-buster' of the 1930s who went a long way towards *'cleaning up the streets of Glasgow'*, as she phrased it.

James noted that Jardine even managed to marry respectably: in 1939 he wed nineteen-year-old Emmeline Dalziel, the daughter of the Worshipful Master of the Worcester Street Lodge. Although arraigned on a number of charges over these years, ranging from tax evasion to money-laundering, nothing ever stuck and Jardine would never find himself incarcerated at Barlinnie again.

What James found interesting was that Jardine began to return to Northern Ireland on a regular basis in the 1930s and '40s, forging strong links with a number of Orange Lodges in Ulster. After the premature death of his wife in the late 1940s, Jardine sent his children to live with a Loyalist family in Omagh. By now he was Treasurer of the Orange Hall on Worcester Street and ran the youth wing of the Lodge. Dunn wrote that the remote relationship between father and only son, Alec, served to engender an acute sense of hero worship in the boy and might well have been part of the reason that Alec followed Billy into the police force in 1963. The article finished by setting up a 'taster' of the second part of the exposé which would focus on Alec Jardine's RUC career in Enniskillen, which was cut short amid allegations of collusion with paramilitary Loyalist organisations during the Troubles. Even more salaciously, Dunn promised first-hand testimonies of serious wrong doing within the Worcester Street Orange Lodge in Glasgow.

Wow.

Out of the frying pan and into the fire, thought James.

He probably shouldn't tell Charlie any of this when he arrived in Glasgow – she would drive up herself and drag him back home – but it reinforced his belief that Jardine was behind it all.

He checked his watch and started looking online for the link to the second half of Moira Dunn's article, but twenty five minutes later as the tannoy asked passengers to return to their cars for disembarkation, James was beginning to think that the article didn't exist.

There was absolutely no trace of it anywhere.

41

Summer, 2018
Glasgow, Scotland

It had been a frustrating three days.

James had arrived at Hamilton House B&B on Tuesday morning and it was now Thursday evening. He had spent that first afternoon scouring microfilm of old editions of the *Glasgow Tribune* at the Mitchell Library trying to locate the second part of the 'Jardine expose' in hard copy – but to no avail. Some basic detective work and a couple of phone calls had led him to the discovery that Moira Dunn had left the employment of the Tribune in 2007 and moved away from Glasgow. She now worked on a local newspaper in Pitlochry – *The Press* – and although James had rung the office number dozens of times, it had always been engaged. Either Pitlochry was in the eye of a current affairs storm or the receptionist had a talkative best friend. So James had sent a couple of emails to the address given on *The Press* website, but was still waiting for Moira Dunn to get back to him.

More promisingly however, late on Tuesday night, after hours of trawling through the millions of hits associated with male members of the Jardine family, James had chanced upon a blog that could be found at *https:/xiiviis.scotsblog.co.uk*. The site was ostensibly a homage to Glasgow Rangers and the Orange Order.

It was filled with links to YouTube clips of football chants and marching songs and there was a gallery of images which James scrolled through. Narrow-eyed men in Rangers tops; their pasty skin scrawled with tattoos, glared from the screen holding cans of Tennent's lager. Click to the right and the same men posed before landmarks in Glasgow, West Londonderry and Belfast now wearing black suits, white gloves, orange collarettes and bowler hats. James followed one of the YouTube links and, accompanied by a playful melody, an animated football bounced across the lyrics:

Hello! Hello!
We are the Billy Boys.
We're up to our knees in Fenian blood.
Surrender or you'll die!
For we are the Brigton Billy Boys!

Charming, thought James. He never ceased to be amazed by sinister truths lurking between the lines of ancient nursery rhymes: the bubonic plague in *Ring a Ring o' Roses*, Mary Tudor's still-born children in *Mary, Mary Quite Contrary* and the incredibly upbeat *London's Burning*. However, to think that this song was still spat at Celtic fans by the bigots who posted on this blog made him question whether anything had changed in three hundred years.

The message board which had lain dormant for most of the year, bar the predicable spleen of malice around the Old Firm derbies, had come to life with a flurry of activity over the last few weeks as the *'Glorious Twelfth'* approached. James had realised that he was on the right track when he spotted that the webmaster, WeeBJ127, had posted that Alec Jardine would be leading the celebrations at the Worcester Street Orange Hall on Saturday 12th. WeeBJ127 had written that he was, *'stoked that Da is back in Glesga for the weeknd! #NaeSurrender'*.

He had found them.

Both Alec and William Jardine Jnr were going to be a couple of miles from where he was sitting in four days' time.

So James had contacted WeeBJ127 that night and pitched what he hoped would be a convincing and intriguing reason for them to meet up. He used the alias *Alistair Dewar*, whom in reality was an acquaintance from university who'd published a couple of obscure sociology texts a decade ago before converting to Islam, changing his name and moving to Indonesia with his new wife. James had decided to work on the webmaster's vanity and claimed in his email that he was researching a book called, *True Brits – The Forgotten Patriots of the British Isles.* He wrote that in the wake of the Brexit vote he'd been visiting the parts of the United Kingdom that clung to a distinctly 'British' identity. It had been when he was interviewing members of the Loyalist community in West Londonderry – he could use Kenneth Fallon's name if he had to – that he had first come across the Jardine clan, and the more he delved into their family history, the more he found that they encapsulated a sense of Britishness that had been lost since the Second World War. He let it be known in his email that he was especially keen to hear about the two elder Jardines' experiences of trying to counter Republicanism in Ireland, and that he was willing to let WeeBJ127 set the record straight over what happened to his brother, Rabb, in 2007.

But since Tuesday; nothing.

James had tramped the streets, visited museums, consumed a lot of coffee and waited. He had checked his emails every twenty minutes or so and pawed his pay-as-you-go phone constantly.

If nobody got back to him, should he try to gate crash the Twelfth at the Worcester Street Lodge on Saturday?

Should he jump in his car now, drive up to Pitlochry, skirt past the chatty receptionist and march over to Moira Dunn's desk and demand answers?

James reasoned that if neither got back to him voluntarily then it was unlikely that either party would appreciate him barging into their lives uninvited.

Maybe it was time to go home to Charlie?

It was at that moment that his laptop informed him he had mail: WeeBJ127 wanted to meet him tomorrow night; the 11th of July.

There couldn't be a more apposite date.

42

Summer, 2018
Pitlochry, Scotland

Moira Dunn was adding the final touches to an article about the local council's plans to remove the recycling containers from the Tesco carpark when the email arrived.

The surname mentioned in the title of the message set off a decade-old sense of panic and Moira started scratching obsessively at a dry patch of eczema on her left wrist. She pulled her arms to her chest, pushed her chair from the kitchen table and stared at the name: Jardine.

Without taking her eyes from the digital envelope that flashed from her inbox, she reached across, almost knocking over a cold cup of coffee and grabbed her cigarettes. With trembling hands she fumbled with the packet, pulled one out and lit it. Inhaling deeply, she regarded the unwanted intrusion into her life. She imagined that if she opened the message, like one of those Trojan horse emails that infect your computer with a deadly virus, she would herself be poisoned by the words it contained.

It had been over ten years since she had published the ill-conceived feature in the Monday supplement. By 9.02 that morning, lawyers had been on the phone to her editor and by midday, the IT team were struggling to cope with the deluge of posts to the newspaper's website that actively incited violence against her.

The editor at the time had been an ambitious arsehole, half her age, who wanted to take on the big nationals. He had played hardball with the Jardines' lawyers telling them that he'd see them in court. All the facts the Tribune had used *and were going to use in the second part of the piece* were verifiable, he claimed; they wouldn't retract a word. Sales for that edition were up 37% on typical Mondays and the editor wanted to capitalise on this interest. He even encouraged the furore that developed over the week. Moira was obviously unnerved by the faceless threats clogging her inbox, but had been 'youngish' at the time and still possessed that crusading zeal that journalists cling to until they realise that life's just too short; so she had been persuaded to stick to her guns and even expand on the article before the next instalment went to press.

It was only when she realised that she'd been followed home by a man in a hoody who stood smoking outside her window that she started to reconsider.

When she received the phone call half an hour later explaining in no uncertain terms what would happen to her if anything was published about the Worcester Street Lodge, she decided to speak with her editor.

And it was when a teenager in a Rangers top delivered her fourteen-year-old daughter back home two hours after school had finished, coolly telling Moira that the streets could be very dangerous for a young lady walking home alone, and that he wouldn't want anything to happen to a bonny lass like her, that Moira decided she was going to pull the plug on the piece.

But it hadn't stopped there. A systematic and insidious campaign of terror was unleashed upon her – but there was never any evidence for her to take to the police. She would be sat on a bus and the professional looking woman next to her would turn and hiss, *"Wee Bill doesnae want ye in Glesga anymair,"* and before Moira could respond, the woman would have disappeared into the bustle of commuters fighting to get off the bus in the business district. Or when the homeless man had left her struggling to breathe after shuffling up behind her on Argyll Street, the wretched reek of soiled clothes choking her as he croaked, *"Next time, tha' wee, lass o' yers willnea make it back home. Wee Bill wants ye oot o' Glesga."*

Moira had spent two weeks off work on stress-leave and then handed in her notice. She had done what they wanted and moved out of Glasgow. As a single mum with very little savings and no job, she'd ended up where she could afford to live. So now she wrote about recycling bins in carparks for a local paper with a circulation of barely a thousand.

Stubbing the cigarette into a saucer, she blew a last lungful of smoke across the screen, selected the unread message from Alistair Dewar and hovered over the image of the trash can.

———

That had been two days ago. It was now Thursday evening. Since then she had received another message from the man – this time just entitled, *'Help me. Please?'*

She had read both messages this morning and recognised that this Dewar's family had been shafted by a Jardine too. If he was to be believed, then his evidence about Billy Jardine's role in atrocities in Ireland would square the circle on the bastard. If she shared what she knew with Dewar, and he published, then she could see justice done at no risk to herself. She'd have to convince him first that her name or any reference to her family was removed and that he would hide the identity of her sources before she'd utter a word – but the threat that existed then wasn't the same now. Her daughter had married an Australian she'd met travelling and lived in Brisbane, and surely the reach of a nasty little Glaswegian gangster didn't stretch that far?

Besides, Moira Dunn hadn't quite lost the indignation at injustice that gnaws at investigative journalists bent on unmasking monsters.

And for her it was personal.

Her father, Malky Dunn, had lived his entire adult life haunted by the things that Billy Jardine had made him, and other adolescent males of the Worcester Street Marching Band do. She had to tell this Alistair Dewar that William Robert Jardine was a sexual predator and arch manipulator who groomed and despoiled the innocence of a string of victims in the 1950s and '60s.

And, of course, he had got away with it.

She picked up her phone and dialled the number on the email.

43

30th June, 1921
Birr, King's County, Ireland

Bronagh had noticed the change in her brother since the spring. Maybe Tommy was finally growing up, or he'd got some sense at last. Either way he'd been unusually quiet around the farm and over the last couple of months she'd watched as he stopped whatever chore he was tasked with and stood stock still, staring at the horizon with those strange eyes of his.

Maybe he was a changeling after all.

When he was young, Bronagh's great aunts, both of whom her father considered malevolent old witches, were convinced that the faerie-folk had stolen her real brother from his cot and spirited him away. Dragging him deep under the hills to their fairy kingdom, they'd left the O'Donagh family with this bizarre child; one eye of emerald green, the other as black as coal. The Sidhe were only attracted to the beautiful, these aunts muttered, and that's why Tommy was chosen: he'd been a fine baby, the most perfect in all of Ireland. They whispered to his mother that this would explain his voracious appetite – faerie children would eat you out of house and home if you let them – that, and the fact the child never said a word for the first four years of his life, proved it. They decided he must be an ancient faerie, sent to live out his days in human form, already aged to senility and now spoon-fed by unsuspecting mortal parents: that was why Tommy '*didn't have a stim o' sense in him.*' When Eamonn heard these accusations, he ordered his wife's kin to leave the house and never darken their doors again. But as Tommy grew older and more strangely beautiful year by year, but never any wiser; people wondered.

He was certainly odd, thought Bronagh: it had always been hard to tell whether he was looking at you or through you, but, without a doubt he was becoming much queerer. She hadn't heard him laugh, nor smile in months and when he slept, he moaned. She wondered whether the faeries had taken their changeling back and left the O'Donaghs with a husk of human boy, haunted by years under the mountain.

She couldn't help but think of the farm dogs as she looked at him: as pups they had no idea that they'd been bred to work and not to play. Unable to resist chasing each other's tails, they yapped and kicked up dirt as they knocked over pails of milk and frightened cattle. But after a couple of weeks of feeling her father's boot on their ribs, they were broken, and they skulked around the farmyard, cowed and insular, both in love with, and in fear of, the man that fed and beat them.

That's how her brother seemed to her now: a spirit-snapped mutt. Once in a while she would wake in the middle of the night to spy his bed empty. She'd wait up, pretending to be asleep as he crept back into the room and sobbed quietly under his covers. The only way she was going to find out what had happened to Tommy was by following him next time he sneaked out of the house.

It was a full moon.

It was always on the full moon that they met, and Tommy felt the familiar sense of dread.

But he knew that if he didn't go, then things would be worse – much worse.

Tommy tiptoed down the stairs. By now he instinctively recognised which creaked and which would not.

The cinders in the hearth smouldered as he padded across the flagstones to the door. Pulling it to behind him, he stepped outside. One of the collies growled quietly, but with a whisper and a rub to its ear, it stilled.

The nights were warm this time of year and the horizon glowed faint turquoise. The fields and trees hummed with life; the stillness of the night attuning his ears to every little sound. Tommy heard the rapid scurrying of small feet in the grass verge, the call of a curlew from the top field and millions of ears of barley shifting in the breeze. As he followed the lane toward town he passed a constellation of fireflies drifting across the hedgerow, casting sliding shadows behind the leaves.

As he approached Tooley's Croft, he began to feel sick. A burnt out old ruin on the outskirts of Birr, it had always frightened him as a child, and he'd flick the whip to induce the colt to trot on past it that little bit faster.

But now it filled him with a very real fear that had nothing to do with ghosts or banshees.

It was to do with a bad man who'd tricked him and twisted things; making everything so dark and awful that it seemed the sun would never come out again.

Tommy didn't understand how things had turned out this way. He'd only wanted to show Brendan and the rest of them that he was to be trusted so that he could be one of them – a real soldier of the IRA.

———

On market days, to impress the boys that hung around the square, and to make them like him more, Tommy had told them that he was a Republican soldier of the South Offaly Brigade. He said that he'd fought the British and had a silver gun kept in a safe place.

But he didn't.

He hadn't.

And he wasn't.

From time to time when men on the run passed through, sleeping in the cots above his father's barn, Eamonn would send Tommy across with milk, cheese and hunks of dry bread. But when he tried to sit with the gunmen, or when he asked to hold their rifles, or hear their stories, they'd tell him this wasn't children's business and he should get back to his mother's kitchen.

They shouldn't have done that: none of this would have happened if only they'd treated him differently.

It was Vinny McMahon, one of the few boys from town whom he knew by name, who'd called him over that day as Tommy returned from market on the trap. He'd tied the horse to the rotten gatepost and stepped through nettles and long grass toward the boy whom he hoped was his friend. Vinny stood, half hidden, behind a large oak tree just off the road.

Vinny had whispered, "Tommy, there's someone inside. He's very keen to see ye, so he is. Don't be feared, he won't hurt ye."

And he'd led Tommy through the empty door frame into the musty front room. Weeds sprouted through sodden floorboards and spider webs, sagging with filthy dust, hung from pocked stonework. In the far corner a Tan sat on an upturned bucket scratching at a scar that ran down his left cheek.

Tommy thought he'd been tricked and brandished his penknife, whirling back and forth between the soldier and the boy he'd thought his friend. He bared his teeth and looked as fierce as he could.

"Whoa, sonny, put yer wee blade away. I'm not here tae hurt ye, I'm only here tae help."

Tommy kept his knife pointing at the soldier.

"Yer looking at my uniform and thinkin' I'm the enemy, right? Well, I'm not. I'm Scottish, an' if there's one group o' folk who hate the English more than the Irish, it's us Scots. Tell him Vinny."

Vinny just nodded.

"Do ye ken, do ye *know*, Tommy, what a 'double agent' is?"

Tommy shook his head. He had no idea.

"Can ye read, Tommy? I've somethin' here ye should see."

The Scotsman held out a piece of paper. Tommy stared at the squat words that all looked the same, line after line, like rows of corn. He recognised the words '*Dublin*' and '*IRA*', and he could see some names, but unless he sat down and spelled out each syllable with his finger, he wasn't going to be able to translate these symbols to words any time soon. Bronagh had been better at her letters when she was five than he was now, and he was angry at himself for not paying attention when she'd tried to help him.

"This is from the Head Quarters o' the IRA in Dublin, Tommy. It reads, '*The bearer of this letter is one William Jardine,*' – that's me: ye can call me Billy – '*and he is working on behalf of the legitimate Dáil Government of the Irish Republic to uncover informers and spies in South Offaly. Grant this man safe passage and endeavour to help him with any requests that he may have. On behalf of the men, women and children of Erin, you have our eternal gratitude.*' An' see here, Tommy, it is signed by Michael Collins, Cathal Brugha and Arthur Griffith in the name of the Irish Republic."

Tommy knew their names: Brendan, Padraig and his father talked of them by the fire when they didn't think Tommy was listening.

"Wha' I'm proposing might put both our lives at risk, but if it helps get the English oot of Ireland, I'm willin' tae take a chance."

He turned to Vinny, "Scram now Vinny. I need tae have a grown up conversation with this soldier here. An', ye will remember *our* mutual friend, won't ye?"

He winked; Vinny ducked out the door into the late afternoon gloom.

"I need yer help, Tommy. Someone amongst ye is gettin' messages tae the Brits in the barracks. My job is tae find the papers wi' their name on – proof. I'm workin' from the *inside*, understand? Yer job will be tae meet wi' me tae tell me if anybody is actin' suspicious an' tae help me narrow doon who I'm looking for. Yer on the *outside*, see? But we're both on the *same side*. Partners. Equals. Together we'll find the spy an' when I give ye the name, it will be yersel' who'll be treated a hero.

"Ye cannae tell anyone about this though, Tommy. Not yer Da, yer family, not Brendan – naebody but me. It's top secret until we find out who's spillin' their guts to Conlon an' the Peelers. Do ye understand?"

Tommy, who still hadn't uttered a word nodded.

"But there's risk that goes wi' responsibility, Tommy, an' I'll nae think any less o' ye if yer too fearful for it. There are lots o' other brave lads who'll do the job, I'm sure."

He paused, gauging Tommy's reaction. "Ye'll get yer own pistol too, if I can sneak one oot of the barracks."

And Tommy now realised that it was at that precise moment when everything in his life had changed: he knew only too well that when a salmon took the bait and the hook tore into its palate, it was all over. The fish could writhe and flip all it wanted, but it would never get to leap upstream to spawn in the shallows of its birth.

They had shared a cigarette and this scarred man had unscrewed his hip flask and let Tommy swig a couple of measures – and it tasted good to be treated as a man and an equal at last.

They'd met in Tooley's Croft for the next six Thursdays as Tommy rode the cart back from market. Billy brought chocolate and gave him the cigarette cards from the packets they smoked together. Tommy told him about the comings and goings on the farm and the Scotsman shared some stories of his time fighting the Germans in Flanders.

And then one Thursday in January it had happened.

He hadn't even known that he was on the hook.

It had grown dark early that day and as Tommy crunched through the frosty grass that now lay solid and horizontal, he could see that the moon was full and already high in the sky. Stepping into the dilapidated parlour, he felt that something wasn't right. Billy was leant up against the wall, sharpening a bayonet that glinted dully in the candlelight. When he spoke, his breath clouded into ghost-like curls of condensation and smelt of sickly sweet spirit. He had a wild look in his eye and Tommy felt scared.

"Sit down, Tommy." He nodded at the bucket.

The frozen metal numbed his backside.

"I have the name here."

Billy carried the candle over and crouched alongside Tommy, another official looking document in his hand. Tommy squinted at the writing and this time he *could* easily recognise the name at the top of the paper: it was his own.

He didn't understand.

"Yer the informer, Tommy."

Tommy blinked with bewilderment.

"It is ye. See here, a list of dates an' meetings an' a list of the bribes that's passed between us…"

"But…?" Tommy started.

"It's all here in black an' white, Tommy. An' there's a copy o' this at the barracks, an' in Tullamore an' no doubt in the hands of Major General Hugh Tudor himself, so don't think that by gettin' some Mick gunman tae knock me off, this problem goes away, Tommy."

Tommy's eyes itched.

"Think on how yer Da will feel tae ken his own flesh an' blood is a traitor. Think what Brendan O'Rourke will do tae ye. Remember Séan Keane, Tommy? Afore my time, but I heard the crow pecked the eyes clean oot o' his head."

Tears had started to roll down Tommy's cheeks. They felt so cold, he imagined them hanging from his chin in salty icicles. He felt very much like a boy and very little like a soldier of the IRA.

"But hush now, son." The Scotsman put his arm around Tommy's shoulder. "I dinnae wan' anything tae happen tae ye. I *like* ye, Tommy. See, we keep meeting up, an' ye keep talkin' and ye promise tae do anything I ask, an' naebody will ever ken about this."

Tommy felt the Scotsman stroke the back of his head – and then with a sudden movement, the Tan swung round in front of him and Tommy found his face cupped tightly between the older man's hands.

Tommy had always struggled to put thoughts into words, but looking into the eyes of the man that late January afternoon, the cold, impassive moon staring down at them through the gaping holes in the roof, he could see that he was in the clutches of a predator.

"But if ye don't keep meetin' me, I'll make sure Brendan gets this, an' after they've put ye in the ground, I'll pay a visit tae yer family. I'll let my men take turns with yer mammy an' yer wee sister an' I'll make yer Da watch. An' then we'll kill them all, Tommy, and burn down the farm. D'ye wan' that tae happen?"

Tommy's mouth was so dry he could only croak and shake his head.

Small pins of sweat glistened on the man's top lip. "But let's not let it get tae that point, eh? Let's stay friends. Close friends that keep each other's secrets – an' that way ye an' yer family will come tae nae harm."

The Tan inched forwards and Tommy could feel his hot, alcoholic breath on his face. He pretended that he was the moon, far away and untouchable, watching through the jagged maw of slates, the twist-toothed scream, as a man in uniform planted his lips roughly on those of the trembling child on a bucket.

That was how it started.

Now every full moon he slipped from the house on the hill to that dank room in the ruin that smelt of rot and decay and he shared his secrets with Billy and he shared himself. And when it was over, he ran as fast as he could up the lane and stood on tiptoes at the top of the bank waiting to catch the first glimpse of sunlight pierce the blackness, just to make sure it would, before slinking back to his bedroom and burying himself beneath his blankets.

———

Bronagh crept closer to the croft at the foot of the hill. A minute earlier Tommy had turned at the oak and made his way into the ivy-clad ruin that everybody said was haunted. She held her breath and very deliberately minded where she placed each step. She could see the flicker of a candle from within and skirted the corner of the building to find a window she could peer through.

From inside she heard a man's voice, then her brother's. She could see two shadows, wobbling like mirages, projected on the uneven stone as she approached a gash in the wall where the masonry had crumbled. She watched as one shadow reached out for the other and pulled it forwards. The shadows merged.

Bronagh inched a foot closer and craned her neck so that she could see across the room to where a man held her brother. He seemed to be whispering something into Tommy's ear but she couldn't see his face.

Her brother knelt down before the man as though genuflecting and disappeared from her line of sight, allowing her to make out the man's uniform, his neat moustache and the line of a scar that traced the left side of his face.

His eyes were closed and it seemed as if he too was reciting some kind of prayer under his breath. Daring to poke her head a fraction higher over the broken brickwork, Bronagh could see that whatever her brother was doing down there, it had nothing to do with God.

44

Summer, 2018
Glasgow, Scotland

It was Friday night in Glasgow and James was standing beneath the Tollbooth steeple on the Trongate. Dislocated snatches of bass-beats tumbled from wound down windows as cars and taxis raced past. Bawling tribes of revellers spilled from bars and clubs and shrieked at each other, or into their phones. Horns blared as hen parties tottered across the road, dodging vehicles with all the grace of toddlers, or sat in clumps on curbs, crying and reapplying makeup. Men in tight tops jostled and larked and strutted cock-like, clutching bottles of Becks and sucking on cigarettes.

James had been told by email to wait by the steeple at Glasgow Cross for *'one o' the lads'* to pick him up. The night was muggy and close and he could feel his back damp with sweat. He checked his watch and saw that it was just after 11pm on the night of the 11th of July: in an hour's time, those of a Unionist persuasion would welcome the Twelfth like it was Hogmany, while the rest of the world would just roll over and plump their pillow or change the channel, oblivious.

Behind him, he heard a thud and a screech of brakes as a car climbed the pavement and juddered to a halt beside him.

"Alistair Dewar?"

James nodded.

"Get in."

James squeezed into the car as the spiky chords of *Killing In The Name Of* by Rage Against the Machine started to blast from the speakers. The driver must have been in his late forties; he had greying sideburns, a double chin and a perfectly spherical belly that hung over his belt beneath a black polo shirt. He released the handbrake, and with a violent twist of the wheel and stamp on the gas, the car jerked off the pavement, across a lane of oncoming traffic and sped towards Saltmarket and the River Clyde.

It was clear from the ear-bleeding volume of the music, the determination of his gum-chewing and his undeviating gaze that the driver was unlikely to engage in pleasantries, so James found himself tapping his thighs arhythmically, furtively appraising his taciturn chauffeur.

He was intrigued by the tattoo that laddered the man's forearm – it looked like it said, SII∧IIX – for the life of him he couldn't work out what that might represent.

"Excuse me? EXCUSE ME?"

With palpable irritation the driver reached over and turned the sound down just enough for James to be heard over the chorus.

"Your tattoo. What does 'siiniix' mean?"

Eyes still resolutely on the road: "Upside down, bud."

The driver reached back across the dashboard and turned up the volume, effectively slamming the door on the nascent conversation.

Upside down?

Oh, I'm reading it upside down, James thought.

X, I, I, V, I, I, S?

Then it made sense: they were Roman numerals with an 's' at the end. XII – twelve, VII – seven: the Twelfth of July. The same letters as on the website address *https:/xiiviis.scotsblog.co.uk*. So the

XIIVIIs must be a gang of some sort and James was on his way to meet the leader, WeeBJ127. Now his web name made sense too.

James was well aware that he was out of his depth. But hurtling over Victoria Bridge, the wind off the Clyde cutting through the sultry night air and cooling his face as Rage Against the Machine screamed their defiant chorus, James didn't care. He'd come too far to go back now. He needed the truth like Connor needed that last fix.

As the song reached its climax, James saw his driver nodding his head with comedic fury. It reminded him of the Bohemian Rhapsody scene in the movie, *Wayne's World;* only this time it was being performed by the bulldog from the Churchill Insurance commercials. James had to clamp his lips together, tight and white like bacon rind, to supress the seismic smile threatening to rupture across his face.

The city centre was a long way behind them now.

They drove down empty residential roads and grim high streets where shutters smothered in graffiti cocooned shopfront windows. Nothing was open apart from a succession of takeaways which pitched paltry squares of ochre onto darkened pavements. Youths, mesmerised by the luminescence of their mobile phones, idled outside. They passed pockets of derelict wasteland caged by chain link fences; the earth scarred with the herringbone tracks of entirely absent JCBs. It was an utterly desolate place, James thought.

The driver made a left turn onto a long, deserted road straddled by squat, ugly tower blocks. Only one in every four street lights seemed to be working and James could just make out the charred and twisted ribcage of an abandoned car in what he supposed must be a playground. He watched a handful of teenagers spin a roundabout with chemically induced aggression, before one of them leapt on it, only to be thrown off, skidding across asphalt to howls of pain or laughter; triumphantly holding his bevie upright.

The car pulled up alongside one of the stocky tower blocks and the driver killed the engine.

"In here."

They walked towards a rectangular entrance way, where another man inked with the same XIIVII tattoo stood smoking. A Staffordshire bull terrier jerked at the leash as they approached. The smoker snapped his arm back violently, silencing the growl that rumbled at the back of the dog's throat. The pair nodded at each other before James's driver led him along a stark corridor to a concrete stairwell that stank of piss and desperation. Broken glass and needles winked at him from dark corners as they climbed to the second floor. Stepping out onto a walkway they were met by two much younger men who were passing a bottle of Buckfast Tonic Wine back and forth.

"Is this him then, Gav?"

"Aye."

The one holding the bottle said, "Bill's waitin' for ye doon there. Ye've nae malkies on ye, eh?"

Whatever a malky was, James didn't think he had one. This didn't stop his partner patting him down as James heard his driver plod back into the stairwell.

"Nah, yer fine. Enjoy the Eleventh!"

James made his way along the walkway. He felt as though he was entering some sort of gladiatorial arena in a lurid, dystopian future: all four sides of the complex squared an open space which, no doubt some dreamy architect of the 1960s had envisioned would see families picnicking on well-tended lawns beneath leafy trees. Instead lifeless grey matter of indeterminate provenance filled every inch of the interior; and dead centre stood a thirty foot pyre. Smaller than the colossus James had seen being built in Shankill, it still towered over the teenage boys who circled it, shaking the last drops of liquid paraffin over scrunched newspaper stuffed between pallets. The triangular structure was decorated with Celtic shirts, images of Sinn Féin politicians, Irish tricolours and even a poster-sized photo of the SNP leader. A young lad wearing a Dutch football top with the words, 'King Billy' printed above the number twelve, adeptly scampered up the sheer face with what looked like a blow-up sex doll. To cheers and pantomime boos from the spectators, the child plopped a mitre on the doll's head and James could see that in a sick parody of a Christmas angel, the current Pope perched at the bonfire's apex ready to be burned alive.

Overlooking this pyre, from every side of the complex, huge Union Jacks and intricately embroidered Lodge banners were draped over the balustrades of all three tiers. Behind them scores of men and women wearing Rangers shirts or orange sashes mingled, tipping Special Brew down their throats whilst packs of children darted between their legs brandishing multi-coloured glow-sticks like wands.

James approached a group set apart from the rest of the hordes. From amongst this cluster, a stocky man with bleached blond hair, closely cropped to a bovine skull, stepped forward and proffered his hand. He could have been no taller than 5ft 4 and as he crunched James's metacarpals it was clear that he had somewhat of a Napoleon complex.

"Bill Jardine. Wee Bill tae ma friends, an' I'd like tae think we'll be buds, Ali."

He nodded towards the unlit bonfire.

"Welcome tae the Eleventh. Wha' could be more patriotic than burnin' those who'd see Britain split up, eh? An' the Pope, of course: ye gottae burn the Pope! Ye can quote me on that in yer wee book if ye like."

"I'm sure I will."

"Ye wan' a bottle o' Buckie?" Bill asked, holding out a tonic wine. "We call it '*Wreck the Hoose Juice*' – jus' the thing tae get the party started."

James considered whether offending the brother of a convicted terrorist whilst surrounded by hundreds of his acolytes was any worse than waking in an underpass with soiled trousers and some interesting new friends: he decided that the latter was preferable. "Sure." He took the bottle and twisted the cap.

Trying not to grimace as the sugary liquor offended his taste buds, he asked, "So, Bill, tell me about tonight. Are there any rules I have to follow? Can I take photographs? Can I record what we say to each other? Will I be able to get a chance to speak to some of your friends here?"

"Nae fuckin' around. I like it. A man who kens wha' he wants, eh? Aye, ye can do all that. But, mind – ye'll not publish a word without our say-so. We willnae have any lies printed about us an' our traditions."

His eyes narrowed.

"I've been tryin' tae find out a wee bit about yersel' an I cannae find much on any author named Ali Dewar. Why's tha'?"

The sickly wine caught in James's throat, but he had gone through all this in his head before he arrived. "No, you wouldn't. I'm not famous or anything – I published a couple of works between '06 and '09; they're probably out of print now. Since then I've been lecturing at a college in Kent. I could direct you to some more recent articles that I wrote for the *British Journal of Sociology* on the ramifications of gender inequality amongst different ethnic groups across the UK if that would interes…"

"Nae bother – I'm not much o' a reader. It's ma Da who wants tae be in a book anyhow."

James glanced round at the men stood around Bill. "Is your dad not here tonight?"

"Nah, he'll be back from Auld Reekie in the mornin'."

"Auld Reekie?"

"Edinburgh, son: he has a lot of business in the capital. Besides, I dinnae think ma Da would be seen dead on this side o' the Clyde. He's more *corporate*, whereas I like tae 'keep it real', so tae speak. Ye have tae keep in step with yer foot soldiers if ye dinnae wannae lose their loyalty. Ye ken?"

Then he surprised James by plucking some Kipling from the accelerant-scented ether, "*If you can talk with crowds and keep your virtue, or walk with Kings—nor lose the common touch…*" He eye-balled James to see whether he was impressed. "My Da does the walkin' with kings bit, an' I suppose ye could say that I'm his *common touch*."

"So do you live here, Bill?"

"Do I fuck!" He choked with laughter, spitting a gobful of Buckie over the balustrade. "Havin' the common touch is one thing, but livin' in an utter shit-hole is somethin' entirely different, son! Nae, I've a couple o' pads around town. Nice places, ye ken? Nae Pakis about."

OK, thought James. Here we go.

"So are there Asians living here? Won't they object to all this on their doorstep?"

"If they ken what's good for 'em, they'll keep their doors closed an' turn up their TVs. I have nae problem wi' darkies as long as they dinnae cause me any strife. Eh?"

"What about Catholics? Are there any living here?"

Bill smirked. "Aye, there used to be a couple of Taig families on the ground floor, but life became…" he chose his words carefully, "*uncomfortable* for 'em an' they moved out."

"But aren't you worried that someone might call the police and complain about the noise and the drinking and – well, the huge fire?"

Bill's eyes locked onto James's with a terrifying assuredness. "Naebody would be stupid enough tae do that, and the polis ken better than tae come out here on the Eleventh."

Bill examined his watch and turned to one of his men. "Is it ready?"

"Aye, it will take yer eyebrows off, Bill."

"Did ye get the right colour this time, Glen?"

"Aye, boss. On eBay: it wasn't easy tae find either – had tae buy one from the States."

Glen bent and dug through the contents of a kit bag, pulling from it a pistol that he handed to Bill.

James started and felt his bowels loosen. Consternation flashed across his face.

"Och! Dinnae pish yersel' laddie. It's only a fuckin' flare gun. Yer gonnae like this!"

Glen handed him a loudspeaker which Bill switched on; a piercing wail of feedback silencing the chatter on the overlooking walkways.

"Brothers and Sisters. Welcome!"

Hundreds stopped talking and turned; even the moving neon of the glow-sticks stilled.

"We're moments away from the Twelfth. Wha' a weekend we're gonnae have! Get ready! My watch tells me tha' in 5, 4, 3, 2, 1…"

He pulled the trigger. An orange flare fizzed from the pistol, arrowing towards the bonfire, straight through the face of Gerry Adams and into the paraffin-soaked kindling.

As the flare sparked and caught at the heart of the structure, Wee Bill bellowed, "Tae Protestantism! Tae King Billy an' tae the Union of Great Britain and Northern Ireland!"

An almighty whoosh sucked the air from James's lungs as the pyre erupted in an explosion of yellow and orange that crackled and spat fat balls of burning debris onto the barren earth below.

This was met with whoops and screams as bottles and cans

clinked together and two huge speakers hammered out a military drumroll before a chorus of flutes picked up the melody and drove a wildly popular marching tune. A spontaneous writhing of limbs washed around the four sides of the block. Couples linked arms and swirled; pumping fists beat out a primitive rhythm and Loyalist lyrics were hollered into the night with frightening intensity.

Bill turned to James, his face aglow in the hypnotic tongues of flame. "Ye've gottae fuckin' love the Eleventh, eh?" His hand disappeared into his jacket pocket. "Ali, smile – yer on candid camera!"

Before he even knew what was happening, Bill had whipped out his iPhone and snapped an image of James. "Nice one Ali! I need tae keep a record of wha' ye look like, jus' in case I ever have tae come an' find ye one day, eh?"

———

Two hours later and James was walking across the bridge that spanned the River Kelvin. Hundreds of feet below, dark waters rushed over rocks toward the slothful flow of the Clyde. The banks were lush with a canopy of leaves; silver-tipped in the moonlight. The university spires burst from the tree-tops, floodlit and beautiful. An avenue of bone-white townhouses peered imperiously over the lawns and fountains of Kelvingrove Park. James imagined the raucous bonfire in the arse-end of town to be no more than a bad dream, so far removed was it from the sumptuous splendour of the West End of Glasgow.

Again, he felt thwarted. Other than confirming that the Jardines were clearly psychotic, James had learnt nothing at all about their family history. Indeed, Bill had flatly refused to speak about his father or grandfather. He'd told James that tonight had merely been a preliminary meeting to gauge whether he was *'dealing wi' a cunt'* as he put it.

Apparently James had passed the 'cunt test' because Bill had invited him to attend the Twelfth celebrations at the Worcester Street Orange Hall the following day. He'd told James that Alec Jardine would address the Lodge before their marching band, *King Billy's Boys,* set off towards Glasgow Green. Bill said that during the hours it took for the hundreds of other bands from across Scotland and Ireland to converge on the Green, James would get a chance to speak with his father. And after that, he could attend the *Orangefest* rally, if he wanted.

Bill had then stabbed a number into his phone and barked at Gav, ordering him round the front in five. He'd asked James which hotel he was staying in. James had lied and said the Crown Plaza – he was determined to fly under the radar this time around.

So after another ride in silence, soundtracked by '90s nu-metal, James had found himself striding confidently past the reception towards the lifts of the massive Crown Plaza Hotel. After pounding the corridors upstairs for a good fifteen minutes, he ventured back to the foyer and surreptitiously surveyed the carpark. His untalkative chauffeur was long gone and James had stepped out into the early morning of the Twelfth and begun the long walk back to his B&B.

Drunk and buzzing from unhealthy amounts of sugar, thanks to the unwise decision to accept three more bottles of Buckie, James gulped the fresh air of Kelvingrove Park. He felt grateful to have made it through the 11th of July unscathed – which, sadly, was more than he could say for poor old Joseph Conlon.

45

1st July, 1921
Birr, King's County, Ireland

Joe Conlon wasn't happy with this.

There were too many civilians about: somebody was bound to get hurt.

It was the Midland Fair: for the last three days the country roads leading to Birr from as far afield as Longford, Carlow and Clare had become clogged with carts and caravans and livestock. An endless stream of farmers, tinkers, breeders and gypsies had converged on the town for the annual fair, considered the largest in all Ireland. The green behind Oxmantown Hall had been transformed into a sea of bleating white, where every second man held a crook. A show ring had been constructed on the land behind the courthouse where stallions and mares, bullocks and heifers were led by farmers in their Sunday best. Canvas tents and stalls cluttered John's Mall; strongmen, magicians, puppeteers and purveyors of the strange and bizarre all competed for the pennies and pounds of the curious and the gullible. The pub doors had been open since breakfast and fiddle music, tall tales and the yeasty fug of warm beer spilled out onto the streets. On Cumberland Square a Methodist brass band entertained the Anglo-Irish nobility. They had come in numbers to experience this quaint tradition whilst being served champagne, cakes and Darjeeling from silver trays by white jacketed waiters hired for the day. Everywhere the blur of chaos, the whiff of toffee apples and animal shit, and thousands of strange faces unknown to Sergeant Conlon.

For him it was the stuff of nightmares.

Especially as it had come to their attention that the IRA were planning 'something big', and according to their source, had managed to infiltrate the mingling masses with scores of gunmen from neighbouring Tipperary. Any one of these strangers could pull a pistol from their pockets and take out a policeman, or a judge or even a bloody Earl.

Because the intelligence that had been seeping up through Acting Sergeant Daly had so far proved reliable, Joe had impressed upon his superiors that this year the fair should be cancelled. Clearly those on a much higher pay grade than his own had decided to ignore this advice, and the go ahead had been given. The message had been relayed down the pecking order finally reaching Head Constable Regan who reiterated to Joe what he had been told word for word; a handful of sentences that in their phraseology encapsulated the futile intransigence of the Crown Forces: 'If we can't stop a bloody rabble of assassins ruining an important show of Anglo-Irish unity with all the might of the British Army and the Royal Irish Constabulary at our disposal, then we might as well bloody quit Ireland now – and the rest of our Empire for that matter. The Midland Fair will go ahead as planned, and that is an order.'

Hundreds of soldiers from the Prince of Wales's Leinster Regiment had arrived this morning from Crinkill Barracks to supplement the RIC. Now they stood in uniform on street corners. They shadowed notables discreetly and searched anybody whom they considered suspicious – which Joe had noticed translated as *any Irish male they didn't like the look of.* They manned armoured cars on all the roads in and out of Birr; their mounted machine guns greeting every soul who made their way into town.

So Joe stood on Cumberland Square and he watched and he waited; scanning every face and every sudden movement.

He was terrified.

Feck.

The place was crawling with them.

Brendan O'Rourke peered from the window of the brightly coloured gypsy caravan. In every direction all he could see were Peelers and soldiers.

Of course Brendan had expected an increased police presence, in fact he'd been counting on it. The more Peelers patrolling the streets, the more targets for his boys to saunter up alongside and end. But the groups were doubled up – if his men took out a pair of policemen, they would be sitting ducks for the soldiers that followed ten steps behind and in clear line of sight.

It was another leak.

Someone was feeding them information and Brendan was damned if he knew who it was.

The attempt last month to blow up the Roscrea-Birr railway as a trainload of British squaddies returned to Crinkill had been scuppered when hours before the train was due to pass, they'd spotted a platoon of Auxies coming up the track on a hand car, a cavalry unit sweeping the embankments on either side. They'd obviously fled, but in their haste, had been forced to leave pounds of valuable explosive partially buried between the sleepers.

Likewise the planned ambush of a convoy of vehicles bringing supplies and ammunition into Tullamore from Dublin had failed after his men had waited for almost eighteen hours in the rain, crouched on a rocky outcrop, before hearing that the weapons had arrived safely in Tullamore after a massive detour north into Westmeath.

Yes, they could both have been coincidences, but Brendan didn't think so.

That's why he'd been determined to make his mark here today. Tom Barry had become a legend the year before with the Kilmichael Ambush, and had gone on to cement his reputation with the engagement at Crossbarry back in March. Michael Collins, Liam Lynch and Ernie O'Malley had also guaranteed their immortality in the pantheon of great Irish guerrilla leaders. Brendan O'Rourke wanted his name to join theirs in the history books. One day he'd write about this moment; a co-ordinated attack on the police and British infrastructure here in Birr. Thirty-five of his own men, supplemented by about forty boys from the North Tipperary Brigade were milling amongst the crowds. Road blocks had been constructed on the Birr-Kinitty Road and motor vehicles waited on the other side to transport his men to safety as they retreated from the operation. If all went to plan, at the twelfth stroke of the midday bell, a fusillade of short range shots would be fired, scores of Brits and traitors would fall and a blow would be struck against those that would oppress them.

However, peering from the opaque caravan window, Brendan could see that if this went ahead, it would turn into a massacre. Many of his men would no doubt die within seconds of pulling their triggers, and after the events of Bloody Sunday, Brendan didn't put it past the British to then open fire on the panicking crowds with machine guns. Instead of glory, his name would be forever associated with the most senseless loss of human life in the conflict so far.

He had a man outside the church now, sober as a judge but drenched in beer, a bottle of poitín in his pocket. If word reached him that the operation was to be aborted, he would stagger inside, overpower anyone who would resist him and leap from the bell ropes until dragged from them, swinging punches and slurring

Christmas carols for good measure. Each of his men knew that if they heard the mad peeling of bells from St Brendan's, they were to disengage and slip away to safe houses in this county or the next and await further instructions.

It wasn't quite 11.30, but Brendan knew that he had to put an end to this before it began. *So much for his name being mentioned in the same breath as Michael Collins*, he mused.

Brendan tapped on the window to get the attention of the lad who was to run to the church, but the boy didn't turn.

Brendan cursed under his breath and tapped again, but that feckin' brass band was drowning out everything else in this corner of the Square.

He moved to the Dutch doors at the back of the caravan and, pulling his cap as far over his face as he could, poked his head outside and hissed, "Boy! Boy!"

The child turned and trotted over.

"Get down to the church now. Tell Pat to ring the bells. Have you got that? *Ring the bells.* Now go!"

He watched the boy scamper through the crowds and turn onto Wilmer Street. He'd be there in a minute.

Good lad, smiled Brendan.

It was at that moment that his eyes met those of Joseph Conlon, and his smile froze.

Joe would have recognised that face from any distance. Pulling his whistle from his pocket, he blew hard as he charged towards the IRA man.

O'Rourke sprung from the caravan like a whippet from traps and wove at speed through the congested square. Conlon screamed, "Stop him! Stop him!" and it seemed as though two passers-by tried: O'Rourke crashed into them, they tangled and he broke free. Only the very sharp of eye would have seen the revolver pass from him to them with sleight of hand.

The same pair then struggled to get out of the way of the chasing policeman but the bulk of Joe Conlon, travelling at speed, bowled them over and sent them pin-wheeling backwards into a bread stall.

O'Rourke ducked down a snickleway, vaulted a sleeping farmer propped against the brickwork, an empty bottle on his lap, and sprinted down the alleyway behind the Georgian houses that fronted John's Mall. Joe followed, pulled the Webley from its holster and without breaking stride, hurdled the drunkard and let off a shot. It missed: a puff of whitewashed wall exploded from a gatepost inches from O'Rourke's skull.

Conlon stopped, set his stance and pulled the trigger again. He caught O'Rourke on the shoulder. The rebel stumbled, regained his footing and continued running towards the end of the alleyway.

Turning sharply down a passage that led out to the street, O'Rourke found a wrought iron gate blocking his escape. If he stopped now he was dead. There was enough room between the top of the gate and the archway above to clamber through. Using his good arm, the wiry man heaved himself up and over.

Conlon turned into the passage just as O'Rourke hit the pavement on the other side. He could see that there was no way he could squeeze over so he aimed at the lock and fired twice as he ran full tilt at the gate. He flung himself at it with every ounce of energy and crashed through it, tumbling to the sound of clattering metal on cobble stones.

Getting up, he saw O'Rourke hemmed in by banks of striped canvas. The rebel hesitated and made to go right before deciding to make his escape to the left. It was all the time that Joe needed: he pumped his legs and threw himself into a tackle that sent them both sprawling into the canvas booth, knocking it over.

A tangle of legs and arms and thrashing punches, complicated by the stunned puppeteer, knotted in his own strings, as tiny wooden limbs were scattered in front of the screaming children.

Conlon and O'Rourke wrestled, but the flesh wound to the smaller man's shoulder meant that the policeman easily gained the upper-hand. Enraged by the recklessness of the operation, a red mist engulfed his senses once more, and Sergeant Joseph Conlon started pummelling the man beneath him with giant fists.

By now policemen and soldiers were yelling conflicting orders as they waded through rapids of fleeing children. It took four soldiers from Crinkill Barracks to drag Conlon off the unconscious redhead, who was by now as inanimate as the marionettes strewn around him.

Head Constable Regan approached the straining Conlon. He emanated a barely concealed rage. "Jaysus, Joseph. My Sergeant breakin' a man's face in broad daylight in front of half of Ireland. Get yourself home and bathe your knuckles, man. Don't go near the barracks tonight. I'll speak with you in the morning."

He looked at the soldiers, "Get him out of here."

And then the bells of St Brendan's started ringing wildly. All across Birr, people looked up, puzzled for a moment, before continuing what they were doing; never knowing that men with cold murder in their pockets were melting away towards the town boundaries.

46

Summer, 2018
Glasgow, Scotland

It was the Twelfth. A succession of trains from Fife, from Stirling, from Aberdeen and Airdrie snaked into Queen's Street Station, their sliding doors disgorging a shuffling stream of charcoal suits, orange sashes, curved brass and stretched oil-skin. Bill Jardine watched this molten flow of marching bands and Lodge members slow and solidify as they approached the ticket gates. He was standing outside WH Smith nursing a nasty hangover with a can of IRN BRU looking out for his father, Alec, who should have arrived on the Edinburgh train five minutes ago.

Bill was irritable: with himself for drinking too much and with his driver, Gav, for crying off and sending his son, Craig, to pick him up this morning. He knew full well that his Da would smell the drink off him long before they shook hands, and regard him with a censorious smile that was always tinged with disappointment.

Suddenly, amongst the myriad of moving faces that bobbed towards the exit, Bill latched onto one particular face: creased and care-worn, leathery and yellowed. Weary and wary at the same time – but it was definitely her.

Bitch.

Fuckin' bitch.

What did she think she was doing?

And today of all days.

If his father were to see her, then all hell would break loose.

Extra police, many of them armed, stood by the ticket office, watching intently as wave after wave of Orangemen filed past them. Bill's aching brain, still toxic with alcohol, tussled with a series of strategies – spiteful, risky, murderous and blunt. *Shit*, he didn't have time to think; so he clutched at one of them blindly.

"Craig, ye've a blade on ye?"

"Aye, of course, boss."

"See that cancerous ol' hag, wi' the tea-cosy on her heed an' the tartan laptop case? The one standin' there checkin' her phone?"

"Aye."

"I wan' ye tae follow her. Do not let her out o' yer sight. When ye find yersel' in a moment o' quiet, away from CCTV and witnesses, I wan' ye to hold the blade tae her throat and tell her these exact words. Nice an' slow so she can hear every one." Bill leant over and whispered into Craig's ear. "Ye got that? Dinnae even think about callin' me on yer phone tae tell me anything. When yer done, ye come an' speak to me alone, face tae face. Nae phones, OK? Ye ken?"

Craig nodded.

"Now give me the car keys. I'll have tae drive the ol' man meself. Go!"

Craig pulled his anorak hood over his head and strode into the stream of one way traffic making for the doors onto Dundas Street. Bill watched as he fell into step with Moira Dunn and prayed that the lad wasn't going to cock this up.

As the boy disappeared, Bill felt a tap on his shoulder and turned to see his father looming above him, terse formality clipping his consonants. "Well this is a pretty poor welcoming party, William. You'd better be sober enough to drive. Come on, take me to Worcester Street, I have a lot to do today."

Moira had explained to James on the phone that she would only meet in a public place out of the city centre. She'd suggested the Kelvingrove Museum and told him to meet her next to Sir Roger at 11am sharp. When James had asked who Sir Roger was, she'd replied that as he was playing detective now, it was up to him to find out.

So at 11am on Saturday 12th July, James found himself sitting opposite a giant Asian elephant surrounded by brown bears, giraffes, leopards, wildebeest and kangaroos. Overhead a full size Spitfire, suspended by steel wire from girders spanning the ceiling, dove incongruously over this miscellaneous collection of stuffed beasts. There were a lot of fangs, thought James. Even the vegetarians looked like they would sink their teeth into you if they got a chance.

A woman in a woollen beret, who had attempted to drown the reek of cigarette smoke with lashings of Lily of the Valley, slipped onto the bench beside him. "Sir Roger was shot whilst eating his breakfast – poor sod. He'd turned on his keeper and wasn't considered safe anymore. No chance of being released back into the wild in 1900 – just a blunderbuss slug in the skull and a date with an ambitious taxidermist. I assume you must be Alistair Dewar?"

"Yes," James lied, "and you must be Moira Dunn? Thank you for meeting me. I know you've come a long way, and I really appreciate it. Thank you so much."

Moira surveyed the tourists and museum staff. She checked her exit routes. Rooting in her purse, she retrieved a blister pack of Nicorette gum and popped two pieces in her mouth.

"I don't want to be here long and I don't want to be seen with you if I can help it. I haven't been home to Glasgow for over a decade, so I am naturally very nervous." She worked her jaws mechanically. "I have only come because you said that you're determined to set the record straight as far as Billy Jardine is concerned. I would like that too – I would like that very much. In fact, I'd like to see the whole family get their just desserts. I think I can help you."

She patted her laptop case. "The man was a monster, and in here I have the evidence to prove it; I've got transcripts of a number of interviews I conducted between 2006-2007. Some of those I spoke to are now dead and those that aren't would be reluctant to talk of it openly, but what they say will blacken that bastard's name for ever. And as for his son, Alec, I have enough on him to start a media storm that could result in prosecution. Ex-combatants on both sides of the conflict in Northern Ireland have signed sworn affidavits indicting him of gross misconduct and fraternisation with proscribed Loyalist Paramilitary organisations whilst serving in Enniskillen. But it doesn't end there: if you've done your homework, you'll be aware that his eldest son, 'Rabb', is currently serving a life sentence for planning acts of terrorism?"

James nodded.

"But what you might not know is that his brother, Bill, known as Wee Bill, is a vicious little gangster who makes his money from drugs, protection rackets and probably human-trafficking and prostitution too. He surrounds himself with a cohort of ultra-Unionist thugs called the XIIVIIs. That's why I chose today to meet: the whole lot of them will be so wrapped up in their big day at the Worcester Street Orange Hall that a washed up old hack should go unnoticed." She looked ahead defiantly. "Besides, there are some things I need to do here in Glasgow that I've left for far too long."

James wanted to show that he too was serious. "I have had the dubious pleasure of meeting Wee Bill. Last night, out in the sticks somewhere to welcome in the Twelfth. I think…"

Moira's eyes flashed in alarm. "Alistair, before you go on, I have to say this: I don't know what your background is, or how far you are prepared to go – but these are dangerous people. *Really dangerous people.* I need to know that you understand what you are letting yourself in for before I give you what I have on them. The Jardine family have ruined my life. They've hounded me out of my home town and turned me into a paranoid neurotic, who lives alone, drinks too much and writes parochial crap that nobody reads. I want to see the truth come out – but I'm not putting myself in the firing line again. If you do this, you'll be firmly in their sights."

"Don't worry, Moira. I have taken precautions: after today, I'm out of Scotland – hopefully with everything I need to finally put the past to bed. They don't know who I am, or where I live. I'm a ghost, so to speak. Alistair isn't my real name, but I suppose you know that already?"

"I was counting on it. Only an idiot would take on three generations of psychopaths, publish a damning exposé on their twisted past and cross their fingers there'd be no repercussions." She smiled bitterly to herself. "So what have you got on Billy Jardine during the Tan War? I'll admit that I drew a blank on that chapter of his life."

James pulled out some of Daniel Fallon's drawings and told her about the taped interviews that Alison had conducted with him. He related stories of rape, pub sackings, dead horses and beaten boys. The journalist nodded politely, but looked distinctly unimpressed. James rallied, citing evidence from the National Archives and Father O'Brien's diary entries the week before the Galross Massacre. It was only when he showed her the drawing depicting the dead priest, the burning farmhouse and the blonde-haired girl screaming from the bedroom window, that Moira visibly started. She grabbed the artwork from his hands and examined it, scratching some dry skin on her arm as she did so. Almost to herself she mumbled, "I never believed it. I thought the bastard was just boasting to frighten impressionable boys."

James waited. "So this makes some kind of sense to you?"

When Moira looked up at him her eyes glistened and her teeth were clenched.

And she told him.

She told him about her father.

About the years he was abused by a supposed bastion of the Unionist community in Glasgow: Billy Jardine; a man so masculine and feared in the East End that absolutely nobody would believe that he hid a predilection for post-pubescent teenage boys. A man that financed and ran the Worcester Street Lodge, who delivered sermons about sin and hellfire on Sunday mornings and slipped his hands down young men's trousers on Sunday afternoons. And she told James about the tattoo that her father had been made to kiss; the tattoo of a cross pierced by dagger on the Orangeman's chest. How he'd boasted as he stroked the back of her father's head that the tattoo signified the struggle against devilish Popery. There were none that God loved more than those willing to take the fight to those arch-disseminators of his Word: the Catholic priests. And, if in the course of one's life, you rid the world of just one of them – you were guaranteed a place at God's side.

Moira's voice trembled as she told James that Jardine had assured her father that he *was* one of those who were thus guaranteed a spot beside the Almighty, so any sins he committed now were superfluous. "My dad never understood what the old perv was talking about when he said that the best thing about it all was that he'd set up another left-footer to take the fall for the killing. Two for one, he joked."

There was a moment of silence between them.

He had done it.

It was circumstantial, he knew, but James was finally convinced of his great-grandfather's innocence.

It was a beautiful moment – but fleeting. James knew he needed more: how had Jardine managed it?

Brendan O'Rourke wrote that when Ciaran Fahy pulled the trigger, he pulled it with the certainty that the man he was killing had not only beaten his brother to death, but had murdered an entire family, razed their farm to the ground and shot a Catholic priest between the eyes.

O'Rourke himself was certain.

Even now, if you typed the words, '*Galross Massacre*', into any search engine, the results were identical: they all regurgitated carbon copies of the original account – O'Rourke's account. Now James understood that this was just fake news made real through replication. If anyone knew how Billy Jardine had pinned the massacre onto Conlon, Alec Jardine would – James had one last chance to unravel fact from fiction and he wasn't going to let it slip through his fingers.

Moira delved into her laptop bag and pulled out a flash drive. "Look, Alistair, or whatever your name is, I have to go. I've been here too long already. You must understand that what's on this memory stick could get you into real trouble. Alec Jardine may be the epitome of establishment values now, but that's what makes him so dangerous: he can't afford to risk that reputation. He won't let his father's name be tainted. He rubs shoulders in Edinburgh with the most important men and women in the Unionist-Conservative camp and although he's publicly disavowed violence and renounced the actions of his errant son, both Rabb and he share the same convictions. If he thinks for a moment that his position is at stake, there are no lengths he won't go to in order to shut you up. He just has to give the word and one of Wee Bill's goons will come looking for you.

"Once you take this from me, I'm walking away, back to my sad little life in Pitlochry – but at least it *is* a life. There will be none happier than I to see that whole family named and shamed – but I'm neither brave nor stupid enough to do it myself." The

USB stick hovered between them. "So before you take it, you have to ask yourself; are you?"

James considered the question. He saw himself at Connor's grave, wretched with guilt. He felt the sting of shame that Pat-Joe had carried with him every day of his life. To be the one to break that cycle; to right a wrong and deliver peace to both himself and his family: yes, he was both brave and stupid enough to take this on.

He reached out and took it.

Moira got to her feet and asked James to wait five minutes before following her out. The pair shook hands awkwardly and wished each other well. James watched as the journalist was subsumed into the shifting throng of denim, camera straps and bum-bags.

But James wasn't the only one watching. Craig had observed the meeting; he'd even filmed some of it on his phone from high above them. Peering through metal cabling, propeller blades and Spitfire wings, he'd seen Moira pass something to the man with dark hair. The moment she stood, Craig had pushed his way through the tourists that clogged the stairs. By the time Moira Dunn stepped out onto Argyle Street he was only ten paces behind her.

47

Summer, 2018
Worcester Street Orange Hall,
Glasgow, Scotland

"I am not afraid to say it; Brothers and Sisters, we are fighting a war, a *cultural* war. Our traditions, our beliefs, our communities, even our faith itself is under attack from a liberal, dissolute press and unscrupulous politicians who would see our nation chopped up into bite-sized chunks!"

Around the hall these words were met with chants of 'Shame on you Sinn Féin!', 'Shame on you SNP!' James noted wryly that Plaid Cymru didn't yet warrant the same levels of opprobrium levelled at the Irish and Scottish Nationalist parties. He toyed with the idea of starting his own chant against those who'd see an independent Wales, but thought better of it.

After leaving Moira he had walked back through Kelvingrove Park to his B&B and spent half an hour skim reading the documentation that the journalist had given him. She was nothing if not thorough. She had grown up within this very community. As a girl she would have sat in this hall and listened to men like Alec Jardine; indeed, more than likely the man himself. Her father and mother had been unquestioning Unionists and remained members of this Lodge until their final years. But the whole time, Malcolm

Dunn had been living with a terrible secret; one he only shared with his daughter after his wife's death. Spurred by disillusion and disgust at what she saw as the hypocrisy of Orangeism, Moira had spent the next eighteen months moonlighting her day job at the *Glasgow Tribune* with a full scale investigation into the Jardine family. Her evidence concerning Billy Jardine's sexual proclivities was substantiated by three other victims, only one of whom was still alive. Her enquiry into Alec Jardine's alleged collaboration with the UVF, the UDA, the Red Hand Commandos, and the Ulster Freedom Fighters was patchy, but telling: in the course of policing Enniskillen, it was probable that he shared British intelligence on IRA activity with the same organisations who were waging war on the Republican community. There was also a very strong suspicion that weaponry and explosives seized from the IRA were redistributed to Loyalist Paramilitary groups with his consent. Before taking early retirement in 1985, Chief Inspector Alec Jardine was under inquiry after claims by a whistleblower that senior RUC officers, Jardine amongst them, turned a blind eye to their subordinates' active participation in organised sectarian violence. Worse, that they then covered up their men's tracks with cursory investigations that came to nothing. Unsurprisingly, like so much that James had read about Ireland, the inquiry into Jardine and his fellow officers was dropped. An unnamed source was quoted as saying that any hint the RUC had been in collusion with Loyalist terrorists would have *"fatally undermined the credibility of the organisation, and possibly compromised overall political stability"*.

So Alec had returned to Glasgow in the mid-80s and now he was Worshipful Master of this Lodge, where this morning he held his wrapt congregation in the palm of his hand:

"We are accused by the BBC, by Sky and by the socialist press of being triumphalist supremacists. They call us sectarian bigots when all we want is the freedom to live our lives without the unscriptured doctrines of the Church of Rome or the dangerous errors of modern heresy undermining our values and traditions!

"Today, Brethren, let us live out those traditions of which we are so proud. Let us celebrate democracy and freedom from Popish rule and tyrant kings. Let us join together to defend our rights to march, to sing and to be joyful on this, the greatest of all days: the Twelfth!"

Rapturous applause engulfed the room and Alec Jardine stepped down from the podium and made his way towards the back of the hall, shaking hands, patting backs and ruffling childish locks.

The Lodge Chaplain took to the stage and tapped the microphone. "Brothers and Sisters, let us now sing a firm favourite of ours; *Hands Across The Water.*"

James felt a tap on his shoulder and was led from the pew by a bear of a man toward the back of the hall. As he passed the rows of eyes, all lit with the same messianic devotion, James listened to the words as they broke into the chorus:

> *"And it's hands across the water*
> *Reaching out for you and me*
> *For Queen, For Ulster and For Scotland*
> *Helps to keep our Loyal people free*
> *Let the cry be 'No Surrender'*
> *Let no-one doubt this Loyalty*
> *Reaching out to the Brave Red Hand of Ulster*
> *Is the hand across the sea."*

48

Summer, 2018
The Necropolis, Glasgow, Scotland

The summer storm that had been threatening all morning unleashed itself as Moira sat at the back of the bus from Kelvingrove Museum to Cathedral Square. On board, sweating Glaswegians were almost relieved to see the lashing rain slice the stodgy atmosphere that had suffocated the city for days.

She took cover in the cathedral whilst angry flashes of sheet lighting lit up the skyline in electric hues. When the squall had abated and the thunder was but a distant rumble, Moira made her way across the bridge towards the Necropolis; the tang of static still fizzing in the air. As she scaled the precipitous stone steps that zig-zagged the face of the hill, torrents of rain water rushed past her bearing flower petals and sodden funeral cards.

Feeling tight-chested at the top of her climb, she vowed to cut back on the cigarettes – yet, just standing in this cemetery for the first time in years, Moira craved a lungful of smoky carcinogen more than ever. She resisted the urge, popped another piece of gum and looked about her. The violent downpour had obviously put off the tourists and scattered the mourners because there wasn't another soul about.

Sombre avenues of obelisks and angels stretched as far as the eye could see; a vast Victorian cityscape of marble. Pillared tombs pointed heavenward, mirroring the multitude of chimney stacks that once choked the horizon, both necessitating and financing the lavish mausoleums. Moira felt her heels sink into the freshly soaked earth as she passed row upon row of macabre memento mori to long dead Scottish dynasties. As she neared the outskirts of the site, the tombstones became smaller and the interment dates became more recent. Half way along a much humbler avenue of headstones, Moira found what she was looking for and knelt at the grave of her mother and father, Irene and Malcolm Dunn.

A single shard of sunlight broke through the dissipating storm clouds and Moira bowed her head, closed her eyes and whispered prayers to them both. When she opened them, she saw a shadow fall across the epitaph. Turning, she squinted up at the silhouette of a hooded man holding a Stanley knife.

Without thinking, she leapt between her parent's headstone and the next, and began to run as fast as she could. Stockinged legs pumping, she slalomed towards the labyrinth of crumbling cherubims and granite needles. Her oxygen-starved lungs were already starting to burn. If she could just make it to the bridge she was bound to come across a gaggle of sightseers on their way up the hill now that the rain had stopped.

Using the towering John Knox monument as a point of reference, Moira twisted and turned her way towards it, grazing knees on sandstone and slate. By now her heels had come off and her tights were torn and mud-splattered. Behind her she could hear the man panting and splashing. It sounded like he was gaining on her.

She reached the brow of the hill and all of Glasgow stretched out before her. Below she could see pockets of people, tiny as ants crossing the bridge. Deciding not to waste time with the winding steps, Moira clutched her bag and began to negotiate the path carved out by rain that ran directly down to safety.

Craig reached the top of ridge only seconds later. The mad auld bat, who was faster than she looked, was slipping and sliding at speed down the face of the bank. He was just about to throw himself headlong after her when he heard her scream and pitch forward. He watched as she cartwheeled downwards at neck-breaking velocity. When she finally came crashing to a halt against a weather-worn sarcophagus, Craig thought that she looked like a tangle of mismatched laundry items, blown off the line and wedged against a garden fence.

Already people were running towards her, some were even looking up and pointing towards him. Craig turned and ran back the way he'd come.

He didn't know whether Wee Bill was going to pat him on the back or stab him in it.

49

Summer, 2018
Worcester Street Orange Hall,
Glasgow, Scotland

Graeme, who led James upstairs to the Worshipful Master's study, wheezed as every square inch of his sizeable bulk strained at the suit that seemed to have been borrowed from a man much slighter than he. James imagined him shaped by dextrous hands, stretched and twisted from one long balloon into human form, his whistling breath some sort of slow puncture.

Alec Jardine sat behind a mahogany desk inlaid with claret leather. He was a trim man with a smooth, domed skull that was entirely hairless. He rose to shake James's hand, and in light of his height and military bearing, James found himself questioning Wee Bill's paternity. That is, until he saw Alec's eyes – hard, unloving; imbued with barely supressed volatility.

"Mr Dewar, take a seat, please. Could I offer you a drink? Tea, coffee, a glass of water perhaps? Unfortunately we don't have anything stronger on the premises – even on a day of celebration like today."

"Black coffee please, two sugars. Thank you."

"It isn't uncommon for those who have spent an evening with my son to require some sort of pick me up the following day,"

Jardine commented drily. "Graeme, I'll join our guest. You know how I take mine, of course."

Graeme's sausage-like fingers pulled the door to.

"So, Mr Dewar, William tells me that you are in the process of writing a book on abiding patriotism in this effete age in which we live. You will have seen today the real sense of Britishness that this Lodge and, indeed, every Lodge from British Columbia to Auckland holds dear to their hearts. There are aspects of Orangeism that you must understand I cannot share with you today. We are a close knit organisation and until sworn in as a Brother, there are protocols and ceremonies that outsiders may not be privy to. However, I imagine them to be irrelevant to your book anyway."

"Of course. I don't want to pry into the Order – I am more interested in human stories, and your family has certainly had…" James weighed his words carefully, "a colourful and strong connection to the United Kingdom over many generations. I would love to know what your father told you about his time in Flanders fighting the Germans and, more pertinently, his experiences in Offaly taking on the IRA. I am equally fascinated to explore how that informed your own decision to join the RUC and how you feel about the situation in Northern Ireland post-Brexit. Meeting with Bill – sorry, William – last night has obviously given me a very contemporary take on how your community feel about Scottish Independence and the SNP. I am keen to explore all these things, so I am really appreciative that you have found the time to speak to me today. May I record our conversation, Mr Jardine?"

"Aye, of course. I have nothing to hide, but I'm not going to say anything that I'll regret either." He laughed briskly.

James's heart sank and he placed the pay-as-you-go phone on the desk and pressed record.

"Ah, refreshments! Thank you, Graeme. Oh, and shortbread too. He's spoiling us, Mr Dewar."

When they were alone again James asked, "So, tell me about your father."

Alec stood and ushered James to the far wall where from floor to ceiling framed photographs filled almost every inch of space. Formal portraits of the Worcester Street Lodge dating from the 1920s hung alongside panoramic prints of parades taken in the last couple of years.

"My father and his regiment in Passchendaele: see how young he looks." Jardine pointed to a blurred image in a wooden frame. "That's because he was, Mr Dewar. So keen to fight for his country, he couldn't wait until he was eighteen to sign up. He was just a wee lad of seventeen when this photograph was taken."

James had seen a couple of images of Billy Jardine thanks to Oisín and Moira, and each and every one of them showed a man staring intensely from the silver-bromide as though he viewed the world and everybody within it as an adversary and he was watchful for soft flesh.

"Here he is with my mother. A truly beautiful woman."

James agreed that she was striking, but she looked positively terrified of her husband. They stood apart like strangers and the young Mrs Jardine, who was no more than a child herself, defensively clutched a baby close to her chest.

"That's me she's holding. It pains me to say it, but I hardly knew her. She was often ill and confined to bed, and after she passed, my sister and I were brought up within the community over in Fermanagh by a couple my father knew well, but had not been blessed with children themselves."

"Didn't you miss your father?"

"Oh aye. But he was a single man with a business to run and he could do without children getting in his way. We came home to Glasgow for holidays, and I returned for good when I turned eighteen."

"So what made you return to Ireland to join the RUC so soon after?"

For a split second James perceived a cloaked truth flit across the old man's eyes. In that moment James understood that Alec *knew* about his father and the boys in the marching band.

"It was the 1960s and the Republican movement was on the rise. I felt that the fight for the Union would be better served by my being in Ulster and not Scotland."

James found himself asking the question before his brain had green-lighted it. "Forgive me if I'm wrong, but weren't the RUC accused of collaboration with proscribed Loyalist organisations whilst you served in Enniskillen?"

"Let me stop you right there, Mr Dewar. I don't like the way that this conversation is going. You told my son that you were here to interview me about my father's war record and the Jardine family's commitment to retaining the Union of the United Kingdom and Northern Ireland in the face of a despotic European cabal and a fifth column of deluded dreamers and Fenian schemers who would see us split up. It was a fact of life back then that good policing required the use of strategic disinformation. Informers, prisoners and suspected spies were fed what we wanted them to hear for purposes that made perfect military sense at the time. Unfortunately in the echo-chamber of Northern Ireland, this led to certain *misconceptions* among the rank and file, and thus erroneous allegations, which I hasten to add were dealt short shrift by the government and thrown out on their ear. I *was* a good policeman, Mr Dewar, just like my father before me, who taught me all the tricks of the trade. So please don't come in here and…"

There was an urgent knocking at the door.

"I'm sorry." Jardine walked over to where Graeme was poking his sweaty head into the room.

They really should install a lift, thought James.

The large man whispered into Alec Jardine's ear before the latter turned to James and said, "Excuse me for a moment."

James was left alone in the study fighting an almost irresistible compulsion to rifle through drawers and cabinets and unearth a secret diary or deathbed confession that would neatly tie up his investigation. But of course he didn't, because he knew they wouldn't exist. If he'd learnt anything, it was that Billy Jardine and his son, Alec, were both exceptionally good at covering up the past.

The door opened and Alec Jardine strode back into the room wearing a grave expression. "I'm afraid we'll have to end it there, Mr Dewar. Another time, perhaps? Graeme will show you out. There's a taxi waiting."

James, taken aback by the abrupt end to the interview, grabbed his phone from the table and followed the puffing Graeme down the stairs. Passing an open door, he saw Wee Bill surrounded by a group of suited Orangemen deep in animated conversation. A youth in an anorak who looked like he was on the verge of tears was gesticulating wildly. Their eyes met for a heartbeat.

James exited the building convinced that the boy recognised him from somewhere, or at least thought he did. He climbed into the cab. In a beautiful fusion of Punjabi syntax and Glaswegian vowels, his driver asked, "And where is it that ye'd be wanting me tae take ye tae, sir?"

Feeling the heavy pounding of Graeme's mass on the pavement before seeing him lumbering at speed towards the taxi, James blurted, "Anywhere in the city centre will do," and because he'd only ever get one chance to say this, "and put your foot on it, my friend."

50

Summer, 2018
The Royal Infirmary, Glasgow, Scotland

James hated hospitals.

He hated the smell of the sour disinfectant that couldn't quite mask the cloying stench of bedpans and infection. He hated the ill-fitting uniforms of grubby blue and scrubs of bird-net green. He hated the grim stoicism in the face of underfunding; the dry rot that infested wall cavities and chest cavities alike. But most of all, he hated the hopeless inevitability that we'd all end up in one, pressing the assistance button with increasing alarm; knowing in our heart of hearts that it wasn't plugged in.

He felt sick to the stomach as he asked at reception where he could find Moira Dunn. He told them he was her son as he suspected that there was nobody else coming for her.

After he'd been dropped off in the city centre, James had panicked for a bit. Why had Graeme come lumbering out of the Orange Hall after him? Who was the boy who had recognised him? Did the Jardine's now know that he was playing them?

He didn't have the answer to any of these questions so he thought that the best course of action was to grab the bus back to the B&B and hunker down for the night. He would close his fake email account, dump his phone and the following morning he'd leave Alistair Dewar, the Jardines and Glasgow far behind him. He could decide what to do about everything he'd uncovered when he was safely back in Yorkshire, living in the skin of James Lucas again.

As he'd packed his suitcase, James had switched on the TV and watched the live coverage of Orangefest. Torn between considering the event unnecessarily provocative and acknowledging that it was culturally important to the communities who participated in it, he'd watched the sadly predictable footage: Blood-smeared Neds tussled with police and chanted abhorrent rhymes about Catholics. They launched cans and bottles into the incensed protesters who jeered back at them from behind flimsy barriers. James thought it was a pity for the peaceable Orangemen and women there today that a handful of louts, high on Buckie and bigotry gave the 'liberal media' exactly what they wanted.

He must have fallen asleep because when his phone buzzed it was getting dark outside. His pay-as-you-go mobile glowed, and only two people in the world had that number. The message simply read. "R U watching the news? Silence is golden."

The sender's number was withheld.

The TV was still on and James flicked through the channels until he found the local news. He turned up the volume. The anchorman was reporting that nineteen people had been arrested over the course of the day: mostly for drunk and disorderly behaviour. Then the next story came on and James paled:

"Police are appealing for any witnesses who may have been in the Cathedral Square and Necropolis area early this afternoon. Moira Dunn, 54, from Pitlochry, was found at the foot of the path that leads up to the Glasgow cemetery. Police suspect that she may have been attempting to flee an unknown assailant. Witnesses claim to have seen

*a male in his twenties at the top of the hill at the time of her fall. The
police would encourage this individual to contact them so that they
can rule him out of their enquiries. Dunn, who once worked as a
journalist for the Glasgow Tribune, now lies in a critical condition in
the Royal Infirmary. Anyone with any information should..."*

James clicked the off button: he had heard enough.

Tearing off the back of the phone, he removed the SIM card.
He folded and twisted it until it snapped. He took the battery out
and stared at the deconstructed device warily.

This was his fault.

Again.

His self-absorbed quest had got people hurt.

He had to see her.

The ICU was on the fourth floor. It was quiet and dark. James
could hear whispers and bleeps and trolley wheels. A long corridor
stretched into the shadows where James could make out a sole
customer struggling with change at a vending machine. There was
a desk behind which a nurse was standing. She had her back to
him and was writing on a whiteboard in marker pen.

"Excuse me? I am a close relative of Moira Dunn's. I understand
that she's on this ward."

The nurse turned. She looked tired, but kindly. "Yes, she's in
a poor way. There's hardly a bone in her body that's not broken.
But she's lucky that there's not too much internal damage. She
has a ruptured spleen and some swelling on the brain – but she's
breathing by herself. We have her in an induced-coma for the time
being, so you won't be able to speak to her."

"She'll live?"

"Och aye, she'll live. She looks like she's been put through
a mangle, but she'll live. There will need to be a long period of

319

rehabilitation, mind. She won't be out of hospital any time soon."

"Can I see her?"

"I don't see why not: that one there." She nodded towards a door half way down the corridor. "Adaoma, could you take this gentleman to see Miss Dunn?"

A young nurse who had been checking and replacing saline drips left her trolley and came over. She led James to a window that looked into a small side-room draped in darkness. Moira lay propped up in the bed, bruised and swollen. There were so many tubes and electrodes attached to her that she resembled a string puppet. Her head was held rigid with a white neck-brace and both her arms were suspended in plaster.

"Would you like to go in, sir?"

"No thank you, there is no need."

"I'll be here if you need me."

The nurse returned to her trolley.

God, what have I done? thought James.

Down the corridor the vending machine whirred, spluttered and trickled the last drops of hot beverage into the paper cup. James stood a moment longer looking at Moira and praying that all would be well. Could it have been a random attack? Maybe it wasn't linked to the Jardines? How could he know?

James glanced up as the man with the coffee approached. He in turn peered at his phone, then back at James and picked up his pace.

As he passed beneath the dim glow of LED light, James thought he recognised the tell-tale stitching of the XIIVII tattoo on his arm.

He backed away from the window and started walking back towards the lifts. He pressed the button, pressed it again, then decided to take the stairs. Pushing through a fire door, he took them two at a time. For a glorious moment he thought that it was all in his head – until he heard the fire door open above him and the slapping of trainer on linoleum.

James now hurled himself down the flight of stairs, almost dislocating his shoulder each time he used the bannisters to make the 180 degree turn every half level. The wan lighting pitched the bottom of the staircase into blackness as James jarred his knees with each juddering stride.

Piling through the fire door on the ground floor, James spilled out into a carpark. It was deserted. Behind him he could hear the pat-ta-pat of rapid footfall. In the distance, James divined movement; emerging from beneath an electric barrier about fifty metres away a small car crawled around the corner.

James started to run towards it, yelling and waving his arms.

It wasn't stopping.

He thrust his hand into his pocket and pulled out his car keys. Attached to the keyring was Joseph Conlon's RIC whistle; the one he'd had on him the day he was murdered.

If I save your reputation, Joe, will you save my life?

James put the whistle to his lips and blew for all he was worth.

———————

Anna Kalniņš had endured a ten-hour shift and could barely see straight she was that tired. She'd only been in Scotland for six months, but already she'd come to learn that if your shift in the Casualty Department was on a Friday night or Saturday evening, then you'd be lucky if you even had time to visit the bathroom. Tonight had been worse than usual though. She couldn't count the number of times she'd been told to go back home as she stitched up slashes made by bottles and pint glasses.

Well, she was going home now. Back to a flat she shared with another girl who would probably be out when she got in. She knew that there'd be no milk left in the fridge and that at 5am her flatmate would come crashing and giggling through the door with a man in tow. Anna would be forced to listen to manic conversation from the kitchen whilst she tried to sleep and then frenzied sex from the bedroom once she'd given up and was toasting stale bread and drinking black tea. And then she had to be back at the hospital for 10am.

Maybe they were right. She wasn't exactly living the dream over here.

As she pulled out from the staff carpark in her rust-bucket Citroen she heard a sound that sent her back to the basketball courts at her school in Jelgava. A whistle was being blown again and again – usually signifying a serious foul had been committed – she slowed the car and saw a man with dark hair and a grey jacket running towards her waving his arms.

She was just about to press the accelerator and leave this mad person to his whistling and gesticulating when she saw the muscular, bald-headed thug sprinting up behind him. He looked the same as all those other hooligans who were happy for her to tend to their wounds as long as she fucked off back to Latvia afterwards.

Anna didn't think twice. She slammed her foot on the break and reached over to the passenger door. She flung it open and called, "Get in!"

51

Summer, 2018
The City Centre Police Office,
Glasgow, Scotland

James was still trembling as he sipped the black coffee. It wasn't fear he told himself, it was the adrenaline coursing through his veins. Of course, he was lying to himself. He'd been terrified, and he still was. But he was also angry: angry that Moira was in an induced coma, angry at himself for setting into motion a chain of events that had led to this and angry at the Jardines, for... well, for being such a bunch of evil bastards.

The interview room was all sharp corners and drab colours. James sat on a grey plastic chair at a grey table that was bolted to the grey floor. Above him a camera blinked impassively. He had been sitting in this tiny room for twenty-five minutes and the dregs of his coffee were cold and tasted like sugared polystyrene.

He was waiting for DI Campbell, the lead officer in the Moira Dunn investigation. In his mind's eye the name conjured up images of a dishevelled detective in his fifties; three-day old stubble camouflaging pockmarked skin. His words would be delivered in a gravelly Glaswegian growl, betraying just the faintest whiff of vodka and deep-seated cynicism. So James was surprised when an ageless man with voluptuous lips, a translucent complexion and hair that was neither blond nor white entered the room. In a soft, almost effeminate voice he thanked James for waiting and sat opposite him, holding a folder.

"Mr Lucas, I am Detective Inspector David Campbell. I am co-ordinating enquires into the injuries sustained earlier today of one Moira Dunn. I understand that you have some information that you believe would be helpful." He shuffled through some papers and glanced down. "I see that you've only been in Glasgow a couple of days and that you're staying in a guest house in the Woodlands area. I have your address as one in Yorkshire? Is that correct?"

"Yes, Boroughbridge."

"Now before we put anything to paper, could you just outline for me what you think you saw or what you believe may have happened to Ms Dunn?"

Campbell clasped his hands together and assumed an air of receptiveness but James got the distinct impression that the detective thought that he was a time waster.

James started by telling Campbell about his meeting with Moira Dunn that morning. He was in the process of explaining the contents of her memory stick when Campbell interrupted him.

"Excuse me, Mr Lucas. Did I hear you say *Alec Jardine*?"

"Yes. You see, that's what all this is about. Three generations of Jardines and all of them criminals: Billy, Alec, and 'Wee' Bill. They've been involved in sexual molestation, murder, intimidation and decades of corruption – and I think that Moira Dunn was silenced by the family because she knew the truth and now I think that I am in danger too." The words tumbled too quickly.

"Calm down, Mr Lucas." Campbell looked interested now. "Tell me everything from the very beginning."

So James did: he started with the chance discovery of O'Rourke's account in a bookshop on the Shambles and ended with Conlon's whistle and the Latvian nurse who'd maybe saved his life and driven him here.

When he had finished, the detective blinked as impassively as the camera behind him. "That is quite a story, Mr Lucas. So, correct me if I am wrong, but you are alleging that Ms Dunn was thrown down the steps of the Necropolis by one of Bill Jardine's – I'll use your word here – '*henchmen*', because she was in possession of sensitive and incriminating information on the Jardine family relating to historical sex crimes, collusion with terrorists and gangsterism on the streets of Glasgow. Also, that one William Jardine, now deceased, was responsible for the murder in 1921 of an entire family and a parish priest, but that he somehow managed to shift the blame onto an innocent police officer who happens to be your great-grandfather?"

With soft and reasonable inflection, he asked, "You're no relation to George Lucas by any chance? This sounds like it could make a very good screenplay."

"What? No, Detective." James was exasperated. "I have the evidence – the tape recordings and the drawings and a laptop full of documents. Surely the hospital will have CCTV. This isn't made up: it's real!"

"And where is all this *evidence*?"

"I told you. Everything is back in my room at the B&B."

"But you say that you've destroyed the SIM card you'd been using to communicate with the Jardines?"

"Yes, but the phone is still there." James massaged his temple. "Look, it might sound far-fetched, but if you take all the pieces together then it adds up."

Campbell smiled benignly. "Mr Lucas, if you believe half of what you say then you are, in effect, making very serious allegations against a family who will have no scruples about seeing you come to harm. Your evidence is based on the ravings of a dementia sufferer and a victim of sexual abuse from half a century ago, both of whom are now dead. More than that, the only other person who can confirm your story is in a coma. If you want my advice, I would forget about all of this. No good can come of it. Go home to Yorkshire and live out your life. Leave this city and its history alone. What you have against the Jardines won't ever make it to a court of law – all you are doing is opening up yourself to mischief. And for what?"

James couldn't believe he was hearing this: "*For the truth*, Detective Campbell. I would see justice served. I would like to make a formal statement please, and if I can't make that statement here with you, then I will go to another police station to make it."

Campbell's gaze hardened.

"As you wish, Mr Lucas. I'll need to speak with my superiors about what we might be landing ourselves in. Another coffee while you wait?"

───────────

Hours had passed: the coffee hadn't been forthcoming.

James had been left in the interview room for another forty minutes before Campbell returned. He had then written up a statement which the two of them had gone through before both had signed and dated it. He'd then been left alone while the detective disappeared again, this time clutching his phone. When he eventually returned, Campbell was holding the statement:

"Think on this very carefully before you go, Mr Lucas. What you've written on these sheets of paper could change your life and the lives of those you care about. It is my duty as a police officer to warn you that, whilst we will make every effort to support and protect you throughout the process, we can't *guarantee* your safety. If this were to come to trial, which I doubt, then life could get very nasty for you. I am not trying to frighten you off: I'm merely telling it to you like it is. It's your call. If you change your mind at any point, then I can make this go away."

He waved the wodge of papers.

"Thank you for your concern, Detective Inspector, but I have to do this. For Moira and her father and for my family."

"Very well." DI Campbell stood up. "It's late and as we need to recover the data from your laptop and collect those tape cassettes and drawings, I'll send you home with a member of my team. Good night, Mr Lucas. Think on what I said."

———————

Constable Sharon Reid pulled up on the double yellow lines outside the Georgian townhouse overlooking Kelvingrove Park. It was 3am and the streets this side of town were absolutely silent.

James was shattered and just wanted to climb into bed and curl up under the covers but he knew that the policewoman would have to bag and tag various pieces of evidence first. He understood that he wasn't going to get to sleep any time soon.

They climbed the steps to the front door and, as James dug in his pockets for the keys, he heard the constable say, "Stand back a moment, sir."

She reached behind her and pulled a torch from her police-belt. Shining it towards the handle, the beam spilt through a sliver of open door and onto the hallway floor behind it.

She inched it open and paused.

"Police. Is there anybody there?"

There was no reply.

"I repeat – there is a police officer about to enter the premises. Come out slowly with your hands up if you are not meant to be here."

Keys rattled in a lock and the door to the left of the hallway opened. A startled woman peered out, squinting into the torch-beam. James recognised the B&B owner, Mrs Dunleavy. She fumbled for a light switch and the hallway burst into warm white.

"Madam, your front door was ajar. Is there anybody other than you in this building?"

She glanced at James, "Well, this young man is staying in Room 4 and I have a French couple in Room 3 upstairs, but other than that no one."

"Could the other couple have left the front door unlocked, Madam?"

"I don't know, maybe."

"Are all the guest rooms upstairs?"

Mrs Dunleavy nodded.

"If you could both stay here for a moment, please?"

Constable Reid climbed the stairs and a couple of minutes later James heard the crackle of her police radio as she returned. He caught the end of her conversation.

"The property is clear. Two of the bedroom doors upstairs have been forced, but as the front door is intact, I would suspect an opportunist has just nipped in and tried his luck. The old dear or one of the guests obviously hadn't locked the front door properly. I'll get them to check for missing items and take statements. Alright?"

She reached the foot of the stairs and turned to Mrs Dunleavy.

"I'm afraid that you've had an intruder, hen. We're going to have to go upstairs and catalogue everything that has been taken."

James had a nasty suspicion that he already knew.

52

Summer, 2018
Boroughbridge, North Yorkshire, England

Charlie awoke abruptly.

It was too hot: the sluggish breeze that pushed and sucked the blinds felt like it had originated in Equatorial Guinea.

Charlie had kicked off the sheets hours ago and was lying naked on the double bed that had seemed large before James had left but now stretched out endlessly and edgelessly on every side. She glistened with sweat; the sheets beneath her were moist and sticky.

There was somebody in her kitchen.

She'd heard the scrape of chair across flagstones.

Slipping from the bed, Charlie wrapped a robe round her bare flesh, reached for the telephone receiver and listened.

Silence.

There was no dial tone at all.

Shit.

Her mobile was in her handbag, dumped with her high heels beneath the coat rack the moment she'd stepped into the house.

Charlie tip-toed to the bedroom door and opened it a crack. She could see the landing and the curve of the stairs.

There was nobody there.

Terrified that switching on the lights would alert whoever was downstairs to her presence, she closed her eyes tight and counted to ten. When she opened them she could discern grey contours and charcoal edging.

She crept along the corridor, crouched at the top of the stairs and peered over the bannisters into the open-plan living space below.

No one.

She listened.

Nothing.

Smack!

Her bedroom door slammed shut and Charlie almost jumped from her skin. The tell-tale blinds tapped against the window frame behind it.

Paralysed with fear, every atom of her being screamed at her to stay still and watch for any movement in the shadows beneath her; but she knew that she had to get to her mobile phone.

Step by step she descended the stairs. Treading with her entire weight on the balls of her feet Charlie skirted the coffee table and padded towards the hallway door. The latch clicked too loudly in the still of the night. She slipped through, closing it gently behind her.

Distant streetlights were refracted in the frosted glass of the front door. Charlie could make out coats and long boots huddled together like Cossacks keeping warm. She knelt at their feet and felt her way through the compartments in her handbag.

She had it.

Unlocking her phone, a painfully bright image of herself and James kissing beneath an Icelandic waterfall glowed from the handset.

She held her breath and dialled 999.

She winced at the volume of the operator.

"Emergency Services. Which service do you require? Police, Ambulance or Fire?"

"Police," whispered Charlie. "There's someone in my house. I am a woman and I am alone. My landline has been cut. My name is Charlie Lucas and I'm at No. 4, Little Ings Lane, Borougbridge. Send somebody now please."

"OK." Charlie heard a clatter of keystrokes. "Someone's on their way. Are you able to lock yourself in a safe place and wait for their arrival?"

"Yes, I think so."

"Can you stay on the line please?"

"I will, but I don't want to talk. They'll hear me."

Charlie looked along the corridor towards the downstairs bathroom, but didn't like the thought of being trapped in a small space with no escape route, so she unlatched the front door, wedged it ajar with a Wellington boot and drew an umbrella from the stand and waited.

Time moved so slowly.

She thought that she heard the stairs creak and then a shutter slide. A couple of seconds later gravel crunched. Between the trees she spotted a shadow flit across the wall on the opposite side of the street. Fifty yards down the lane rear lights lit the tarmac red, and an engine growled into life.

Charlie knew instinctively that the house was empty. She whispered into the phone. "I think they might be gone."

"Don't move. Stay where you are, love. The police are on their way. They'll be with you in a matter of minutes."

But Charlie wasn't listening. She walked through the living room into the kitchen. She saw that the French doors were open onto the patio. She slid them shut. Swapping the umbrella for a large kitchen knife, Charlie made her way to the foot of the stairs. She flicked the light switch and began to climb.

Her bedroom door was open again.

Somebody had been up here whilst she'd been downstairs.

Cautiously she approached their room, the phone nestling

between shoulder blade and ear, the knife gripped with both hands.

She felt the gust of sultry air before the door slammed shut.

And she started to scream.

The phone fell to the floor, a tiny voice imploring, "Talk to me. What's happening? Are you alright? Ms Lucas, are you there? Talk to me!"

But Charlie couldn't hear the operator anymore. All her senses were focused on the blood-red hand print on her bedroom door and the weeping rivulets of scarlet streaming onto the carpet.

53

Summer, 2018
Glasgow, Scotland

Slumped in a tartan armchair in a strange Scottish room, James stared numbly at the upturned suitcase and at the trousers and T-shirts tossed across the quilt.

From the corridor he could hear Constable Reid relaying an update to her boss back at the station.

Everything was gone: his laptop, the pay-as-you-go phone, his external hard drive, all the USB sticks and the box of cassettes and sketches. This 'opportunist' had even seen fit to rifle through the used tissues and empty sugar sachets in James's wastepaper basket to retrieve the twisted chip that used to be a SIM card. Despite the fact that the empty room next door had also been forced and a kettle and alarm clock taken, James knew full well that the only thing *opportunistic* about this burglary was the opportunity afforded by his extended interview with the only man in Glasgow who knew his real name and where he was staying.

Thus James wasn't entirely shocked when Sharon Reid popped her head around the door proffering her mobile. "DI Campbell would like to have a word with you."

Campbell was delicate and deadpan. "Mr Lucas, I hear your day has gone from bad to worse. Constable Reid has filled me in on the details. This is either an unfortunate coincidence or something else entirely; but I did warn you. When I went upstairs to speak to the top brass, a lot of ears pricked up at the mention of Alec Jardine. Your personal details are available at the click of a mouse from lowly desk Sergeant to Chief Constable, so…" He left the words hanging. "I think it's easier for all concerned if we just treat this as an unrelated incident. Obviously, I have to inform you that without any of the evidence that you claimed to be in possession of, we are no longer in a position to pursue your allegations any further at this point. Do you understand that, Mr Lucas?"

James still didn't respond.

"I hope this doesn't put you off Glasgow, eh? You know, they say that bad luck comes in threes, so considering what I've just told you, I think it might be prudent to phone home and check that everything's OK?"

But James didn't need to because that very moment his mobile began to ring and it was Charlie.

54

Summer, 2018
Todhill Services, M6, Cumbria, England

James had had to pull over.

It was all too much: Swarms of thoughts assaulted his sanity. Snatched snippets of conversation, swirling images and switching emotions looped through exhausted synapses. Threading through them all were the final words of Charlie's phone call: *"James you promised this wouldn't happen – you promised me! Don't think I don't understand what a fucking red hand symbolises! What have you done? Who have you pissed off? You have to end this now and come home."* She paused, waiting for his response. *"Especially as things are going to change; I didn't want to have to tell you like this, but I'm pretty sure that I'm pregnant."* She began to laugh and sob at the same time.

And that had been the moment when the penny dropped.

He'd paid Mrs Dunleavy in cash, thrown his clothes back in the suitcase and he'd jumped in the car and started driving. He hadn't wanted to stop until he pulled up outside their front door and saw Charlie at the window. However, as he crossed the border at Gretna approaching Carlisle, his aching brain threatened to send him careering through the central barrier, so now he sat in his car watching the weak sun break through the clouds over the Cheviot Mountains.

He was beaten.

He had to give up; the groundswell of guilt that had driven him since reading those first few chapters of O'Rourke's book, spiked by his suspension from school had made him reckless. And look what had happened: to Moira and now Charlie. He was a selfish man who was putting other people's lives in danger trying to exculpate his own sins.

As always when it became too much, James sought solace in the songs that sound-tracked a time of his life before it all got so dark: the time before Connor died and James began a daily battle against the black tumour he carried with him everywhere. He reached into the glove compartment and grabbed a tape. Labelled 'Celtic Calm', James recalled that he had recorded each track individually from vinyl and had given it to his mother one Christmas. It was a collage of bitter-sweet ballads by artists like Christy Moore and Clannad. It had some Pogues and some Sinéad O'Connor too. In fact, James had liked it so much that he'd spirited it away to university a couple of years later. James could remember playing it one night to Charlie while they lay in bed surrounded by candles, overfull ashtrays and empty bottles of cheap wine: she hadn't been impressed.

Ejecting the cassette already in the machine, James saw that the very last recording of Alison Fallon's interviews with her grandfather had escaped the burglary. What good would that do him now? He tossed it to one side.

Celtic Calm slipped in: he pressed play.

The ghost of a needle scratching and catching the grooves of the record gave way to quivering strings that rose and fell. Sinéad O'Connor whispered an ancient prayer. The words couldn't have been more pertinent: *'God grant me the serenity to accept the things I cannot change, the courage to change the things I can, and the wisdom to know the difference'.*

He felt goosebumps on his forearm and a strange chill on the back of his neck as he realised the serendipity of the moment. *I've done what I can; I'm going to have to let it go*, he thought.

The song was called *Feel So Different* and he'd heard it a thousand times, yet he was certain that *this* was the precise moment he was meant to understand it. James smiled wistfully at how we project our current circumstances onto simple stanzas, dressing and redressing them over the years whilst the words themselves never change.

We only hear what we want to hear.

Certainly O'Rourke had wanted to believe that Conlon was responsible for all the murders in Offaly. And all those who read his book or stamped their feet to *Ol' Mad Eyed Joe of the RIC* were fed a tale they wanted told.

Fed a tale they wanted told: James froze.

A throwaway sentence uttered by Alec Jardine collided with a turn of phrase in O'Rourke's book.

And everything made sense.

Finally James understood what had happened on the 11th of July 1921. With crystal clarity, he saw how Billy Jardine had brought about Joseph Conlon's death, and by the same token, damned him for all eternity.

He turned the ignition key. James knew what he had to do to end this, but first he needed to muster the courage to change the things he could: he was going to have to return to London and pay a visit to Brenda McCleary.

55

10th July, 1921
Birr, King's County, Ireland

The parochial house on Wilmer Street was a large, suitably austere building. At the turn of the century it had housed four priests who between them had served the local community and outlying parishes and conducted Mass for the nuns of St John's Convent. However, since the troubles began, only Father Patrick O'Brien and Father Boniface O'Carroll were full time residents. Whereas O'Brien tended to the spiritual needs of the parishioners of St Brendan's, it was Father O'Carroll who was tasked with celebrating Mass at the religious houses of Birr and Gloster.

Father O'Brien had risen early as he had a busy day ahead: Boniface was on retreat in Tullamore and thus his duties had transferred to the shoulders of the older priest. O'Brien had barely slept a wink. Indeed, he had slept fitfully all week. Since Eamonn O'Donagh's little girl, Bronagh, had confessed to him what she had seen in the derelict building on the edge of town, the cleric had wrestled with his conscience. If what she said was true, and he had no reason to doubt her, then Joseph Conlon needed to know. The announcement of the truce between the Crown Forces and the rebels was common knowledge about town, and although the priest thanked the Lord for an end to hostilities, he feared that if he didn't say something then it may be too late. Once the ceasefire came into effect the following day, who was to know what would happen to the swollen police force here in Birr? He imagined that they might be redeployed elsewhere and the man who had committed these heinous acts would escape justice.

Before he had taken to bed the night before, O'Brien had prayed for hours on wooden floorboards for guidance. He'd confided in his diary that today he would press the girl to speak with the Sergeant – but on reflection, he didn't think it fair to force the child to relive the experience, especially with a man who was not of the cloth. So, Father O'Brien had resolved to speak to Joseph himself. His conscience told him that he wasn't breaking the seal of the confessional because he wasn't revealing the sins of the confessor, but the sins of a monster to whom he was not bound.

———

Ciaran Fahy buried his face into the pillow as Maggie threw open the curtains.

"Top o' the mornin', brother dearest. Mammy's baking boxty and there's porridge in the pot, so there is. It's amazes me what the return of the prodigal son will do to a mother keenin' for her first born. It's not like Carmel or I get this treatment, but I suppose we should enjoy it while it lasts."

"Jaysus, Maggie. What time is it?"

"Time to be up, Ciaran. You're not in the city any more, you're home in the country, an' it's getting late!"

Ciaran groaned and rolled onto his back.

It *was* good to be home. He had missed the fresh air, the bleating of sheep and barking of dogs. He'd missed his mother and her baking and he'd even missed his sabre-rattling father and sisters. He hadn't been home since November when Carmel wed

Brendan up in the hills, and even then it had been a fleeting visit. He supposed that after what had happened to Micheál, he'd come to consider the green fields around the farm poisoned with his brother's blood – and his father responsible for encouraging him to take up arms in the first place.

Ciaran wasn't a soldier: he could never have pulled the trigger on Seán Keane like Brendan. He liked to think that the act of killing a man in cold blood was beyond him. But neither was he naïve enough to imagine that the words he'd written in the *Western Gazette* hadn't inspired somebody else to commit an equally callous deed in the name of the Republic. Being at arm's length from the bloodshed suited Ciaran and his talents. That was why he was back in Birr. The announcement of the ceasefire afforded an opportunity for Sinn Féin to set up a circuit of Dáil courts in the rural areas and Ciaran was responsible for co-ordinating that process here. If Brendan hadn't been arrested at the Midland Fair a week earlier then Ciaran would now be working with him and the South Offaly Brigade to that end. However, as far as he understood the terms of the truce, with the cessation of violence on the 11th, there would also be an amnesty of political prisoners, so the Fahys were hopeful of Brendan's release on the morrow.

Ciaran had assumed that Carmel would be ecstatic at the imminent liberation of her husband, but in the few short days he'd been home he'd not once seen her smile. His youngest sister appeared guarded and distant and, despite the warm weather, she hid herself under layers of material. It was only last night, after Carmel had retired to bed and Ciaran had commented on her behaviour, that Maggie had whispered to him that their sister had lost a child before Christmas, and that mammy and daddy didn't know. She would say no more on the matter and swore her brother to secrecy. In the uncomfortable silence that followed, Ciaran watched as Maggie gnawed her lip and stared into the embers wearing a pained expression that he couldn't read.

Like Father O'Brien, Brendan O'Rourke had not slept well, but this had nothing to do with his conscience and everything to do with an infected shoulder and a straw mattress that was utterly devoid of straw.

Dr Burke hadn't changed his bandages in two days and Brendan couldn't lift his right arm. The healing process hadn't been aided by the earlier interrogation at the hands of Conlon. The big man had pressed him to give up the locations of the safe houses his men had fled to after the debacle of the Midland Fair but O'Rourke wouldn't speak. Handcuffed to a heavy wooden table, he regarded the policeman with contempt and licked his bruised lips.

"Ye can't win, Conlon. There's no place for yer sort in Ireland anymore. The whole town saw what ye did to me. They won't forget and neither will the IRA – no one ye love will ever be safe." And then, just for good measure. "Ye can't stop what's gonna to happen here, Peeler…" He grinned.

"What? What's going to happen here? What have you got planned? You'll tell me, damn it!"

Brendan just grinned more broadly.

Conlon rose from his chair slowly, his dark irises glowering with hatred and walked behind O'Rourke and out of his line of sight. White pain shot from skull to fingernails as the policeman clamped his huge hands around both shoulders, leant in and whispered, "I asked you politely, what has been planned?"

His grip tightened and Brendan screamed in agony. Conlon stepped back, but Brendan continued to scream and scream.

The door was flung open and an older man with bushy, white sideburns burst into the room. Seeing the blood welling from Brendan's bandages and Conlon standing behind the prisoner wiping his left hand on his trouser-leg, he barked, "Sergeant, a word please."

Since then O'Rourke had neither seen nor heard Sergeant Joseph Conlon. He'd been taken back to his cell where an hour later the doctor changed his bandages, and then he was left alone.

That had been two days ago.

However, in those two days Brendan had come to appreciate that his words of bravado about the inevitability of an Irish Republic might not be so far from the truth after all. The makeshift cell in which he was detained had once been a larder and was just off another smallish room that had been the Workhouse scullery. It was now home to a desk and cupboard in which the cell keys were kept. Bare of any other furnishing, this wing of the barracks echoed even whispered conversations and Brendan could hear almost everything that passed between the Peelers as they changed shifts. And he had heard that there was to be a ceasefire.

Tomorrow, he might be free.

"Joseph, wake up."

Joe Conlon could feel Kitty's lips on his forehead. His eyes opened to a sight that never ceased to humble him: this beautiful, sensuous woman regarding him with adoration.

He didn't deserve it.

If truth be told, he'd failed her. It was his subordinates who'd stepped up, not him. If it hadn't been for the intelligence passed to him by Daly then the town he'd vowed to keep safe could have been drenched in blood at the Midland Fair. More than that, he'd allowed his rage to get the better of him more than once this week and he knew full well that there were mutterings about his suitability to represent the Crown. Both those of a republican bent, and those who were not, believed him too handy with his fists. From the highest echelons of establishment Birr, the message had filtered down that he had to watch his step.

That is why Head Constable Regan had pulled him from the interrogation room and told him to stay away from the barracks until O'Rourke was gone:

"God knows, Joe, that your heart's in the right place, but remember what I said to you when the Tans arrived: it's *them* that should be getting their hands dirty – we'll have a job to do once they're gone. Christ, how much dirtier could you have got your own hands this week? And in front of the chattering classes as well! I can't have you in the barracks, Joe. Take a break. You have a pregnant wife to look after and I'm sure that Kitty could do with some help around the house. O'Rourke's like a red rag to a bull with you, he'll goad you into doing something you'll regret. Stay away, Sergeant. Let us deal with him."

So for the last few days, Joe had not worn the uniform and he'd spent time with his daughter and he'd laughed with his wife. When news began to emerge that there was to be a ceasefire on Monday, Kitty had taken his head in her hands and planted a lingering kiss on his lips.

"You did it, Joe. You promised to keep us safe and you have. In a couple of months, things could be back to normal. With peace coming we can put this behind us. Our babies can meet my mammy!"

Kitty had beamed with unrestrained joy as Joe gently touched her rounded belly. That night they had fallen asleep in each other's arms.

In this bubble of idyllic domesticity, Joe had almost forgotten the world outside the window. She was right, once things were over maybe there might be reconciliation with the Sheehans. If his bridges were burnt in Birr, which looked to be the case, then Joe couldn't care less where he lived, as long as it was with Kitty.

She was stroking him now, her dark hair tumbling and tickling his cheeks. "So, husband, are you planning on getting up at all this morning? I have some more chores I would love for you…"

Kitty was cut short as their daughter, Bridget, came squealing into the bedroom and clambered onto her father's chest. "Daddy, do we *have* to go to church today? Can't we walk along the river instead? Please?"

Joe feigned a look of outrage. "Bridget Cathleen Conlon! I never heard the like. If you want to be an angel one day, then yes, we do."

Bridget pouted.

"Come here, Bridie, and give your daddy a kiss. We can walk along the river afterwards. Cross my heart, hope to die."

Joe would never know how different things could have been if he'd only stayed away from St Brendan's that Sunday morning and skimmed stones across the water and caught sticklebacks with his daughter.

56

10th July, 1921
Birr, King's County, Ireland

As if attending a wedding every Sunday, the congregation of St Brendan's had conspicuously divided itself into two camps: the larger of the two supported the status quo and was primarily made up of shopkeepers, land owners and those that worked in the legal profession. They sat on the right. On the left were the tenant farmers, the teachers, the very young and the very old – some of whom were veterans of the Land Wars of the 1870s. Although Father O'Brien never deviated from his message of love and reconciliation, there had been precious little of that between the pious Catholics on either side of the aisle since 1919.

Bridget was already dragging her father from the pew before the dying note of the final hymn had dissipated. The Conlon family shuffled patiently with the rest of the congregants towards the porch where their parish priest accepted platitudes, shook hands, smiled and nodded.

Joe noticed O'Brien glancing down the aisle, through the milling throng, as though looking for somebody. When their eyes connected, Joe realised that the person was he. When he reached the priest, O'Brien pulled him close, smelling as he always did of incense and communion wine.

"Sergeant, I would have an urgent word with you, but not now. I must first celebrate the Eucharist with our sisters at Gloster then here at the Convent, but later this afternoon I would appreciate it if you would grant me the time to lay out a delicate matter; a delicate *police matter*. I wouldn't ask if it wasn't important, Joseph. Would you take tea with me at the rectory at four?"

Somewhat puzzled, Joe agreed and stepped out into the churchyard. It was a glorious day and he had a couple of hours to spend with the two people he loved most in the world.

———————

Despite the warmth of the sunbeams catching crystal on the drinks tray, Joe was chilled by what Father O'Brien told him. Bronagh O'Donagh's description of a scarred policeman with a tidy moustache could only be one person: William Jardine.

Joe had never liked the man: he possessed a dark charisma the other men found attractive. Even though only a constable, it was clear to Joe that he was the de facto leader of the 'Protestant clique' that had evolved within the ranks. Acting Sergeant Daly may well be his superior on paper, but he danced to Jardine's tune. Joe now suspected that he knew where the intelligence that Daly had been feeding him had originated: Eamonn O'Donagh had been the wary old farmer at Micheál Fahy's funeral and the boy at his side was this 'Tommy', of whom the priest spoke. Somehow Jardine had got his claws into the boy and was despoiling him and dredging him for information at the same time.

Joe felt the old rage rise inside him. Not only at the deeds of the Glaswegian, but at the fact that something so sick and sordid could have infected this most perfect of days. The butterflies, giggles and stolen kisses of the riverside seemed as though they'd happened in another world. Now O'Brien's words had dragged him back

346

to this one: a gritty and unforgiving place where men committed unspeakable acts in the name of God or nation or neither. More than that, Joseph hated that he could not let it go. His sense of duty impelled him to follow a path he innately understood could lead to no good. A less principled, but maybe wiser man than he would have returned home to his supper and forgotten all about it. But Joe wasn't that man.

When he arrived at the Workhouse Barracks, it was almost deserted. There were two men on sentry duty, but all the vehicles were out on patrol. Nodding at the desk officer as he stepped into the station, Joe asked for the duty roster. As he scanned the names, he heard an explosion of laughter from the mess hall followed by a barrage of expletives. Amongst them he could make out the recognisable vowels of a Scotsman.

He dropped the roster on the desk and strode towards the refectory. Pausing outside the door for a moment, he listened. The men were boasting about their marksmanship. He recognised the Cockney twang of Simons:

"You could 'ardly 'it a barn door at five paces, mate!"

"Fuck off. I'm a better shot than ye'll ever be." The Scottish accent again.

Then Joe heard the hard consonants of an Ulsterman. "Danny, go on, tell 'em about my shot. Took out a horse from behind a trap at what must have been a hundred yards, on a bend, in the woods. One in a million shot that was. Go on Danny, tell 'em."

Joe felt adrenaline spike the blood that ran cold in his veins.

He stepped into the room and saw Daly, Fallon, Simons and the Scotsman, Taggart, sitting at the table. There was no Jardine.

Daly stood. "Something wrong, sir? Ye look like ye've seen a ghost."

Conlon could barely conceal his animosity, "Jardine. Where is he?"

"On patrol. Him, Evans and Flynn are sweeping the border roads into Tipperary, sir."

"You tell him that I know about Tommy. You tell him that he's not going to get away with it." Joe's voice was getting louder and starting to tremble. "And don't think I didn't hear what you just said, soldier."

Daly smirked, "I don't know what ye think ye heard, sir. We're just talking shite at the table on the last day of war."

"I know full well what you were talking about, Daly, and I'll see you charged for it."

Daly stepped forward and squared up to his Sergeant. "If ye have something to say to me, *sir*," he spat insolently, "then say it to my face."

Joe clenched his fists and felt any restraint that he had thus far shown drain from him. Fury welled up once more.

"You will do nothing of the sort, Sergeant!"

From behind, the angry and exasperated Head Constable Regan continued, "If you have something to say about any of the men under your command, you'll damn well put it into writing and you will bring your complaint to me and you and I will discuss the merits of your suspicions. You will not come barging into the barracks spoiling for a fight. Do you hear me, Sergeant?"

"Yes, sir."

"First thing tomorrow, I want a written statement that clearly outlines whatever suspicions you may harbour about members of the Constabulary on my desk up at St John's Mall. I do not want to see you in this building again. Are we clear on that, Sergeant?"

"Sir."

"Now this is the last time I will tell you, Joseph: go home and be with your family."

Regan turned to the men at the table. "And as for the rest of you, do you think the highways and byways of King's County are going to police themselves? Get out there and make sure not a drop more blood is spilt before we sign the truce. Go!"

———————

Kitty had been immediately fearful of Joe's grim expression on his return from the barracks but could get nothing more from him than grunts as he stomped upstairs. Within minutes Joe realised that he needed a more detailed account from the priest before he began to write his deposition. He was also acutely aware that he couldn't bear to be in the same house as Kitty as he committed to paper the suspicion that all this time he had worked with and even promoted the man who'd beaten her cousin to death. Surely it was going to seem to everyone as though he'd protected Daly these past two years?

As he brushed past her, he muttered, "I wish I'd never seen the damn priest today. I've got some grim work to do Kitty. I'll be back later."

Father O'Brien was still at the rectory when Joe arrived. The policeman recounted what had happened with Regan and asked the priest to write a statement that he in turn would type up. O'Brien had hurriedly scribbled a side of prose in an elaborate hand before apologising that he had to make his way back to Gloster for vespers. He told Joe that he was welcome to stay at the rectory and use his study if he was uncomfortable at home. Joe thanked him and accepted his offer.

As O'Brien left, he regarded Joe sympathetically saying, "God can give us fortitude in many different ways, Joseph, but I find that a little brandy helps too."

Joe listened to horseshoes on cobbles and rolling wheels as the priest's trap trundled past the open window and along Wilmer

Street. He reached for the decanter and poured a generous measure. Joseph Conlon breathed deeply, slipped the thick, cream paper between the platen and paper-table, cracked his fingers and started to type.

––––––––––––

Joe typed for hours.

He wrote and rewrote. All the while expecting O'Brien to return, but with his own lids drooping and the document finished, he clipped the sheets together, closed the black attaché case and left the rectory without having had the chance to thank the priest for his hospitality.

The lights were out on Main Street as he tiptoed upstairs and slipped into bed beside his sleeping wife. He leant over, stroked her hair and kissed her on the cheek. He knew that this time she wouldn't object to the resignation letter that he had attached to the affidavit he was going to present to Regan in the morning.

57

10ᵗʰ July, 1921
The O'Donagh Farm, Galross,
King's County, Ireland

Father O'Brien had only arrived at the farm a quarter of an hour earlier. It was a long trek from Gloster to Galross, but his conscience weighed heavy on him. It was the *boy* who needed to confess or he wouldn't have his sins absolved. Without absolution he surely risked eternal damnation.

The O'Donagh's were surprised to see him at this time of night, but fussed over him anyway, offering tea and Barmbrack. When Bronagh had spied the priest, she had fled upstairs to her bedroom dragging her brother with her.

O'Brien was sitting at the kitchen table contemplating how to broach the issue with the boy's parents when he heard the snarl of an engine approaching the farm. His heart sank as he realised that it would probably be Joseph, on his way to take an official statement from Tommy. The Lord knew that this was going to become awkward for everybody.

At the sound of the engine, Eamonn O'Donagh cast a wary glance at his wife and sprung to the curtains with an agility that belied his years. Wearing an expression of alarm, he exclaimed, "It's the Peelers, Father. Three of them in an armoured car."

O'Brien frowned and went to the window. The man he saw climbing from the mud-spattered vehicle wasn't Joseph Conlon.

It was him.

The man that Bronagh had described.

Danny Fallon watched as Daly and Jardine jumped from the truck. Billy Jardine walked towards the cottage door while the Acting Sergeant skirted round to the rear of the croft. Fallon remained at the Lewis gun, his fingers slippery with sweat on the trigger. Candle light flickered behind the curtains and two shadows hovered behind them.

When Jardine had returned from patrol an hour earlier, Daly had taken him to one side and relayed Conlon's message. If Jardine had been concerned, he hadn't shown it. He asked Daly to repeat *exactly* what the Sergeant had said and then he'd lit a cigarette and closed his eyes in contemplation. A moment later he'd announced to the pair of them, "I think it's time we found out wha' the wee laddie's been sayin', eh? We cannae have Fenians bleatin' about our business, can we?"

When they'd pulled up at the O'Donagh's they'd seen that there was a horse and trap tied up in the yard. For the first time a cloud of consternation had crossed the Scotsman's face.

Now he stood statuesque before the cottage holding a revolver above his head. Releasing a round into the night, he yelled, "Come out wi' yer hands up, ye Fenian fuckers! We ken yer in there. Yer surrounded. We *will* open fire!"

There was much muttering from within and then the cottage door opened. A priest and an old farmer emerged with their hands on their heads.

It was clear to Fallon that this turn of events had both confused and enraged Jardine.

"A fuckin' priest breakin' bread wi' an IRA traitor, eh? If that's

not proof of a Catholic-Republican conspiracy, I dinnae ken wha'
is. What ye doin' here, priest?"

The priest didn't seem to be afraid. A strange calm possessed
him. "I'm here to save the soul of one you defiled. I *know* you
soldier. You are an abomination in the eyes of the Lor…"

A single shot rang out.

A perfectly spherical black blot materialised dead centre of the
cleric's forehead. He rocked on his heels for a split second before
crashing backwards into the dust.

Dumbfounded, the old man backed away towards the wedge
of light that spilled from the door waving his hands before him as
if warding off evil. "Don't do this!"

Jardine pulled the trigger once more and the farmer grunted
and fell to one knee.

Daly came sprinting from behind the cottage just as a boy burst
from the door screaming, "Daddy! No!" He scrambled to where
his father knelt, doubled up in pain and coughing gobs of blood.
Holding his head the boy whispered. "I'm so sorry. He tricked me."

The red froth on the farmer's lips stopped bubbling and he
went limp. Very gently the boy laid him on the ground. He looked
up at Jardine. "Ye said ye'd never hurt them if I stayed quiet. Ye
told me! Yer a liar!"

Pulling a tiny knife from his pocket he made a lunge at Jardine.
He had no chance. Shot from the front and side simultaneously,
the boy was dead before he thudded onto his father's corpse.

Daly and Jardine gave each other a smile, both their barrels
smoking.

From inside a door slammed.

"Danny, do the honours."

Fallon gulped as the Lewis gun stuttered into life. In seconds
hundreds of rounds had smashed through windows and walls.
Everything disintegrated into mortar dust, wood chip and shards
of glass.

Amid this maelstrom, the priest's horse, mad with fear, reared and snapped its bridle. The terrified animal and trap clattered away along the Athlone Road.

The racket quelled as the machine gun spat it's last. Fallon's finger was still locked on the trigger and the smell of scorched saltpetre choked him.

"Whoa, laddie. I think they're all killed!"

Jardine called to Daly. "Jonny boy, help me shift these inside, then let's light this place up."

The crumpled father and son. A priest spread-eagled in the yard. A crucifix on a chain sunk in the mud beside him: all these images burned themselves into Fallon's consciousness. And as the flames ate up the cottage with vicious glee, Fallon lifted his gaze to see a girl at the window.

On the way back to barracks the three men were silent; each coming to terms with what had just happened.

"For Christ's sake, Billy, ye've just gone an' shot the feckin' priest! Why the feck did ye do that? We're done for." Daly gripped the wheel with knuckles smeared in the blood of three different people. "Conlon knows about Danny an' me killin' his wife's cousin. I told ye, he's after writing' a report layin' it all out in black an' white. Regan will have it in the mornin', so he will. An' now this as well! Feck, Billy, we'll be court martialled at the very least, an' if the Fenians find out, they'll string us up, for sure! I say, we make a run for it. Go north into hiding – there's people up there will understand. Hell, some o' 'em will buy us a pint."

Billy Jardine was unflustered. "Nae bother, Jonny. When we get back, tell Flynn ye'll do night duty. I've an idea that will solve all our woes. Trust me."

58

11ᵗʰ July, 1921
The Workhouse Barracks, Birr,
King's County

It had been an unusually quiet evening. Most nights Brendan was serenaded with the inebriated bawling of the town drunks, flung into cells further down the corridor, but tonight all he could hear was the occasional fart and the scratch of nib on paper. The glow of an oil lamp around the corner was the only light that penetrated the shadows of his cell. Feverish with infection, he drifted in and out of consciousness.

It must have been well after midnight when Brendan was woken by a shift change.

"Flynn, get yerself to bed. I'll take it from here."

"Many thanks."

Departing footsteps and again silence.

Then Brendan heard a commotion as another set of heels clicked across flagstones.

"Jaysus, what's happened to ye?"

"Feck, I tell ye, I've just seen some dark shit, so I have."

Brendan moved from his mattress to the cell bars and listened. Had he been able to see around the corner he would have been witness to a strange sight. Two policemen leant against the jailer's desk holding hastily scribbled scripts while a third orchestrated their conversation.

O'Rourke recognised the accents as Irish. From the north somewhere: Ulster or Donegal.

"Conlon's just led a raid on a farm full of Fenians out on the Athlone Road. A feckin' bloodbath it was. I'd not want to get on the wrong side o' that man's fury. Feckin' fearless he is."

"What happened?"

"He was tipped off there was an IRA safe house up on the hill near Galross an' he wanted to have one last pop at the Fenians before the ceasefire. When we got there he tossed a grenade through the window and waited. I don't think he was expectin' a priest to come runnin' out, mind. I swear, once he started shootin' he couldn't stop. He killed the priest stone dead an' when this auld man comes stumblin' out o' the smoke with a shotgun, he put one in his guts too. Then he jumps up into the turret on the truck and lets off a couple o' hundred rounds into the cottage. I tell ye, I've not seen the man so wild since he danced a merry dance on that boy's head up on the Riverstown Road: his own wife's cousin, so it was. *'Family counts for nothin' if yer a Fenian'*, he said."

Brendan knew it!

Proof that Conlon was the murdering bastard he'd always thought he was. It made him feel better about the execution of Séan Keane.

"Anyway, I've just had word through from Tullamore that we're to release any politicals. Have we any Shinners in there?"

"We've only got O'Rourke. Do gunmen count as politicals?"

"O'Rourke?" His voice dropped to no more than a theatrical stage whisper, "He can't hear us can he? Is he not the one whose woman Conlon had fucked senseless by the side of the road last Christmas just to teach the Fenian a lesson in respect?"

"The very same."

Inside the cell Brendan clenched the bars and clenched his teeth and wondered which would shatter first. Carmel had never said a word.

"Feck, there'll not be many left in Birr with a good word to say about him when this is over, so there won't."

"Well, the Sergeant won't care. Have ye not heard? A letter came through sayin' he's been promoted 'for showing the utmost resolve in the face of revolution'. Well, that's what I heard him telling Flynn anyway. He's off to Dublin in the mornin' to make the necessary arrangements before he takes on a full time post at the castle."

"Well, if ye earn yer stripes by the number o' bodies ye bury, then he deserves it. I'd wager there's no Irishman fought harder for the British Crown than he. Anyway, by my watch it's past midnight. It says here that Lloyd George has agreed to release all political prisoners including POWs. He's been forced to concede they were fightin' for a legitimate Irish Republican Army after all. Bullshit, but that's what it says. So it looks like it's O'Rourke's lucky day."

"Is it safe to let him out on the streets before the ceasefire's come into effect?"

"From what I've heard, the man can barely hold his cock with his right hand, let alone a gun. Besides, with no prisoners to guard we can have a drink to celebrate, eh?"

Brendan listened as keys rattled and footsteps approached his cell.

59

11th July, 1921
The Fahy Farm, Birr, King's County, Ireland

Brendan had been led, almost disbelievingly, from the barracks by a mean looking Peeler with a scar down the left side of his face. He was sure that he was going to feel the muzzle of a gun on the back of his skull before the lights went out, but the policeman walked him past the sand bags and barbed wire, past the sentry who dozed at his post and out onto the pavement.

"Now dinnae ye be goin' an' gettin' yersel' in any bother, eh?" he'd chuckled before slamming the gate shut.

The streets were empty. Brendan knocked on a couple of doors and had quiet conversations with men he knew could be relied on. Then he'd made his way down Main Street, turned right at Craughwell's and followed the Riverstown Road to the Fahy farm.

There were a lot of tears: some of joy, but most were shed in anger and sorrow. Carmel was mortified her secret had been shared and terrified that Brendan could never look on her the same way. Padraig, who'd been hiding in the Fahy cowshed for the last week pulled a revolver from his holster. He vowed to empty the entire chamber into the policeman.

Surprisingly, thought Brendan, it was Ciaran who took control. He firmly wrested the pistol from Padraig's hand, kissed his youngest sister on the cheek and quietly spoke:

"No, it has to be me. For what he has done to this family. For what he has done to God knows how many families. Father was right: I've been a coward. I've spent too long hiding behind legal benches and inflammatory editorials. The kind of justice Conlon deserves can't be delivered by Dáil Court or any court, for that matter. This will be his justice." He slipped the revolver into his jacket and turned to Padraig. "Come, the sun's nearly up. We'll do this together: for Micheál, for Carmel; for Ireland."

Epilogue

The Serenity to Accept

Late Summer, 2018
St Patrick's Rock, Cashel,
County Tipperary, Eire

Shafts of early morning sunlight sliced across the hilltop bleaching the dewy tips of grass a blinding white. Three generations of Devlins huddled around a headstone in the shadow of Cormac's Chapel. Aunt Catriona, wrapped up well at this ungodly hour, was tickling the shaggy-haired Colm behind the ear and feeding him dog-biscuits from a garish bum-bag. Aoife was bleary eyed and nursed a Thermos flask of black coffee. Her sister, Orla, who worked for Heritage Ireland and had sneaked the family onto the site hours before the ticket office opened, prodded and swiped at a smartphone attempting to set up a FaceTime connection with brother, Liam, in San Francisco. The toddlers, teens and cousins of Uncle Mikey's family perched on camping stools. His wife, Bernadette, passed around hot sausage sandwiches wrapped in kitchen foil. Other than Noel, who refused to have anything to do with it, every member of the Devlin clan who still lived in Ireland had made it to St Patrick's Rock for sunrise.

James had flown out the night before and rented a car at the airport. Unlikely though it was, he feared that reports of a claret Morris Minor on the byways of Tipperary would somehow filter back to the ageing Provo who'd followed him from Birr to Belfast; and James wasn't prepared to risk that. Glancing toward the access gate that Orla had left unlatched, he checked his watch again.

They still weren't here.

James felt surprisingly self-conscious and wondered at how somebody who martialled classrooms of adolescents for a living could be so nervous at the thought of speaking to a tight-knit group of relatives. He scanned his notes one last time and prayed the girls arrived soon. Charlie had texted him an hour earlier to tell him that they'd *picked up the package and were on their way*. After grave misgivings, she'd relented, and from the sound of her text was even revelling in the clandestine nature of the arrangement. If they didn't make it in the next twenty minutes, then Orla's colleagues would begin to turn up for work and she'd have a lot of explaining to do. Worse, it could generate unwanted attention for the Devlins in Cashel, and James knew that Noel would never forgive him for that.

He heard their chatter long before he spotted them; but that was no surprise. When his mother got together with Charlie and Phoebe it was hard to get a word in edgeways. It was understandable his father had opted to stay in London.

He watched the quartet make their way through the headstones up the hill. Charlie and Cate walked side by side, Charlie steadying her mother-in-law over the uneven ground. Phoebe pushed the wheelchair which glinted metallically as it caught the sun, bumping and jolting over tufts of turf. Holding his cane and wearing a bemused expression beneath a woolly hat, great-uncle Pat-Joe bounced gracelessly towards the final resting place of his mother, Kitty Conlon.

Since the moment that James had made the connection between an innocuous clause in O'Rourke's book and a throwaway comment from Alec Jardine, he'd been determined that Pat-Joe should hear the truth along with the rest of the family. But it wasn't just about the living: Kitty had died without ever knowing for sure that her husband was an innocent man. So it had to be here, at her grave, that James explained to Joseph Conlon's descendants how he'd been set up.

The pertinent passage from the book followed a long and typically verbose description of the massacre itself, and because it merely qualified what had gone before, James hadn't questioned the subtext of this particular paragraph at the time. O'Rourke had written: "*It was common knowledge about the town that Conlon had led the raid on the O'Donagh farm. It is less clear whether he knew that there would be a priest present, but then he didn't care for the fact that there were children within either. What is certain is that it was he who pulled the trigger and strafed the croft with machine gun fire, and he who ordered for the farmhouse and outbuildings to be razed to the ground. Indeed his men even boasted of his actions after the deed. Unable to hold a gun straight, I cursed that it could not be me who delivered the justice the man deserved, but on release from incarceration, it was I that coordinated the operation...*" O'Rourke had then recounted how Padraig Nolan and Ciaran Fahy had slipped into Birr on the morning of the 11th and waited for Conlon to leave his house before sinking three bullets into him. It was the line about Conlon's men *boasting of his actions* along with O'Rourke's timely release that had made James recall what Alec Jardine had said about feeding disinformation to prisoners and informers in Enniskillen in the 1970s. The Worshipful Master of the Orange Lodge had gone on to say that this example of *good policing* was one of the *tricks of the trade* passed down from father to son.

It was the oldest trick in the book: feed false words to someone desperate to believe them, and there's nothing they wouldn't do. Just ask poor Desdemona.

The priest had written of *'unspeakable acts'*, and thanks to Malky Dunn's testimony, James had a very good idea what they were – you don't suddenly wake up one morning a fully-fledged pederast. Conlon had obviously discovered the Scotsman's secret and was about to unmask him in the letter that never reached Head Constable Regan's desk. Fallon's drawings and recordings put Jardine at the scene, and his macabre tattoo and boastful claim that he'd set up another Catholic for the murder of the priest proved it: *'Two for one'*. Billy Jardine had got rid of the only people who knew the truth. It all added up: Jardine had allowed O'Rourke to believe that it was Conlon who'd wiped out the O'Donaghs, and then released the rebel onto the streets to do his dirty work for him. What better way to cover his tracks?

In the weeks following James's return from Glasgow he'd discovered that Moira Dunn was conscious and stable. She'd been transferred to a private hospital near Edinburgh to recuperate. He suspected that he knew who was paying for her rehabilitation along with her renewed silence; and he had absolutely no intention of putting her in any further danger.

Besides, he knew the truth now, and that was all that mattered. In fact it was the truth that had finally set him free. A week ago he had found himself sitting face to face with Brenda McCleary in a compact flat in Kilburn. A framed depiction of Our Lady regarded him coolly from the wall above the sofa, while faded photos of Connor and lots of people he didn't know smiled at him from the gas fire and window ledge. She'd married and acquired two strapping step-sons and a gaggle of grandchildren. She was happy. She was even happy to see James. There had been awkward small-talk, a mug of instant coffee and some ginger snaps and then James had dove in. He told Brenda about that last night, about how he had paid for the drugs that killed her son and how he should have told her at the funeral. When he was finished, there were tears streaming down his face and a chasm of silence between them.

He could hear the second-hand on the carriage clock mechanically tick out time.

She blinked slowly, stood and walked toward his chair. She very gently held his head in her hands and placed a kiss on his temple. "James, yer an awful eejit, carryin' around a burden like that all this time. Ye didn't kill Connor any more than I did by working every moment God gave me, or those feckin' wasters he hung around with. *Heroin killed him*, James; junkies will find the funds to feed the habit from anywhere – from my purse, from your pocket; it doesn't matter. He was a grown man, an' he made his own choices – it's just that they were usually the wrong choices. Connor was his father's son, so he was. But one thing he wasn't, James, was a liar."

James had wiped his eyes and looked up at her.

"As it happens, he didn't lie to ye that night: the fifty quid was for rent. It was for *my* rent. He came round late; pissed he was, but happy to have seen ye and he handed me the notes, gave me a hug and he was away. Maybe he was guilty about skimming from the biscuit tin where I kept my bills money; maybe he was ashamed to see me go cap in hand to people like your mother to make ends meet. Either way, his last act was one of the kindest."

James, who had been holding his breath while she spoke, exhaled; he felt a malignance leave him. And when he breathed in, it was though he could taste the air for the very first time; the angora wool of her cardigan, the sweetness of the ginger snap, the faint whiff of pine from the toilet down the corridor.

It was nothing and everything.

Just like today.

God, grant me the serenity to accept the things I cannot change: James couldn't change the hatred felt towards his great-grandfather by Republicans in Offaly any more than he could change the sectarian bigotry of Wee Bill and the XIIVIIs. He needed to focus on the things he could influence. He could be a better husband, a wiser teacher and hopefully he'd become a good father to his unborn child. Standing here on a Tipperary hillside with his kin, there was one thing of which he was certain; he *could* change the past for this one family – and who else mattered anyway?

He cleared his throat and began.

"On the 11th of July, 1921 Sergeant Joseph Conlon kissed his wife goodbye and left his house carrying a briefcase that contained a document that identified three men, Jonathon Daly, Daniel Fallon and William Jardine as the perpetrators of a string of atrocities in and around the town of Birr during the Irish War of Independence. He never made it to the barracks that morning because he was shot dead by two members of the IRA who wrongly believed him guilty of the very crimes he sought to expose. I think it's time we all understood the truth…"

As James spoke, he observed his family's reactions: His mother gripped Phoebe's hand and fought to hold back the tears, Orla nodded sagely, angling her phone so that Liam could follow events from the States. Catriona and Aoife had linked arms, Aoife resting her head on her mother's shoulder. Mikey Devlin kept a watchful eye on his brood, who all listened respectfully with heads bowed. Pat-Joe had pulled himself from the wheelchair and stood with one hand on Kitty Conlon's headstone; the other clutching his gnarled, wooden cane. Although his eyes glistened with moisture, he looked more joyful than James had ever seen him.

When he finished, he pulled Joseph Conlon's RIC whistle from his jacket pocket, dug into the soft earth and buried it along with Kitty.

James stepped back and appraised the tombstone. Chiselled into white marble, the original epitaph simply read:

Here lie the remains of Catherine Conlon
1897-1939
Beloved Mother of Bridget and Patrick-Joseph

Now, beneath this inscription, a sliver plaque had been added with the words:

Loving wife of Sergeant Joseph Conlon, RIC
1885-1921
Together may they sleep the blissful sleep of the innocent

Pat-Joe planted his cane carefully and stepped towards James. He embraced his great nephew and whispered, "Ye've done a grand job, Seamus. I knew ye would. Míle maith agat – *a thousand thanks.*" He turned to the rest of the family. "When my time comes, and it's fast approachin', so it is, this is where I want to be: with my mother and the memory of my father, looking out on the Golden Vale. Now, will one of ye's get me somewhere warm and give me a drink afore ye take me back to St Michael's holding pen."

As the group made their way down the slope, Charlie slipped her arm around her husband's waist. "I'm so proud of you, James. You've made an old man very happy. You worked everything out in the end. Maybe that history degree of yours is worth something after all."

James smiled. "Well, not everything. For the life of me I still don't understand what Daniel Fallon was going on about in that final recording. I remember the image – he'd drawn himself without the stitching in his lips – but on the tape he raves about bed-fellows, irony and absolution. If only I could..."

"Stop." Charlie placed her finger on his lips. "Some things we're not meant to know. Besides, what fun would there be in history without a little mystery?

James kissed her finger and the pair walked hand in hand back to the car.

15th July, 1922
Crinkill Barracks, Birr, County Offaly, The Irish Free State

"Strange bed-fellas, eh? A Fenian an' a Peeler fightin' for the Irish Free State."

The two men crouched below the shattered window that looked out onto the parade ground at Crinkill Barracks. On the far side of the square, entrenched behind sandbags and fallen masonry the Irish Irregulars had penned in the surviving soldiers of the Free State Army.

St Swithin's Day, 1922, saw an Ireland devouring itself: men who'd fought side by side to see the British expelled from their land now trained their sights on each other. It was over six months since Michael Collins had returned from peace talks in London with a Treaty that he'd quipped would be his own death warrant. This agreement gave the newly created Irish Free State full control over domestic affairs and legislature, but stopped short of delivering full independence. For some this was a victory – a stepping stone to ultimate freedom – but for others it was a betrayal of those who'd spilt their blood fighting for nothing less than a full Republic. By late spring Ireland had slipped into a Civil War, fought between rationalists and idealists, who paradoxically both craved the same end.

In Birr the abandoned Crinkill Barracks had been occupied by the Pro-Treaty forces. Amongst them were ex-IRA officers, Sinn Féin deputies and even former policemen who were prepared to fight for a partially emancipated Free Southern State as long as it was still bound by allegiance to the Crown.

Danny Fallon wiped the sweat from his brow, smearing ash and grime across his forehead. He wore the rictus smile of those who suspect they face certain death.

"There'll not be any quarter given, will there? These bastards will kill us if they get their hands on us."

Ciaran Fahy nodded, knowing full well that for men like Brendan O'Rourke, who was probably one of those peppering the dormitory walls with rifle shot, betrayal to the cause was punishable only by death.

A volley of fire rang out and a bullet ricocheted off the far wall, embedding itself in the mortar next to Fallon's ear. He paled. "Now I'm no Catholic, but d'ye suppose that things will go better for me on the other side if I admit my sins?"

Ciaran heard the rat-a-tat of machine gun fire and a howl of pain in an adjoining block. "Feck, you've nothing to lose…"

The Donegal man closed his eyes, bowed his head and blurted out a series of sentences that would make little sense to anyone in the world but Ciaran Fahy.

He spoke of a boy who loved his horse too much. Of a bride raped days after her wedding. Of a family murdered, a priest shot and a policeman set up to take the blame for it all.

When he opened his eyes, Daniel Fallon could see the trembling black blur of a revolver inches from his forehead and behind it, in sharp focus, the face of Ciaran Fahy, twisted into an expression of utter anguish.

Ciaran cocked the gun.

At that moment a grenade came hurtling through the window. It hit the wall and skittered beneath the bunk beds in the corner.

Both men covered their heads and flung themselves to the ground.

Ciaran was unsure whether he was dead or alive. He had no idea how long he'd been lying here. He could taste dust in his mouth, but he could neither see nor hear anything. He pushed at the planks of wood that entombed him. A pale gloom penetrated the smoke that curled around the mound of debris in which he was buried.

He could see that the far wall had been blown clean away and on the other side of the fallen bricks and mortar, the open fields rolled upward towards the Slieve Bloom hills.

As if in a dream, for he couldn't hear the sound of tumbling masonry as he pushed it from his chest, he tried to sit up. Pain ripped through his abdomen and when he touched his stomach his hand came back bloodied in thick, viscous indigo-red. Forcing himself to examine the wound, he saw that a jagged slat from the bunk beds protruded from his guts.

Almost fainting in the process, Ciaran dragged himself to his feet and crouched in agony behind part of the fallen wall. There was no sign of the Donegal man – most likely he too had been buried by the blast, or maybe captured. Ciaran didn't care now.

On the other side of the parade ground he perceived some movement and realised he was far from safe. He staggered away from the wall and across the field towards the hills.

It was early evening. The ground was soft and the smell of sheep shit hung ripe in the air. Ciaran stumbled through gorse and bracken and climbed the slope, ever higher, slipping and tripping as he did so. At the summit a chalk-white standing stone pointed heavenward, faintly luminescent in the setting sun.

Ciaran propped himself against the ancient stone that had stood for millennia, watching impassively as wave after wave of invader had fought over the rich fields that stretched away into the distance: Celts, Vikings, Normans and English had all claimed this land as their own at one time and now, below him, the Irish themselves were killing each other for control of it.

Ciaran pressed the palms of his hands into the thick grass, closed his eyes and whispered to the earth.

"I failed you, Micheál."

The act of speaking brought on a bout of breathless rasping and he coughed up a mouthful of dark blood. Wincing in pain, he dug his fingers into the moist soil.

"Forgive me, Kitty. Forgive me, Joseph."

The sun slunk behind the horizon, shrouding the green fields of his childhood a sombre grey. As the dusk swallowed him whole, Ciaran heard the bells of both Birr's churches begin to toll the hour. As ever, only a heartbeat out of time and a semi-tone out of tune – yet enough in this fractured isle of his, to turn godly peals of tempered bronze into a clanging din of dissonance.

Acknowledgements

There are many people whom I would like to thank for their support and advice over the last few years. Firstly, the readers of the early draft deserve a special mention; Jools, Wizzy, Frank and Anita – thank you for your encouragement.

Without Abigail, I wouldn't have been in a position to write the book at all – I will never forget that you gave me the chance to commit to the project full time. Thank you.

Imogen Robertson, in her role as reader for the Literary Consultancy, gave invaluable feedback and encouraged me to give James some 'demons'; your advice was spot on and the narrative is all the better for it.

Huge gratitude must also go to everybody at the Book Guild, all of whom have worked tirelessly to publish and promote this novel.

Finally, I would like to take this opportunity to thank my family in Ireland and England. Special mention must go to Natasha, Janet and Bill for believing and Tony for printing off reams of paper. I will pay you back for the ink one day!

Thank you all.
Finn Dervan
December 2018.